S.R. Witt
J. A. Hunter

The Artificer:
A Viridian Gate Online Novel DLC 1.1

S.R. Witt and J. A. Hunter

Dedication

To great partnerships, and awesome people.

S.R. Witt and J. A. Hunter

ONE:

Maintenance Sweep

Robert Osmark watched his death approaching in vivid ultra-high definition on a ninety-inch holotable display. Only a handful of people on the planet could see what Osmark saw, and most of them didn't understand what they were looking at. Not even the smart ones. He zoomed in as close as the satellite's telescopic lens would allow. He wanted to get a good look at his nemesis, 213 Astraea. A nine-mile-wide rock shot through by twisting veins of ice, the whole thing wreathed in a halo of burning gas. When it filled the entire display, Osmark walked up to it and stared at its pitted surface.

"Never before has something so uninteresting held so many in awe," Osmark whispered to himself.

It was a shame, really. But he wasn't surprised. Humans weren't impressed by the amazing and awesome things happening all around them—unless it was burning, naked, or life-threatening, most people wouldn't notice a miracle if it bit them on the nose.

Osmark Technologies had revolutionized life in every corner of the world, but that hunk of rock in the sky had eclipsed all of its achievements the second it revealed itself to the Arecibo Observatory, down in Puerto Rico. In the end, the people of the world would be more impressed by an unfeeling, unthinking hunk of stone hurled at their planet by an indifferent universe than by the countless technological miracles Robert Osmark had brought into their lives. Ingrates.

"Let's go check on the New World," he said to the empty room. Osmark left the asteroid behind. It didn't care about him, or the billions of others it would kill along with him, so why should he care about *it*?

Besides, in many ways, the asteroid was the best thing that had ever happened to him.

He turned, heels click-clacking on the gray stone floors, hands neatly folded behind his back, and beelined for the gigantic steel blast door separating his private quarters from the rest of the sprawling underground facility. Leaving the comforts of his suite behind was always a shock and more than a little disorienting.

His room was a work of art: old gray stone walls, polished dark wood floorboards underfoot, a massive fireplace with a mocha-brown leather sofa sitting close by. Arched windows littered the room, overlooking a forest filled with an assortment of pines and firs. They were holo-projections, of course, but the most convincing kind. Built-in nooks and crannies held priceless sculptures—the *L'Homme au Doigt* by Alberto Giacometti here, the *Tete de Femme* by Picasso there—or world-changing paintings. Just over his fireplace hung a Nymphéas, by Monet.

All works of art the world couldn't stand to lose.

Testaments to human brilliance.

But one step took him from the luxurious and into a bland white tunnel lined with naked pipes and exposed conduits. At first glance, the walls appeared to be painted concrete, as did the floor and ceiling. A closer examination revealed the truth.

Salt.

When Astraea plowed into Central America and ended life as humans knew it, this bunker, carved into the world's largest salt deposit, would preserve some of the earth's wealthiest inhabitants.

Or it would preserve their minds, at least.

He whistled as he walked down the tunnel, pointedly ignoring the mute and immobile weapon emplacements mounted at regular intervals in the walls and ceiling. Once the largest and deepest salt mine in the world, Osmark's new home had also been a military installation of last resort before it found its way into his hands. He couldn't help but wonder how the architects of this place, who'd built it to stand up to a nuclear assault that paled in comparison to the disaster heading toward Earth, would feel about the improvements he'd made.

His first stop was the ventilation and cooling plant. Though there were technicians and engineers tasked with making sure every vital piece of the bunker's machinery was in perfect order, Osmark wasn't going to leave anything to chance. If he'd learned one thing as the head of Osmark Technology, it was that someone always missed something. Always. It was as inevitable as the turning of the seasons. If he wanted to be sure something was done correctly, he'd have to check it himself.

"How's it going, Harry?" he asked the security guard stationed inside the clean room leading to the plant. Names were such a little thing in the grand scheme, but he'd found they held a tremendous power. He knew the name of every subordinate—he even knew the names of their family members—because those small details cemented loyalty better than anything else.

The guard, a former Marine with beef-slab arms, stood a little straighter when he addressed Osmark. "Boring, which I guess is an improvement over what's going on topside." He jabbed a finger toward the roof.

A broadcast monitor mounted near the ceiling inside the clean room showed Osmark scenes of rising anarchy. With the literal end of life on Earth approaching at an alarming rate, things were breaking down. With so little time left, people were doing exactly what they wanted, when they wanted, to whom they wanted. When you had no future, maybe the best you could hope for was to enjoy your present to the fullest.

Unfortunately, that meant your good day could turn into someone else's very, very bad day.

Rioters rampaged across the monitor, weapons raised in mindless defiance. Fires burned in blackened storefronts. The wounded ran screaming, their mouths carved into black circles beneath the horrified caverns of their dark eyes.

An overhead view erased the individual rioters and pulled back to show the scope of the insanity. "Where is this?" Osmark asked.

"Dallas," Harry said flatly. "I've never seen anything like it. The scary thing is what's missing."

Osmark zipped into his white Tyvek suit and raised his mask to his face. Before he strapped it on, he asked, "What's that?"

Harry's eyes narrowed as he watched the chaos dance across the monitor. "Cops. Firemen. Ambulances. No one's trying to stop it. No one's trying to help."

I am, Osmark thought as he fastened his mask in place. "Show me Osmark Stadium."

Harry nodded, hands quickly working at the control panel. The chaos in Dallas was replaced by an interior view of a massive football stadium in San Diego. The difference was immediate. Ashen-faced people milled around in orderly pockets, each clutching a lone suitcase with the last of their earthly belongings. Soldiers patrolled the perimeter and weaved their way through the crowd; their boxy, matte black assault rifles kept the masses in check. These were the survivors. Well, *potential* survivors. The few lucky enough or wealthy enough to win A.R.C. lottery tickets and a place in one of the deep-earth bunkers scattered around the globe.

The whole setup was nice, neat, and orderly.

"And the Silicon Valley facility?" Osmark said, leaning forward as he inspected the monitor.

Once more the holo-screen flickered and morphed. A giant warehouse with concrete walls and harsh halogen lighting appeared. The space was filled wall to wall with state-of-the-art NexGenVR capsules—a sea of glossy, black plastic coffins. Here too, order reigned. Nurses, orderlies, guards, and tech service support personnel loaded people into capsules or carted bodies away for incineration. Five thousand capsules per facility, and five hundred facilities operating at max capacity worldwide. The greatest evacuation the world had ever seen.

I am, Osmark thought again as he waved to Harry and stepped into the plant.

The noise inside was incredible, deafening even. Even with the state-of-the-art earplugs, Osmark could hear the plant's unearthly racket. A steady bass drone underlined rhythmic hissing and an oscillating rumble. The bunker was close to two miles beneath the surface, hidden below the sleepy town of Independence, Missouri. Getting air that deep into the earth required a staggering number of powerful fans, which constantly buzzed in the background like never-ending white noise. And each one of those fans added heat to the air passing through its whirling blades.

The mine's engineers had dealt with the heat by adding enormous cooling chambers between the fans. Exhaust vents dissipated the heat through narrow channels leading back to the surface. It was an impressive feat of engineering, and if it ever failed, everyone in the bunker would die through a painful combination of suffocation and slow broiling. There was no chance of it failing anytime in the next hundred years, however. Osmark had seen to that personally. He'd hired the best engineers on the planet to improve the system, pushing it far beyond the capacity its creators ever imagined. Standing on the catwalk overlooking his End of the World air conditioning system, Osmark couldn't help but smile.

Everything was working precisely as he'd planned, and it would keep on working long after he died.

"Perfect," he whispered, leaving the plant behind for the last time.

Briskly, he marched down a dozen different hallways after he left the cooling and ventilation plant—left, right, left, left, straight, right—taking each turn without the least hesitation. The broadcast monitors scattered around the mine kept him apprised of the situation on the surface. He did his best to tune it out because it pained him to see people behaving like animals. He was living proof that they didn't have to be that way. A little effort, a little luck, some brains, and one man could move the world.

Several levels down from the ventilation plant, Osmark reached his next stop. With a wave of his hand, another steel blast door swung open on silent hinges, revealing a stark white hallway, which connected to a darkened chamber. The security guard was half out of his chair before he recognized Osmark.

"I didn't know you were coming today, sir," the man said with a sheepish grin.

"Relax, John," Osmark said. "I'm just making the rounds."

His last stop had been all about cooling things down, but this room was for heating things up. OLED panels lined the walls, each displaying information about a critical subsystem. The center of the far wall was what drew Osmark's attention, though, because it gave a readout of the whole system at a glance.

That display had a tiny pictogram representing the salt mine at its top. A thick tube led from the mine down to the earth's vast darkness. The mine's geothermal well. It descended more than ten miles below the earth's surface to a vast lake of superheated, pressurized water. That water, heated to almost five hundred degrees Fahrenheit, was pumped up to the power plant under intense pressure. The steam generated turned turbines, which generated electricity. As the water cooled, it flowed back to the lake that provided it. The closed loop was efficient, nearly perfect. It would keep electricity flowing until the end of time, powering the Overmind servers, which ruled Viridian Gate Online.

The central display was a solid shade of blue, telling Osmark everything was running as expected.

"Of course it is," he whispered to himself. "I made it."

Satisfied, he turned and left, waving goodbye to John for the last time, and he headed deeper into the earthen bunker, past the food stores and clean water wells, the housing quarters for the transition team, and the drone vaults. The drones were Osmark's final project.

After Astraea did its dirty work and debris stopped falling from the sky, the bunker's artificial intelligence units would direct the drones to the surface. There, they'd clear away rubble and debris from the entrance just in case one of the mine's residents needed to head outside. But, more importantly, the drones would be able to deploy a sophisticated solar cell system once the atmosphere shed the worst of Astraea's pollution. Those cells would allow the drones to recharge on the surface so they could continue exploring the dead world left behind.

Osmark paused, rubbing his suddenly sweat-slicked hands over his pants. There was only one last area to check before he made the plunge: the servers themselves, buried in an area the staff jokingly referred to as the Underworld. No one liked to go down there. Not the techs. Not the engineers. Not the guards. And if Osmark were honest, he'd include himself on that list. Still, this was the most important check—the one the whole world of Viridian Gate Online rode on—and he couldn't put it off any longer. Reluctantly, he made his way down the catwalk to a stainless-steel elevator, which plunged even deeper into the earth.

When the elevator door dinged opened, the trio of guards standing at attention didn't apologize for pointing their weapons in Osmark's direction. It wasn't until the lead guard recognized Robert that he motioned for the others to relax. "One last check, sir?" the guard, a whip-thin man named Marcus, asked.

"Better safe than sorry," Osmark said, giving the men each a nod as he passed them.

The black door they were guarding had no handle or lock. A single glowing green panel marked its center. Osmark placed his palm on it and spread his fingers wide to give the sensor a clear view of his prints. Red light flashed in each of his eyes, scanning his retinas and confirming his identity. Without a sound, the door vanished into the wall.

Osmark licked his lips. He wasn't afraid, not of a machine he'd helped create, but he couldn't hide his apprehension. What he'd accomplished here wasn't just a feat of technology. It was miraculous.

And that made him just a little nervous.

The black box was ten yards on a side, and five yards tall. It looked like a chunk of polished obsidian resting on the salt floor. Thick cooling tubes descended from the ceiling to connect to the box's sides and top like metallic umbilical cords. The faint whooshing of forced air was the only sound inside the sacred chamber.

Osmark approached the room's only other object: a black monitor resting on top of a short pillar. When he stopped in front of it, a low mechanical voice droned, "Hello, Robert."

The monitor flickered to life, displaying a dizzying array of charts and graphs. None of them were labeled because no one would ever see this screen other than Robert. He knew what each line and bar graph meant; he understood intimately what every colored pixel was telling him. This was an overview of the world he'd created. The virtual reality realm where close to four million men, women, and children would live after Astraea wiped out the rest of humanity—not to mention the eight million or so NPCs generated by the Overminds. Like everything else, it was close to perfect.

So close that the imperfections rose to the surface like jarring notes struck in an otherwise melodious orchestra. "Damn it," Robert snarled.

The Chinese had assured him their donation would work flawlessly. And it had, until recently. There was something off with the Thanatos Overmind. There were no severe anomalies, but almost constant fluctuations above and below normal operating thresholds disturbed Robert's otherwise flawless system.

"Maybe it's the reflection core, I could just tweak …" Robert muttered absently, then bit his tongue. With only a little more than eight days remaining before Astraea plowed into the earth, there was no point in tinkering with the arcade built. It would be more than good enough.

It had to be.

TWO:

Upload

Osmark's most trusted ally, Sandra Bullard, glared at him as he entered the transition chamber. She was a slight woman with a severe face, made even more so by the tight bun fixed at the back of her head. She leaned casually against the sleek black tube that would soon be his grave and tapped a pen against her chin. "You're late."

"For a very important date?" He chuckled and shook his head. "There's still plenty of time."

Sandra frowned at Robert. "What has been your favorite saying since we began this project?"

"The end of the world isn't an excuse to slack off," he said with a sigh. "And that's true, but I wasn't slacking."

"Robert, we have highly qualified staff to check all of those systems. Let them do the work you hired them to do." She raised her clipboard and turned it toward him. "You have a schedule to keep."

"Ah, mom," Osmark said with mock exasperation. "I don't wanna die, yet."

His assistant tried to hold it together, but she couldn't suppress a single giggle. She covered her full lips with her clipboard until the fit had passed. Though both of them were aggressive, high-performing personalities, their long-standing relationship gave them a firm enough foundation to let loose with one another occasionally. With the stakes so high, and the need to keep up appearances so great, Robert couldn't resist sharing an occasional joke with his chief operations specialist, personal assistant, and primary bodyguard.

"Let me give you a rundown on our current situation," Sandra began. She ran her finger down the single sheet of paper on her clipboard and tapped the conductive ink with the micro transponder embedded in the lacquer covering the nail of her right index finger.

In a blink, the transition chamber's northern wall transformed into a deep black tapestry. One by one, photographs of Osmark's primary contributors to the V.G.O. Project floated up through the darkness and into view. "As you can see, most of our esteemed guests have already arrived at the bunkers assigned to them. Transitions are already in progress, and I don't foresee any difficulties with the guests I've highlighted."

Robert noted two photographs that were not highlighted. "Carrera and Sizemore are already stirring up trouble?"

"You're half right," Sandra corrected. "Carrera's being a good boy. I doubt that's going to remain true for long, but at present, he's minding his manners and doing as he's told. He's a pragmatic man, and he understands that his survival rests in other hands. *Your* hands." Robert couldn't hide his smile. Though he'd achieved far more in his life than any of the guests who'd contributed to his project, most of them had not viewed him with the respect he deserved.

Once the money had changed hands, his genius disappeared in their eyes. He'd been paid, and now he was the help.

Be a good boy and build us a new world to conquer.

He'd let them believe that. But Osmark was more than prepared to show them the truth after the transition period was over.

"If he's playing by the rules, why did you flag him?" Osmark asked.

A grim smile tightened Sandra's lips. "To remind us both to keep an eye on him. He's playing nice *now*. But once we're all inside, the gloves will come off. Remember that."

Osmark nodded and raised his hands in surrender. Sandra had made her point, and he wasn't about to challenge her on it.

"And Sizemore? What's he up to?" His eyes narrowed as he spoke. Sandra traced her fingernails over the top of Osmark's high-tech coffin. The way she treated it with such indifference annoyed him, though Osmark would never let it show. He was going to die in that capsule, but that didn't mean anything. His superstitious dread of the grave was embarrassing, and he chewed on the inside of his lip in frustration.

"Are you listening?" Sandra asked.

Osmark cleared his throat. "Sorry, just a little preoccupied."

"As I was saying," Sandra said, annoyed at having to repeat herself, "Senator Sizemore has contacted several of the other guests. Including our Chinese contingent."

Robert clenched his teeth and forced a deep breath through his nostrils. He'd needed Sizemore to get the project off the ground. Without the senator's help, they wouldn't have the salt mine and all the goodies that came with it. More importantly, Osmark would never have received the Yama system from the Chinese. Sizemore had greased those international political wheels so smoothly and efficiently that Robert had immediately taken a dislike to the man. Anyone who could get concessions from the Chinese in less than twelve hours couldn't be trusted.

"I should've known," Osmark said. "He was too close to Peng. I assume you have some idea of what they're discussing?"

Sandra sketched an abbreviated bow. She grinned and said, "I know you love to watch."

The transition chamber's east wall displayed a crystal clear still shot of Sizemore handing a drink to the Chinese contingent's spokesperson. It lurched into motion, and immersive audio made Osmark feel as if he were standing in the room with the men.

"You understand we cannot allow him to control our destinies once we transition," Peng said as he accepted the drink. "We must forge our own paths."

Sizemore's trademark smile flashed like a megawatt laser, his teeth immaculately white and straight. At fifty, the senator was just a few years older than Osmark, but he looked a decade younger. His tanned skin showed no wrinkles, and his dark hair had just the right amount of gray peppering the temples. The man would've been as at home on a movie set as he was stalking the halls of Congress. A classic politician in every way.

"I couldn't agree with you more, sir," Sizemore said with a deferential bow. "Osmark's brain is valuable, and he's done us a great service, but if he thinks I'm going to let him run the place, he's got another thing coming."

The Chinese spokesperson shot Sizemore a dubious glance. "Surely he has contingencies in place to deal with those who would rise against him. The man who built the world will have given himself insurmountable advantages."

Sizemore drained his glass in a single long pull. For a moment he didn't speak, instead refilling his glass as he considered his next words. "You'd think so, but it doesn't work that way. Osmark has advantages, the same as the rest of us, but he's not a god. No matter what he wants us to believe, the truth is the simulation can only be stretched so far. It has rules that can be bent, but breaking them is impossible. He's formidable, but not indomitable."

Peng tapped the rim of his glass with one bony finger, his lips pursed into a thin line. "You have a plan, then?" he asked.

Sizemore touched his glass to Peng's. "I do. And I've already told it to my allies."

"Ah, but it appears you have forgotten one of your allies." Peng smiled. "It seems we have much to discuss."

Sandra killed the replay with the tap of a finger. "Once you begin your transition, I could have Sizemore dealt with on a more permanent basis—"

Robert raised his hand, shaking his head in protest. "No, that won't work. It'll set a bad precedent moving forward with the rest of the Imperial Alliance Board. Besides, Sizemore's security force is *formidable.* You're extremely capable, but taking him out at this point isn't worth the risk. I'll deal with him in game."

"I'm sure I could handle it," she protested, hands placed on her hips. "There's room in the schedule for me to adjust my transition time. I'll arrive a couple of days after you, but it's worth it to deal with this problem before it can blow up in our faces."

Robert folded his hands behind his back and offered her a thin, tight smile. "This isn't open for discussion. I'll handle him in game. Is that clear?"

Concern flashed across Sandra's face like a raven's shadow. "Handle him how?"

"Let me worry about that," he replied coolly. "You have more than enough on your plate already."

Sandra wanted to press him for more details, Robert could see it in her flashing jade eyes, but she held her tongue. They'd been together long enough not to question one another in certain areas. When it came to his safety and the operation of his company, Sandra was more than welcome to challenge Osmark. But on this project, his iron will and snap decisions were the only forces guiding them to the finish line. She couldn't afford to doubt the choices he made.

"Fine," she said. "Peng has been in contact with Bulger and Whitehead. That connects them to Modhi and the rest of the subcontinent billionaires. If they do plan a coup, you're going to have your hands full."

"That's why I'm bringing you along. I'll make the plan, but somebody has to execute it."

A quiet chime rang through the transition chamber.

It was time to die.

Sandra clutched her clipboard to her chest and stepped around Osmark's coffin. For a moment, the two of them stood silent and motionless. Their eyes locked. He wanted to reach for her, to wrap his arms around her shoulders and pull her across the narrow gap that separated them. They'd always been professional, but this was different. If everything went as planned, they would both be dead before they saw one another again.

"On the other side," she said quietly. "Safe travels."

And then she was gone, her flats whispering across the floor as she swept from the room.

A trio of nurses swooped into the space left by Sandra like air rushing into a vacuum. They wore blood-red surgical gowns and caps, and their faces were professional masks. The lid swung open and carefully, slowly, he climbed in, conscious of the eyes scrutinizing his every motion. He lowered himself down, adjusting and readjusting his body on the conductive memory foam, then slipped a modified VR helmet into place. The lid automatically closed, leaving Osmark in a claustrophobically tight space filled with pulsing blue light.

As he lay there, Osmark doubted everything. *Everything.*

There was no going back, though. This was the way forward, the way of survival. And he would survive the transition—the highly trained nurses would ensure that.

"Initiate Viridian Gate Online," he said to the trio of nurses.

"Of course, Mr. Osmark," came a curt reply from the lead nurse. "Please lie as still as possible."

The capsule let out a *click-buzz*—the lid locking mechanism—followed by the *whoosh-whoosh-whoosh* of a whirling MRI. Abruptly, everything went black as the VR headset engaged, quickly replaced by a white loading screen as anesthetic gas hissed into the capsule. The gas was an added precaution to help with the upload and the transition. Osmark breathed deeply and began the long process of dying as the machine kicked into overdrive, the whirling picking up in intensity. *WHOOSH, WHOOSH, WHOOSH, WHOOSH.*

"Traveler," boomed a hard-edged male voice, "prepare to enter Viridian Gate Online!"

THREE:

V.G.O.

The all-encompassing white loading screen faded from Osmark's vision as his consciousness transitioned into the world he'd created. He stood on a grassy knoll; long blades of green bent beneath his feet, giving the ground a cushioned, almost springy feel. The grass spread in every direction like a sea of rippling emerald. The air was so thick with the scent of growing vegetation, Osmark could taste it on his tongue and feel it against his skin, carried by a stiff breeze slapping at his face and tugging on his rough garments.

He lifted one foot, examining the flattened grass below. Flawless.

The rolling plains stretching beneath the cloudless azure sky were stunning not just for their sheer size, but for their incredible detail. Osmark had known the world of V.G.O. would be impressive—he'd seen plenty of footage from the beta runs—but he hadn't understood the scope and magnitude of his creation. Not really. Not until this moment. Guided by AI-curated algorithms, his technology had woven a creation more enchanting than he'd imagined possible. The graphics quality—if such a crude term could even be applied—was indistinguishable from real life.

This world was *better* than reality.

Osmark took a tentative step; his legs wobbled uncertainly beneath him, then gave way. He landed on his hands and knees, scraping one palm along a jagged piece of rock protruding from the grass. A muted flash of pain zigzagged up his arm, there then gone. Curious, he turned his hand over, inspecting the flesh. Vivid green streaks from the grass stained his skin along with a few splashes of red. Incredible. He shook his head and turned his attention to a small army of ants scurrying along nearby with scraps of leaves and tiny clods of earth in their mandibles. A flock of ravens with glossy blue-black feathers cried out to him as they flew high overhead, and unseen ground squirrels and chipmunks chattered in annoyance at his presence.

"How is this even possible?" Osmark asked himself. The NexGenVR capsule's NerveTech was fantastic technology. He knew that from his time developing it, but the cold measurements of the technical specifications and design diagrams hadn't conveyed just how stunning the result would be. A surge of pride welled up inside Osmark. He'd *made* this. The worries he'd had about V.G.O. seemed so petty and insignificant in light of this fantastic experience. The transition would be agonizing, there was no getting around that, but this world was so much more perfect, so much purer, than the disaster Osmark had left behind.

He couldn't wait for Sandra to join him here.

But, before that could happen, he had a ton of work to do. As beautiful and enthralling as this peaceful little slice of paradise was—and it was—he didn't have time to sit around and take in the sights. Osmark's enemies had a small, but significant, head start on him, and that couldn't stand. No doubt they were already on the move. Already forming their factions and building their defenses. If he wanted to beat them, he needed to get moving and do what he did best: outwork the competition.

With a grimace, Robert gained his feet and brushed his dirt-stained hands on his trousers.

First, he needed an avatar.

The simulation responded to Osmark's desire instantly. A semitranslucent image of him materialized into view. His dark hair and lean figure were the same, as were his hawkish features and smooth-shaven jaw, but his custom-tailored clothing was gone, replaced by a rough burlap tunic, matching britches, and ill-fitting canvas boots, which covered his feet and the lower half of his calves. A coarse rope around his waist served as a belt. The clothes irritated Osmark immensely. They were uncomfortable and ill-fitting, but that wasn't what bothered him most. The tattered clothing made him look *weak. Poor.*

Appearances were critical. If Osmark wanted to be respected, then he had to look like someone who *should* be respected. New clothes moved to the top of his to-do list.

The thought faded as a glowing white interface bar with a variety of options—race, build, sex, face, name—blinked to life around his character's image. He already had his race and build in mind, but he couldn't help scrolling through the options one last time. A final system check before he made the leap.

Osmark focused on "race," and a series of new options popped up, showing Osmark all of the character choices available to players. The elves topped the list, Dokkalfar and Hvitalfar representing the dark and light side of the fey races, followed by the stocky, bearded dwarves, known as the Svartalfar. Where the elves were lean and graceful, the dwarves were built like cubes of muscle, fat, and gristle. Their natural crafting abilities and aptitude with Smithing and Enchanting would be a huge plus in the advanced profession Osmark had in mind, but he could never be a dwarf.

He could never be comfortable in that body.

His eyes flashed over the Dokkalfar, and the display shimmered and changed to show him what he would look like as a Murk Elf: brown hair gave way to black, and the avatar's skin took on a dusky, gunmetal-gray tone. Though he approved of the Dokkalfar's rugged physique and mysterious appearance, he wasn't fond of the Murk Elves' favored class, Rogue. A common thief simply wouldn't get the job done. Besides, he had his sights set on the Viridian Throne, and taking that seat as a rebel Murk Elf would be next to impossible. He'd need an Imperial-friendly race.

Next came the Wodes. They were much taller and more muscular than the Murk Elves, with lustrous golden hair and pale skin. Osmark was struck by their impressive appearance, raw size, and sheer physicality. Osmark took a closer look, and an information panel shimmered to life:

Wodes (Human): The most numerous of Eldgard's races, the Wodes are a flexible and resilient people known for their impressive stature and steadfast nature. Though Wodes are not blessed with any particular affinity for one class or another, they also suffer no penalties to any class. This adaptability has allowed the Wodes to spread far and wide, making them as at home in the mountains as the forests or plains.

Good, but not for him. Not for what he had planned.

The Accipiter, or Winged Race, followed, and though they looked like an option that would be a lot of fun to try, he knew it would get old in a hurry. The ability to fly was impressive, certainly, but there were plenty of downsides balanced against a powerful skill like that. By design, the Accipiter were physically weaker than most other creatures, their class choices were severely restricted, and worst of all? They all spawned in the Barren Sands, which was about as far west in Eldgard as an adventurous player could go.

That was no good since he needed to be on the easternmost side of the continent.

He dismissed the Risi—half-ogre creatures with powerful frames, thick muscles, and green-tinged skin—without a second thought. They were scary and intimidating, true, but they were also suited almost solely for up-close physical combat—tanking— something Osmark had zero interest in. Not to mention, he refused to look like a damned monster for the rest of the foreseeable future.

That left him with the only real option left. He scrolled over to the Imperials.

The avatar twirling in the air before him changed from the green-skinned Risi to a human Imperial. The Imperial's features were similar to Osmark's natural appearance, though they were more chiseled and refined—made sharper and more perfect through virtual reality magic. Without his glasses to hide them, his eyes had become an intense sapphire blue, burning with a fierce intelligence. Osmark's brown hair was a touch darker and a bit longer, but otherwise looked more or less like it always had.

If it's not broke, he thought, *why fix it?*

Imperials (Human): Though less numerous than the Wodes, the Imperials have carved out their place in the history books. Their military might and political strength have no equal, and their empire stretches from one horizon to the other. Imperials are not gifted with any resistance bonuses, but all initial stats begin at 12, except for Intelligence, which starts at 15. As with other humans, Imperials are not restricted in any way as to the classes they may pursue as they advance.

"Perfect," Osmark whispered, casually lacing his hands behind his back.

He spent a few moments making minor refinements to his avatar's appearance—he made his shoulders a touch broader, his chin a bit more defined, and removed the stubble from his cheeks—and then clicked the "Create" button.

A new prompt appeared. "Please select a name."

Osmark considered his options only for the briefest moment.

"Robert Osmark," he said. If he changed his name he might be able to fly under the radar in these crucial early days, but the minor benefit wasn't worth it. Not by half. He'd clawed his way up from the bottom of a Brooklyn gutter, and he wasn't going to give that up. Not for some political gnat like Sizemore and his cabal of sycophants. Everyone in V.G.O. knew who Osmark was, and what he'd done. They were all alive because of his initiative. That was a reputation boost he couldn't afford to throw away, even if it did plant a target on his back.

"Are you sure you would like to create Robert Osmark the Imperial?" a booming baritone voice asked. "Once you create a character, you will not be able to change your racial identity or name. Please confirm?"

"Confirmed."

Though Osmark had designed the opening cinematic, that didn't prepare him for the explosion of music that surrounded him. A powerful orchestral anthem crashed through the air like a thunderstorm. Drums rumbled, cymbals clanged and clashed, and a host of warbling stringed instruments washed through his head.

"The year is 1095 A.I.C.—*Anno Imperium Conditae*," the disembodied announcer bellowed over the music. "Dark power and the stirrings of war ride upon the winds of Eldgard, the provincial outpost of the Great Viridian Empire."

Suddenly, Osmark soared above a massive lorica-clad army led by a man in golden platemail riding a black stallion. The troops' armor gleamed in the sun, and the marching column shone like a great steel serpent winding its way across the landscape. A cloud of dust rose from a snaking line of heavy, mounted cavalry, blotting out the horizon behind the army as if stomping hooves had obliterated the roads they traveled and left nothing in their wake.

"Imperial legions," said the announcer, "allied with the forces of light, march from the east, bringing the natives of Eldgard to their knees through flame, magic, and steel. Bringing progress. Building roads. Cities. *A kingdom.* Civilizing the dark-natured Wodes, the swamp-dwelling Dokkalfar, and the Accipiter of the far-western deserts, enlightening them in the ways of the ever-victorious empire.

"But the natives of Eldgard are not so quick to give up the old ways—to heel for foreign masters. Though the rebellion is yet small, they fight on. Hour by hour, day by day …" A massed throng of howling Wodes surged from the forest lining the wide road and charged toward the Imperial forces. The enormous blond warriors hoisted oversized battle-axes above their half-naked bodies. Their muscles writhed beneath their skin, coiling like serpents preparing to strike.

The Imperials held their ground, faces hidden behind metal helms, weapons held steady as their mounts pawed at the earth. The forces slapped together with the ring of metal on metal and the cry of horses. For a moment, it appeared as if the Wodes had won the battle before it even began: The front ranks of the Imperials vanished beneath a swarming tide of flashing steel and tattooed flesh. For a moment, the war cry of the Wodes drowned out all other sounds.

A pang of doubt speared through Osmark's gut. Had he made the wrong choice? In his designs, the Imperials were the dominant force on Eldgard, but the Overminds were more than capable of adjusting the game world as needed to keep it challenging and exciting for the players. An unavoidable part of the content design.

A second later, the wave of barbarians swallowed the golden leader and his black stallion.

Osmark's heart stopped.

And then, in the blink of an eye, everything changed.

The Imperial foot soldiers formed a tight wedge of interlocking shields and thrust out barbed spears that pierced the main body of the encroaching Wode force like an arrowhead through unarmored flesh. An Imperial cavalry contingent slammed into the side of the barbarian army, trampling their opponents beneath steel-shod hooves. The golden Imperial commander emerged amidst a circle of dead Wodes, his rugged face covered in blood, a wicked, victorious grin splitting his face as he raised his sword high and unleashed a piercing battle cry.

The soldiers responded with furious war cries of their own as the Wodes broke, fleeing the field for the safety of the tree line. The Imperials showed no mercy, however. The barbarians had raised arms against the Empire, and now they'd pay the price.

A galloping line of armored knights circled the fleeing horde, brass horns blaring, the ground reverberating as they mounted a charge. Shining steel lances pierced rough hide armor and burst through Wode backs in showers of blood and gore. Heavy maces and blunt-headed warhammers smashed bones and caved in steel helmets. Hooves crushed men into the earth and churned their guts into reeking, bloody mud. Even knowing this wasn't real didn't make it any easier to watch. Eventually, the cavalry pushed through the dying mob to rejoin the rest of the Imperial troops.

They left a gory trail of dead and mortally wounded in their wake. Their lances dripped red as they wheeled into position.

The Imperial army marched on.

The scene faded, shimmered, and changed as Osmark rose higher and higher above the marching army. He watched in awe as the Imperial forces transformed the untamed wilderness. Roads carved their way across the plains to connect the Imperial outposts that sprang up in strategic locations. As he watched, those first meager settlements swelled and expanded their borders to become villages, then walled towns, then gleaming cities.

"But even as the Empire spread, the natives learned and adapted to their strange and deadly ways." The announcer narrated as Osmark's point of view sped east like a steel-tipped bolt fired from a ballista. The scattered forces of the defeated Wodes joined with Murk Elf war bands. They transformed from ragged bands of isolated tribesmen into organized troops with one purpose in mind: destroying the Empire.

"For even the mightiest armies cannot do battle without teaching their enemies how to resist them. The Empire is a power to be reckoned with, but their enemies grow in strength and numbers with every passing day."

A great map unfurled before Osmark, showing him the current lay of the land. Crossed swords marked battlefields. Thick dashed lines stitched along territorial borders. Though much of Eldgard had fallen beneath the shadow of the Empire's banners, the days of explosive expansion had reached their end. Now, every inch was hard fought and soaked in blood. The rebel forces rallied by the natives held the Empire in check. Neither side could risk pushing their advantage in one area, as the enemy was always poised to steal back any territory left unguarded.

"The war continues, but its fires have cooled. Cooled until one side can gain a decisive advantage. But while the Imperials and their enemies struggle for dominance, a greater evil is rising." Without warning, the scene exploded in a shower of light, and Osmark found himself deep beneath the earth, craggy stone pressing down all around him. Burly, heavily bearded dwarfs labored in a mining tunnel. Their bodies were slick with sweat and darkened by the powdered rock they created with their hammers and pickaxes.

"In the far north, the Svartalfar ignore the strife beyond their borders. Their illustrious Merchant's Council pushes them to ever greater feats of engineering. They delve deep into the earth, uncovering riches undreamt of by the other races." The narrator's tone grew solemn, and a chill cut through Osmark like a winter breeze. "But the dwarves have uncovered something dark. Something which should have remained untouched and unknown."

A stout man with a massive potbelly lashed out with his pick, sinking it deep in black stone. Chunks of rock crumbled from around the pickaxe, and the earth groaned in protest. The gap widened, and a foul stench gushed through the cleft. The dwarf who'd breached the earthen wall collapsed, his face turning purple, his hands clawing frantically at his throat. The other dwarves backed away in horror as a guttering green light emerged from the crack, dancing in the air like a plume of smoke.

Osmark knew he was watching a scene from the past, but he couldn't convince himself there was no cause for fear. An eye appeared, glaring at him through the gap in the stone. A venomous green iris, shot through with visceral red streaks, split in half by a vertical pupil filled with an abyssal black.

"A great darkness is coming. Serth-Rog, Daemon Prince of Morsheim, has awakened. The dwarves have breached his long-forgotten prison and woken him from an ancient slumber. The great evil cannot yet escape from the vault that holds him. But his whispers infect the minds of those who worship evil and coax them to work toward his dark ends. Soon, much too soon, he will be freed."

A malicious grin split the face of one of the Svartalfar. She dropped her hammer and snatched the pickaxe from the hands of her fallen brother. The monstrous demon laughed, a guttural grinding sound like a rockslide, as the pickaxe took on a bloody red hue. The corrupted dwarf wheeled around and buried the pick in the head of the dwarf next to her.

The scene collapsed around Osmark as darkness consumed the dwarves—dissolving the stone around him—and left him standing in a formless void.

The narrator's voice thundered through the black. "It is an age of heroes. It is a time of great villainy. A new battle looms on the horizon. Imperial. Rebel. Light. Dark. Living. Dead. Which side will you choose?"

S.R. Witt and J. A. Hunter

The darkness erupted in a swirl of opalescent light and violent motion, wind whipping at Osmark, snatching his breath away as he tumbled and fell. Down, down, down.

FOUR:

Ambush

A gentle rocking and the creak of wood dragged Osmark from the depths of unconsciousness. He didn't open his eyes as he came awake, instead he let his other senses feed him bits and pieces of information about his surroundings. After the emotional introduction to V.G.O. and the terrifying fall, Osmark felt as wrung out as an old dishtowel. He wasn't ready to face the world just yet.

Maybe I should've made that entry a little less intense, he thought, his fingers slowly tracing over the rough burlap beneath him.

He breathed deeply, filling his lungs with clean, fresh air and his nose with the rich scents of turned earth and recently picked produce. He'd been to more than his fair share of farmers markets—Silicon Valley was bursting with snobs who swore by locally sourced produce—but he'd never smelled *anything* so fresh or enticing as the aromas tickling his nostrils. *What is that?*

Osmark reluctantly cracked open one eye. He was lying in a lurching box with low wooden walls and an arched canvas ceiling supported by curved bows.

Bulging burlap sacks overflowing with ears of corn, mounds of wheat, lumpy dirt-smeared potatoes, and gleaming red apples surrounded him. Sturdy wooden crates pressed against the soles of his boots, which forced his knees to bend at an awkward angle. He must have been in the same position for too long because his back and calves ached and burned.

It took Osmark a moment to realize where he was, and then he couldn't suppress a wide grin.

A covered wagon, he thought. *Maybe all those years messing around with that ancient Oregon Trail game will pay off after all.*

"Finally awake, are you?" a woman's voice teased from across the wagon. "I was starting to think you'd sleep through the whole trip."

Osmark opened both eyes and gave the woman a thorough once-over through a narrow gap between a rough sack overflowing with beets and another bulging with its load of apples. She was handsome, though just short of beautiful, with a strong nose, blue eyes, and the dark hair so common to Imperial citizens. Unlike Osmark, she wore clothes of finely woven linen dyed a deep red and edged in silver thread. If that wasn't enough to mark her as a member of the Empire's merchant class, the gold hoops dangling from her earlobes and the elaborate silver necklace coiled around her throat certainly made her wealth apparent.

The necklace shifted, and Osmark spied a splash of golden ink glowing at the hollow of the woman's throat.

Ability: Keen-Sight

A passive ability allowing the observant adventurer

> to notice items and clues others might not see.
>
> *Ability Type/Level:* Passive / Level I
>
> *Cost:* None
>
> *Effect:* Chance to notice and identify hidden objects increased by 6%.

He dismissed the notification with a wave of one hand and squinted, studying the mark: a tattoo of three gold coins. Interesting. That mark, he knew, identified her as one of the Empire's favored mercantile interests. She was an important person, and a good first impression could make his life much easier going forward, at least in the short term. On the other hand, a bad first impression could cause him all sorts of problems down the road. The starting scenario was unique to each player, painstakingly crafted by the Overminds to test the person. A hyper-advanced Myers-Briggs Type Indicator used to determine what type of class and quests each player would be best suited for.

The starting scenario ramifications could be sweeping.

"I'm awake," Osmark said. "I think." He offered her a charming, lopsided grin.

"Then maybe it's time to sit up. The rest of us would like a little room to stretch our legs, too." The woman's impish grin took the sting out of her words, but the underlying tone of command told Osmark she wasn't making a request.

Osmark scrambled up to give the woman room. He cracked his head against one of the wagon's wooden bows and immediately plopped back down with his legs crossed. Sparks of pain danced behind his eyes, and a thin splinter drove itself into the palm of his hand as he shifted position to try and give the merchant as much space as possible. The wood beneath his hands was rough, and Osmark felt its grain rasp across the tips of his fingers.

Once more, he was amazed at how *real* everything felt. He didn't enjoy pain, of course, but the sensation was astounding. The fact that he could experience pain at all made it *almost* enjoyable. The algorithms had far exceeded even the lofty goals he'd set for his team. *Make the game better than the real world,* he'd told his developers. *Make the players so happy to be there, they never want to leave.*

The woman's sharp gaze drew Osmark's attention. He must've looked like a complete moron, staring off into space and rubbing his hands over the wagon's floor.

"I was asleep," Osmark explained. "I mean, I was alone when I went to sleep. If I'd known…"

She sat up straighter and grinned at him over the top of a crate. "That's better," she said and slithered her slim legs through the gap between two burlap sacks. "I'm not usually this cranky, but my calves have been curled up under me for the past hour, and they're killing me."

"Where are you coming from?" Osmark asked, trying to change the topic.

She gave him another grin, glancing down and absently picking imaginary lint from her dress. "From the south," she finally offered.

"And you're headed to?"

Her grin widened as she glanced up. "Same as you. North."

That was surprisingly vague and unhelpful. He took a moment to pull up his user interface, scrolling over to the in-game map, the same map he'd stared at a thousand times during the design phase. He sighed in relief. He was on the West Viridia side of the continent, trundling north, apparently headed toward the sleepy town of Tomestide. Perfect. Everything was going according to the plan Osmark had settled on before beginning his transition to V.G.O.

While most of the other players were scampering around chasing after the familiar and predictable base classes like rogue or warrior, Osmark intended to beeline for one of the most advanced classes offered to players of Viridian Gate Online. He had his sights set on the Mechanical Artificer profession, which would grant him a host of unique skills and powers. A tricky class to play: weak initially, but profoundly powerful if managed correctly due to the combinatoric marginal mechanics of the kit.

Osmark couldn't cheat the game's systems without endangering the whole virtual world, but with his knowledge of V.G.O.'s designs and its many secret classes and quests, he wouldn't need to break the rules to gain a significant advantage.

And if he was near Tomestide, he was ahead of schedule. Even better. The caravan he'd been lucky enough to join would deliver him right to the doorstep of his allies and the training he needed to put his plans into motion. He closed out of the map, his smile widening.

"You seem pleased with yourself," the woman said with a wink. "Copper for your thoughts?"

Osmark chuckled and licked his lips.

He didn't know this merchant, and he wasn't going to tell her even a fraction of the truth about his thoughts. She might be nothing more than an NPC, but tipping his hand to *anyone* this early in the game could be a fatal error. And V.G.O.'s NPCs were far from the standard MMO fare. Though the NPCs were procedurally generated by drawing on a host of information from all over the internet—history books, Facebook profiles, novels, movies, games—each one could pass the Turing Test with ease. They could be just as cunning and just as dangerous as any of the player characters.

"I'm just glad I woke up in the same place I fell asleep," he replied with a shrug. "How far to Tomestide?"

She grinned. "So you do know more than you're letting on. For that, I'll tell you what the driver told me this morning. We'll likely reach Tomestide by nightfall."

Osmark grunted and glanced at the sun, which was dipping below the horizon, painting the land with streaks of gold, red, and dark purple. Another hour until full dark, at least. That was an awful lot of precious time to waste in the back of a wagon. "I'll just check with the driver. Maybe we're running ahead of schedule," Osmark said, gaining his feet and squeezing past the woman.

The wagon wasn't more than fifteen feet long, but walking through it took Osmark most of a minute. Between the uncertain footing caused by the wheels bouncing through ruts and the jumbled cargo occupying almost every free inch of floor space, it was far more of a challenge than Osmark would've liked. He'd almost reached the driver's bench when the wagon suddenly veered hard to the left, the horses shrieking in protest up ahead.

Osmark lunged, grabbing at the back of the bench before he crashed to the wagon's floor. The pain filter was amazing, but he wasn't too keen to experience any more pain than strictly necessary. His fingers closed over the rough wood, earning him a few more splinters. "What the hell?" he shouted, a flash of anger swelling in his chest.

The driver turned to Osmark and shouted right back at him. "Get down! There's—"

Blood jetted from the man's mouth and splattered across Osmark's chest. The driver slumped to the side with a thick arrow jutting from the side of his throat, dead. The smell of fresh-spilled blood panicked the horses, and they reared back, legs flashing in the air as they crashed into one another. Osmark tried to grab the reins from the dead driver's nerveless fingers—to restore order to this mess—but the leather was slick with blood. It slithered through the guard's hands and vanished over the lip of the driver's bench. Gone.

Bestial howls filled the air.

The terrified horses screamed and bolted from the road, but in their blind panic, they tangled in their traces and lost their footing. The horse on the left, its hair black as midnight, crashed onto its side and dragged its partner, a chestnut brown, down on top of it. The screaming beasts slid down the grassy embankment next to the road in a jumble of kicking legs, gnashing teeth, and thrashing heads.

Osmark saw the disaster coming but was helpless to stop it. The falling horses dragged the wagon hard to the left, pulling it down the hill behind them. The wheels dug into the dirt like plows, and broken earth mounded up before them. The wheels on the wagon's downhill side burst under pressure, splinters of wood and bits of iron flying free like shrapnel. The front axle lurched and dropped, burying itself in the dirt as a thick wooden pole bucked up against the bottom of the wagon and momentum did its work.

In seconds they were airborne, the wagon flipping onto one side with a groan.

Osmark sailed away from the driver's bench and toward the field beside the road, tumbling head over heels before crashing into the dirt with bone-jarring force. The impact knocked the wind out of his lungs in a muffled bark. Everything went black, and then a new game message floated into view:

Debuffs Added

Stunned: Movement reduced by 75%; duration, 1 minute

Concussed: You have sustained a severe head injury! Confusion and disorientation; duration, 1 minute.

Blunt Trauma: You have sustained severe Blunt Trauma damage! Stamina Regeneration reduced by 30%; duration, 2 minutes.

Osmark lay on his belly and struggled to fill his lungs with air. A high-pitched ringing filled his ears. His vision drifted out of focus, snapped back, and then drifted away again. His body felt like someone had dumped him into a burlap sack and then kicked him for a few hours. Lying in the grass seemed like the best idea he'd had in a long time. His eyes slipped closed, and he took a deep breath of the cold air. But the smell of burning hair curled in Osmark's nostrils like a barbed wire noose and immediately brought him back into the moment. The stench ignited a primal fear that screamed for him to move.

To run, before he, too, was burning.

Osmark fought to gain his feet, but his current debuffs made it almost impossible. Crawling was all he could manage, so that's what he did. He wormed away from the wagons and the screams and the fire, pulling himself along an inch at a time, his fingers and knees scrambling for purchase while his head throbbed and his thoughts bounced around inside his ringing skull like rubber balls thrown against a brick wall. *What the hell happened back there?*

When Osmark reached the tall grass a few yards from the road, he turned back, scanning the road and the chaos. Most of the wagons had crashed and spilled over in the road or beside it, their dead horses still tangled in their rigging. A frightening number of arrows had punched through the faithful beasts' hides, and the pooling blood had turned the dirt into a muddy mire.

Figures moved through the bloody wreckage in the red light of the sinking sun, their faces lit by the dancing flames of the torches they clutched in their meaty fists. Some were human, their golden hair and pale skin marking them as Wodes. Their allies, however, were much too large to be men. Standing a good foot taller than their human companions, these creatures' bodies bulged with misshapen muscles. Their faces were distorted by tusks that jutted from the sides of their mouths beneath their wide upturned noses and piggish nostrils.

Risi.

Osmark inched forward another inch, then two, watching the unfolding carnage with wide eyes.

The Wodes and their Risi allies stalked through the wreckage, kicking at burlap bags, smashing open wooden crates, and butchering any survivors they came across. Wicked axes and pitted steel swords scythed through the merchants and guards who tried to stand their ground and fight. It was a hopeless battle; the guards and merchants were outnumbered five to one, and most were injured from the wreck to boot. Quickly, Osmark surveyed the battlefield for any signs of the female merchant from the wagon. He saw dead guards and slaughtered horses, but there was no sign of the woman.

Had she run? Maybe.

That hopeful notion died when he saw one of the few remaining drivers break and flee into the night. Shaggy-maned wolves, larger than any Osmark had ever imagined, exploded from the shadows to pursue the fleeing man. They were massive creatures with gray hair, oversized jaws filled with far too many teeth, and beady yellow eyes. They were almost hyena-like.

Fifteen yards from the road, the wolves caught up to the runner, circling him like sharks smelling blood in the water, their lips pulling back in silent snarls. The obvious leader—a great white beast with a black blaze marking his forehead—howled. Then he lunged, and his pack joined in the slaughter. The man's screams went on far longer than Osmark would have believed possible.

He was torn to shreds before his cries faded away.

Despite the horror of the situation, Osmark had to admire the artistry of the scene. He'd created this, even if only indirectly. His tools, his machines, his programming, had fashioned this barbaric scene from the nothingness of electronic space. It was *incredible*, in a cold, pragmatic way.

And it would've been even more amazing if those impressive beasts his programming had spawned hadn't turned and headed in his direction.

The bulk of the bandits were busy divvying up the spoils of their attack, but a lone Wode had split off from the rest of the group to search for survivors. He followed a trio of wolves, their black noses pressed to the ground. Sniffing. Searching.

They have my scent, Osmark thought. Fear, real and primal, took root in his guts. He froze, unable to run, unable to even think. The wolves were less than thirty feet away. If he moved, they'd see him and run him down in seconds. If he stayed put for much longer, they'd stumble right over him, then shred him into dog chow. He needed to do something. Anything was better than lying there like a terrified rabbit waiting to die.

But what to do? He didn't have a weapon. He didn't have any skills.

The search party drew nearer to Osmark.

Osmark eyed the towering Wode leading the little party. The blond thug had a massive battle-axe resting on his shoulder and a blazing torch in his offhand. Sapphire-blue tattoos curled from under his mane to frame his face in intricate and fearsome designs, which made him look almost as monstrous as the Risi. The Wode's blond hair was plaited into elaborate braids that dangled down his back like golden ropes, swaying past his belt as he turned his head from side to side in search of prey. His armor was nothing more than crude hides that revealed almost as much of his skin it covered.

The lead wolf threw back her head and howled. She lowered her muzzle, and her eyes blazed like swamp fire in the last rays of the dying sun. The wolf charged.

Straight at Osmark.

His paralyzing fear shattered.

He hadn't come this far, accomplished this much, to be gutted on his first day in V.G.O. He leaped to his feet and ran, only realizing his host of debuffs were gone when he didn't immediately fall to his knees again. His head still ached from the wreck, but he wasn't injured. Now, he just needed to stay that way. Before he'd taken three steps, however, a jolt of savage pain tore through his calf as jagged fangs clamped down, puncturing skin and digging deep into the muscle below. With a guttural snarl, she jerked him off his feet and tossed him away with a twist of her head. Stars flashed across his vision as his head bounced off the dirt road.

The wolf snarled again and curled back onto her haunches, muscles tensed to lunge.

Osmark stared into her wild eyes. Blood stained her muzzle and slicked her daggerlike teeth.

His blood.

Well, this is a disappointing start, he thought. He wasn't even scared anymore. Frankly, he was disgusted by his failure. Yes, he'd respawn, but it would cost him precious time he didn't have to waste. He'd lose eight hours, which wasn't much in the grand scheme of things, but with the Imperial Advisory Board meeting just days away, he needed every minute to accomplish his goals. He had to establish his presence in Tomestide, earn both his class and specialization, and come up with a plan to deal with Sizemore before the senator could undercut all his efforts.

No, death was far too inconvenient at this point.

The wolf leaped for his throat, its slathering jaws spread wide.

And then it yelped, and blood splattered across Osmark's face. The hot and sticky spray blinded him, but temporarily blinded was better than dead. Osmark cleared his eyes with the palms of his hands and stared in disbelief at the dead wolf sprawled in the dirt, its yellow eyes already glassy.

A lean man wearing burnished leather armor loomed over the fallen wolf, his feet spread wide, his gaunt face tense, a gleaming silver sword raised and at the ready. In an instant, he lashed out at the next animal, splitting it almost in half with a two-handed chop that caught it mid-leap. The third wolf, surprised and off balance, didn't have a chance. The man feinted left, shot right, then lunged, driving the bloodied tip of his blade through the wolf's gray hide and into its heart.

"Don't just lay there gawking, lad," the man said, jerking his weapon from the dead wolf's twitching corpse. "My name's Horan and I'm here to help. But if you want to live, you best get ready to fight."

FIVE:

Blood Rage

The tattooed bandit rushed to the attack before Osmark could stop staring at the dead wolves, much less prepare himself for the brutal onslaught. The Wode charged through the tall grass with his gleaming axe spinning over his head. A chilling hunting cry burst from his open mouth as he brought the axe down at Horan's face. For a split second, Osmark thought his guardian NPC was as good as dead.

But Horan was an experienced soldier, steeped in discipline and technique.

The barbarian's reckless attack cleaved the empty air left as the mercenary pivoted away, and the axe buried itself in the earth instead of Horan's skull.

Horan darted forward with a grimace, his sword whistling out in a tight arc, slicing through the off-balance Wode's unprotected throat. A fountain of blood gushed from the wound, painting the evening air with a vivid crimson mist. The barbarian warrior leaned heavily against the haft of his axe, a stunned look sprinting across his face, then keeled over onto his side to vomit up his last, bloody breath.

"We should get clear of these maniacs, sir," Horan said, his voice gruff and no-nonsense. He wiped his blade on a fistful of green grass and shoved his weapon back into its sheath. "I was hired to keep this caravan and its passengers safe, and this place is a hell of a long way from that."

The thieves continued to loot and slaughter as they prowled through the burning remnants of the caravan. It was clear they intended to take anything valuable, kill anyone who opposed them, and burn whatever they didn't feel like dragging away.

Horan was right. This place wasn't safe.

But Osmark didn't give a shit about safe. Who did these animals think they were to attack an Imperial caravan? A cold rage stuck in his chest like an icicle through his heart. "We're not leaving."

Horan glanced at Osmark, lips pressed into a tight, thoughtful line. "Then you'd best grab a weapon, lad. The killing ain't over for those who stay here."

A weapon, Osmark thought. He padded back toward the caravan with Horan beside him, stealing along the tree line to avoid detection. *But it can't be just any weapon.* Every choice made in V.G.O. had consequences, especially during the opening sequence. Most players didn't understand the scope and depth of the game's analytical tools. Even those who did know that every action, even every word, was recorded and picked apart by V.G.O.'s AI gods, didn't understand just how much their choices changed the world around them.

Osmark, on the other hand, knew exactly how his decisions affected V.G.O. The Master Artificer character class would give him an edge over his enemies, but qualifying for it was extremely difficult.

To even have a chance of gaining that class, he'd first have to find a trainer. And then he'd have to convince that trainer he was a good candidate for a student. If he didn't make just the right choices now—including which weapons to use—he'd never have a chance of passing that test.

Horan elbowed Osmark in the ribs to knock him clear of an attacking Wode who burst out from behind a fat elm. An axe as long as Osmark was tall whooshed through the air over his prone body.

The golden-haired berserker howled in rage at his missed attack, spinning with the momentum of his wild swing, redirecting the axe blade toward Horan's face. The veteran fighter staggered back to let the hungry crescent sweep past his eyes.

"Get a weapon, man!" Horan shouted, his sword flashing out, batting aside another attack.

Osmark scrambled away from his guardian NPC in search of a crossbow. The engineered weapons relied on brains rather than brawn, and its mechanical design would earn Osmark faction points with the Master Artificers. Plus, he'd much rather stand at a distance and pepper his enemies with streaking black bolts than go toe to toe with the filthy warriors.

An enormous Risi charged at Osmark from behind a burning cart. The massive ogre wore spiked black platemail and wielded heavy black blades in each hand, the weapons poised for both offense and defense. The barbaric creature snarled at Osmark, its face a rictus of rage, its tusks dripping with foaming saliva. Osmark knew instinctively that even with a weapon, he was no match for that thing. Not on his best day.

Osmark was many things, but a brawler wasn't one of them. Without a weapon, though, he'd be sliced into bite-sized chunks before he could so much as kick the Risi in the shins.

He did the only reasonable thing.

He ran for all he was worth.

This is getting to be a habit, he thought.

The ambush had been a disorganized charge. The wolves had terrified the horses, which sent the wagons spilling in every direction. Most of the overloaded carts had splintered their wheels and shattered their axles as soon as they left the road. Their contents were scattered across the grass and dirt, ripe and ready for looting, pillaging, and burning. Not every cart was getting the same amount of attention, however, and the one ahead of Osmark was still upright. Its right wheel was shattered, true, and the horses had burst from their traces, but the bonnet was still intact, and it wasn't on fire.

Best of all, the dead guard was still on the bench with a fistful of arrows punched through his face and chest.

Osmark beelined for the crippled wagon and prayed he would be faster than the Risi on his heels, eating up the distance between them.

Behind him, Horan shouted in victory or pain, it was impossible to tell which, and Osmark didn't have the time to stop and check on his only ally. Osmark knew his guardian NPC was a grizzled fighter with years of experience, but there were a *lot* of bandits still in the fight. Osmark silently prayed Horan was skilled enough to hold off their attackers until he could contribute to the fight.

The Risi's rasping breaths echoed in Osmark's ears. The barbarian was close—and getting closer every second—but so was the wagon. Osmark thought he had enough of a lead on his enemy to gain the high ground on the driver's bench before he was cut down.

It was the only chance he had.

A yellow bar flashed in the upper corner of Osmark's vision. The thing was almost empty, which meant Osmark was running out of Stamina. He'd exerted himself to the edge of his low-level capabilities, and if he didn't stop running soon, he'd end up exhausted. And if that happened … Well, he'd be even more helpless than he was now. Unable to run or fight. Unable to so much as stand. He'd be an easy target.

He was only feet from the wagon when a sharp pain ripped across his shoulder.

Between the crash, the wolf's bite, and the Risi's sword stroke, Osmark had lost close to half his hit points. He wasn't out of the fight, but another hit like the last one might be the end of him.

Pushing through the pain, Osmark scrambled up onto the wagon's driving bench. His hands and boots slipped on the wet blood coating the wood, and he fell hard onto his back on the floorboards. Sparklers of pain erupted through his spine and burst behind his eyes, his teeth bit down hard on his tongue, and Osmark tasted blood in his mouth. He groaned, clutching at his shoulder, which burned like a red-hot poker. Maybe installing a one hundred percent pain threshold had been a mistake. The pain was meant to be a deterrent to reckless play, but this? This was too much.

He shoved the thought away as the Risi clambered up onto the bench and raised both blades overhead. The barbarian grinned and angled his weapons until they were aimed straight at Osmark's chest, then howled in victory and plunged the blades down. Without a thought, Osmark tucked his knees up to his chin and drove them forward in an explosive kick. His ragged boots slammed into the Risi's fat belly and pushed the ogre off balance. The Risi tottered uncertainly, his arms windmilling in a valiant effort to keep from falling, but the swords were throwing him off balance. After a long beat, he let the weapon in his left hand clatter to the ground as he grasped for the edge of the bench to stay upright.

Osmark didn't wait to see if the Risi would fall. The moment he landed his kick, he twisted and scrambled across the floor of the wagon. The dead guard stared down at him, his torso littered with arrows.

"Rest easy," Osmark said as he ripped the crossbow from the loop on the man's belt. He also snatched a steel-tipped bolt from the quiver on the bench next to the corpse. Osmark held the bolt between his teeth to free both of his hands for the crossbow.

Osmark glanced right, muttering under his breath as he worked. Unfortunately, the Risi had regained his balance, and worse, he seemed to recognize the danger Osmark now posed. He lunged with a roar, his heavy fur boot slamming down on the wood between Osmark's legs. The Risi switched to a two-handed grip on his remaining sword and cocked it over his shoulder like a major leaguer readying for a home run blast.

Osmark braced the crossbow against his knees and seized the string with both hands. He knew he'd need a tool to cock the weapon properly, but there was no time to search the wagon for it. So, with a shout, he yanked back, manually cocking the crossbow and leaving skin and blood along the coarse string for his reward. The injury was just the price he had to pay for his haste.

It was a hell of a lot better than taking a sword to the face.

The Risi's blade fell like a streaking meteor aimed at Osmark's skull. The massive creature's wide eyes glowed with a ferocity Osmark had never seen before. He was amazed the ogre hadn't fallen on him with tooth and claw instead of a weapon.

Time slowed to a crawl as Osmark dropped the bolt into the crossbow's channel. There was no time to aim—no time to think. He hefted the weapon with quivering hands and squeezed the firing lever. *Twang.*

The crossbow's string hummed as it hurled the bolt through the air, moving so fast Osmark wasn't sure it had even fired.

A heartbeat later, the Risi's sword smashed into the wood next to Osmark's head and sprayed his face with bloodstained splinters. Then, like a felled tree, the bandit collapsed on top of Osmark, and his blood splattered across his chest in a hot, red stain. A message flashed across Osmark's vision, momentarily blinding him.

Skill: Engineered Weapons

Engineered weapons, such as crossbows, ballistae, muskets, and flintlocks, require a great deal of skill to

---

use to best effect. Though the simpler versions of these tools of destruction can be found in the hands of common soldiers, the more advanced weapons are suitable only for experts trained in their use and maintenance.

Skill Type/Level: Passive/Level 1

Cost: None

Effect: Increases engineered weapon damage by 5%.

Osmark dismissed the new notification as he struggled to breathe. The impact of the creature's body slamming into him had driven the air from his lungs, and he suddenly had a terrifying vision of dying under the Risi's filthy bulk.

Not like this, he thought, panicked.

With an effort that drained almost all of his remaining Stamina, Osmark shoved against the enormous body with his arms and legs, his muscles straining against the immense weight. *Slowly,* the Risi's body tipped to the side but hung up on the wagon's front and started to sink back down onto Osmark. With a pained shout, he shoved the barbarian's corpse up again, wedging it against the front of the driver's bench, allowing him just enough space to slither free.

Osmark used the wagon's seat to haul himself to his feet, then wheeled around, stealing a look toward Horan to see if the old man was all right. His NPC was battling a Wode wielding a burning flail. The spiked weapon shrieked through the air like a comet with a flaming tail.

"Dammit, Horan, can you stop finding fights every five seconds?" Osmark gasped.

Horan fended the blazing weapon off as best he could, but its flexible chain bent around his sword, ripping it from Horan's hands as its burning head slammed into his chest like a wrecking ball.

Osmark watched in horror as his NPC stumbled and then fell onto his back, his sword now lying in the dirt to his right. The Wode spun his weapon in a blurring circle overhead, preparing to crush Horan's skull into the mud and end him for good. Though players could respawn, NPCs only had one life to live. And this was it for Horan—unless Osmark could do something.

Osmark grabbed another bolt and shed yet more skin from his fingers to cock the crossbow. The pain was intense, but he had no other option. He lifted the crossbow, pressing the rough buttstock to his shoulder, and rested his cheek against its wooden length. He needed to act fast, but he also only had one chance to get this right. Osmark sighted down the bolt and did a rough mental calculation to account for the distance between the crossbow and his target. After careful consideration, he raised the end of the crossbow just a hair.

A new message floated into view:

Ability: Engineered Weapon Precision

You understand the proper use of Engineered Weapons. Whenever you make an attack, you may use your Intelligence bonus in place of your Dexterity bonus for both to-hit and damage.

Ability Type/Level: Passive / Level I
Cost: None
Effect: Substitute your Intelligence bonus for your Dexterity bonus whenever using an Engineered Weapon.

"Not today," he whispered, squeezing the crossbow's lever.

The string twanged for a second time and the bolt shot free. Osmark held his breath and prayed the Wode would fall.

But instead, *he* fell.

Strong hands grabbed his ankle and flipped him forward. He lost the crossbow and tumbled free of the wagon to land in the grass, face-first. The taste of green blades and blood-soaked earth flooded his lips as his open mouth scooped up a bite of the ground. Before he could catch his breath, Osmark's attacker flipped him onto his back. The wounded Risi—with Osmark's bolt still jutting from the left side of his chest—screamed into his face and threw a wild haymaker.

A keen survival instinct spurred Osmark to roll to one side, and the attack just missed his head as a fat fist sank deep into the loamy soil where his head had been moments before. He was far from in the clear, though. The bandit grabbed Osmark by the throat with his other hand and dragged him up to his knees. "Die, Imperial!"

Osmark's fingers scrambled through the grass looking for his crossbow, but the Risi's meaty fingers kept him from turning his head to search for the weapon. All Osmark could see was the man's fat gut and the belt that held the barbarian's loincloth in place.

A warning flashed across his vision.

WARNING: You are suffocating. You will suffer 10 points of Stamina damage each second until you can breathe once more.

If your Stamina reaches 0, you will die.

Current estimated time of death: 25 seconds.

Osmark's fingers clawed at the thug; his nails raked at sweat-slicked skin in a desperate attempt to free himself from the man's deadly grip. Osmark drew blood, but his opponent was relentless, driven on by blind fury and consuming hate. His thick fingers were like iron bands clamped around Osmark's throat, pinching off his air and the flow of blood to his brain. He only had seconds to live.

And then Osmark's fingers brushed against something at the Risi's belt. A handle.

A dagger's handle.

With the last of his Stamina flickering away, Osmark drew the creature's knife from his belt and put it to use. The bandit was so focused on choking his prey, there was no chance for defense. Zero. Osmark stabbed the creature, again and again, punching the blade into the Risi's belly in a rapid flurry of wild strikes. Blood soaked through Osmark's clothes and turned the dagger's handle into a slippery rod. But he didn't stop. Couldn't stop. A fifth strike and a sixth followed.

Osmark's Stamina bar was down to the slenderest of slivers, flashing a neon yellow in warning.

The Risi stumbled, but he wasn't letting go of Osmark's throat.

Just die, Osmark thought as he desperately thrust the dagger up under the Risi's heaving ribs one more time.

Finally, the Risi's fingers went slack, and he collapsed backward, blood gushing from his many wounds.

Osmark drew a great, whooping breath into his lungs, and his Stamina bar began to refill. With a strangled shout, he rose to his feet, raised the stolen dagger high over his head, and fell on the Risi's body, driving the knife into its chest.

Rough hands landed on Osmark's shoulder and dragged him off the dead bandit a moment later.

Osmark spun with the bloodied weapon in his hand and glared at whoever had dared to touch him.

Horan stepped back, a worried frown on his face, his hands raised in defense. "That's enough. That un's good and dead, I'd wager."

Yes. Right. Of course. Perhaps he'd overdone it a bit there in the end. The black rage of battle slipped away from him in fits and starts, leaving him shaking and weary. "You're all right?" Osmark asked.

"Thanks to your shot." Horan clasped Osmark's shoulders. "These rebel hooligans are retreating with their spoils, lad. We need to be on our way as well. Best to get as far from here as we can before they decide to come back and finish off the survivors."

Osmark shook his head, wiping the bloody blade on his trousers. He had another plan.

SIX:

Loot

Osmark watched the outlaws march north, their backs bowed under the burden of their ill-gotten booty. The dwindling purple of late twilight painted their shadows in long black strokes across the waves of emerald grass. The towering Wodes and hulking Risi roared with laughter as their captives—ropes and chains scavenged from the caravan wrapped around their ankles and wrists—struggled to keep up with their captors' loping strides. He counted eight prisoners total, a mix of elite guards and velvet-robed merchants, including the tattooed woman from his wagon.

Osmark turned his intense gaze away from the bloodthirsty mob ahead of him to the burning caravan at his back, giving it another look. He frowned and shook his head in disgust. They'd decapitated the horses and stacked the heads in a pile in the center of the carnage like a grisly monument to their victory. The monstrous wolves had ripped open the horses' guts and strewn their innards across the road like kittens playing with bloody balls of gory yarn. The few horses that had broken free from their harnesses had bolted a long time ago.

Only a fool would remain behind, and horses were no fools.

Smoke rose in thick, choking clouds from the burning wagons to join the dark gray clouds gathering in the sky overhead. Bodies marked by horrific wounds lay scattered around the wagons like discarded dolls. In the matter of a few minutes, the attackers had transformed the peaceful caravan into burning piles of kindling and scattered meat.

Osmark put the awful scene from mind and took a moment to review his stolen weapons, which were every bit as shoddy as he'd feared.

Heavy Crossbow

Weapon Type: Missile

Class: Uncommon, Engineered

Base Damage: 15

Base Range: 20 yards

The crossbow was a bulky contraption of rough wood, blackened steel, and coarse rope, which had seen better days. The crossbow wasn't imbued with any magical abilities—not that he expected a find like that so early in the game—but it carried one unique trait that made it worth its weight in gold to Osmark: It wasn't just a conventional missile weapon. It was *engineered*.

That classification would earn Osmark hidden affinity points, boosting his chances of gaining the Master Artificer class later on. Most players had no idea those affinity points even existed. Every time he fired the weapon, he would earn more of those precious affinity points, leveling up the skill little by little. And he'd be an excellent shot with it, thanks to his Engineered Weapon Precision skill.

The crude steel dagger with its yellow bone handle was even less impressive than the crossbow, though it held a certain grisly appeal to Osmark. Its slightly curved black blade bore no ornamentation. It was a tool built to perform one function to the best of its ability.

Risi Gutting Blade

Weapon Type: Dagger

Class: Common, Light

Base Damage: 5

As a light weapon, the gutting blade used Osmark's Dexterity bonus to determine his odds of landing a blow in combat. Master Artificers needed decent Dexterity to boost their chances of successfully crafting the intricate items that were their stock in trade. Using the gutting blade would earn him affinity points, which his hoped-for trainer would find irresistible. Assuming everything else went according to plan, of course. The weapons were a good start, but Osmark needed a lot more gear before he was ready for the next part of his plan.

Hopefully, the caravan's wreckage would provide most of what he needed.

Osmark glanced at the sun, now almost below the horizon. He didn't have much time to lose if he wanted to do this.

"Horan," he said to the stern and bloodied figure standing next to him, "we need to gather supplies before heading out."

The NPC grunted as he continuously surveyed the landscape, but he didn't object to Osmark's command. "Lead on," he said with a nod.

Osmark beelined toward the wagon where he'd fought the Risi. It was at the head of the caravan, and would likely have some of what he needed. First, he scampered up onto the driver's bench and took the belt from the same dead guard who'd provided his crossbow and cinched it around his waist. After hanging the crossbow from the belt's hook, Osmark slipped the dagger into a sheath dangling from his hip. The worn leather holster was a bit large for the blade, but it would have to do for the moment.

Osmark would worry about finding a proper set of gear during his visit to Tomestide.

There was enough undamaged gear among the dead guards to put together a decent suit of leather armor, but that wasn't what Osmark needed. Master Artificers were scholars as well as tinkerers, which meant he needed light armor, which was more for show than protection. Still, he was nearly penniless at the moment, and the gear would bring some extra change once he got to town, so he gathered everything he could while continuing his search.

What he really *needed* was a nice set of robes.

What he eventually *found* was a scratchy woolen dressing gown made from some material that seemed purposefully designed to scrape Osmark's skin raw. Despite the gown's irritating construction, it was perfectly suited for the profession he'd chosen.

Neophyte Scholar's Robes

Armor Type: Medium; Cloth

Class: Rare

Base Defense: 5

Primary Effects:

- +5 to Intelligence
- +6 to Reputation with all Friendly Factions

"What do you think, Horan?" Osmark asked, cocking one eyebrow as he fastened the scavenged belt around his waist then raised his arms to model his new gear.

"I think it'll show blood right well," the mercenary said with a wry grin.

Osmark waved off Horan's smartass comment and headed for the next wagon in line that wasn't burning. His keen blue eyes scanned the bloody mire of the road for what he needed. "Grab some rope, Horan. As much as you can find. We're going to need it for what I have in mind."

"I'm not that kind of mercenary, you know," Horan said with a gruff snort that made Osmark laugh.

"Who were those bastards anyway?" Robert asked Horan.

The mercenary paused in his assessment of a pair of fur-lined brass greaves he'd lifted from a dead

Wode. "They looked like the Wolf's Fangs. Got some loose ties to the *Òrdugh an Garda Anam*—the Order of the Soulbound—which is part of the rebel front. In reality, though?" He paused, hooking his thumbs into his belt. "A bunch of brutal monsters is what they are. The whole lot of 'em. They use the war as an excuse to murder and pillage." He leaned over and spit into the dirt. "They've harassed the Empire's caravans for months now. Nobody's been able to stop 'em, and now I see why. They appear like ghosts, slaughter the guards and take the rest prisoner, loot the wagons, and then disappear as if they were never here."

Osmark didn't hear anything after Horan mentioned the Empire. If the Wolves were stealing from the Empire's wagons, they were stealing from *him*. He couldn't allow that. He might be a nobody right now, but that would change in a matter of days. "They're hardly ghosts. I can still see them out there, skulking away like a pack of jackals."

Horan grunted noncommittally. "Aye, but they're as good as gone. You'd need a fast mount to catch up to them, now."

"Don't worry about that," Osmark said, heading over to another bit of wreckage. He found what he needed among the splintered timbers jumbled up near the edge of the road. He kicked the pile apart to reveal coils of hemp rope. "Grab these. Three of them," he said, jabbing a finger at the rope. Before the NPC had even finished hoisting the rope over his shoulder, Osmark had moved on in search of the next items on his list. The sun was almost gone, slowly replaced by a waning silver moon, and he had an exhausting amount of work and travel left to see to before the day ended.

He found some empty canvas rucksacks scattered around another pile of broken crates and grabbed a pair of them. He tossed one to Horan, who slipped it over his shoulders without comment. Osmark held the other one like a sack so he could fill it quickly.

"What is it you're looking for?" Horan asked, genuine curiosity lacing his words.

Preoccupied with dark thoughts, Osmark shook his head. Once he had a plan in mind, it consumed his thoughts. Checklists and blueprints flashed across his mind's eye. He'd always been this way, ever since he was a child. He knew it wasn't an endearing trait, but he didn't care.

Osmark's laser-hot focus had made everything around him possible. He wasn't about to start doubting it now.

One of the overturned wagons was loaded down with an assortment of farm tools, and Osmark stopped there as a dark joy filled him with warmth. "This should do," he said, more to himself than Horan.

He snatched up a pair of short shovels—the wood cracked, the metal pitted—and handed one to Horan. From the same pile of crude tools, he fished out a pair of hatchets, dropping one into his inventory and tossing another one to Horan.

The NPC raised an eyebrow at him. "What's all this, then? You planning on building yourself a cozy little cabin out here, maybe?"

Osmark grinned, his eyes burning like embers in the last dying light of the sun. "I'm building something, all right. But it's not a cabin. Now come on." He jerked his head toward the next wreck in line, and continued his hurried scavenger hunt. By the time he finished, the pair were loaded down with even more supplies.

"Maybe it's not my place to mention it, but I notice we didn't grab any food," Horan said with a rueful grin. "No wineskins, either. Might be I'm wrong"—he offered a lopsided shrug—"but I'm afraid we may not get far carrying these heavy tools instead of gear that might help us survive."

"We don't need food where we're going," Osmark said, distracted by the next step of his plan. Before V.G.O., he'd never bothered to explain what he was doing or why he was doing it to the help. But, here, he still had to prove himself as a competent leader. He might as well start with his sole follower. "I don't think it's far, and I'm sure there'll be plenty for us to eat once we're finished with our work."

Osmark left the wagons and headed north; Horan hurried to keep up with him. They walked in silence until the flames and carnage were far behind them. Osmark didn't look back but kept his eyes locked on the far horizon ahead of them. The bandits had long since vanished from sight, but Osmark had no trouble following the path of crushed grass and churned earth they left in their wake.

Horan cleared his throat. "What exactly are we doing? If you don't mind my asking."

"Looking for a place to build," Osmark said, a cryptic grin quirking the corners of his mouth.

The pair said nothing for another half hour. In that time, they'd closed the distance to the bandits, moving from rolling green plains with a spattering of trees to a lightly forested area. The shadowed bulk of the horde was on the horizon, now, so close it hurt. Loaded down with loot and burdened by hobbled prisoners, the Wodes and Risi were slower than Horan and Osmark by a fair margin.

"Not sure if you noticed," Horan whispered, "but there are a hell of a lot more of them than there are of us. And while you're a passable marksman, I don't think you'll be able to shoot 'em all before they slice us up to feed to their wolves."

Osmark chuckled at the NPC's nervous words. "I thought you were a soldier, Horan."

"That I am," the older man said with a disgruntled sniff, "but I'm not an army."

They walked in silence until thick tree cover rose up on the horizon, quickly swallowing the marching bandits from view. Horan put a hand on Osmark's shoulder. "Them's the Blackwillow Woods, my friend. If that's where the thugs are headed, then there'll be more of 'em in that forest than we've seen so far."

Osmark grinned. "You're saying they're all hiding in the woods?"

Horan shrugged, nodded. "Likely so."

"Looks like a good place for me to build, then," Osmark replied.

His words were cold and determined, like the ring of a warrior's sword drawn from its sheath. Their savage attack had set his plans back and had delayed his arrival in Tomestide. More importantly, these thieves had dared to attack him, an Imperial citizen, which couldn't be allowed. The real world was on the brink of annihilation, and V.G.O. was one of the few refuges left for people to survive, to start over. And with millions of grief-stricken people permanently flooding into the server from all over the world, there would need to be a steady hand at the helm of this ship.

His hand. And that meant the Empire needed to be stronger than ever. This new world needed unity—so an example would need to be made here. Open rebellion couldn't stand. Couldn't.

"And what is it you'll be building?" Horan asked, an apprehensive edge creeping into his words.

"A tomb," Osmark replied flatly.

SEVEN:

Death Trap

The forest was a dense mixture of old-growth giant oaks and supple young pine trees spreading their needle-clad limbs past the edges of the path Osmark and Horan followed. The undergrowth was so thick and tangled around the tree trunks it formed an almost impassable barrier of grasping vines and ankle-breaking roots to anyone trying to leave the path winding through the forest.

"Nice place," Osmark said. "It'll be great for our project."

Horan watched Osmark with narrowed eyes, brow furrowed in skepticism. "I hope your plan's less crazy than you're acting. You know this forest is swarming with bandits?"

Osmark waved away Horan's concerns, restlessly scanning the trees. "There are bandits here, but they're hardly swarming. Right now, they're drinking themselves stupid and squabbling over the spoils they stole from my caravan."

The mercenary raised an eyebrow at Osmark's choice of pronoun but didn't comment on it. "You're so sure of that? What's an Imperial like you know about bandits living rough?"

They walked in silence for a few moments while Osmark considered his words. "I don't know anything about bandits. But I know people. And men like that? They're the kind of scum who have never created anything in their lives but feel entitled to everything. They can't look further ahead than their next meal. Trust me—they're celebrating without a care in the world right now."

Enjoy it while you can, Osmark thought.

The bandits had been loitering in the forest long enough to ruin its natural beauty with the presence of their sprawling, ugly, unsophisticated camp. Their boots had worn a crude path through the undergrowth and between the trees, leaving a rutted dirt trail, which threaded its way into the woods along the route of least resistance. It curved around the larger trees and jutting boulders that rose from the earth like the skulls of long-dead giants buried in shallow graves. The serpentine path was wide enough for two men to walk abreast, but only if they paid attention to where they put their feet.

"I find it hard to believe no one could track these mongrels down," Osmark said, kicking absently at the dirt. "I'm not exactly a woodsman, and I could find it." He paused, glancing left then right. "I mean, they've left a path any blind man could follow."

"Mayhap the matter isn't finding the *prey*, but finding enough determined *hunters*." Horan rubbed the gray bristles running along his square jaw. "If what we saw was a raiding party, how many do you reckon are waiting in their camp?"

Osmark had already done the calculations as they walked.

Their small caravan had less than a dozen guards, and there'd been twice that many outlaws in the raid, maybe three times as many. Assuming most of the thugs didn't head out every time they attacked a passing caravan, and assuming those who'd been on previous raids were recovering from wounds they'd picked up, Osmark's mental arithmetic pegged the upper bound of the bandit's forces at around one hundred. That didn't account for the wolves, and he had no way to be sure how many of those might be waiting in the night, ready to chew off his face.

He decided it was best to keep his actual estimate to himself, however. Horan was acting a bit skittish; Osmark didn't want to spook him into uselessness. "Two dozen or so. Maybe a few more," he hedged. "But I doubt they're all in fighting shape. That caravan was carrying liquor and ale, so most of them will be drunk senseless by the time we crash their party."

"I hope you're right," Horan said, shifting the straps of his heavy backpack to take the strain off his shoulders. "Because I don't think I'm in any shape to fight twenty men by myself, and I doubt you're up to the task, either. No offense intended."

"Oh ye of little faith," Osmark said through a steely grin. If his plan went as expected, very few of those bandits would see the sun rise tomorrow. He pointed at a guttering orange light leaking through the trees at a bend in the path ahead of them. "Looks like we've found the place."

Osmark held a finger to his lips and motioned for Horan to follow him. He picked his path carefully, placing his feet with slow and measured steps to make as little noise as possible. He was sure the bandits were too confident and intoxicated to bother setting guards, but he wasn't taking chances. His plan relied on stealth, smarts, and dirty tricks. If the bandits discovered Horan or Osmark before the time was right, they were both dead.

When he reached a massive oak towering over the path near the bandits' camp, he stopped and leaned against the tree. A new message flickered to life in the air before him:

Skill: Stealth

Stealth allows you to creep through the shadows, making you harder to detect by hostile forces. Successful attacks from stealth mode activate a backstab multiplier for additional damage.

Skill Type/Level: Active / Level 1

Cost: 10 Stamina

Effect: Stealth. 7% chance to hide from enemies.

The percentage seemed low, but Osmark wasn't worried. The forest provided ample cover as long as he stayed off the road, which gave him a substantial bump to his odds of success when sneaking around. The buzz of insects and sounds of wildlife crashing through the underbrush would mask most sounds he made, as long as he was careful.

The outlaws had erected a crude stockade around their camp. The thick boles of oak trees, their tops carved into wicked points, formed the stockade's walls. The bases of the cut trees were buried in the earth and bound together by lengths of sturdy rope and scavenged vines. It was no architectural marvel, but the stockade provided shelter and would keep all but the most determined intruders outside of the camp.

The only way into the stockade was a primitive gateway hacked through the trunks of three trees. A crude door, fashioned from scavenged planks of wood nailed together with crooked iron spikes, hung from a pair of rusted hinges that were probably stolen from some poor farmer's barn.

"That's quite a fortress they've built for themselves," Horan said offhandedly, before licking parched lips. "You reckon we should just knock and politely ask them to surrender?"

Osmark snorted at the remark. "You think I want to go inside that cesspit? No, it'll be much easier to get them to open the door and come out for a chat."

"Think you could convince them to bring me a wineskin to wash the dust out of my throat, eh?" Horan asked. "Humping all these supplies is thirsty work. Could be, I deserve a bonus when this is all said and done with."

Osmark chuckled again, but he wasn't really listening to the warrior. The stockade was an unexpected wrinkle to his plan, but it had only taken him a few moments to iron it flat. In some ways, the enclosure would make his plan work even better.

Mental diagrams flashed through Robert's head, and he made decisions based on what he knew and what he suspected. The walls were nothing more than an engineering problem. His enemies were inside the stockade, and he needed them to come out where he could kill them.

Horan distracted him with a question that Osmark missed at first. He glared at the NPC. "What?" he asked a touch more sharply than he intended.

"I asked you what that was under those torches by the gate," Horan said, hooking a thumb toward the front of the stockade.

Osmark stared at the row of low stakes protruding from the earth in front of the gate. It only took a moment for him to recognize what he was seeing, and when he did, a cold wind stoked the fires of his anger. "Heads," he growled. "Those are heads." They'd killed the prisoners, all of them. Even the lovely Imperial merchant from his caravan.

Horan gulped, squatting down on his haunches as though he might be sick. "Aye. That's what I was afraid you'd say."

Osmark dropped to a knee and motioned for Horan to do the same. "Rest while you can. We're about to be very busy."

Without another word, Osmark turned to an ancient oak tree and scrambled into its branches like a squirrel. Before coming to V.G.O., he hadn't been a natural athlete, but he'd done his best to stay in shape. Rock climbing had been one of his hobbies, and it served him well here. The tree's branches were nowhere near as challenging as even an artificial wall in a gym, which made it easy for him to clamber to the top in short order.

Unfortunately, it was so easy to climb the tree that he gained no skill from the process. That was all right, though, because he was about to rack up some very impressive EXP. Whatever Horan thought,

Osmark was confident he could put an end to the bandits. All of the bandits. The thought of that juicy experience was almost as enticing to Osmark as the idea of wiping out the Wodes and Risi.

Almost.

From the top of the tree, he surveyed the forest surrounding the camp. His estimate had been off—there were well over a hundred of the bastards inside the stockade's walls.

But he had also overestimated their strength. Many of the bandits were wounded, and their blood-soaked bandages and wooden splints were evident even at this distance. The raucous cries rising into the night also told him those who hadn't been out raiding had been drinking even before night fell. And while a few Wodes had wolves at their sides, most of the shaggy-maned beasts were locked up in iron-barred kennels next to the stockade's back wall.

Other than the wolf cages, the bandits had no permanent structures inside their shoddy walls. Canvas tents and lean-tos carved from saplings served as their sleeping quarters, and a raised platform hewn from raw logs held their chieftain's wooden throne and a rough-hewn dining table loaded down with charred wildlife and burlap sacks of stolen fruits and vegetables.

Everything looked rudimentary, dirty, and well-worn. Clearly, they'd been here a while, which worked in Osmark's favor. They were in their home territory, and they weren't afraid of anyone or anything. Not here. Here, no one challenged them. Which bred complacency. Complacency meant no guards and even less caution about how much they ate or drank. Low-hanging fruit, if Osmark had ever seen any.

The rough road Osmark had followed to the stockade widened into a bare earth loop around the camp's perimeter. Smaller paths led away from the perimeter to features Osmark noted on his mental map.

A crooked row of shoddy privies occupied the end of a path leading to the northwest.

To the east, a well-worn trail led to a well, and beyond that to a burbling stream.

Another path pointed north, where it snaked right and disappeared into the forest, out of sight.

He'd seen enough. Though the glow of the setting sun had vanished completely below the horizon, the silver light of the moon provided plenty of light to do what he needed to do. He scrambled down from the top of the tree, mind racing as he wiped bits of bark and sticky sap onto his robes.

It was time to get to work.

He padded back through the trees in a low crouch, his modest Stealth ability active, to where Horan waited patiently, tucked away in the deep shadow of a leafy oak. "All right, here's the plan," he whispered as he squatted down near the grizzled warrior. "Take that barrel of oil we liberated from the caravan. Soak the base of the stockade, just above where the trunks are buried in the earth. When you're done, come back here and wait for me."

"What if there's not enough oil to do the job?" Horan asked.

Osmark's eyes locked on the man with a steely, calculating stare. "Make it enough."

He didn't have time to babysit.

Osmark snatched a shovel from the base of the tree, then slung the leather straps of his rucksack over his shoulders. His Stamina had replenished after their long walk, but he'd have to monitor it carefully as he went about the rest of this night. He couldn't afford to exhaust himself at an inopportune moment. Any misstep would cost him dearly.

His first stop was the privies. They weren't impressive structures, but they were exactly the kinds of landmarks the bandits would look for in the dark. Fortunately, they were constructed from pine branches that were chosen more for concealment than sturdiness. In a few minutes, he had dragged the privies off of their reeking holes and repositioned them a few yards back from their original position.

Osmark held his breath while he dug away the earth between the privy holes. It was hard work, made even harder by the foul reek rising from the primitive toilets, but he managed to transform the six holes in the ground into a wide trench. Though he was winded, he'd finished it much faster than he would've been able to IRL. V.G.O. prided itself on reality, but it made concessions in certain areas. Crafting was one of those concessions.

You're all dead, he thought. *You just don't know it yet.*

With a spring in his step, Robert headed off the path. He used his shovel to clear a path through the undergrowth, and it only took a few minutes to find the exact pine trees he needed. They were young and had branches a little thicker than his thumb.

Robert switched his shovel for the handaxe in his backpack and set to work. A few strokes of his axe earned him a bundle of sturdy but flexible branches, which he dragged back to the hole he'd widened.

He cut the sticks into foot-long rods and used the hatchet to shave their tips into barbed points. Satisfied with his handiwork, he pushed the blunted ends into the earth a few inches below the lip of the pit. He smeared the white tips with moist earth to hide them from a casual observer. A new window appeared the moment he finished his task:

Skill: Trapper

This skill enables you to build a wide variety of traps used to capture everything from small animals to large predators.

Including men.

Experimenting with this skill may unlock Plans, which can be upgraded to build traps that cause more damage or have other effects. Characters with the appropriate skills can upgrade Plans to Blueprints, which are more powerful constructs.

Skill Type/Level: Passive / Level 1

Cost: None

Effect: One or more of the following

- 20% build time reduction
- 10% increased damage
- 25% increase in area of effect
- 15% increase in duration

Note: Attempts to add more than one effect to a trap

> may increase build time, materials consumed, difficulty, or all three.

Plan Discovered: Spiked Pit Trap

Build Time: 10 minutes

Difficulty: Easy

Materials: Shovel, 20 wooden sticks (consumed)

Area of Effect: 125 cubic feet

Effect: Target immobilized for 1 to 5 minutes

Base Damage: 15

Osmark surveyed his handiwork. He'd opted to keep the pit trap fairly shallow between the privy holes so he could make it longer and wider. The finished trap was a rough trench about four yards long, one wide, and a few feet deep. Perfect.

"One down," Robert muttered, circling behind the palisade to the road heading north.

Horan hooted like an owl and waved at Osmark as they passed one another. With a start, Osmark realized he would never have seen the older man if he hadn't made a noise. He wondered what other tricks the mercenary had up his sleeve.

Angry voices rose through the night air, and Osmark ducked off the path to hide, pressing himself up against a scrubby wayward pine and hesitantly peeking his face out, hyperconscious of the starlight filtering through the leafy canopy. A few moments later, he realized the bandits inside the camp were squabbling over ale or women. Maybe both. He was safe for the time being.

Morons, Osmark thought, unable to suppress an eyeroll as he stole back into the night. Silently, he headed over to the northern path and diligently set about his work, stringing up another vicious surprise.

The next half hour flew by in a flurry of hammering, digging, sharpening, tying knots, securing traps, and tightening trip lines. By the time Osmark returned to Horan, he regretted not picking up something to drink before they'd left the caravan. Quickly, Osmark pulled up his character screen, navigating the menu until he found the section listing all of his active effects and debuffs. He had a few active buffs, courtesy of his scratchy robes, but he also had a small list of status debuffs:

Current Debuffs

Tired (Level 2): Skills improve 10% slower; Carry Capacity -20lbs; Attack Damage -17%; Spell Strength reduced by 20%

Thirsty (Level 2): Health, Stamina, and Spirit Regeneration reduced by 25%

Hungry (Level 2): Carry Capacity -30lbs; Health and Stamina Regeneration reduced by 30%; Stealth 25% more difficult

Unwashed (Level 1): Goods and services cost 5% more; Merchant-Craft skills reduced by (1) level

---

The list of debuffs was a not-so-subtle reminder that this wasn't IRL. He couldn't afford to make simple mistakes like that anymore. He dismissed the window with a nod and turned his attention on Horan. "All done with the oil?"

The mercenary sketched a lazy bow. "As Your Highness commanded."

"Don't," Osmark said in a voice so harsh it even surprised him. That title would be his soon enough. He wanted it to be respected, not mocked. "Not yet."

The two men stared at one another for a moment, and Osmark realized Horan was afraid.

And not of the bandits.

He was afraid of Robert.

"All right, then," Osmark said, trying to lighten the mood. He took a seat on the oak tree's knuckled root and patted a spot next to him. "Take a load off. We've got some time to kill before it's time to kill."

Horan grinned at the turn of phrase and Osmark returned it with a wink. "Here's how we're going to fill the tomb I've been building."

EIGHT:

Burn it Down

The fire's acrid tang loitered in the air as its burning talons clawed their way up through plumes of black smoke and across the wooden palisade walls. Robert had expected a hearty blaze, but he hadn't been prepared for its size or sheer intensity. In moments, hungry flames engulfed the stockade, unleashing a hellish roar and the *pop-crackle* of snapping wood as they devoured the outer defenses. With his crossbow cocked and raised, Robert watched the stockade burn from a safe distance, tucked away in a thicket of pines near the southwestern corner.

These thugs had dared to interfere with his plans, and now they'd become an object lesson to anyone else foolish enough to get in his way.

The bandits—passed out cold after an evening of fighting, gambling, and drinking—scrambled from sleeping rolls, howling in outrage and panic. Robert could only imagine their fear and confusion: one moment they were safe, sound, and victorious, the next, their comfortable home had become a pyre. A cold glimmer of satisfaction flickered deep in his heart. He wasn't a violent man, never had been—he was an innovator, a tech-genius, a business man—but he believed in fighting fire with fire.

In this case, literally.

Wolves howled as the flames danced along lines of spilled booze and reached their kennels; Wodes answered those plaintive squeals with anguished cries of their own, but there was nothing they could do. Not now. It was too late for that. The flames had transformed the night into a chaotic storm of raised voices and staggering men searching for their allies.

Osmark watched the murderous scum stagger through their burning gate on drunken feet, hands shielding eyes from the blaze or covering mouths against the harsh smoke. Soot stained golden hair, and the terrible heat left blisters in its wake. The Risi fared no better, though they bore their crisped and blackened skin in stoic silence. Robert tried to count the survivors, but the swirling smoke and capricious light from the fires made it hard to get an accurate number. At a rough glance, less than half of the bandits made it out onto the path before the fire gnawed through the base of the stockade and the towering walls fell inward, leaning against one another like a crude flaming pyramid in the center of the Blackwillow Woods.

The Risi, Wodes, and wolves trapped within the burning walls shrieked in panic, their voices rising to a choking crescendo as the flames strained ever higher.

And then the walls suddenly fell in on one another with a series of brutal crashes that rang through the forest like the voice of early morning thunder. The wails of the trapped bandits died with the last crash, leaving the night strangely quiet, save for the crackling hunger of the fire.

x2 Level up!
You have (10) unassigned stat points!
You have (2) unassigned proficiency points!

Nice, Osmark thought as his experience bar filled, filled again, and once more, stopping just short of another level. It wasn't as much experience as he'd hoped, but he knew V.G.O. wasn't giving him full credit for every bandit who died in the fire. If the game gave every player the full ration of experience points when a trap killed an enemy, the whole world would be littered with tripwires and spiked pits.

The bandits were so stunned by the chaos and fire they could do nothing but watch in wide-eyed terror as their camp burned. The survivors moved like car-crash victims, lurching and swaying, hands hanging listlessly at their sides as they finally gathered on the road and stared into the flames consuming their comrades. They watched silently, mournfully, as sparks leaped into the air and caught in the thick boughs of the towering oaks near the collapsed palisade's perimeter.

"How does it feel?" Osmark whispered and unleashed a crossbow bolt. A Risi with a heavy scar encircling his neck jerked up onto his tiptoes as the missile smashed into an unarmored temple. *Critical Hit.* With a strangled cry, he collapsed against a Wode, groping uselessly at his head as he died. Surprised, the blond warrior shouted and shoved the Risi away without even sparing a glance; he flopped onto the dirt path, eyes glazed over, blood leaking down his cheek like a tear.

No one noticed.

Osmark wrenched the goat's foot lever into place, cocking and loading his crossbow again. He fired into the mass of bandits, not bothering to aim. A second thug swatted at his chest and staggered toward the perimeter of the group with a splash of dark crimson running down his lips and into his sandy beard.

That got their attention.

A frightened shout rose through the night, carried by a multitude of voices, as the remaining bandits gathered around their fallen brother and eased him to the ground. A few of the smarter—or maybe soberer—thugs eyed the woods, but none of them spotted Osmark.

Useless, Osmark thought. *They can't even find me when I'm* trying *to get their attention.* Obviously, subtlety wasn't the way forward.

"How does it feel to be on the wrong side of an ambush?" Osmark shouted, stepping out from between the trees and firing into the crowd again. His bolt flew true, punching into the throat of a leather-clad Wode thirty yards away. *Critical Hit.* The blond giant tore at the injury, eyes wide with shock, and collapsed a moment later, his HP bar plunging to zero. The attack put him over the top, and a new notification appeared:

x1 Level up!
You have (15) unassigned stat points!
You have (3) unassigned proficiency points!

"Deactivate notifications during combat," Osmark muttered, dismissing the popup.

"Alert," came a male, British voice inside his head, "notifications have been deactivated during combat." The default AI assistant.

Osmark put all of that from mind as a small group of bandits finally spotted him. Those who'd had the presence of mind to grab their weapons before fleeing their home-turned-tomb raised them in Robert's direction, rattling them at the night air in defiance. Others grasped burning sticks from the rubble to light their way, and soon the survivors were headed Osmark's way, legs pumping, arms swinging, eating up the distance as quickly as their tired feet would carry them.

Osmark fired a final shot, then turned and darted into the tree cover, not bothering to see if the bolt found its mark. The time for playing Robin Hood was over. The bandits were furious and wouldn't think twice about chasing him down and sticking whatever weapons they still had into his guts. Any mistake— even the slightest miscalculation—would be the end of Osmark. With the bandits howling for his blood, Osmark fled north along the path. The choking smoke billowed around him, and blazing embers tumbled into the sky.

Carried on swirling columns of heat rising from the stockade's burning wreckage, the flames churned upward and engulfed the crowns of the nearest trees.

Eventually, the smoke grew so thick Osmark wasn't sure he was still headed in the right direction. Tiny flashes of panic and doubt clawed their way into his mind, but he shoved them away—now was not the time for second thoughts. That way lay fear and indecision, which was the worst possible thing in a situation like this. He took a deep, calming breath and pulled up his map, double-checking his position, before minutely readjusting his course. With that done, he closed the interface and coaxed his legs into motion once more.

Everything is fine, he reassured himself.

When he believed he'd reached the right spot, Osmark ducked away from the path and curved off to the northwest. He picked up the pace to a slow jog, but almost immediately rammed his toe into a buckled root that snatched his left foot out from under him. Robert windmilled his arms and caught his balance at the last second, the fingers of his left hand grazing the undergrowth before he righted himself. *Slow is smooth, smooth is fast,* he thought, replaying one of Sandra's favorite refrains. Once he regained his balance, he reloaded the crossbow and beelined for his next point of attack.

A bit more cautiously this time.

The looping course took him behind the line of privies, and as he stepped out from between the wooden huts, he caught a glimpse of the pursuing outlaws. They were on the path straight ahead of him, scanning the forest with their crude torches. Perfect.

"Over here, you ugly bastards," he hollered, cupping one hand around his mouth to amplify the noise. A host of angry gazes landed on him, and almost as one, they charged, driven by rage and bloodlust.

Robert raised his weapon and fired another bolt, catching a Wode square in the chest. No quick, clean kill, but it sure amped their anger to new heights. Infuriated, the bandits screamed and rushed him, spreading out as they charged down the path, forming a line that left Osmark no room to escape. He held his ground and rested his hand on the pommel of his gutting knife. There was no time to reload. The line of warriors burst through a windblown veil of smoke and put on a final burst of speed, desperate to reach Osmark. Their weapons glowed red in the firelight, and the soot painted across their cheeks and foreheads gave them demonic snarls.

Osmark waited stoically, a smug grin on his face—the picture of self-assurance.

The front-line bandits came to an abrupt stop and dropped three feet into the earth, screaming as sharpened pine stakes plunged into their bodies, piercing their thighs, guts, and groins.

Those in the second rank had no time to stop before stumbling into the pit themselves, colliding with their fallen allies, driving the spikes deeper into the pinned first rank.

Those in the third rank almost managed to stop, but the headlong charge of bandits behind them threw them forward even as their heels dug into the earth. Down they went, right into the brutal spiked pit trap.

In confusion, those in the rear trampled those in the lead, snapping bones like damp wood. "Halt! Halt, burn you all! Pull yourselves together, you drunken louts!" their chieftain barked from the rear of the hasty formation. Finally, slowly, the troop obeyed, grinding to a reluctant stop while those in the front moaned and groaned in pain.

Osmark faded like a ghost back between the privies, circling the tangled crowd of injured bandits; a grim smile split his face as he imagined the fates of those who'd fallen prey to his trap. The first rank was almost certainly dead, and maybe the second rank with them. Likely the third and fourth would survive, but the stakes would cripple them temporarily, and even more would be too injured to keep up the pursuit. Left untreated, the puncture wounds would fester from infection. Long term, that could be deadly in its own right.

Most of you won't be around to worry about that slow death, Osmark thought as he made his way through the forest and onto the path well ahead of the injured and befuddled bandits.

NINE:

Loose Ends

When he'd reached what he considered a safe distance, Osmark ducked behind a thick shrub and cocked his crossbow again. He waited as his Stamina regenerated. The smoke ripping at his lungs slowed his recovery, but he was all right with that. Everything was going as expected, other than the forest fire spreading around him. The stockade had gone up much faster than expected, and the fire had spread with a ferocity he hadn't anticipated. Before he could puzzle out why the forest fire had taken off like a spark tossed in a fireworks factory, bandits strode through the smoke.

Osmark raised his crossbow, drew a bead on the chieftain's leading leg, exhaled slowly, and fired.

The bolt streaked through the swirling smoke and licking flames, disappearing from Osmark's view. The chieftain screamed a moment later, the sound echoing through the night as Osmark emerged from his hiding place like a vengeful apparition. An opportune gust of wind parted the smoke and fire, revealing Osmark's soot-stained visage to the band of outlaws.

"Hello, gentlemen," Osmark crowed. "Shame about your camp. And your friends. Fire can be such a dangerous and unpredictable thing."

"Bring him to me!" the bandit leader shouted, his face contorted with pain, the bolt protruding from his thigh like an accusing finger. "I want to kill this one myself."

Osmark laughed. It was a haughty, taunting sound that rang through the forest like the braying of a hunter's horn. His pit trap had been even more effective than he'd hoped. A quick count told him there were fewer than twenty-five of the rebel thieves left. Between the fire and his trap, he'd killed or incapacitated three-quarters of their numbers.

He felt invincible.

The remaining bandits hesitated, suddenly much less enthusiastic than they'd been just moments before. The screams of the wounded had demoralized them, just as Osmark knew they would. Killing a soldier took him out of the fight. Crippling a soldier took the fight out of his companions. Robert stood his ground, arching an eyebrow as he leisurely cocked his crossbow. He needed them to see his contempt. He needed them to hate him with such intensity they couldn't think of anything other than gutting him like a fish.

"Lost your will to fight?" he asked, voice condescending. "This is why the Empire stomped your people into submission in the first place. You're weak. Our children have more spine than the lot of you."

He watched their resolve harden in real time. One moment they loitered uncertainly, the next, they surged forward like a wave, ready to grind him down to nothing. Good. He laughed again and ran.

The path hooked around the burning pyre of the palisade, and Osmark followed it. He didn't need the bandits to be close to him for this next trap, but he couldn't help but look back.

After engineering his most impressive death traps, Robert had taken a few extra minutes to gouge deep holes in the path with his hatchet before scattering fallen branches around them. They weren't deadly, but they did their job just fine. Careless feet plunged into those holes and bandits toppled like dominos, ankles and legs snapping in the process. Easy game.

The more alert bandits realized Osmark had pocked the path with leg breakers. So, rather than risk a crippling injury, they darted into the woods on the north side of the haphazard trail. The undergrowth slowed them, and the tree branches slapped and scratched at their faces while tugging mercilessly at their cloaks. Snarling with frustration, the bandits shoved one another forward, heedless of their surroundings as they struggled to forge through the woods. At last, they burst through the dense tangle of vegetation and onto the road heading north from the perimeter path.

As they crossed the tree line in a furious rush, their feet snagged a trip line carefully strung between several trees. The sudden strain released Osmark's next trap. With a furious *whoosh*, a young sapling, studded with heavy iron nails—looted from the caravan and hammered into the tree's supple trunk—whipped across the road in a vicious arc. The nails pierced armor and flesh like crossbow bolts punching through sheets of target paper. Impaled by the spits of iron and stuck to the tree, the Risi and Wodes couldn't pull away from the trap without injuring themselves even worse, which was a thing of beauty in Osmark's mind.

He stopped on a small hill, purposely sky-lining himself so the remaining men could see him admiring his handiwork. He laughed again, taunting the bandits even as the cries of their wounded hounded them like dogs in the night. "You like to attack innocent people?"

"Your people aren't innocent," a burly Wode in leather armor shouted as he strode toward Osmark, shouldering his way past the other bandits. "This isn't your home. Your people invaded this land. Sacked our cities. Killed anyone who refused to bend the knee to you and yours." He cocked his head, snarled, and spit a wad of bloody phlegm into the dirt. "And now you levy crushing taxes on us and conscript our young folk to fight your wars of conquest."

"And you think you have what it takes to topple the Empire?" Osmark asked, eyes narrowed. "The Empire is civilization. It's progress. It's the future. And this"—he gestured toward the trail of broken bodies and scattered dead—"is the fate of all who would stand against us."

"Your trickery will not stop us, Imperial," the Wode replied in turn. "You may kill many of us, you may cripple many more. But us?" He slapped his chest. "We're only one small part of the rebellion, and as long as the rebellion lives, *you* live on borrowed time."

Osmark laughed right in his face. "Your home has burned to the ground. Your men grovel in the dirt from the wounds *I* gave them. How many of you remain? Fifteen? Less? The night is young, my tall friend, and I will end all your lives before the sun rises. Then I'll do the same to your rebellion. As I said, the Empire is the future."

That should do it, Osmark thought when he saw blind hatred twist the remaining bandits' features into demonic masks. Lightning flared from the clouds overhead, transforming the night into day. Osmark glared down at the dirty and bloodied men coming for him.

It was true he'd killed almost all of the rebel scum, but those coming now were the hungriest, smartest, and most fearsome the Wolf's Fangs had to offer. There was only one trap left, but it was the one he hoped would end this fight.

He darted away once more, keeping to the path, which had no more traps along its length. By the time he reached the trailhead near the well, the rebels were hot on his heels, their labored breaths rasping in his ears. Osmark could almost feel the heat of their unwashed bodies crawling across his back. He threw on a burst of speed and gained ground, praying it would be enough. He couldn't afford to be caught, not so close to the finish line. True, he had the upper hand, for the moment, but he had no illusions what would happen if they captured him:

His head would join those stacked on the path before the burning gate.

With a gasp of smoky air, Osmark hurdled a low-hanging rope stretched across the path and reached the well. Dense forest surrounded the wide stone-lined structure, and there was nowhere left for him to run. He turned to face his enemies, crossbow hanging from his belt, one hand on his dagger's pommel, his back pressed against cool rock.

The giant of a Wode who'd threatened him earlier stopped a few yards away from Osmark, just in front of the rope crossing the path between them. "This another of your godsforsaken traps, Imperial?"

Osmark shrugged, aiming for chagrined. "It is. I'm sad that you've seen it. I thought I'd hidden it better than that."

All of the remaining Wodes and Risi were gathered behind their leader, now, pawing at the earth with their boots, grinding their teeth in savage frustration.

"I demand the right of honorable combat," Osmark shouted. "You, big man, I'll fight you."

This time, it was the Wode's turn to laugh. A deep belly chuckle shook his whole frame. "I don't honor your ways," he finally said as the laugh guttered and died, "but this sounds like fun. First, let me do away with this trap of yours." As he leaned over to flick the rope away, Osmark made his move.

Without a sound, Osmark threw himself over the lip of the well and plunged into its depths, snatching frantically at the rope he'd dangled over its edge earlier.

That rope ran from the well to a thick-trunked tree, went up and over a gnarled bough, and connected to a host of other ropes painstakingly hidden in the forest around the spot where the bandits stood. The line went taut in Osmark's palms, and he thudded hard against the stone wall, stopping his meteoric fall, but eating up a chunk of his HP in the process. He couldn't see a thing from the belly of the stone well, but a chorus of startled curses told him everything he needed to know.

Osmark dragged himself up, one hand at a time, digging his toes into the craggy wall to ease his climb. At the well's rim, he lashed the rope tightly around one of the supports holding its bucket, then straddled the lip with a tired groan and slipped back onto solid ground. His net hadn't lifted the bandits off the ground, but that wasn't the plan. The ropes and vines had tied them together in a knot so tight it would take them most of the night to free themselves.

Osmark stood a few feet away, arms crossed, staring into the burning eyes of the Wode who'd taunted him. "For the record, my name isn't Imperial—it's Osmark. Robert Osmark. Say it so I know you'll remember. You're going to be hearing it again very soon."

The Wode spat into the dirt at Osmark's feet. "My name is Balmar Garmson. Say *my* name so it may haunt your nights until I find you and tear out your heart."

Osmark drew his crossbow and cocked it. The outlaws watched him with nervous eyes. All except for Balmar.

That one needed a lesson.

Robert fired at his thigh. The black bolt speared through the Wode's leg and crunched into the bone. Blood welled around the missile, dripped down leather trousers, and drooled onto the dirt path.

"Try again," Osmark said as he lazily reloaded the crossbow. "What's my name?"

A glint of cold hatred flashed through Balmar's eyes as lightning raced across the sky. "Osmark. Robert Osmark the Imperial. I won't forget. Trust me on that."

"See that you don't," Osmark said. He turned on his heel and stalked along the path away from the well.

One of them called out. "You're leaving us here to burn?"

Osmark smiled over one shoulder at them. "I'm giving you a chance. To escape. To redeem yourselves.

The Empire is the future, but that future can include you too if you're wise enough to see it."

"You just don't have the stones to kill us yourself," Balmar roared in anguished frustration, his pale fingers clutching at the thick ropes of his temporary cell.

"No, I just don't care to waste my time with you. Look around. The fire is hungry. Maybe you can cut yourselves free before you burn. Maybe not." Osmark held out one hand to catch the first drops of rain falling from the swollen clouds scudding across the face of the night sky. "Maybe the rain will douse the fire and save you. Maybe lightning will strike the lot of you and do us all a favor. Make the best of it," Osmark said, leaving the bandits behind, a wide grin splitting his face.

TEN:

Buried Treasure

Robert had a spring in his step as he left the last of the stranded rebels behind. They shouted and pleaded for him to cut them loose before the forest fire reached the final trap, but he ignored their cries. They'd made their choices, they'd *earned* this end, and it wasn't his duty to absolve them of their sins.

Plus, he *had* given them a chance. Those who spent their time trying to free themselves might escape before the flames burned them alive. Those who spent their time crying and whining for someone else to save them would have to rely on the gathering storm to douse the conflagration before it reached them. The rain was only spitting into the fire now, but even that scant moisture was slowing the spread of the fire. Maybe Mother Nature would spare the trapped Wodes and Risi.

Or maybe not. He was indifferent.

Experience alert messages flashed yellow in the upper right corner of Robert's vision, but he ignored them—there would be time for them later. He needed to find Horan, who was somewhere nearby, following through on their plan, executing the thugs who'd fallen prey to the traps. It was grim and dirty work, but the mercenary hadn't complained when he'd been told his part in cleaning out the forest. Osmark was glad the man hadn't kicked up a fuss, because he needed pragmatic allies who could do the work he needed to have done. Even the ugly, gritty, distasteful parts.

Retracing his steps through the burning forest led Osmark to the victims of his swinging spike trap. Blood loss had already claimed several of the bandits' lives, and those who hadn't died yet were pale and shivering against the tree that had impaled them. Traps in V.G.O. were funny like that: they might not kill right off, but they ate slowly and steadily away at HP unless the victims could free themselves in time. Rain splashed on their blue-tinged faces and mixed with the blood oozing from their wounds.

"Please," a young Risi with bright red facial tattoos and a necklace of splintered bones around his neck croaked at Osmark. "Cut me loose. I can help you."

In response, Osmark pulled the gutting knife from his belt and promptly drove it into the man's left eye. *Critical Hit.* The young criminal sputtered and gasped as the signals from his brain short-circuited and died. The rest of the survivors cried out and raised their hands to defend themselves, but Osmark was having none of it. He ended each of their lives with a single quick stroke—his motions brutal, efficient, and merciless. Finally, when the last of the pinned bandits gave up the ghost, Osmark turned his attention to their belongings.

Despite their looting and pillaging, the bandits were far from rich, but at this point in the game, anything they had was worth taking. Osmark stripped the corpses of their belt pouches, crude gold and silver rings, and any rusty weapons, depositing the haul into his almost-empty inventory. Armor came next—a combination of thick leathers and shoddy fur hides—followed by a spattering of coins. Mostly copper and the occasional silver. A few had necklaces studded with bits of gold and yellowing bones; Osmark gladly added all those to the jumble of loot as well.

Have to start somewhere, Robert thought as he left the dead bandits bleeding in the rain.

He continued retracing his steps, pausing only to snuff out the lives of incapacitated bandits he happened to find along the path. A throat slit here, a dagger through the skull there. The scattered bandits didn't even plead with him; the cold glint in his eye told them it wasn't worth wasting the last of their breath.

Killing and looting the wounded was a boring, ugly grind, but Osmark took a grim satisfaction in the work.

It could have very easily been him on the receiving end of a killing blow. Just hours ago, he'd been at the tender mercy of these cruel bastards, and he doubted they would've given him a clean death. Outnumbered and surrounded by enemies, Osmark had snatched victory in V.G.O. the same way he had in his previous life: by coupling his brilliant mind to his iron will. Sometimes, winning in games or life just took the guts to keep going when your enemies had long since stopped.

It turned out that founding an empire wasn't all that much different from the start-up grind of a tech company's early days. Sure, there might be more blood spilled, but it was all just *work*. Executing the plan. *And your enemies,* Robert thought with a grim smile.

Building a company might have even been easier if I'd been able to raid rival outfits and put their CEOs to the sword.

When Osmark met up with Horan a few minutes after dispatching the last bandit, the rain had intensified from a steady drizzle to a crashing thunderstorm. Though the fire still clawed its way through the treetops, the downpour was choking the life from its hungry flames. That was all right, though; the blaze had done its work admirably. Raindrops crashed through the blackened boughs and carried ash to the bloody mud of the forest path, transforming it into an inky ribbon.

Horan nodded at Osmark, then tilted his head back and opened his mouth, sticking the tip of his tongue out. Black drops splashed into his face and dribbled from the corners of his lips, but Horan didn't seem to mind. "Killing's thirsty work," he said with a shrug. "How'd it go on your end?"

"Good. Better than I'd hoped. Almost all these monsters are dead, and they were kind enough to offer up some decent loot for the trouble," Osmark said. "Not exactly a king's ransom, but enough to pay you your damned bonus."

Horan laughed at that, a hearty thing that billowed up from his gut. "You think? I don't know that we ever agreed on an amount for that bonus."

Osmark rolled his eyes and hitched his heavy belt back up over his hips. "Did you get the big prize?"

"This way," Horan said, jerking a thumb to the right.

The duo tromped through the sticky black mud to the northwest corner of the fallen stockade. Osmark instantly recognized the hillock he'd taunted the bandits from and just as easily recognized the chieftain with a black bolt protruding from his thigh. The fat Risi hung from Osmark's snare trap by his wounded leg like a rabbit ready to be killed, skinned, and cooked. Blood from the puncture wound painted a crimson stain from the man's leg, down his torso, to his pale and bloated face. Wide white eyes stared out of the red mask coating his rough, leathery features.

"I'll kill you," the man growled, his words full of hate and resignation in equal measure.

Osmark's attack had been a long shot, but it had succeeded beyond his wildest hopes. Slowed by his injuries, the chieftain hadn't been able to keep up with his enraged men. The wounded Risi had made his way to the hillock for a better view of the pursuit, and his clumsy foot had landed right in Osmark's snare trap. Perfect. People were easy to predict and anticipate if you were observant and patient.

Robert glanced at the thug and then grinned at Horan, folding his arms in smug satisfaction. "Oh, dear. This terrifying rebel chieftain is going to kill us."

Horan clapped his hands to his cheek, and his mouth formed a terrified O. "Whatever shall we do?"

"You think you're smart?" the Risi growled. "The Wolf's Fangs don't stand alone, fool. Our allies in the rebellion will make sure you pay for what you've done here. When this is over, I'll piss on your grave."

Before the chieftain could blink, Osmark was at his side. Robert held the tip of his gutting knife against the Risi's groin, the razor tip piercing the leather and drawing a thin bead of red. "That'll be a good trick when I'm through with you, though I suppose you could squat over my grave."

Under the mask of blood, the Risi's face went pale, his lips trembling minutely. "What kind of monster are you?"

"The kind that doesn't take kindly to other monsters stealing from him. What kind of idiot are you to think you'd be able to keep robbing the Empire's caravans and killing its people without paying the price? There's always a price to be paid."

Osmark ground the tip of his knife into the chieftain's crotch, ensuring the big bloke was paying attention. He was surprised at the depth of his anger, at how quickly he'd adopted the persona of an Imperial citizen, but then he realized he'd been living V.G.O. longer than anyone. Before the VR rigs, before the first line of code had been hammered out, Robert had helped design this world. He was god here, and this world was his child. If he felt like an Imperial citizen, it's because he was, and had been for years.

The chieftain winced and licked his cracked lips nervously. "I have money. Gold and silver. Jewels. Fine weapons and armor. Let me go, and they're yours. I swear by the face of my father it will be so."

"Oh? And what's to keep me from taking it after I kill you, anyway?" Osmark withdrew the dagger and pointed it at the blazing stockade. "Besides, something tells me all of your bargaining chips just burned up in a tragic accident."

"Cut me down, Imperial," he begged, words brimming with panic. "Cut me down, and I'll show you where it's hidden. The best stuff was never inside the stockade—only a shadow-blighted moron would keep the real treasure there, surrounded by a bunch of thieves and cutthroats. It's out in the woods, but you'll never find it without me to guide you. Never."

Osmark weighed his options.

The chief could be lying. No, he probably *was* lying. Scum like him would lie to their mothers if they thought it would give them even a temporary advantage. Faced with execution, they could spin the most fantastical tales to add a few more minutes to their scheming lives. On the other hand, the chief could be telling the truth. His explanation made a certain sort of sense. Releasing the chief was a calculated risk, the kind Osmark had taken many times while building his business empire.

And, in the grand scheme, this was a small gamble, substantially outweighed by the potential reward.

He spun on one heel, his dagger slashing through the falling rain to sever the rope holding the man off the ground. The Risi fell like a bag of wet concrete, landing on his skull with a meaty splat. He groaned, flopping over into the mud, clutching his injured leg with both hands, then cautiously examining his groin. After a long beat, the pitiful fat outlaw pulled himself into a sitting position, propping himself up with his arms, his legs sprawled out in front of him.

"Tie his hands," Osmark commanded Horan.

The mercenary responded instantly. He seized the Risi's belt and flipped him facedown on the muddy path, adding insult to injury, and dropped a knee into the chief's back to hold him in place. Then, with practiced ease, Horan wrenched the Risi's hands back and lashed them together with loops of coarse rope, quickly tying a complicated knot, which he tested with a firm tug. The grizzled mercenary grunted and nodded in satisfaction with his handiwork, then dragged the bandit up onto his feet and presented him to Osmark with a flourish. "Your prisoner, sir."

The Risi glared at Osmark. Under all the fat and blood, Robert recognized a fierce warrior who'd killed dozens, if not hundreds, of innocent men and women. If the Empire had thousands of enemies like this to contend with, Osmark had a serious challenge ahead of him.

The Risi tried to hold Robert's gaze, but the hardened crook didn't have the strength of will to match the human before him. His yellow eyes shied away from Robert's pitiless stare.

Osmark inched up to the chief and pressed the tip of his dagger under his double chin just hard enough to pierce the skin. "You're going to lead us to this treasure. If you're lying, if you try to run, if you look at me the wrong way, my friend here is going to hold you down, and I will use this knife I took from one of your dead men to empty your guts out. Do we understand each other?"

The chieftain gulped and bobbed his head. "It's this way," he said, eyes downcast and dazed as he waved toward the tree line.

The rebel staggered into motion, one uncertain step at a time. His bad leg sagged and buckled whenever he tried to put too much weight on it, but the Risi never fell, thanks in part to Horan's steadying hand. Still, Osmark had to give it to the chief—he was hard as nails even with the Grim Reaper watching over his shoulder. A trait Robert could respect.

They wound their way through the forest, around a clump of spruce, then through a patch of young pine, before finally stopping at an enormous blackened oak tree. Its bark was charred and splintered, but not by the fire Osmark had set. Sometime in the distant past, a lightning bolt had carved the oak almost in half, leaving its destructive mark like a planted flag. But the ancient tree had refused to die despite the damage, and over the years, it had healed the worst of the wound and had grown ever taller.

"There," the Risi said, nodding at the base of the tree. "That's where I buried it."

Osmark pulled a short shovel from his inventory and thrust it toward Horan. "I'll keep an eye on our friend while you dig."

With a sigh, the mercenary sheathed his sword and took the shovel. "I didn't sign on for manual labor, you know."

"I'll add it to your bonus," Osmark shot back with a grin, then offered him a *move-it-along* gesture with one hand. Though Robert didn't say more, he was secretly relieved the mercenary was following orders. Leading was an art, and Osmark hoped to perfect it as his forces grew. It wouldn't do to have his first follower pushing back against his orders.

Horan grumbled under his breath but set to work, hunching forward and shoving the steel shovel blade into the leaf-covered ground. The earth was moist with fallen rain, and there was a pocket at the base of the tree where no roots had grown. The mercenary threw shovel after shovel of wet earth over his shoulder, and the hole grew ever deeper.

Osmark didn't watch the NPC dig. He watched the Risi, who fidgeted with his bound wrists and shifted the weight from his wounded leg to his good one, then back, every few seconds, his piggish eyes sliding side to side as if searching for an escape route.

"If you're lying," Osmark said, "you're dead."

The Risi snorted. "I'm dead anyway. What you burned back there was what I owed my fence in Tomestide. When I don't show up with the next shipment, he's likely to hire a necromancer to raise my corpse just to kill me again. The Resistance might be fighting the Empire, but it's also a business—and you just cost 'em a whole lot of coin."

Before Osmark could pursue the line of questioning about Tomestide, Horan shouted. "By the gods, the bastard wasn't lying!"

Horan tossed the shovel into the dirt next to the hole, crouched over, and dragged what he'd found from its resting place beneath the earth. The bundle thumped down on the ground with a sound loud enough to pique Osmark's interest. Robert stepped to the chieftain's side but kept the dagger pressed to the Risi's throat. He wanted a better look at the find, but not at the expense of losing the strategic advantage over his enemy. Priorities were important.

Still, he easily spotted a long heavy bundle wrapped in a waterproof canvas tarp, secured with thick ropes, which wound from one end of the package to the other.

Horan sliced through the dirt-caked ropes holding the bundle together with a short dagger, and the tarp's edges flopped open to reveal sacks of coins, a gleaming black breastplate, a trio of long swords wrapped in coils of braided black leather, and an assortment of other miscellaneous items. Osmark had to admit the treasure was more than he'd believed the Risi had to his name. How many had to die so this piggish thief could be rich?

"That's it?" Osmark asked, jabbing the dagger upward, drawing another drop of blood. He wanted to be sure the bandit wasn't holding out on him. "If so, I'm not impressed."

"Open that black bag," the Risi said, jerking his head toward the bundle despite the knife tucked beneath his chin. "The little one, tied to the swords."

Horan looked to Osmark for confirmation, and Robert nodded.

The NPC freed the small sack from the bundle of blades, pulled its mouth open, and upended the bag over his outstretched hand. A single pearlescent orb the size of a tennis ball dropped into his open palm. "A pearl? That's your big prize?"

"No," the Risi explained. "That's no pearl. It's a port-stone."

Osmark's eyes widened in genuine surprise.

During V.G.O.'s development, there'd been some heated discussions about just how realistic they wanted to make things. The virtual world was huge, roughly the size of Texas—a state larger than many European countries—which made travel a constant topic of conversation and point of contention. Some developers wanted to keep the sense of scope and wonder by making players travel everywhere through mundane means. That camp imagined players hiking, riding horses, and taking boats wherever they needed to go. Osmark understood the appeal in that.

Eventually, though, he sided with the opposing camp that wanted the players to be able to see more of the world they'd created.

For Osmark, fast travel was simply an issue of pragmatism. After all, V.G.O. had originally been designed as a video game, not a life-saving escape pod. In the end, he knew gamers would be discontent with having to spend weeks in travel to accomplish quest objectives. And that led to the creation of summoning scrolls, magical gates, and a few other supernatural means of quickly getting from one point in V.G.O. to another. But the development team had intentionally made these magical travel modes expensive to use, disposable, or rather inconvenient.

A port-stone, however, wasn't any of those three things, which made it a shockingly valuable prize.

"You're lying," Osmark said flatly. "A single port-stone is worth more than your whole pack of thieves."

"Aye," the Risi replied solemnly. "Which is why my fence is going to be so pissed when he learns I've lost it. He acquired it for me, to make it easier for me to move back and forth from our camp to Tomestide. Now, a deal's a deal. It's time to cut me loose, I think."

"You're right," Osmark said. "You're free."

The gutting blade sliced across the chieftain's throat with a faint hiss. A curtain of blood burbled from the wound and cascaded down the Risi's chest. The man's legs crumpled, and his HP bar flashed vibrant red and plunged as he fell to his knees, gasping like a fish out of water. He stared at Osmark, his lips forming a single question. "Why?"

Osmark didn't bother answering.

Instead, he lifted his boot and planted a harsh kick into the Risi's chest, pushing the dying man onto his side.

Horan stepped around the puddle of spreading blood and handed the stone to Osmark. "You think he's telling the truth?"

"There's only one way to find out," Osmark said. "Grab the rest of the loot. We're taking a trip."

ELEVEN:

Tomestide

Horan shouted in surprise, then collapsed to his knees next to an enormous bush studded with bright red berries. He groaned and clutched his stomach, which unleashed a series of alarming burbles. "By the gods," he choked through a rattling belch, "you've turned me inside out, I swear to my father you have."

Osmark chuckled weakly, then raised a hand to his mouth, stifling a wave of terrible nausea. It felt as if someone had reached down his throat, grabbed a fistful of his guts, pulled them out of his mouth, and then spun him around for a good hour. Meanwhile, flashes of rainbow light danced behind his eyes, his brain throbbed like a rotten tooth, and the world wobbled unsteadily beneath him. Travel by port-stone was instantaneous and convenient, but also thoroughly unpleasant. "Let's not do that again for a while," he agreed.

Robert held onto the fist-sized pearl and glanced at the description, just to give himself something to focus on other than his reeling senses and protesting belly.

Port-stone

Activation allows instantaneous travel between the user's current location and a predetermined location (the port anchor).

The anchor may be changed to the user's current location by willing the update.

Cooldown: The port-stone requires a cooldown period of 1 hour after each use.

Current Anchor: Tomestide

"I guess the Risi wasn't lying," Robert said as he carefully tucked the priceless item into his belt pouch. "We made it to Tomestide, and in record time." Or at least, he hoped they had.

Osmark and Horan were standing in the middle of a copse of leafy apple trees ringed by a thick hedge of carefully manicured raspberry bushes. The aroma of ripe apples, loitering heavy in the air like perfume, made Osmark's stomach grumble again, this time from hunger. No, he wasn't just hungry, he was *famished.* He snatched one of the red fruits from the tree branches above and tossed it to Horan with a flick of his wrist.

"You know what they say, an apple a day keeps the doctor away," Osmark said. He grabbed another for himself and took a hearty bite. The skin was crisp under his teeth, but not tough or fibrous, and the flesh was firm and juicy. The tart taste calmed his stomach even before he swallowed.

Horan devoured half his apple in two bites. Juice spilled from the corners of his mouth and ran down his chin in twin rivulets, sluicing away the dried blood and dirt to reveal lines of tanned skin. "I don't know much about doctors," he offered, his mouth full, "but this is a damned fine apple."

From the other side of the raspberry bushes, a voice called out, "And whose apples do you think you're eating, eh?"

Before Osmark or Horan could react, gauntleted hands parted one of the bushes, and a pair of hard gray eyes peered at them through the foliage. A moment later, a stoop-shouldered [Legionary] with a doleful face and segmented lorica armor pushed his way into the clearing.

Horan's hand shot toward the hilt of his sword, but Osmark caught his wrist before he could draw the weapon. "We're just travelers," Robert said to the guard, raising his hands to show he was unarmed. "Travelers looking for a place to stay for the night."

The man frowned then adjusted his leather skullcap. "Travelers, you say? Well, I suppose the mayor won't miss an apple or two," he finally grunted. "He pays me to guard the gate, not keep a few apples out of the bellies of road-weary Imperial travelers. The pair of you look quite a fright, though. Thought maybe you were highwaymen or the like. You're welcome to stay here, in the orchard, but you might be more comfortable under the inn's roof. Assuming you have the coin to rent a room in our village, of course."

Osmark plucked a pair of silver coins from the pouch hanging from the left side of his belt and rubbed them together for the guard's benefit. The silver flashed in the moonlight. "We have a few bits to rub together, no thanks to the bandits we faced on the road here."

The man shook his head and sighed sadly. "That's a crying shame, friends. Truly. The roads used to be safe, but the rebels have made a right fine mess of things lately. Used to be, they'd target Imperial troops and armed patrols, but these days they've turned their attention to softer targets. Merchants. Imperial caravans. That sorta thing. A crying shame," he said again, slouching in weary defeat. "Well, let's not dwell on that, eh? Let me show you to the gates. Best to get cleaned up and settled before someone mistakes you for the bandits you've escaped."

The guard turned smartly on his heel, forcing Horan and Robert to push their way through the raspberry bushes and hurry to catch up. The effort left Osmark's lungs aching for air while his muscles burned—he needed to rest, and he needed to do it soon. His Stamina recovered at a glacial pace, and if he didn't find somewhere to lay his head, he'd be passed out on the grass like a hobo.

Tomestide didn't look like much to Osmark's discerning eye: a little one-horse, layover village of maybe five hundred people. The kind of place that offered a handful of low-level quests for new players looking to kill rats for minuscule amounts of experience. Idyllic, beautiful, but not much more than a blip on the map.

A rough stone wall encircled the village, providing a token protective shield against roaming monsters and lazy brigands. It wouldn't stand up to an actual army, but Osmark had picked this village as a likely base of operations because it wasn't likely to face such a threat anytime soon. Its unassuming appearance was its real strength. Tomestide was far enough off the main travel routes to afford Osmark the privacy he needed to pursue his agenda. Simultaneously, it was also near enough to other major trading posts that Osmark would be able to get the supplies he needed without too much travel.

Not to mention, his Artificer class trainer just so happened to reside here as well.

After planning his visit to the village for so long, it was startling to *arrive*. Osmark slowed his steps to absorb it all. It was very much as he'd pictured, but there were enough differences to assure him this wasn't all in his head. Tomestide was as real a place as New York or Los Angeles. He started when the Legionary banged the butt of his spear against the wooden gate and called out to the watchman inside, "Open up, Bingley, I found a pair of wanderers in need of rooms for the night."

A moment later, the gate swung open on well-oiled hinges to reveal another watchman, this one shorter than the first and significantly stouter around the middle. "What've we got here, then?" he asked suspiciously, eyeing Osmark and Horan in turn.

"Are you daft, Bingley?" their escort interjected. "I just told you. Good Imperial visitors in need of a place to sleep. Don't be a right sod. Just let 'em in, eh?"

Bingley eyed them for a second longer, cataloging their weapons and gear, studying the lines of their faces. "Alright, then," he conceded eventually. "Welcome to Tomestide. Don't cause no trouble, there won't be no trouble. Understand? You'll find the Saddler's Rest straight down this road on the left. Rooms and food at reasonable prices. Might even convince ol' Murly to draw you a bath if you've got the coin to burn." He sniffed as though to say, *by the look of you, I very much doubt you have the coin to burn.*

"Thank you," Osmark said, tossing a silver coin to each of the guards. "There's more where that came from if you hear any interesting rumors or see any strange folks skulking around. My man and I will be staying here for the next few days, and I'm always willing to pay for interesting news."

Robert sketched a hasty salute to the sentries, then he and Horan made their way down a gray cobblestone street. The gate banged closed, and the gentle sounds of a village at night rose up to greet them. From the outskirts, Osmark heard cows lowing and the contented clucks of hens in their roosts for the evening. Stone and wood-framed houses with peaked roofs lined the street; from beyond glowing windows came the sounds of cooking fires crackling beneath bubbling pots of thick stew. The voices of families gathered around their tables for dinner reminded Osmark of the burbling of a gentle stream.

This place felt good. It felt *right*.

"You think it was a good idea showing those bumpkins your coin?" Horan asked, sliding up next to him. "What's to keep them from kicking in our door tonight and taking the rest of our hard-earned loot?"

Osmark's hand landed on the pommel of his gutting dagger. "You think the two of them pose much of a threat to us? We're the killers of the Wolf's Fangs. We have nothing to be afraid of. Especially not here." He thumbed his nose conspiratorially. "Trust me on that. Let's get some food in our bellies and get some rest before we pass out from starvation and exhaustion. Ah, here we are," he said, nodding toward a boxy two-story building with a stone foundation, a red-tiled roof, and a host of windows bleeding warm yellow light onto the street.

[The Saddler's Rest]

With that, Osmark threw open the inn's polished wooden door and strode in.

Sputtering candles and flickering lanterns filled the common room with dancing light. The inn was quaint and cozy, with worn cobblestone floors, white plaster walls, and a double handful of sturdy oak tables flanked by long communal benches. A roaring fire burned happily in a stone fireplace on the right-hand wall, and a long sleek bar—well-stocked with large wooden barrels—ran along the left. There was a small wooden stage near the back, but it stood empty despite the hour. Strange.

Osmark had expected to find a pack of weary travelers huddled over warm meals, or maybe a group of local old-timers wagering on the outcome of a chess match. There were no travelers, though. No old men. No games. What he found instead was a small group of well-armed adventurers watching him with flinty eyes and grim mouths. There were three of them, obviously all together, and just as obviously hostile to strangers. They congregated around one of the rectangular pub tables, their backs to the fire, their eyes on the door as if expecting trouble.

A younger man with a swath of dark hair, bronze skin, and deep brown eyes folded his arms over his chest and said, "Well, look what the cat dragged in. A pair of wanderers up to no good."

The woman next to him, her black hair piled high on top of her head, and her slim body sheathed in a jade-green robe, nodded and patted the man's bare arm. "I'd say you're right, Dorak. What do you think, Garn?"

A Risi rose from behind the table and cracked her knuckles. Unlike the chieftain Osmark had just killed, there wasn't an ounce of fat on this warrior. She wore oiled black leather armor that strained to contain her bulging muscles, and a weapons harness adorned with so many daggers Osmark was afraid he'd cut himself just looking at her. "The inn's closed for the night, boys," she offered tersely, idly examining a wicked half-moon axe tucked into her belt. "The whole place is booked for a private party. So, it's time to move it along, unless …" She let the sentence trail off.

Horan tensed next to Osmark, but the mercenary didn't move. Neither did Robert. He'd killed the bandits because he'd had the advantage of surprise and the time to put his mind to the problem. If the adventurers decided to start a brawl, he had no illusions about his ability to win a fight. Not at this point. He was too tired to draw his dagger, much less use it. But he didn't think it would come to that, not if these three were who he suspected.

The Risi drew a monstrous crossbow—adorned with more gears and pulleys than seemed possible—from the rack across her shoulders as she approached Robert. "So, are we gonna have a problem or did my payday just arrive?" She arched a dark eyebrow, letting the question hang heavy and threatening in the air as she cocked the crossbow with a simple twist of her wrist.

"Ms. Garn," Osmark offered, praying he was right, "if you don't give me that crossbow right now, you're fired."

After a moment's pause, the Risi threw back her head and laughed so loud she shook the rafters. "Some things never change, Mr. Osmark. It's damn good to see you—almost didn't recognize you in that potato sack you're wearing. Come have a bite with us, and we'll brief you on everything."

Horan caught Osmark's arm before he could join the adventurers. "What was that all about?"

Osmark shot a wink to his NPC. "Nothing you need to worry about, Horan. These fine folks work for me—and they're going to help make us incredibly wealthy. Just stay close and try not to get in the way, okay?" He clapped the man on the shoulder and steered him toward the table.

The pair of them took seats, and Osmark groaned with relief. It felt like it had been weeks since he'd rested, and muscles he'd never known he had ached from the day's exertions. Every inch of his skin was caked with blood and mud, and all he really wanted was a hot bath and a soft bed, but first he needed to eat. A horse, or something larger if he could find it.

The Risi reached across the table to Horan and pumped his hand with a vigorous greeting. "Good to meet you. My name's Garn. The witch at the end of the table is Aurion, and the twitchy little man sitting next to her is Dorak. Nice work getting the boss"—she nodded deferentially toward Osmark—"here in one piece."

Osmark ignored her and snatched a pair of wooden plates from the center of the table. Time to eat. He passed one to Horan, dropped the other on the table in front of himself, and grabbed a roast chicken from the serving platter. With a grimace, he tore it in half with his bare hands and slapped half the chicken onto each of the plates. "Let's eat," he said to Horan.

Aurion rolled her eyes as the men laid into the food. "You're late, boss. We thought something had happened."

Osmark wiped a spot of grease from his lips with the back of his hand. "Something *did* happen. I took care of it."

"Anything we should be concerned about?" Garn barked, her eyes hard, her brow creased in concern.

"I took care of it," Osmark replied flatly. "Let's move on. I'd like a status report on our progress so far."

"Of course, Mr. Osmark," Garn replied, glancing away.

Dorak cleared his throat and raised one hand, extending each of his fingers as he counted off their various accomplishments. "First, we've established ourselves in town, per your request, and made some solid connections with both the mayor and the inn keeper, Murly. Second, we've each managed to hit level ten, and we've each established our primary class kits: I'm a Mystic Sage, Aurion's an Ice-Lancer, and Garn is an Inquisitor. Third, we've scouted the immediate area, hit the local dungeons pretty hard, and grabbed as much useful loot as we could. And lastly, we've been here eating and drinking on your dime, waiting for you to show up." He grinned good-naturedly, trying to lighten the mood a bit.

Osmark said nothing until he'd finished most of his chicken. The food was plain and barely spiced, but he couldn't remember the last time he'd had a better meal. His stomach groaned, this time because it was filled to bursting. A notification window popped up as he savored the drink:

Buffs Added

Roast Chicken: Restore 75 HP over 21 seconds

Well-Fed: Base Constitution increased by (2) points; duration, 20 minutes.

He dismissed the notice and turned his attention back to the delicious food. Despite the ache in his belly, Osmark wasn't about to leave the last of the chicken on his plate. He scooped it up with his fingers and shoveled it into his mouth before leaning back in his chair with a satisfied grin. "Good," he finally said, eyeing his three assistants, "you've earned your keep. Now, please show me what you have for me."

Garn pointed at the black crossbow with one finger. "This is Heart Seeker. It's a little fancy for me, so you can have it."

She pushed it across the table, and Osmark scrubbed his palms against his thighs before taking it from her. His shoddy crossbow had worked fine in the field, but this was a much more powerful weapon. He could feel restrained energy thrumming beneath the black lacquered stock and the gears attached to the cross bar. "Very nice," he said, pulling up the stats and giving them a quick peek:

Heart Seeker

Weapon Type: Engineered; Crossbow

Class: Rare, Two-handed

Base Damage: 25

Primary Effects:

- +4 Dexterity Bonus
- +5% Base Ranged Weapon Damage
- Intelligence Bonus = .25 x Character Level

Secondary Effects:

- Increases all Engineered Level Skills by (1) while equipped

---

"There's more," Garn continued, "but it's up in the room we rented for you. Better robes than that burlap junk you're wearing. A selection of daggers for your stabbing pleasure. Some armor and weapons for your friend."

Osmark wanted more chicken, but he was too tired to ask for it, much less to eat it. "You've all done well," he said appreciatively, "but I'm beat. Let's get some rest and start bright and early tomorrow morning."

He pushed back from the table and rose to his feet, tottering on exhausted legs. As weary as Osmark was, he was also excited. After all the planning, it was finally happening.

His world was waiting for him to claim it.

TWELVE:

Wind Down

O smark staggered into his room, closed the door behind him, and fumbled the latch into place. He tried to shrug out of his robe, but it tangled around his arms before he could lift it over his head. It took him an embarrassingly long time to get free of the sodden cloth's filthy embrace; clots of drying blood and blobs of sticky mud flaked away from the scholar's robes as he finally wrestled the garment off. He let the robe fall on top of the mess he'd made. There'd be time to worry about it in the morning.

Or, more likely, he'd just leave a few extra coins on the nightstand for the help. Because truthfully, Robert didn't see much spare time in his future. Thanks to the port-stone, he'd made up all of the time the bandits had cost him, but that wouldn't make the next day any less frantic. The to-do list in his head was a mile long, and getting longer every time he thought about it. There were just so many details he needed to nail down, so many little tasks that he needed to accomplish. Always one more thing to do. One more thing to tweak. If he just had more time …

But time was the one thing he didn't have.

His rivals were already marshaling their forces, no doubt, and every minute he wasn't pursuing his goals, they were getting closer to achieving theirs. The thought of that clock ticking down made Osmark want to push through his exhaustion and forge on to the next phase of the plan immediately. But that would never do—the game would punish him *mercilessly* for trying something like that.

So instead, he begrudgingly stripped out of his britches and positioned himself in front of the room's rickety wooden dresser. A large basin of water rested on top of the chest of drawers with a stack of clean linen towels off to the right. Wisps of steam wafted from the water's surface, curling toward Robert like inviting fingers. Either the innkeeper had done an amazing job preparing the room just before Osmark headed upstairs for the night, or there was some magic at play, keeping the basin heated enough for a comfortable wash.

If it was the former, he'd need to tip the man well; if the latter, he had some Dev to find and thank.

Robert dredged the edge of the first towel through the water and scrubbed the coarse cloth across his face, wiping away grime, blood, and layers of old sweat. There was no point in trying to rush his plan tonight because the contact he needed to meet for his Artificer class kit quest would already be asleep—he might be an NPC, but NPCs in V.G.O. were as good as real people. The dwarf would rise early the next day to open his shop, though, and Osmark planned to be on his front step as soon as the doors opened for business. Until then, all Osmark could do was get cleaned up and catch some sleep.

He dipped the cloth back into the soothing water, then absently wiped at his chest while pulling up the interface menu. According to the experience messages he'd hidden during his combat with the bandits, he had five levels' worth of unspent Proficiency points and Stat points to distribute. It wasn't quite as much as he'd hoped, but he'd suffered a pretty steep penalty for using traps and fire to kill the rebels—not to mention most of them had been either drunk or wounded, which further reduced EXP.

Still, five levels for his first day's work was beyond decent.

"Open inventory menu," he said, and the game responded by pulling up a list of every item he currently possessed. Coins were at the top of the itemized menu, and Osmark was pleased to see he had a substantial stash. There were only three gold marks—each equivalent to around one hundred US dollars—but he had more than three hundred silver marks and almost a thousand coppers. He also had a handful of semiprecious stones and a single fine ruby. He'd have to appraise those when he had more time and energy, but he guessed they would fetch him another fifty silvers.

Next, Osmark headed over to a narrow wardrobe in the corner, eager to see what other trinkets his crew had gotten for him. He threw open the hardwood doors and immediately a wardrobe inventory screen popped up, filled with gear that was far more intriguing than a collection of coins or a fistful of baubles.

Tinkerer's Jacket

Armor Type: Light, Cloth

Class: Rare

Base Defense: 5

Special: (2) hidden pockets of small capacity

Primary Effects:

- +5 to Intelligence
- +5 to Reputation with all Friendly Factions

The sturdy jacket was embroidered down each arm with metallic threads that formed intricate designs and complicated sigils. Robert admired the flashy armor, running a thumb over the beautiful scrollwork, and made a mental note to add a bonus to whichever employee had secured it for him. Probably Aurion, who'd been a world-class professional gamer before the comet showed up and short-circuited her career.

She had a good eye, a quick mind, and even quicker reflexes. He was a bit surprised she'd ended up as a sorceress, though. She had next to no experience playing as a glass cannon, but that was why Osmark had other allies, he supposed. Dorak's mystic class kit gave the group a significant healing boost and an upgrade in the hand-to-hand combat department, and Osmark had a sneaking suspicion Garn would be an unstoppable tank once she got rolling.

Plus, there was Horan. He was an unexpected addition to the team, but Osmark had to admit he enjoyed the man's company. Not only was he competent, there was something surprisingly refreshing about just having a friend—as a tech billionaire, it'd been ages since he'd had a real friend. Not since his father passed away, years before.

Osmark put Horan from mind and focused on the task at hand. He'd scrubbed the filth and grime off half of his body, but he was still far from clean. He set to work on his legs while he reviewed the rest of his gear. He had a matching pair of leggings to go with the jacket, which, when compared to his old Scholar's Robes, effectively doubled his Defense and Intelligence bonus. *Serviceable,* he thought as he reviewed the stats.

Tinkerer's Breeches

Armor Type: Light, Cloth

Class: Rare

Base Defense: 5

Special: (2) hidden pockets of small capacity; (2) pockets of medium capacity

Primary Effects:

- +5 to Intelligence
- +5 to Reputation with all Friendly Factions

His crew had also acquired a pair of gloves with a +2 boost to both Vitality and Constitution, a drab gray cloak with a +10% bonus to Stealth, and a Signet Ring with a +5 to Intelligence and +4 to Spirit. Overall, a pretty decent haul. Exhaustion was clawing relentlessly at him, and he could barely keep his eyes open, but there were still a few things left to be done. He pulled up his main interface, only to be flooded by a wave of new notifications:

Skill: Light Armor

Though Light Armor doesn't offer the same defensive benefits as Medium or Heavy Armor, it is far less bulky and heavy, granting the wearer decent protection while simultaneously offering significantly increased speed, dexterity, and maneuverability. Light Armor is perfect for classes that rely on speed and distance, such as ranged warriors or spellcasters.

Skill Type/Level: Passive / Level 1

Cost: None

Effect: 7% increased base armor rating while wearing Light Armor.

Skill: Bladed Weapons

Bladed weapons, such as claymores, swords, daggers, and cutlasses, can cause massive damage to foes. Bladed weapons are especially effective against animals and lightly armored opponents. This skill is always in effect and costs no Stamina to use.

Skill Type/Level: Passive / Level 1

Cost: None

Effect: Increases blade weapon damage by 5%.

Skill: Engineered Weapons

Skill Type/Level: Passive/Level 2

Cost: None

Effect: Increases engineered weapon damage by 7%.

Skill: Trapper

Skill Type/Level: Passive / Level 5

Cost: None

Effect: One or more of the following

- 25% build time reduction
- 15% increased damage
- 30% increase in area of effect
- 20% increase in duration

Note: Attempts to add more than one effect to a trap may increase build time, materials consumed, difficulty, or all three.

Osmark quickly read each notification, before scrolling over to his "Character" screen—he had points to divvy up, after all. At level six, he had 25 Stat points to invest; he dropped 7 into Intelligence and 5 into Dexterity, but saved the remaining 13 points for later. Yes, Robert had a good idea of what his class kit would require, but he wanted to have enough wiggle room to make adjustments to his attributes on the fly. The AI constantly tinkered with class requirements, and the last thing Robert wanted was to be caught with his pants down.

It might take a little longer, but, in his experience, the patient man with the long view always won in the end.

V.G.O. Character Overview					
Name:	Robert Osmark	Race:	Imperial	Gender:	Male
Level:	6	Class:	Unassigned	Alignment:	Unassigned
Renown:	0	Carry Capacity:	295	Undistributed Attribute Points:	13

Health:	200	Spirit:	220	Stamina:	200
H-Regen/sec:	3.9	S-Regen/sec:	4.31	S-Regen: 1.10/sec	2.2

Attributes:		Offense:		Defense:	
Strength:	12	Base Melee Weapon Damage:	5	Base Armor:	12
Vitality:	14	Base Ranged Weapon Damage:	25	Armor Rating:	21.6
Constitution:	14	Attack Strength (AS):	57	Block Amount:	6
Dexterity:	24	Ranged Attack Strength (RAS):	77	Block Chance (%):	12.06
Intelligence:	38.5	Spell Strength (SS):	57.75	Evade Chance (%):	5.4
Spirit:	16	Critical Hit Chance:	5%	Fire Resist (%):	3.35
Luck:	5	Critical Hit Damage:	150%	Cold Resist (%):	3.35
				Lightning Resist (%):	3.35
				Shadow Resist (%):	3.35
				Holy Resist (%):	3.35
Current XP:	2,750			Poison Resist (%):	3.35
Next Level:	3600			Disease Resist (%):	3.35

Osmark eyed his character sheet, then, satisfied with what he saw, he closed his interface, toweled off with the last clean scrap of cloth, and made for his bed. He flopped back with a groan, his muscles aching and his head pounding. He couldn't remember the last time he'd worked this hard, both physically and mentally. There was something about fighting for his survival that pushed Osmark to a whole new level of effort.

It wasn't fear. It was something else. Something stronger, more visceral, than he'd ever imagined possible.

He closed his eyes—prepared to sleep—when an annoying *ping* dragged him from the edge of unconsciousness. He glanced up at the small envelope icon, and a message unfolded across his vision.

Personal Message:

Robert,

I'm in, but I've started farther north of Tomestide than we originally anticipated. Fortunately, the *Mystica Ordo* has a branch in Glome Corrie. If everything goes according to plan, which it hasn't so far, I'll be in Tomestide by tomorrow.

If I'm late, don't wait for me—stick to the schedule. You have a busy day tomorrow. Here's the itemized list we discussed earlier:

1. Meet with Rozak, the dwarven artificer. Hopefully, you've remembered to stick with engineered weapons or those that require dexterity. If you forgot, he's likely to turn you away until you've repaired your faction standing.

2. After you finish your class kit quest, get to your restricted area, and retrieve the faction seal. I can't tell you what you'll face because the AI's in charge of populating it, but be smart. If I'm not there to see you through it, make sure you bring more hirelings than you think you'll need. Better safe than sorry.

3. Your meeting with the Imperial Advisory Board is scheduled for the day after tomorrow, late afternoon. With any luck, I'll be at the meeting with you, so you won't have to remember who all of your allies are. If I'm not there, zip your lip and play it close to the vest. No one expects you

to remake the world on the first day. Or the second day.

One last note and this is very important. Sizemore is already on the move. My eyes and ears tell me he's put a price on your head. I'm not sure if there are any takers yet, but he's offering 1,000 Imperial Gold Marks to anyone who can prove they took you out. He's in Wyrdtide, and you need to get some eyes and ears over there as soon as you can.

Be careful!

I'll see you soon,

—Sandra

Osmark could almost hear his assistant's voice as he read the message. Despite how exhausted he was, he couldn't help but smile at her sarcastic tone and gentle reminders. It wasn't likely he would've forgotten anything, but Sandra didn't take chances. She was paid to be extremely thorough, and she was nothing if not a professional.

He drifted off before he could muster the energy to blow out the candle, and enjoyed the dreamless sleep of the dead.

THIRTEEN:

Apprenticeship

A deafening trumpet blasted Osmark awake. He kicked the sheets away, stumbled out of bed, and tried to get his bearings. His head felt as if a herd of elephants had been using it as a soccer ball, and his thoughts were too scattered and disorganized for him to corral them into some sort of sense.

The rough and uneven wooden floorboards tripped him up, and he stumbled again, barely avoiding the chest of drawers against the crudely plastered wall. Through sheer force of will, he lurched over to the washbasin on unsteady feet, bracing his hands on either side of the porcelain bowl as he stared at the wavering image in the mirror. He recognized the face staring back at him as his own, but subtly different. His eyes were a steelier shade of blue than he remembered, and his jaw was a bit more pronounced.

What the hell is going on? Osmark thought. *And where the hell am I?*

The trumpets blared again, echoing through Osmark's head with painful force. What was that noise and why wouldn't it stop?

When in doubt, Osmark always fell back on what he knew. First, he took stock of his surroundings. His room was cramped and populated with furnishings straight out of a Renaissance faire. The rickety bed was rumpled and obviously slept in, so clearly he'd spent the night here. The tallow candle in the sconce on the wall had burned down to a nub, further confirming that he'd been there for a while, and letting him know that he'd been so tired he hadn't thought to snuff the flame.

The trumpets brayed once more, a brazen call like a hunter's horn, and Robert's world snapped into focus around the painful spike of sound.

"Alarm, off," he snapped. The sound had been in his head; it was all part of the game.

No, part of his new *world*. V.G.O. was much more than just a game.

"Welcome, traveler," said a friendly female voice, "my name is Silvia, and I'm your customer support representative. Our system records indicate you've spent your first full night in Viridian Gate Online. Congratulations! Many fellow travelers have reported severe disorientation and head pain after their first night of in-game rest; these symptoms are common and are not a cause for concern. The confusion will pass in a few minutes, and a hearty meal at your nearest inn or tavern will help with any head pain or other lingering aftereffects. Thank you for playing."

Robert had known about the side effects of transitioning to V.G.O.

The NexGenVR capsules achieved full sensory integration by injecting microscopic nanobots into the bloodstream. The nanobots traveled to the brain and mapped out the mind in precise detail. The technology was revolutionary and perfectly safe—under the right conditions. If the nanobots stayed active for longer than seventy-two consecutive hours, however, the body shut down and the brain entered a state of catatonia before the player simply died. The NexGen capsules all had neural inhibitors to prevent that sort of thing from occurring—kicking players out after six hours of play—but those had been disabled with Patch 1.3.

On paper, the transition symptoms sounded unpleasant but manageable. Some nausea, disorientation, a headache. The technicians had made it sound like the side effects of riding a particularly vigorous roller coaster.

"It's a good thing I can't fire you," he muttered, cursing the lab jockey who'd understated just how painful dying would be. Osmark returned to the uncomfortable bed and flopped down on its grubby sheets, cradling his head in his hands while he rested his elbows on his knees. He'd suffered migraines as a child, and this agony reminded him of those distant days. He closed his eyes and waited for the flashing aura to recede and the pain to diminish to manageable levels.

For a moment, in the grips of the vise crushing his skull, Osmark suffered tiny flickers of doubt. Maybe this had all been a mistake. Maybe he wasn't going to be one of the ones who made it through the transition. Despite the swarms of expert medical professionals monitoring his transition, there was always a chance something would go wrong.

And, of course, there was a chance there weren't any medical professionals at all. What if his people had lost their nerve at literally the last minute and bailed out of the bunker? Or, even worse, what if packs of marauders had breached the bunker? Maybe a group of military grunts had decided to take it for their own.

"Food," he snapped, irritated with the doubts gnawing at him like the pangs of hunger stirring in his aching belly. He just needed breakfast.

He dressed in the new tinkerer's clothes his crew had secured and admired himself in the mirror. He looked damn fine, maybe a little *too* fine. He wasn't a total newbie to V.G.O., but he wasn't exactly a powerhouse either—not yet, anyway. It was always possible some griefer might take a liking to his new threads and decide to take a poke at him. Osmark straightened his back and smirked into the mirror. "Let them try," he whispered to himself as he left the room.

Horan and the rest of his allies were waiting for him in the common room. They were at the same table they'd been at the previous night, and thankfully, it was piled high with food. Pancakes, biscuits, an earthenware bowl of boiled eggs, dishes of butter, crocks of honey, and a massive platter of sausages and rashers of bacon had Osmark drooling before he sat down. He had to hand it to whoever had designed V.G.O.'s food; it was better than anything he'd ever had in the real world.

"Good morning," Robert said with a smile, eyeing the food. He split a roll down the middle with his fingers and dredged a table knife through a thick slab of creamy butter. "It's going be a busy day, boys and girls, so listen up."

Osmark ate as he outlined the day's plans. A pancake soaked in syrup disappeared down his gullet, followed by crispy bacon strips and a pair of biscuits oozing a molten mixture of rich honey and heavenly butter. "As we expected, some of our esteemed guests have gotten a little too ambitious for their own good. I'm going to need the three of you to hightail it over to Wyrdtide."

Garn frowned as she speared a sausage link with her fork. It vanished between her gleaming white teeth in a single bite. "You're the boss, but Sandra is going to skin me alive if she finds out I left you all alone here."

Osmark swirled a piece of bacon through the puddle of syrup on his plate. "You let me worry about her. The reason I need you over there is that Sizemore is gearing up to take his shot."

Aurion raised an eyebrow. "Shot at what?"

"Yours truly," Robert said before devouring another mouthful of carbs and protein. He washed it down with a glass of fresh milk that tasted richer and creamier than anything he'd ever imagined. His belly was already groaning at the quantity he'd shoveled down his throat, but he wasn't about to quit eating when everything still tasted so *good*—not to mention, the food did wonders for his aching head. "I don't know what his plan is, but rumor has it that he's put an open contract on me."

Dorak mopped up traces of runny egg yolk from his plate with the edge of a flaky biscuit. "You want us to return the favor?"

That's exactly what Osmark wanted to happen. Even better, he'd like to dispatch a team of specialists

IRL to take care of Sizemore in a more permanent fashion, assuming the man hadn't already fully transitioned. Unfortunately, he couldn't do that—there were too many protections wrapped around Sizemore—and killing him inside of V.G.O. would accomplish little since Sizemore would simply respawn in eight hours. Meanwhile, his other rivals would see the infighting, take it as a sign of weakness, and leapfrog ahead of him. If he wasn't careful, he'd end up with a dozen advanced factions trying to squeeze him out.

"No, that's not going to work." Osmark nibbled at another biscuit while he considered his options. "But I do want you to keep an eye on his wife and son. We need to know exactly where they are at all times."

Aurion's eyes narrowed to angry slits. "No civilians. That was the deal."

For a moment, Osmark regarded the sorceress as if seeing her for the first time. He wiped his mouth with a linen napkin and carefully folded the cloth into a neat square that he placed across his lap. With slow, deliberate actions, he squared the silverware on either side of his plate until everything was in perfect alignment. Then he stared at Aurion until she paled under his gaze.

"I'm sorry, I didn't hear you," Osmark said with a flat, dead voice. "What did you say?"

Garn opened her mouth to reply, but Osmark silenced her with a raised finger. "I want to be very clear. I am in grave danger for the next few days. Which means all of *you* are in grave danger as well. We'll do what has to be done to make sure we get through this. *All* of us."

His eyes swept the table, and even Horan looked away from the cold steel flashing in Osmark's gaze. "Aurion, find Sizemore's family. I want to know where he's keeping them. Who's protecting them. What kind of defenses he's set up around them. Am I clear?"

The sorceress wouldn't look at Robert. She steepled her fingers over her plate and stared into the gaps between them. She took one deep, slow breath. Then another. Finally, she nodded. "Okay, sir, I understand. I'll take care of it."

"Good!" Osmark said, his voice returning to its usual warm and charismatic tones. "I know this is hard. I know none of us is at our best right now, but we have to pull together if we want to succeed. We only have a little over a week until the asteroid hits, and we have so much to do before then." Osmark extended his hand to the middle of the table and clenched his fist. "Bring it in."

His allies, Horan included, extended their hands until all of their fists touched in a tight circle. Osmark nodded and said, "Okay, you're on the clock. Get outta here."

Horan rose to follow the rest of Robert's allies out of the common room, but Osmark stopped him. "Not you. I've got something else in mind for us."

He motioned for the mercenary to sit back down, and Horan obliged. "My contract's not exactly open-ended, sir, but I'm open-minded."

Robert chuckled at Horan's choice of words. "I thought you said you weren't that kind of mercenary?"

Horan didn't laugh. "Honestly, you're the kind of man that scares the shite out of me, sir. And that's the only kind of man I want to follow. I reckon if you've got the coin, I can be any kind of mercenary you want me to be."

"Don't worry about running out of coin," Robert said with a laugh. "And don't worry about what I have in mind. It's not what you think."

With that, Robert pushed back from the table and tossed a fistful of silver coins onto its chipped and worn surface. He knew he was paying far more than the meal was worth, but he wasn't just buying the meal. He was buying loyalty. He planned to be in Tomestide for a while, and he wanted to stay on Murly, the innkeeper's, good side.

Horan followed Osmark out of the inn. The pair of them wandered down the small town's main cobblestone street, admiring the boxy houses of wood and stone as they went. Tomestide wasn't big, which made it easy to find the business Robert was trying to locate. They hadn't walked more than one hundred yards before he heard the musical ring of a hammer against iron. "This way," Osmark said, excited.

The side street he turned down ended in front of a sizable stone-front shop edged with intricately carved wooden trim and studded with windows, the shutters thrown back. The wide front doors likewise stood open, revealing a small forge, its belly glowing with intense heat, and an anvil. [The Iron Anvil]. As they got closer, Osmark could see sparks flying away from the anvil in rhythmic bursts. Closer still they could see what was causing the ruckus.

A sweat-soaked dwarf, clad in a thick, black leather apron and sporting an even thicker black beard, glared through a set of goggles at Osmark the instant Robert's foot landed on the first step leading up from the road to the shop. The dwarf hefted his hammer in one hand and blew a gusty breath through his thick mustache. "What are you two louts looking at? Ain't never seen an honest day's work before?"

Osmark bristled at the insult, then caught himself before he could lay into the dwarf. It was taking him longer than he'd like to admit to shed the remnants of his old life. Two days ago, no one would have dared to speak to him like that. Now, he was a peasant, and if he wanted to be more than that, he was going to have to earn it all over again. "Actually, sir, that's what we've come in search of."

The dwarf, his great shaggy beard waggling in front of his prodigious belly as he stomped around the anvil, adjusted the goggles covering his eyes. He appraised Osmark openly, raking his gaze up from Robert's dusty boots over his fancy pants and finally to his plain shirt and embroidered jacket. "Those don't look like work clothes, son."

"They're the only clothes I've got, sir," Osmark said, careful to keep his tone in check. "And despite appearances, we're willing to work hard."

Horan raised an eyebrow at the remark but didn't contradict Osmark. Under his breath, he muttered, "Oh, this bonus is going to be glorious."

With a grunt, the dwarf shouldered his enormous smith's hammer and motioned for Osmark to follow him inside. "We'll see if you're cut out for this work, fancy boy. I'm Rozak, by the way. You can call me Sir."

The interior of the workshop was warm, but not unpleasantly so. Osmark was impressed by the complicated system of gears and pulleys attached to the fans whirring overhead with a constant hum. The far end of the system was connected to a yard-high wheel that contained two smaller wheels, one red and one blue. The red wheel seemed to chase the blue wheel, which, in turn, spun the larger wheel and kept the fans moving.

The dwarf slammed his hammer on the floor next to Osmark's feet with a *thud*. "I ain't paying you to watch my wheels turn, boy."

"I've never seen anything like it," Osmark said, trying to appeal to the dwarf's pride and satisfy his curiosity at the same time. He honestly hadn't ever seen anything like it before. "Can you explain how it works?"

The dwarf, unmoved by Osmark's flattery, shrugged. "Course I can. I built the damned thing, but I'm not going to explain the inner workings of an Elemental Pursuit Confluence to someone so ignorant they don't even know what to call it. Now, you wanna work, you come this way."

The surly dwarf led them past the forge to the dimly lit recess of his shop. Piles of ore were stacked on shelves that ran from floor to ceiling. "I need you to turn these"—the dwarf's hammer banged off the nearest rack—"into these."

The dwarf's grimy hand pointed at a neatly stacked pile of iron ingots against the far wall. "Think you can manage that?"

Osmark's eyes darted around the interior of the shop. He spotted a brick-lined circular smelter in the back with a bin of coal next to it. There were a few steel-ribbed barrels full of water, a metal-topped workstation, and a variety of tools hanging on the far wall. Heavy mallets, grooved swages, calipers, and an array of vises and rasps. Ingot molds hung from pegs on the wall above the coal, and a massive pair of thick tongs dangled next to them. "Where are the crucibles?"

The dwarf hiked a thumb over his shoulder. "That corner over there, Mr. Smarty-Pants. Don't get excited just because you know the basics, though. After you get them ingots made, turn 'em into sheet metal. I need flat sheets, curved sheets, and hammered sheets."

Quest Alert: A Dwarf's Dogsbody

Help the gruff dwarf Rozak transform raw ore into finished sheet metal. You must create thirty ingots, which must then be worked into three different types of finished product.

Quest Class: Rare, class-based

Quest Difficulty: Moderate

Success: Make ten flat sheets, ten curved sheets, and ten hammered sheets.

Failure: Fail more than five skill checks before achieving success

Reward: Class change; faction increase; 500 EXP

Accept: Yes/No?

Robert's lips quirked into a smile. He drew a deep breath and accepted the quest.

Time to get to work.

FOURTEEN:

Iron and Ingots

Rozak swaggered away with a dismissive frown that told Osmark all he needed to know. The dwarf thought he was going to fail miserably at the task—it was etched into every line of his stout body—which set Osmark's teeth on edge.

"You're about to find out that betting against me is a sucker's bet," Robert muttered after the dwarf, hands curling into tight fists. Then, louder, to Horan, "Time to earn your keep."

"I thought that's what I was doing when I saved your arse from the bandits," Horan said with a grin. "What do you need?"

Robert opened his interface and reviewed the blueprints that had landed in his inventory when he'd accepted the quest. Each of the metal sheets he had to manufacture required a single ingot, and each ingot required three pieces of ore. So far, so good.

Then Osmark took a closer look at the instructions for creating ingots from the raw ore—the process was surprisingly complex and involved for such a relatively simple task. He needed to light the smelter and get it up to temperature, load a crucible with raw iron and heat it, before finally pouring the molten metal into an ingot mold. Successfully crafting each ingot required four passed skill checks, and Robert needed thirty of the damned things. Osmark didn't like the odds of getting through 120 skill checks, even easy ones, without failing five of them and blowing the quest.

Even if he had the skills he needed—and he most certainly didn't—the law of averages put Robert at a severe disadvantage.

Just the way I like it, he thought.

Time was a concern, too.

Some of the crafting steps were long, tedious, and guaranteed to burn through a lot of time. Starting the fire took five minutes, and getting it up to temperature took another five. For thirty ingots, that alone would eat up five hours of Osmark's day, which would never work. Not with Sizemore out there actively gunning for him. He needed to reduce the production time, or he'd be stuck in the surly dwarf's shop all damned day. Robert took a deep breath, closed his eyes, and then opened them slowly to clear his thoughts.

He surveyed his surroundings and formulated a plan.

"Okay, we can do this," Osmark said, mostly for himself. "Horan, head over to that closet and grab as many crucibles as you can carry. Line them up on the floor there in front of the forge."

"Aye, aye, cap'n," Horan replied, hurrying to the closet to begin his work.

In the meantime, Osmark snatched up an armload of gritty coal from the bin to load into the smelter's belly. The soot-stained structure reminded Robert of a beehive. It had the same general shape, though the dwarf had fashioned it from red brick, not dirt and bee spit.

Robert pulled a drawer out from the side of the smelter near its base and dumped his armful of coal into the drawer, before clapping the black dust from his hands. A shelf on the side of the smelter held small twigs and dried leaves to use for tinder, and Robert pushed these into a mound in the center of the coal.

Osmark found a flint and steel on the same shelf that held the tinder, but after a few moments of staring at the fire-starting tools, he shook his head. No. He was a tech genius, not a woodsman, and he'd certainly never started a fire without a lighter. Trying to start one with flint and steel was an experiment better left to a time when he didn't have to worry about every errant spark ruining a critical quest. Fortunately, he didn't need to screw around with primitive tools.

Robert grabbed a pair of tongs from the tool rack on the wall. He pinched the air experimentally, then headed toward the front of the shop.

Rozak lounged at the small desk near the front door. He had his hobnailed boots up on the furniture's scarred and dented surface and held an enormous, vile-smelling pipe clenched between his lips. He blew out a plume of dark smoke when he saw Robert and cocked a *failed-already* eyebrow. "Your business is on the other side of the shop, boy," he said flatly, nodding toward the back room.

Robert bobbed his head respectfully but didn't change course. Instead, he beelined to the large forge near the front of the shop and used the tongs to pull open the drawer on its side. A wave of intense heat gushed out of the opening, stinging Robert's skin and making his eyes water. Undeterred by the warmth, he fished a single glowing ember from the forge's belly, then kicked the drawer closed.

"Cheeky cheating bastard," Rozak grumbled and sent another cloud of reeking smoke at Osmark's face.

Robert ducked away from the plume to hide his grin and hurried back to his corner of the workshop. He dropped the orange ember into the open smelter drawer, and the tinder immediately burst into flame with a *crackle*. The other lumps of coal smoldered as the ember nestled in among them, sending up a few wispy curls of smoke.

Osmark's chest swelled with pride.

He shoved the drawer back into place and sealed the latch to make sure it didn't slide out. Ruddy light rose through the thick stone slats that made up the floor of the smelter, giving the structure a menacing glow. It reminded Osmark of the time he'd spent lava surfing on the big island with Sandra and the rest of his senior team. A twinge of loneliness pricked at Osmark's thoughts, but he pushed it aside. He'd be with his people soon enough.

"I've got your crucibles," Horan said, gesturing toward a row of porcelain cylinders in a neat column. "I think I'll head back to the inn and fetch an ale, maybe kick up my feet—"

"Or you can head outside and work the bellows," Osmark said with a wink, cutting the man short. "I'll let you know when to stop pumping."

"That's what she said," Horan muttered on his way outside.

With his NPC outside, Osmark took a good look at the racks of ore on the wall. There was another puzzle here, one which he was sure the dwarf hadn't expected him to spot without a lot of trial and error. The ore came in all different sizes, but every ingot needed exactly three pieces of ore. Select a piece that's too big, and he wouldn't be able to fit another pair into the crucible with it. And if he screwed up filling a crucible, that was a failed skill check. Five of those, and he was a washout. Everything he'd worked for would end here in this dingy little shop.

No, I don't think so, Robert thought as he reviewed the blueprints for any clue as to how he could get around this challenge with minimal risk.

A heavy grating noise echoed from deep within the brick-lined smelter as Horan worked the bellows. The orange glow brightened to a harsh red glare as heat billowed out, tightening Osmark's skin against his bones where it touched him. He'd have to be careful working around the contraption if he didn't want to end up as a crispy critter.

Osmark turned his attention back to the task of picking pieces of ore from the hundreds stacked up before him. He shrugged out of his backpack and opened the flap, holding it out as he scoured the pile for the smallest bits of ore he could find, plucking them as he went.

Five minutes later, he had ninety pieces he hoped would fit the bill.

Next, Robert crouched down in front of the first crucible in line and dropped in three tiny pieces of raw iron; a wide grin spread across his face as he watched them morph, shimmer, and swell, suddenly filling the crucible right to the rim. The blueprints called for three pieces of ore in each crucible, but it didn't say anything about those pieces needing to be a specific size. Though V.G.O. looked indistinguishable from the real world, Robert reminded himself that it *was* still a game. Three minutes later, Osmark had emptied the ore into the thirty crucibles without a single failure.

Then it was time for the first scary part of the process: loading the blistering hot smelter.

Osmark retrieved the heavy leather gauntlets from the shelf next to the molds and pulled them over his hands, wiggling his fingers in place. The thick leather would save his skin from the forge's heat, but the gloves also made his hands dumb and clumsy. He couldn't feel anything, and if he wasn't careful, he'd end up making a terrible mess moving crucibles in and out of the smelter.

There wasn't much danger of an injury while loading them in, but once the iron was molten and ready to be moved to molds, it would be hellishly hot. Horrible visions of liquid metal splashing out of the crucible and melting the flesh from his bones rose to the surface of Robert's thoughts.

"One step at a time," he said, picking up the curved crucible tongs from their peg on the wall.

Robert stooped to pick up the first crucible and realized he'd made a mistake. Several mistakes, really—about thirty of them. He stood, his brow furrowed, and regarded the cylinders. Damn.

His first error was putting the crucibles on the floor. There was a rolling table against the wall, and its marble surface was at the exact height of the smelter's opening. If he'd been thinking, Osmark could've easily had Horan load the crucibles onto it, and then it would've been a simple matter to fill the crucibles and move them into the forge without having to bend at the waist every single time.

"I've seen that face before," the dwarf said with a hearty guffaw. Rozak had ambled over from his desk to watch Osmark's progress, arms folded, smug satisfaction on his weather-beaten face. "Probably should've used the table, aye?"

Osmark refused to give the dwarf the gratification of seeing him angry.

He took a long, slow breath and crouched down to grasp the first crucible between the curved surfaces of the tongs. It took more strength than Osmark had thought to close the tongs and keep them secured against the crucible's sides. For a beat, he even considered throwing a few points into Strength to see if that made it easier, but he quickly dismissed the idea since he didn't want to squander his Stat points so frivolously. Especially not on something as useless to his future class as Strength.

Five minutes later, he loaded the last of the crucibles into the smelter. The fiery breath of the bellows had built the heat inside the stone hive until

Osmark could barely stand to be in front of it. The fine hairs on his forehead had long since burned away, leaving a faint dusting of powdery ash on his face, which mingled with the sweat to leave his forehead and cheeks black and sticky. Osmark didn't care, though. By loading all the crucibles into the forge at the same time, he'd cut the number of skill checks for this phase of the quest in half.

"Think you're smart, do you?" the dwarf barked around his pipe's filthy stem. "What happens if you overcook 'em, eh? You ever think about that, Mr. Fancy Pants? I reckon you'll lose all your work in one fell swoop."

Robert's guts tightened at the thought. Would that be one failed skill check? Or thirty?

The sweat dotting his brow was no longer just from the smelter's heat.

Robert scooted back a few paces to watch the crucibles from a safe distance, and it wasn't long before a faint glow lit each vessel's interior. The ore was smoldering. Melting.

Osmark headed out the shop's back door to fetch Horan. The cool morning breeze lapped at the beads of perspiration covering every inch of his flesh, and suddenly Osmark wanted nothing more than to find a frosty mug of ale and a shady spot to sit. When this quest was over, he'd need two drinks just to soothe his jangled nerves.

Horan looked as sweaty as Osmark felt, his face drenched, hair mussed, linen shirt clinging to his chest. "We done yet?" he wheezed, sounding half dead with exhaustion.

Osmark nodded and moved his hand in a seesaw motion. "You're done out here. But there's more to do inside."

With a grunt, Horan released the bellows, stretching his back with a wince. The heavy counterweight slammed down onto a thick grounding plate with a loud *clang*. The dwarf shouted something inarticulate and furious from inside the shop, drawing a grin from both Horan and Osmark.

Back inside the shop, Osmark started laying out their next plan of attack. "Pull that rolling table over to the smelter. We need to wrap this up. Time for some teamwork."

Osmark pointed at the wall next to the forge. "Put five molds across the table. I'll start filling them from my left. When I finish with the third, the first one should be cool enough to dump in that bucket of water next to the smelter. From there?" He paused, shrugged. "Well, we'll just keep up that cycle until we're done."

"Let me find another pair of them gauntlets, and we'll get to it." Horan left to find his protective equipment, and Osmark pulled his gloves back on. He hefted the tongs and went through the motions in his head: Open the tongs. Slide them around the crucible. Close the tongs. Pull the crucible out. Twist at the wrists to pour the metal into the mold.

It seemed like an easy enough task, and Osmark was sure he could handle it. At least, he thought so until he started filling the first crucible. As soon as he twisted his wrists, his muscles strained to keep the tongs closed. The awkward angle robbed Osmark's arms of their strength, and his eyes widened in horror as he lost control of the tongs.

The ceramic vessel slipped just a hair, and a hot blob of red-hot metal the size of a quarter burped out and splattered on the floor near Osmark's feet, sizzling on impact. He struggled to right the tongs, but his grip was too weak. He was losing it. *No, no, no.* In his head, he envisioned the crucible flipping over and splattering boiling metal down his legs. He imagined the agony of hot iron coursing through his flesh in screaming streams. Even worse, he imagined the pain of *failing*.

If he lost this crucible, he'd have to fire another one, risking more skill checks, wasting more time.

But just when it seemed he was on the brink of absolute disaster, Horan lunged across the table and steadied the tongs with his gloved hands. His eyes met Robert's. Osmark caught his breath, braced himself, and nodded to Horan. "Thanks," he said quietly.

"Whoa, careful there," the dwarf called out, his tone oddly delighted at their near catastrophe. "I don't need you burning the place down. Do I need to come over there and show you girls how to hold a pair of tongs?"

Osmark ground his teeth. He refused to respond to the dwarf's gibes because he didn't have any mental or physical energy to spare for banter. His hands and arms ached, but he wasn't going to let the dwarf beat him. He *would* finish this. Horan said nothing, his forehead creased in concentration, his gaze fixed unwaveringly on the ingot molds. They had stout iron handles jutting from their back ends, which made it easy enough for him to transport them and swap them out.

The work was exhausting, true, but with the pair of them working together it was manageable. Before Osmark knew it, they had ten ingots cooling in the bucket and three more poured.

Despite the aches gnawing on his muscles and hammering at his back, Osmark pressed on. In less than an hour, he'd fashioned all thirty of the ingots he needed.

Unfortunately, he also was completely exhausted. The yellow Stamina bar in the upper corner of his vision had drained down to next to nothing, and he needed time for it to refill. Time he didn't have to waste.

"I need a break," Osmark begrudgingly admitted, angry with himself.

The dwarf snickered from his post near the wall, and the sound burned Robert's ears as surely as the splattered molten metal had burned the floor.

Osmark's temper flared hot as the forge. He wanted to slam the tongs alongside the surly dwarf's skull, and consequences be damned. It would feel *good* to shut Rozak's hairy mouth. Too good.

Knock it off, he told himself. *You need him, no matter how much of a pain in the neck he is. Pull it together.*

Robert forced himself to turn and walk away without looking at the dwarf or his mocking, bearded face. A deadly calm had descended over him, cooling his emotions like an arctic breeze and stilling his thoughts. The dwarf's jabs didn't matter, not really.

They were painful to his ego, but not to the quest. He was in great shape really—far further along than he'd expected and with only one minor slipup. *Slow is smooth, smooth is fast,* he reminded himself.

He'd take a break. He'd catch his breath. And then?

Then he'd show the cocky, disgruntled dwarf the best sheets of metal he'd ever seen.

Even if it killed him.

FIFTEEN:

Artificer

O smark walked away from the forge and leaned against the wall, his body aching, his throat raw from inhaling the smelter's scorching breath. Horan took up a spot next to him, mopping the sheen of sweat from his brow with the back of one soot-stained hand.

"You want me to do the next part? I was just shuffling molds. I'm pretty fresh," Horan offered, even though he looked far from fresh. Not that Osmark was in any better state—he was much worse. Straddling the line of complete burnout, even.

Osmark shook his head. "I'd let you, but I need to do this myself. Need to. I have to earn it."

Horan raised an eyebrow. "You're the first boss I ever had who didn't want me to do the grunt work. And what makes this different from all the shoveling and pumping you had me doing?"

Robert considered the question. Maybe this was part of the test. He didn't have the Strength or Stamina to keep bowling through every challenge that popped up in front of them. He needed to keep increasing his Intelligence and Dexterity, which meant someone else

161

was going to have to be the muscle. Wasn't that the same as any team he'd ever led? There had to be a leader, and there had to be followers. This was exactly the thing Sandra had warned him about before they'd transitioned to V.G.O.

Her voice echoed in his head. *"If you hire someone, let them do the work you've paid them to do."*

"Alright, let's give it a try," Osmark conceded, a plan forming in his thoughts. "But do exactly what I tell you to do. No more, no less, understand?"

Horan nodded. "That's what I do best."

Begrudgingly, they left their spot against the wall and returned to the smelter as Osmark considered the blueprints. He reviewed them again and again, until he understood precisely what each step required.

"First, put on the gloves, and grab those tongs." He waited as the man complied. "Take one of the ingots from the bucket with the tongs, and put it in the smelter," Robert said, guiding Horan.

The smelter had cooled considerably once Horan had stopped pumping the bellows, but it was still hot enough to soften the ingots and make them more malleable.

When the metal's surface glowed a dull red, and its crisp edges slumped into gentle curves, Osmark gave Horan his next order. "Now, grab the nugget and set it on the metal slab to the right of the smelter."

Horan followed Osmark's instructions to the letter, grinning like a fool as the ingot sagged into a glowing mound on the flat anvil. It wasn't molten, but it had softened to the consistency of warm wax.

Robert grabbed a massive hammer from the rack next to the forge and exchanged it for Horan's tongs. "Next, it's time for the labor-intensive portion of our experiment. Smash that ingot flat as a flapjack."

The mercenary nodded and took to the task with gusto. He planted his feet, squared up his shoulders, and swung the hammer into the ingot so hard the anvil rang like a church bell. The metal smushed and spread, nearly flattened with the first blow. By the third strike, it was a uniform sheet. So far so good.

Racial Ability Unlocked: Overseer

Because of their reliance on social institutions for survival, human races (Imperials and Wodes) can acquire the racial ability Overseer. This ability allows you to command one NPC for every ten experience levels you have gained. The guided NPC uses its physical abilities, skills, and attributes, but the NPC uses your mental abilities, skills, and attributes to determine its success at the skills used under your command. The Overseer ability can be leveled through practice and use, but any additional specialized skills must be unlocked with Proficiency Points. All unlocked specialized Overseer skills can be upgraded a total of seven times (Initiate, Novice, Adept, Journeyman, Specialist, Master, Grandmaster).

Ability Type/Level: Racial, Active / Level 1

Cost: Racial Skill, Once a Day per 5 Character Levels (C.L.)

Effect 1: Command friendly NPCs in your party or faction to perform non-combat tasks.

Effect 2: Commanded NPCs temporarily gain the Overseer's mental abilities, skills, and attributes for the given task.

Effect 3: Increase the skill increase rate of the NPCs under your command by 5%.

Osmark's breath caught in his chest as he read and dismissed the notice. When he glanced up, he saw the dwarf glaring at him from across the shop, and Osmark grinned back so hard his jaw creaked. This was it, the game changer he needed to ensure his place on the Imperial Throne, and now that he'd figured it out, nothing could stand in his way.

With Horan's strength and Osmark's mind, the duo hammered through the rest of the sheets in less than twenty minutes. As Horan quenched the last of the hammered metal in the bucket of water next to the forge, Osmark noticed another game prompt awaiting his attention.

Crafting Profession Unlocked: Blacksmithing

The blacksmithing profession allows you to create finished metal products from a variety of different types of ore. This crafting profession requires a blacksmith's shop for maximum effectiveness.

There are eight primary Crafting Professions: Cooking, Enchanting, Alchemy, Tailoring and

Leatherwork, Engineering, Merchant-Craft, Blacksmithing, and Lapidary (Jeweler). All Professions, both Gathering and Crafting, can be unlocked and leveled through practice and use, but any specialized skills or abilities within a given profession must be unlocked with Proficiency Points. All specialized profession skills can be upgraded a total of seven times (Initiate, Novice, Adept, Journeyman, Specialist, Master, Grandmaster).

Gathering Ability Type/Level: Passive / Level 1

Cost: N/A

Effect 1: Increase quality of created items by 5% OR reduce required materials by 15% OR reduce production time by 15%.

Effect 2: All Stamina Costs associated with Blacksmithing are reduced by 10%.

Effect 3: Randomly increase damage of created weapons by 1-4 points OR randomly increase the base defense of created metal armor by 1-4 points.

That second one would have been useful, Osmark thought ruefully.

Horan winked at Osmark. "I guess you really can teach an old dog new tricks."

Osmark rubbed his chin. "Wait, are you saying you gained skills?"

Horan nodded. "Aye. Picked up a little blacksmithing. Was I not supposed to?"

A flicker of excitement lit up Osmark's thoughts. This was even better than he'd first thought.

If he could use the Overseer ability to train NPCs at the same time he trained himself, there were limitless possibilities. As he gained levels, he'd be able to train even more allies, which would give him access to more physical abilities, which would give them access to his mental abilities...

"Pretty pleased with yourself, eh, Mr. Fancy Pants?" the dwarf asked through a puff of choking black smoke, cutting Osmark's thoughts short. "Let's take a look at this garbage you and your henchman have turned out—see if I might not be able to salvage some of it."

Osmark nodded, patiently ignoring the dig, and gestured toward the neat stacks of metal sheets he and Horan had created. "I think you'll be surprised at the quality."

The dwarf grunted and frowned. "I'll be surprised if there is *any* quality."

Robert watched anxiously, hands folded behind his back, as the dwarf strutted over and slowly appraised each sheet of metal in turn. He tilted them to look at their edges, running a calloused thumb along the side. Next, he pulled a pair of calipers from his worn leather belt and measured them at various points from the center. He even lifted one of the painstakingly hammered sheets and bit down on it with his thick front teeth. The dwarf's craggy face betrayed no emotion. Beneath his massive beard, he could've been smiling from ear to ear or scowling in fury, and Osmark wouldn't have been able to tell.

Finally, after what felt like an eternity, the dwarf set the last sheet down, folded his arms across his barrel chest, and nodded to Robert. "I have to say, Fancy Pants, you've surprised me."

"I think you'll find I'm full of surprises if you hang around me long enough," Osmark replied flatly, though inside he was practically glowing with pride from having discovered a way around the physical limitations of his class. As long as Horan was around, that was no longer a concern.

"Suppose I could use an apprentice," Rozak mused, scratching absently at his beard. "Just one apprentice, mind you, which means one salary. I don't care if the old man works with you—lends a hand here or there—but I'm not paying him. Course, if you choose to compensate him from your pocket, that's none of my business."

Horan cocked an eyebrow and glanced at Osmark. *I damned well better get paid,* that look said.

Robert muttered, "Don't worry, you'll get your money."

The dwarf reached beneath his beard and pulled out a smooth leather roll, bound with a piece of twine. "If you want the job, it's yours. Just take the toolkit, and we can get started."

Robert didn't hesitate, not for an eyeblink. He snatched the leather bundle studded with tools from Rozak's hand and felt a wave of relief wash over him. He expected a flurry of system messages informing him of his new class kit and at least one level gain. But there was nothing except blank ominous silence, which could only mean one thing: the quest hadn't ended.

"Don't go getting all goo-goo eyed on me," the dwarf said. "There's still one test left for you. If you can't pass this, I won't have much use for you as an apprentice. Most fools can figure out how to forge a sheet of metal with enough time and patience, but being an Artificer requires more than that." The dwarf headed across the shop to an ornately carved door set into the east wall. It swung open on silent hinges as he approached, and had almost closed behind him by the time Horan and Osmark caught up.

The smith's shop had been a dusty, dirty, crude place. The room beyond the door was something else altogether.

There were no hammers or mallets here, no blazing forges or hunks of iron waiting to be smelted. Instead, the walls were lined with glass-fronted tool cases, all filled with delicate tools. Osmark couldn't even begin to identify all of the devices and gadgets, though he knew one day he would have to master every one of them.

"Don't stand there gawking, boy," the dwarf growled as he plopped his bulky body into a padded chair in front of a workbench and stripped off the thick goggles he'd been wearing. "I have work for you, yet." His stubby fingers gingerly lifted another set of goggles, these much more intricate and fitted with hinged and telescoping lenses, from a rack above the bench. "You'll need these."

Osmark rested his toolkit on the bench to free both hands for the goggles. He slipped them over his head and adjusted the straps until the lenses were seated snugly over his eyes.

The dwarf tilted his head to one side and said, "Nah, you've got them all off-center. Catawampus."

With a few deft motions, Rozak adjusted the contraption, and suddenly everything snapped into focus for Osmark. His vision had been serviceable before, but the goggles showed him the world in a way he hadn't seen it before. Everything was sharper and rendered in finer detail—the fibers of Rozak's clothes popping out, the smudges on Horan's face taking on new dimension—but it wasn't overwhelming. It just *was*.

"You can stare at tree leaves on your own time," the dwarf said. "I want you to look at this." He tapped his stubby fingers against an elegant weapon on the workbench—a cross between a flintlock pistol and a Tesla death ray—then pushed it toward Osmark. The weapon was all bright brass, polished dark wood, and copper tubing meshed together into something new, exotic, and beautiful. Carefully, Osmark picked up the pistol, examining the barrel, which was covered with elegant patterns and flowing runes. In his gut, Osmark knew those odd sigils meant something, but he couldn't tell what exactly.

Not yet.

The barrel butted up against a firing chamber, which sprouted a pair of fine copper pipes from its rear, and instead of a firing pin, this weapon sported a bulging brass cylinder covered in decorative scrollwork. Osmark tried to puzzle out what he was seeing. "What is this?"

"It's a repeater," the dwarf replied. "A weapon no Artificer worth his salt would be without." Rozak hooked a thumb toward the wall behind him, which housed a number of similar weapons on wooden shelves. "This one's busted, though. Fix it, and it's yours. Don't fix it, and you're done as my apprentice. I've no use for someone that doesn't have the sight"— he tapped at the corner of one eye—"or the wits to use it."

Carefully, Osmark set the broken repeater down on the tabletop and focused as if his life depended on it because in many ways it did. True, he might be able to fight off Sizemore and the rest of his bloody thugs without the unique skills of an Artificer, but that wasn't in the plan. He'd have to retool, reconsider everything.

There wasn't time for that.

Robert's eyes played over the weapon from one end to the other. He felt a flutter of panic in his stomach. The pistol was exquisite, crafted with obvious care and attention to detail. He couldn't see anything wrong with it.

He paused, dry washing his hands as he thought. *"I've no use for someone that doesn't have the sight."* That's what Rozak had said a moment before. The goggles had to be the key here. They'd shown him the world in a way he'd never imagined, but maybe they could show him even more.

Robert swiveled a green lens in front of his left eye, and the world plunged into an emerald sea. But he saw nothing different about the repeater, so he rotated the lens away from his eye and back into its place. He stared at the weapon, forehead creased in concentration, and rotated a telescoping lens over his right eye. He adjusted the dials and tiny levers alongside the lens but discovered nothing new about the repeater.

Frustrated, Robert flicked one lens after another over his eyes, experimenting with a variety of different combinations, desperate to unravel the mystery the dwarf had placed before him. If he couldn't fix Rozak's repeater, all of his planning would come apart at the seams. No. He wouldn't let this defeat him, not when he was so close.

Flick.

Nothing.

Twist.

Nothing.

Slide.

Noth—

Something.

A blue magnifying lens over Osmark's left eye revealed a vivid red streak like a blood vein within the pattern running the length of the repeater's barrel. The undulating line flowed from the weapon's front sight all the way back to its firing chamber.

The crimson line within the pattern, however, was slightly different from the wave form it occupied. There was a tiny break in the red light midway down the repeater's barrel, a minuscule rupture. Osmark leaned in to get a closer look, resting his elbows on his thighs, and noticed a jagged notch gouged through the complicated pattern etched into the metal. "Here," he said, pointing to the damage.

"Good eye," the dwarf offered with grudging admiration. "Being an Artificer is more than just knowing how to build machines. It's more powerful than science alone and more flexible than the spells you'll see mages bonding to weapons and armor. What you'll learn bridges the natural and the supernatural, science and sorcery, in ways others can only imagine in their wildest dreams. There are a few who can manage what we can—mostly the Weaponeers and their ilk—but the gift is exceedingly rare."

Rozak opened the case to his left and extracted a tool with a narrow shaft and a wicked point at its tip. "This is an engraving awl, and a finer one an amateur like you is unlikely to see. Take it. Use it to fix the repeater."

Osmark returned his attention to the weapon before him and hunched over it to focus on the task at hand. The dwarf continued talking, his words not distracting, but soothing, calming, and focusing Robert's thoughts.

"We control the secrets of the Divine Geometry," the dwarf continued. "We combine ancient symbols and diagrams of power with the force of steam and ingenuity of science. We merge the two worlds to power our inventions."

Osmark drew light strokes across the notched gap on the repeater's barrel. Each movement left hardly a scratch, but Osmark knew he was making progress. The hair-fine lines he engraved into the weapon's surface were nothing individually, but they were building on one another into something much greater than the sum of their parts.

"I could teach anyone the basic scrivening you're doing, but the higher orders contain secrets only the most talented can master. A true artificer can craft mechanical minions to do his bidding. Some even claim to have re-created the ancient Weapons of Sundering."

Osmark healed the repeater's broken pattern with a final line etched with his steady hand. Blue light shot away from the tip of the engraving awl with a sizzling crack and flowed through the repeater's restored pattern. The luminance soaked into the brassy metal and oiled wood, breathing new life and power back into the damaged contraption.

Rozak took the engraving awl from Osmark's nerveless fingers. "Well, don't just stand there, boy, pick up your new weapon. Take a moment to appreciate the work of your hands."

Osmark raised the repeater from the bench and admired its ornate construction, feeling the comforting weight in his hands and breathing a deep sigh of relief. It seemed at once too delicate to be a weapon and yet too refined to be anything else. A series of game prompts flashed across his vision.

x1 Level up!
You have (18) unassigned stat points!
You have (6) unassigned proficiency points!

Quest Alert: A Dwarf's Dogsbody

You have completed the tasks set before you by Master Artificer Rozak Kulrath. He has recognized the value of your work and agreed to train you in the ways of the Artificer in exchange for your apprenticeship here in his workshop.

You have permanently received the Class Basic Artificer and have been granted a scalable toolkit from Rozak Kulrath.

Also, you have raised your reputation with the Tomestide township to Friendly.

You have also been rewarded 50 renown for completing this quest!

Class Unlocked

Congratulations, you have been granted the Basic Artificer class and have unlocked the Basic Artificer skill kit! Each class has a variety of locked skills/abilities, which can be unlocked and improved by investing Proficiency Points earned while leveling up your character. Many skills require you to reach a certain character level before unlocking, and each unlocked skill can be upgraded a total of seven times (Initiate, Novice, Adept, Journeyman, Specialist, Master, Grandmaster).

"A word of advice before you bugger off into the great wild. You won't be able to use that repeater until you unlock the Firearms Skill in your new class tree. Weapons like these are specialty items, and only those with the proper know-how can use 'em, understand?"

"Understood," Osmark replied, burning with excitement to examine his Basic Artificer Class Kit Skill Tree.

"Good enough," the dwarf grunted, pointing to the leather holster hanging from the end of the workbench. "Now, why don't you strap that on," Rozak said, "and then get the hell outta here and go do something useful, like a good and proper apprentice. You'll find a list of supplies I need you to gather on my desk in the main room. Take the paper." He paused, eyeing Osmark with a mixture of hope and suspicion. "Don't touch anything else. Nothing."

Osmark bobbed his head and hurried out of Rozak's workroom before the dwarf could change his mind and reclaim the repeater. He shrugged into the shoulder holster and pulled up the weapon in his interface screen, eager to see what it could offer him.

Shoddy Repeater

Weapon Type: Engineered; Firearm

Class: Rare, One-handed

Base Damage: 20

Capacity: 10 shots (Ammunition can be created using the Blacksmithing skill and any ore; it takes 1 minute to create (10) shells)

Primary Effects:

- +10 Dexterity Bonus
- +10% Base Ranged Weapon Damage
- Intelligence Bonus = .25 x Character Level

As he scanned the repeater's stats, a new text window appeared, this one an informational overview regarding his mysterious new weapon:

Repeater Tutorial:

The repeater is a refined weapon ideally suited for Artificers. Its exceptional accuracy and range allow the wielder to dispatch opponents at a distance to minimize risk to their persons.

The repeater is also highly customizable, allowing Artificers to tailor them to specific needs.

The basic repeater has three firing modes:

Single Shot is the most accurate, allowing one shot per trigger pull, and incurs no penalties while firing.

Burst Fire unleashes three shots in a single action. Burst Fire cannot be aimed and suffers double range penalties. Burst Fire can be used once every fifteen seconds.

Automatic Fire empties all remaining shots from the repeater's magazine in a single action. Automatic Fire cannot be aimed and suffers triple range penalties. When using Automatic Fire, the damage inflicted by critical hits is reduced by 25%. Automatic Fire can only be used once per minute.

Excellent. After reading and rereading the information, he closed the screen and secured the repeater in its holster; out of the corner of his eye,

Robert caught Horan smirking at him. "What?" he asked the old merc.

"You look like a kid who just got handed the cookie jar," Horan replied, hooking his thumbs into his leather belt. "It's that nice of a toy, eh?"

Robert couldn't help but chuckle. "Let's go find out just how nice."

SIXTEEN:

Level Up!

Osmark checked the in-game clock as he walked to the dwarf's desk near the shop's entrance. It was just before noon, which meant he only had a few short hours to spare before he needed to head down to the restricted area and claim his Faction Seal. And they would be busy, busy hours: He had to check in with his allies to see how they had progressed on their surveillance of Sizemore and meet with Sandra before heading into the restricted area. That didn't leave him much time for anything else, but if he hurried, he could complete this quest for Rozak and still meet his other obligations.

"Here we are," he said as he snatched up the list of supplies the dwarf had mentioned. A popup appeared, revealing a new quest.

Quest Alert: A Dwarf's Dogsbody, Part 2

Rozak needs supplies to continue his work. Gather the following and return them to Rozak for your reward:

- 20 Oletharin Leaves

- 10 Moridon Fungus
- 5 Chunks of Starfall Ore

These items can be found in most forests, though Starfall Ore is only found near mountains.

Quest Class: Rare, class-based

Quest Difficulty: Moderate

Success: Return all required supplies before day's end.

Failure: Fail to return all required supplies before day's end.

Reward: Class change; faction increase; 2,000 EXP

Accept: Yes/No?

"Yes," he confirmed absently, before turning to Horan. "Oletharin leaves, Moridon fungus, and Starfall ore. Where's the nearest forest?"

Horan scratched the salt-and-pepper stubble on the right side of his chin. "Across the river to the east, in the foothills, before you reach the Kelos Peaks. It's not far, but do you have time to waste on a fetch and carry mission for that grumpy old dwarf? Seems to me, a man like you might have more important business to be about."

Robert frowned and motioned for Horan to follow him over to the bulky forge nestled in the front of the shop. He needed bullets, but he also needed to make some noise so he could talk to Horan without the crotchety dwarf overhearing.

He gathered some ore, rattling the nuggets in their rack to drown out his conversation. "Yes, I have the time. Even if I didn't, I need to make the time. I need that dwarf to like me if I'm going to succeed here in Tomestide. And I need him to like you, too, so easy on the insults within earshot of him."

A few minutes later, Robert had filled the ammunition straps on his holster with twenty shells and dropped another thirty into his inventory. He spent another minute creating ten more shells to load the repeater, then showed his handiwork to Horan. "This'll make a nice hole in anything that gets in our way, I bet."

Horan grunted noncommittally at that and followed Robert out of the shop and down the eastern road out of Tomestide. They waved at the bored guards at the gate, who nodded at them as they departed.

"Safe travels," the taller of the two guards called as they passed.

Robert turned on one heel. "Thank you for the well wishes. And what's your name, good man?"

The taller guard doffed his leather skullcap. "Tarlson, sir. And this here's Gurt."

"Well, Tarlson, you and Gurt enjoy a drink on me after your shift." He fished a silver coin out of his belt pouch and flicked it to the guard.

Horan waited until they were out of earshot of the guards before grumbling, "They don't even work for you, and they're getting paid better than me."

Osmark rolled his eyes. "You're getting paid. And you get a *bonus*, remember?"

Horan grunted but didn't challenge Robert.

He knew which side of the bread his butter was on.

A few minutes after leaving town, the duo reached the river, which rushed beneath a stone bridge. The swiftly moving waters crashed over hidden boulders, kicking up whitecaps with a rumbling roar that made it impossible to carry on a conversation. Robert admired the turbulent water as they crossed over, his boots click-clacking on the cobblestones. Its determined flow had changed the face of the earth over the centuries. No matter what obstacles rose in its path, the water found a way around them.

And if it couldn't go around a barrier?

It would simply wear the obstruction away with its tireless, incessant efforts.

Not long after they left the bridge behind, Robert and Horan reached the forest's edge. The wood was not as dense as the Blackwillow nor as intimidating—just a loose gathering of towering elm trees covering the gently rolling hills. The trees were widely spaced, and the forest floor was free from the tangled undergrowth that had clogged the Blackwillow Forest, though occasional berry bushes dotted the ground. The shadows looked cool and inviting below those trees, and Osmark couldn't hide his smile as they entered the forest.

This was certainly a marked improvement over his last foray into the woods.

"We need twenty of the Oletharin leaves, ten of the fungus, and five pieces of ore. You know what any of that looks like?" Robert asked Horan.

"Aye," Horan replied, coming to a halt as he pulled a waterskin free from his belt, fingers working at the cap. He took a long pull, stifled a soft burp with one hand, then stashed the water. "Oletharin leaves have seven points and a red stem, and Moridon fungus grows on the south side of elm trees. Has these bright blue edges. Damn hard to miss, that stuff. As to Starfall ore"—he seesawed his head, left, right, left, right— "well, it looks a bit like copper nuggets, I suppose. But it has green veins running through it." Horan clasped his hands behind his back and kicked a rock from the path. "I guess I'm a foraging mercenary now."

Osmark cocked a finger at the NPC. "Don't let anybody tell you you're not quick on the uptake."

Horan grumbled and tilted his head to the north. "I'll head over this way and start poking around. Just holler if you need me, sir."

Before Horan could take a step, Osmark lunged at him and hooked an arm around his throat. "Don't move."

The NPC gasped for air and choked out, "Ease up on the neck, I'm not moving."

Robert released his grip slowly, ensuring his friend wasn't going to take a step in the wrong direction before he understood the danger. Osmark pointed at the ground ahead of Horan, where a slender strand of twine was drawn tight through the sparse undergrowth. "You just about strolled into a trap."

The duo traced the trip line over to a nearby elm, where a carved wooden trigger held it taut. From the trigger, a coarse rope ran straight up the side of the elm, looped once around a sturdy branch, and ended at a suspended bundle of jagged rocks.

Horan let out a long, slow whistle. "That might have cracked even my thick skull."

"Doesn't look like whoever set this trap was worried about camouflaging it. Probably a fur trapper or hunter trying to bag some game without sitting in the woods all day," Robert said. "Still, if there's one, there are likely more. Just keep an eye out, and you'll be fine."

"Aye, I'll do that. The last thing I need is to get laid out by a hunter's trick." Horan eyed the rocks again. "If I see anything that looks dangerous, I'll give you a shout."

Robert nodded and turned his attention back to the trap, squatting down and scrutinizing it thoroughly. The trip line ran across an almost-invisible rutted game trail, and the crude trigger resembled a simple fallen branch if you didn't know what to look for. "A rockfall trap," he read from the system message as he added the trap's plan to his repertoire.

"I wonder just how many more of these things are scattered through this forest," he mused, vowing to keep a close eye on his surroundings. If he focused too much on finding the supplies Rozak needed, there was a good chance he'd blunder into one of the hunter's other surprises. He considered disarming the rockfall, then shook his head. It was inconvenient to have to keep an eye out for someone else's traps, but better that than destroying someone else's livelihood.

He needed to get searching, but Rozak's words of warning rang in his head like a gong—he wouldn't be able to use his repeater without first acquiring the skill from his class tree. And honestly, he was excited to see what other options would now be available to him. His skill tree would morph and expand once he acquired his final, specialized Artificer class kit, but now that he was officially in the fold, he felt safe to divvy up his Stat Points and start unlocking a few of his new abilities. He spotted a large flat-topped rock butting up against a stout elm and took a seat as he pulled up his interface.

He toggled over to the character screen; he'd only managed to hit level seven so far—though he was only a handful of experience points away from eight— but that was okay. Once he got to his restricted zone, chock-full of high EXP mobs loaded down with loot, he'd power level in no time.

Currently, he had 18 Stat Points to invest, and he knew just what to do with them. He immediately dumped 13 points into Intelligence, then dropped the last 5 into Dexterity. A small part of him was sorely tempted to invest a few into Constitution and Vitality, but he knew min-maxing his most important stats would pay big dividends in the long term.

With that done, he pulled up his character sheet and examined his work:

V.G.O. Character Overview					
Name:	Robert Osmark	Race:	Imperial	Gender:	Male
Level:	7	Class:	Basic Artificer	Alignment:	Unassigned
Renown:	0	Carry Capacity:	300	Undistributed Attribute Points:	0

Health:	210	Spirit:	230	Stamina:	210
H-Regen/sec:	4	S-Regen/sec:	4.46	S-Regen: 1.10/sec	2.31

Attributes:		Offense:		Defense:	
Strength:	12	Base Melee Weapon Damage:	5	Base Armor:	12
Vitality:	14	Base Ranged Weapon Damage:	22	Armor Rating:	21.6
Constitution:	14	Attack Strength (AS):	65	Block Amount:	6.75
Dexterity:	27	Ranged Attack Strength (RAS):	82	Block Chance (%):	14.47
Intelligence:	51.75	Spell Strength (SS):	77.63	Evade Chance (%):	6.1
Spirit:	16	Critical Hit Chance:	5%	Fire Resist (%):	4.78
Luck:	5	Critical Hit Damage:	150%	Cold Resist (%):	4.78
				Lightning Resist (%):	4.78
				Shadow Resist (%):	4.78
				Holy Resist (%):	4.78
Current XP:	3,900			Poison Resist (%):	4.78
Next Level.:	4480			Disease Resist (%):	4.78

Satisfied, he closed out from the character sheet and pulled up the Basic Artificer Skill Tree screen. The kit seemed rather basic at this point—though Osmark knew he'd gain more options once he earned his specialization—and appeared to be broken down into three primary groups: Offensive Firearm Skills, Traps, and Passive Abilities. Most of the awe-inspiring skills and abilities were blocked at the moment, due to level restrictions, but there were still a few options available. Osmark slumped back against the tree trunk, crossed his ankles, and carefully reviewed the different choices.

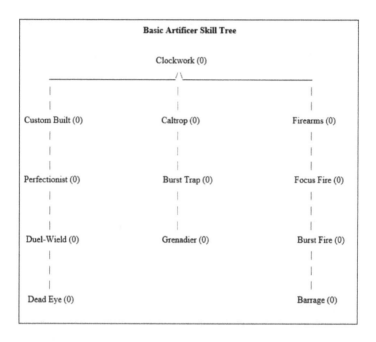

After several minutes of careful examination, Osmark knew what he wanted to invest his meager stock of points into. Since Clockwork was his first prerequisite skill, he dropped a single point there, then selected two active skills—Firearms and Focus Fire—as well as the Caltrop defensive ability, which seemed to function as a powerful crowd control technique.

Skill: Clockwork

With a fundamental mastery of science and physics, engineers can transform raw materials and resources into deadly ranged weapons, uniquely modified armor, terrifying mechanical minions, and deadly traps built with the use of reason, steam, and gears instead of magic. The Clockwork skill increases the mechanical efficiency of all crafted items.

Skill Type/Level: Passive/Initiate

Cost: None

Range: N/A

Cast Time: N/A

Cooldown: N/A

Effect 1: Engineered Weapons Base Damage increased by 5%.

Effect 2: Trap and Turret durability increased by 5%.

Effect 3: Sigil efficacy increased by 5%.

Skill: Firearms

Eldgard is a world of lethal weapons and deadly magic, ruled by sword, bow, and spell. Yet a new item is slowly invading the realm: firearms, a powerful type of ranged weapon. Since they are fueled by gunpowder and steam, however, only a select few have the inclination and know-how to build, maintain, and wield such weapons.

Skill Type/Level: Passive/Initiate

Cost: None

Range: N/A

Cast Time: N/A

Cooldown: N/A

Effect 1: Wield firearms, a class of restricted weapon.

Effect 2: Increases firearm damage by 3%.

Effect 3: Increases weapon reload speed by 3%.

Skill: Focus Fire

Focus Fire gives the Artificer accuracy and damage bonuses to successive attacks against the same target. This ability, when activated, can stack with repeater fire modes and Burst Fire.

Skill Type/Level: Active/Initiate

Cost: 50 Stamina/Sec

Range: 40 Meters (Line of Sight)

Cast Time: N/A

Cooldown: N/A

Effect: +60% Accuracy against same target.

Effect 2: + Physical Damage (100% x Spell Strength); + 5 pts Burn Damage/sec; duration, 15 secs.

Skill: Caltrop

Deploy a Caltrop bomb, which explodes when enemies approach, causing minor damage and temporarily slowing all hostiles in range and badly hindering movement. Up to (4) Caltrop bombs may be placed at one time; set bombs remain active for (1) hour.

Skill Type/Level: Trap/Initiate

Cost: 50 Stamina per Bomb

Range: 35 Meters

Cast Time: 1.0 seconds

Cooldown: N/A

Effect 1: Physical Damage (50% x Attack Strength).

Effect 2: Hindering enemy movement by 55%; duration, 45 seconds.

He wouldn't be a powerhouse in the melee department anytime soon, but with Clockwork, Firearms, Focused Fire, and Caltrops at his disposal, he would stand a chance, so long as he played things smart and didn't take too many uncalculated risks. He still had two points left, so he decided to pick up Custom Built and Perfectionist—both passive abilities:

Ability: Custom Built

The Custom Built ability allows Artificers to destroy found or crafted items, salvaging them for usable parts, while additionally granting them the chance to discover blueprints for how those items are made. Additionally, this ability allows Artificers to use blueprints to modify existing weapons, armor, and mechanical items.

Skill Type/Level: Passive/Initiate

Cost: None

Range: N/A

Cast Time: N/A

Cooldown: N/A

Effect 1: Destroy any player-controlled item and receive 50% of the original building material.

Effect 2: Destroying a complex crafted item gives the player a 40% chance of discovering a "blueprint" for the item.

Effect 3: The Mechanical Artificer can add one "blueprint" modification to a compatible item.

Restriction: Can only destroy found or crafted items—potions, scrolls, and books do not count.

Ability: Perfectionist

The Artificer's meticulous eye for detail saves them time and money when slaving away in their laboratories, crafting innovative and often dangerous machines. With the Perfectionist ability, both the cost and time requirements of crafting or modifying items are drastically reduced, increasing overall productivity.

Skill Type/Level: Passive/Initiate

Cost: None

Range: N/A

Cast Time: N/A

Cooldown: N/A

Effect 1: Production costs (coin, ore, lumber, oil, gears, and all other gathered ingredients) are reduced by 12%.

Effect 2: Production time for crafting or modifying items is reduced by 12%.

He closed out of the skill tree, but immediately noticed a new tab in his interface: "Artificer Build Mode." Curious, he scrolled over and opened the new screen. Inside was a "Salvage" section with a list of gear he currently possessed that could be broken down and reclaimed for items or blueprints. Below that was a "Modify" section, followed by a "Manufacture" option with a scant list of items he could build, including ingots, bullets for his pistol, and something new, which flashed in hazy yellow in his vision. *Caltrops.*

When he selected the Caltrop option from the "Manufacture" menu, a new screen appeared with a squat metal orb, a little larger than a baseball, floating in the air, rotating slowly.

Next to the orb was a craft button, and beneath that was a short list of necessary supplies. In this case raw Iron Ore—which Osmark had plenty of thanks to his time in the smithy—and Stamina. He added the few pounds of raw ore from his inventory, then shrugged and hit the create button, interested to see what would happen. A wave of dizziness smashed over him like a baseball bat and an eyeblink later, the ore vanished, replaced by four of the odd metal grenades.

He slumped forward, wheezing and shaky limbed, black creeping in on the edges of his vision. His Stamina bar flashed manically in the corner of his vision; his jaw dropped as he realized his Stamina had plummeted from 210 down to a mere 10 points, all in the span of a single heartbeat. Interesting. So, the Stamina cost came during the creation of the items, not during their deployment. If that was the case for all Artificer creations, it held some interesting possibilities—namely, with enough resources and preparation, he could be virtually unstoppable.

He closed his eyes for a few minutes, letting his Stamina recover. Eventually, he stood with a groan, stretching his sore back and achy legs. He eyed the flat rock longingly, thinking about how much he would enjoy lounging around a bit longer; at this point, though, he couldn't afford a luxury like that. After all, the Imperial Throne wasn't going to just fall into his lap. Plus, he suspected there would be at least a few monsters lurking around these woods, and he was curious to put his new skills and inventions to the test.

SEVENTEEN

Fungaloids

After a frustrating half hour's search through the forest, all Osmark had to show for his troubles were sore feet and the locations of two more traps—another rockfall and a trip line snare.

He pulled his goggles down from their perch on top of his head and seated them over his eyes. "There must be something on these that'll help me find what I need," he grumbled, giving the goggles a thorough examination. He'd left Rozak's in such a rush, he hadn't taken the time to investigate this odd new piece of gear.

Basic Artificer's Goggles

One of the most important tools in an Artificer's bag of tricks are his goggles. The basic model has four different lenses, each of which provides a different bonus:

Magnifying Lens (clear): Provides a +10 bonus to any Engineering task involving intricate or detailed work.

Engraver's Lens (blue): Provides a +10 bonus to any Engineering task related to engraving Divine Geometry patterns.

Harvester Lens (green): Provides a +10 bonus to any Engineering task related to disassembling engineered items for parts or plans.

Surveyor Lens (telescoping): This lens provides a +10 bonus to any Mining task.

"Ah, there you are," Osmark said to himself. He found the telescoping lens and pulled it over in front of his right eye. It took a few moments and several adjustments to get the focus right, but once he had it dialed in, the benefit was immediately apparent.

Robert swept his gaze across the surrounding terrain, and several points flashed with vivid yellow light like sparklers on a moonless night. After a few seconds, the bright spots faded to a ginger glow that was still visible without being distracting. Maybe this would be easier than he'd thought.

When Robert arrived at the first glowing orange spot, he found a chunk of plain gray rock. He picked it up, examined it, and discovered it was nothing special. He grunted and tossed the stone back into the brush. Apparently, the goggles would show him likely places to find ore, but that was no guarantee there'd be anything of value at those points. Still, he supposed it was better than wandering aimlessly through the forest looking for the right kind of rocks.

Robert brushed his hands free of dirt and hustled to the next spot, which turned out to hold a hunk of silver ore the size of his fist. Though it wasn't what he was looking for, it provided him with a small experience point boost, not to mention, he could always use it for crafting in the future. Robert dropped the rough chunk of stone into his inventory and continued following the clues highlighted by the surveyor's lens.

Thirty minutes later, his inventory bulged with a variety of gathered materials—including three chunks of the Starfall ore. He'd also earned himself another level, bringing him up to eight, gaining another 5 Stat Points, which he dropped into Intelligence, and an additional Proficiency Point, which he saved. Always good to have an ace in the hole. He pulled up his interface, glanced at the time, and decided it was time to find Horan.

With any luck, the old merc would be almost done gathering the rest of the materials and Osmark could focus on finding the last two pieces of Starfall ore. Even with his small break earlier, he was running ahead of schedule and wanted to keep it that way. He wheeled around and backtracked, heading off in the general direction he'd last seen Horan foraging. After a few minutes of steady progress, he heard a rustling near a thick tangle of bushes and promptly picked up his pace.

Only it wasn't Horan making the noise.

A trio of naked, deformed creatures huddled around the body of a stag that had been ensnared by a hunter's noose. They pawed at its tattered flesh with thick, blunted fingers and shoveled pieces of dripping red meat into their mouths. Oozing blisters covered their pallid flesh in thick, weeping growths that drooped from their skin like stalks of rotting vegetation.

Robert crouched, silent as a field mouse, and ducked behind a gnarled trunk before the creatures spotted him. He pushed his goggles up onto his forehead, then turned and peeked out to get a better look at them. A descriptor tag, [Fungaloid Hosts], hung over their deformed heads for a moment before vanishing. He couldn't be sure of their level, but the in-game Overminds of V.G.O. were good about spawning scaling creatures, appropriate for any given traveler. Appropriate, but rarely easy.

They hadn't seen him yet, though, so if he chose, he could just leave them be and go about his business.

Osmark considered that option but discarded it. To reach his Master Artificer specialization, he needed more than just the Honored reputation with Rozak he'd get from completing his fetch quest. He also needed to be at least level seventeen, and these Fungaloid Hosts were perfect for grinding out some extra experience. "Sorry, mushroom men," Osmark whispered as he drew his loaded repeater, "but it's time to serve the greater good."

Osmark adjusted the weapon's firing mode and aimed it at the huddled Fungaloid Hosts. Slowly, he exhaled and squeezed the trigger; the repeater barked three times in rapid succession, and the weapon kicked in his hand. Flashes of blue-green light erupted from its barrel and jets of steam hissed from the firing chamber as the burst sent three shots roaring toward the monsters.

All three rounds peppered the nearest Host's back, puncturing its shoulders with puckered red entry wounds. *Critical Hit.* The shots exploded from the Fungaloid's chest in a spray of viscous slop that painted the face and chest of its friend, sitting on the other side of the deer. The wounded creature toppled onto its side with a wheeze, revealing the ugly wound Robert's attack had left in its torso. There were no vital organs or bones in that hole, just a lot of sticky blood and walls of pale spongy meat shot through with fibrous black cords.

All the same, the sight was quite disturbing.

But Osmark put that from mind as he exploited the advantage of surprise by firing a single shot into the head of another creature. The Fungaloid Host's skull erupted in a fountain of gore and pale, flying meat. It jolted to its feet, flailing its arms in shock and horror as thick, irregular grunts escaped from its slack-jawed mouth. The lobotomized creature turned to stare at Osmark with milky eyes bulging from their sockets, then toppled like a felled tree, landing with a meaty *thud.*

The third Fungaloid Host vaulted over the remains of the deer carcass and past its mortally wounded companion, shrieking madly, its mouth open wide and its spatulate fingers hooked into claws.

Surprised by the creature's speed, Robert retreated from the onslaught, backpedaling as he fired at the onrushing monster. Naturally, the hasty shot went wide, streaking past the Fungaloid's head and smashing into the side of a tree with a *crack.*

"Shit!" Osmark shouted, fumbling to get the weapon up and ready.

The Fungaloid Host's moist hands latched onto Robert's shoulders and pulled him into its crushing embrace. The creature's humid breath washed over Robert's face like the rotting stench of a ripe compost heap. Robert struggled against the Host, but the creature was far stronger than he'd imagined, and its bear hug robbed him of any leverage.

The Host's mouth stretched open wider and wider; for a terrifying moment, Osmark thought it was going to chew his face clean off. Instead, a strange hissing noise worked its way up from deep inside the creature's chest and erupted from its gaping mouth along with a sticky gray spray.

Before Robert could think to hold his breath or plug his nostrils, the gray mist was in his mouth, clawing its way down his esophagus.

Debuff Added

Choking: You have inhaled Suffocating Spores, reducing your Stamina by 10% and causing 5 hit points of damage per second; duration, 30 seconds.

Osmark's lungs burned, and a heavy weight settled on his chest, slowly squeezing out the air. He gasped for breath like a fish out of water, but only sucked in more spores, gagging as the things invaded his mouth and nose. The choking damage wasn't enough to kill him, but it would knock off three-quarters of his Health. Worse, if he didn't get free from the creature, it might be able to finish the job simply by squeezing him until his ribs fractured.

Robert struggled against the Fungaloid Host, wriggling his shoulders and bucking his hips, but the lack of oxygen had sapped what little strength he had. Brute force wouldn't be enough to get him out of this jam.

The repeater, he thought desperately.

It was still in his right hand, but he couldn't aim it. He snarled in pain and twisted the gun until the barrel pressed against something firm but yielding—hopefully, the Fungaloid Host's belly and not his own—then squeezed the trigger yet again. Blood sprayed the trees behind the Fungaloid and dripped from its branches in glutinous red cords. Undeterred, the creature roared in Robert's face, and its crushing grip intensified.

Osmark's ribs creaked under the monster's thick arms, and black invaded the edges of his vision as his HP continued to plunge.

He tilted the gun's barrel up, slightly, and fired again.

This time, the monster's mouth flopped open, and threads of smoke wafted out between its flat teeth. It groaned and flung Robert away, staggering drunkenly as it clutched its wounded abdomen with its stubby, shaking hands. Blood ran from between its squared fingers and splattered onto the leaf-strewn forest floor.

Osmark, still wheezing from the suffocating spores, raised his weapon once more and fired, blowing a chunk out of the Fungaloid's left shoulder.

But somehow—almost miraculously—the creature survived the shot.

It lurched forward as Robert fought to clear his head.

Less than a yard away, it opened its mouth wide and inhaled, preparing to launch a fresh assault despite its terrible wounds and plummeting HP.

"No," Robert choked out as he rammed the repeater's slender barrel past the Fungaloid's spongy lips and deep into the creature's gaping mouth.

On instinct, his thumb stroked the fire selector on the back of the weapon's grip and his index finger convulsed on the trigger. The repeater roared, *crack-crack-crack,* but Osmark couldn't see the bursts of light from the barrel—not with the muzzle lodged so deeply in the creature's mouth. The effects were immediately evident, however. The attack obliterated the Fungaloid's head and coated Osmark's face and eyes in a thick layer of fetid red slime. From now on, he was leaving the goggles in place.

Osmark reeled and fell to the ground, temporarily blinded by the remains of his foe.

For a moment, he just lay there, wheezing in agony as the spores chewed away at his lungs and Health in equal measure. Finally, the debuff wore off, and he mustered the strength and energy to flip over onto his belly and drag himself across the forest floor, blinking his eyes in an attempt to clear the goop away.

"What," a familiar voice asked, "you decided to use your fancy popgun like a club instead of shooting the monsters from a reasonable distance? You've got guts and blood all over your face, man."

"Can't see," Osmark gasped, reaching a hand blindly toward the sound of Horan's voice.

The merc clasped Robert's hand and pulled him to his feet.

"You mind holstering your weapon?" Horan asked, his words coated with worry. "Not that I don't trust you, but I'd feel a mite bit better if you weren't flailing that thing around where someone innocent might get shot."

"Good idea," Osmark replied, frantically wiping the goop from his eyes; slowly the world swam into focus through a blurry red haze. He found the mouth of the shoulder holster and slipped his repeater inside. Finally, he glanced back at the carnage from the battle, taking in the three dead creatures. He felt nothing but disgust at the scene—disgust with the beasts and with himself for coming so close to failure. Back IRL he might've been king, but here in V.G.O. he still had a lot to learn. "How'd you do?" he asked Horan, purposely turning away from the mess.

The mercenary grinned. "Got the leaves and the fungus. How about you?" he offered, wisely avoiding any mention of the Fungaloids.

Osmark took a deep breath, savoring the clean air that filled his lungs as his Stamina bar crept back toward full. "Not bad," he replied. "I just need to find a couple more pieces of ore, but I think there're some good spots near here." He waved a hand vaguely toward the east.

Horan walked behind Osmark and put the supplies he'd gathered into his employer's bag. "You'll probably want to turn these in yourself."

"Thanks," Osmark replied. "Now, let's get the last of the ore and head back to Tomestide." He faltered and looked down at his fancy new clothes, now covered in gore. "I could use a nice, long, hot shower."

Horan gestured for Osmark to proceed. "You lead the way, sir."

Robert rubbed the goo from his goggles, slipped them into place, then adjusted them for foraging. The telescoping lens revealed a few likely spots nearby, and a few minutes later they had everything they needed. Osmark dropped the last chunk of ore into his inventory, relieved to be done. "That's the last of—"

A series of low groans echoed through the forest from all points of the compass. The odd mewling sound raised the hairs on the back of Robert's neck. "What in the hell was that?"

"Your new friends," Horan replied with a devilish smile. "The Fungaloids can smell their dead. Like flies to shite. No doubt, they're on their way to this mess." He swept a hand to the three corpses not far off. "We should probably make ourselves scarce before they start looking for revenge."

Osmark imagined a horde of Fungaloids blasting spores at him from every direction and shuddered. Killing them all would earn him a huge chunk of experience, but he didn't see himself surviving a fight with a swarm of enraged mushroom men, not without better weaponry and a way to stop them at a distance. If they got in close and all started spewing spores into his face, he'd be a dead man in no time.

If he could set up some traps, that might be enough to tip the balance in his favor. He imagined a killing field crisscrossed by pit traps and rockfalls with him waiting at the other end, pistol drawn and ready. Setting that up would take hours, though. And even if the Fungaloids weren't on their way that very moment, Osmark didn't have that much time to spend on anything not directly related to finishing his tasks for the day.

"Let's check these three for treasure, then get the hell out of here," Osmark muttered, waving at the nearby creatures. "I don't have time to fight off a whole army of those monstrosities."

Quickly, Osmark searched the bodies but didn't find any coins or gemstones. The miserable beasts didn't even have any weapons. The only thing he found of value was on the second Fungaloid Host he'd shot in the face. The grievous head injury had left the torso intact, which is where Osmark found a [Pristine Spore Sac]. Gingerly, he removed it with his gutting blade and held the strange organ up to Horan. "What do you think this is worth?"

"Your life," Horan replied darkly, edging away a few feet. "Those spores are what the others smell."

Osmark shrugged and stowed the sac. "They can't smell them if they're still in the organ."

"Just don't break it," Horan said with a grimace before glancing around. "Let's get out of here, eh? All of a sudden I feel like trouble's headed our way."

"Aw, so soon?" A voice came from the branches overhead. "We were hoping you might stick around."

Osmark spun and drew his repeater, scanning the forest canopy. He spotted black-clad figures crouched among the tree branches, their faces covered with heavy veils. Assassins. One by one, the newcomers drew their weapons and aimed at Osmark's face.

EIGHTEEN:

Gray Death

R obert weighed his options and found all of them wanting. "Get ready to run," he whispered to Horan. "We need to split up."

The figures overhead remained as motionless as statues. Some held crossbows; others had short bows with arrows nocked. They looked intimidating, but Osmark knew the archers were at a disadvantage: their shots were as likely to be blocked by tree limbs as they were to find their marks.

"Not a good plan," Horan muttered back, his hands slowly creeping toward the sword at his hip. "I like six against two better than three on one."

Robert frowned and his spine stiffened. He didn't have time to negotiate. He had a plan, and it needed to be executed. "Not asking, telling. Head south, I'm going north."

Without waiting for a reply, he sprinted away, not even glancing back to see if Horan would follow orders. Osmark needed time to prepare for a fight, and he wasn't going to get that time standing around, twiddling his thumbs while he waited for his enemies to attack. Arrows and crossbow bolts whistled through the air around him, but Osmark's gamble paid off. The bolts struck wood, not flesh, or threaded through the forest's canopy only to crash harmlessly into the ground, kicking up swirls of dirt on impact.

The inviting forest turned hostile as Robert sprinted through its depths. Walking at a leisurely pace made the trees easy to navigate around and the obstacles simple to avoid. Running, however, turned every rock into a potential trap and every tree root into a snare waiting to bring Robert to his knees. He focused like a laser, putting everything else from mind as he ran. If his attention wavered from the path ahead of him, even for a moment, Robert was a dead man.

His enemies slipped through the canopy above like wraiths, the sound of their footfalls pursuing him through the woods. Every time he glanced over his shoulder, they seemed closer. One black-clad figure darted through the brush, while two more vaulted from one tree limb to the next, agile as monkeys and relentless as bloodhounds, quickly eating up the distance between them. Even though there were only three on his trail, that was still more than he was willing to face in a straight fight.

If he wanted to survive, he had to even the odds. Fortunately, he had a plan.

He always had a plan, though pulling this one off would be a tricky thing.

A crooked elm with a drooping branch caught Osmark's eye, and he veered toward it, ducking beneath the low-hanging bough and dodging a jutting snarl of bushes. His feet found a rutted game trail, and he followed its twisting course deeper into the forest, hooking left, then swerving right.

A crossbow bolt buried its barbed head in a nearby tree, and a moment later, a bright flare of pain exploded in Robert's left shoulder as his HP bar dropped by a fifth. He cursed softly under his breath as he noted the black steel head of a crossbow bolt peeking out from his armor, covered in deep crimson. He blocked the pain from mind, though, and continued his course despite the sliver of fear worming its way through his guts.

Changing his plan now invited disaster.

In the distance—but drawing closer with every passing moment—the Fungaloids hooted, the eerie noise reverberating in the air. It was a sound filled with rage and despair as if they knew their kin were lying dead in pools of their blood and they desperately wanted vengeance.

An arrow hissed past Robert's left ear like an enraged serpent, and vanished into the forest, leaving behind a trail of clipped leaves and snapped twigs. Robert was still hurting from his battle with the mushroom men, and with the arrow protruding from his shoulder, he couldn't afford to take much more damage. A critical hit from one of those bolts might be enough to kill him. And something told him the archers were more likely than not to land a critical strike—these guys were pros.

Robert didn't know who the well-trained killers on his trail were, but he didn't have to know *them* to know who'd *sent* the assassins. Sizemore.

You'll pay for this, Robert thought as he continued his madcap sprint.

Osmark's mind raced along with his feet as he mentally reviewed the contents of his backpack, searching for something he could use. He had ore, rope, a hatchet, and a few other useful scraps, but there wasn't any time to dig a pitfall or even the ankle breakers he'd used against the bandits. He needed something faster and more effective. Like the new Caltrops he'd just unlocked. He wasn't sure how well the traps would function against the thugs leaping through the canopy, but it would most definitely work against the one dogging his heels on the ground.

He fished one of the orbs from his inventory and hurled the ball over his shoulder at the encroaching assassin. The ball landed harmlessly on the ground with a thunk, but a heartbeat later it exploded in violent fury as the hooded thug drew into range, releasing a plume of cloying gray smoke and a hail of small black spikes, each one no bigger than a quarter. The spikes didn't do all that much damage, but the man faltered, skidding to a near standstill as the barbed prongs dug into his legs and feet, drawing tiny pinpricks of bright blood.

Osmark grinned despite the awful situation and turned back toward the game trail. He put on a renewed burst of speed and jumped over a rotting log, rounding a sharp bend. His grin widened as his eyes landed on the thing that might save him. Robert just hoped he had enough strength and endurance left to pull off the dirty trick he had in mind.

Osmark kept his eyes glued to his target. If he misjudged, even by an inch, he'd be dead before he knew it.

More arrows streaked toward him. At the last possible second, Robert hooked right and dashed toward an ancient elm with a rope trailing down from an overhead bough. One of the hunter's traps. He bolted around the tree's gnarled trunk and latched onto the line with both hands, kicking the trigger loose from the peg holding it in place. Robert's shoulders screamed in protest as the trap released and the rope dragged him high into the air. He clung to the line and ignored the fiery pain.

There'd be time to hurt later. Now it was time to fight.

As Osmark rose up, the heavy bundle of rocks on the other end of the trap crashed down through the treetops. A hundred pounds of stone slammed into the lead assassin and knocked the man from the branches like a freight train.

The killer hit the forest floor with a meaty thud, and the rocks landed on him with savage power a moment later, forcing a scream out of him as blood spurted from his broken body.

One down, Robert thought. He caught a nearby branch with the toe of his boot and pulled himself onto it.

"Bastard!" another assassin shouted. The dark-garbed man rushed toward Osmark with uncanny agility, his feet finding tree limbs unerringly as he leaped from one elm to the next with simian grace.

Still holding onto the rope with his left hand, Osmark drew his repeater with his right. He leveled the hand cannon, fixed a bead on the charging assassin, and squeezed the trigger.

The weapon's firing mechanism *clicked*, and a pitiful wisp of steam escaped from the firing chamber. Osmark had forgotten to reload the repeater after his battle with the Fungaloids. "Unfortunate," he muttered under his breath.

He reached for the rounds in his bag, but it was too late—the assassin was already on him. There was no elegance in the killer's attack. He kicked off from a tree limb, somersaulted, and landed on Robert's branch. The instant the assassin's soft boots made contact with the limb, he launched a flurry of jabs with the gleaming short swords in his hands.

Robert had no reliable melee weapon, which left him with only one option to defend himself. He leaped away from the tree limb—holstering his weapon midair—wrapped both hands on the rope, and swung toward the elm tree's twisted trunk, silently praying he could get away in time.

The assassin lunged forward, thrusting both of his weapons at Osmark's momentarily exposed back.

Robert had anticipated this attack, however, and used his momentum to spin around the tree, which shielded him from the deadly assault. In an instant, Osmark landed on a stout branch and braced his feet, leaning back against the rope so he could see on either side of the elm. Then he waited patiently for the assassin to expose himself, knowing it would only be a matter of time. As soon as the masked face appeared on the tree's right side, Osmark leaped to the left.

His maneuver sent him sailing around the elm once more; he swung like a pendulum, and his orbit carried him behind the assassin. Before the killer could turn, Robert twisted on the end of the rope and drove both feet into the man's back.

In theory, the attack should've knocked the assassin off balance and sent him plummeting to the forest floor below.

But the man was more agile than Robert had anticipated, and his reaction speed was terrifying.

The second Osmark's feet landed, the killer threw the weapon in his left hand away and twisted on his right heel, hooking an arm around Osmark's leg. Before Robert could react—before he could even think—the assassin used his momentum and body weight to whip Osmark around in a tight arc. Robert's back slammed into the tree, shaving off another chunk of his Health.

It wasn't a killing blow, but it wasn't meant to be.

Pinned against the tree with his feet on the branch, Robert couldn't dodge the assassin's follow-up attack. The hired murderer's short sword plunged into Osmark's side, just below his floating rib, and a wave of cold agony ripped through him.

The Fungaloids howled again, the sound a fierce wail so close it raised Osmark's skin into goosebumps.

"Robert!" Horan shouted. No, no, no. His call was too close, much too close. The idiot had ignored Osmark's orders.

There goes your bonus, Osmark thought, wriggling in a futile attempt to free himself from the sword.

The assassin released the weapon pinning Robert to the tree and drew a black stiletto from a sheath on his left hip. A startlingly blue fluid dripped from the weapon's tip, and Robert knew he was dead. One scratch would no doubt send poison coursing through his veins, and as wounded as he was, Robert had no illusions about his chances of survival.

But that didn't mean he would go down easily.

The assassin prepared for a thrust, but Osmark was ready. Unable to dodge, he used what little strength he had left to sling the rope around the killer's head with his left hand, catching it with his right.

Confused, the assassin hesitated.

Robert didn't.

With a roar, Osmark drove his boot heel into the killer's midsection, clinging desperately to the rope with both hands, and bracing himself against the branch with his other foot as best he was able.

The assassin slipped from the tree, his eyes wide above the black cloth of his mask as he fell.

Robert shouted in pain when the assassin's full weight landed on the rope. It almost yanked him off the bough, too, but the sword jammed through his side actually saved him from going over.

The killer struggled like a landed fish, bucking and jerking against the noose around his neck, unable to get his fingers beneath the tightened rope.

Horan darted into view and skidded to a halt on the game trail Robert had raced down a few minutes before. "Robert!" he shouted again, panicked, eyes sweeping the treeline.

"Run!" Osmark hollered, drawing the man's gaze. "Get the hell out of here, you idiot." Another black-clad assassin dropped from a tree, landing on the path just ahead of Horan.

The NPC feinted at the killer, then juked to the right and sprinted toward Osmark's tree. "I'm coming," he hollered at the top of his lungs. "Just hold on a little longer, blast you!"

Robert watched as Horan drew closer, pursued by four assassins.

The other assassin, dangling below Osmark from the rope, gasped and flailed wildly, fighting to dislodge Robert from his perch. Worse, it was working. Holding onto the dying man drove the sword's cutting edge deeper into Osmark's body, and further ate away at his Stamina and Health. A stream of blood ran from the wound and soaked into the wood between his feet. "Just die already," Robert hissed, glowering at the man below.

One of the assassins on the ground shouted and reeled away from Horan, his face bloody, one eye swaying on a string of glistening sinew.

A second assassin lunged toward Horan, but the older man sidestepped the attack, parrying the stroke with practiced ease, before driving the pommel of his blade into the thug's face. The assassin fell back, lost his balance, and landed on his back.

Horan raised his blade for the killing blow, but the attack never landed.

Yet another assassin darted in from his blind side, moving like the wind. A precise slash parted Horan's armor and opened the NPC's side. Horan grunted, groping at his ribs with one hand while he lashed out at his attacker with the other. Unfortunately, his blade went wide, and a third assassin took advantage by coming in low and slicing across the back of Horan's left leg, damn near hobbling the man.

The rope Robert was holding onto suddenly went slack.

Alarmed, he tore his eyes away from Horan and glanced over the edge of the tree limb; somehow, the assassin had twisted around and grabbed the elm's trunk.

The man was no longer hanging.

He was climbing.

Robert's heart sank as he stole another look at his friend on the ground. Clearly, Horan's wounds were sapping his strength, making it impossible for him to fight back against the assassins. All four of them were on their feet, and they circled the NPC like a pack of wolves. Their blades flashed and darted, too many, from too many different directions, for Horan to defend himself.

They were going to kill Horan. And when they finished with him, they would come for Robert.

He couldn't allow that. He had too much to do. Too much to accomplish.

There was only one way left, and Osmark already hated himself a little for thinking of it. But there was no other way—and he would always do the hard things, the awful things, if that's what it took to win.

Reluctantly, Osmark reached into his belt pouch and pulled out the fleshy organ he'd carved from the Fungaloid's chest. He hesitated for a beat, feeling sick to his stomach. Then, without a word, he threw it into the fray below.

The sac plunged through the trees and hit the ground with a sharp *pop*, releasing a cloud of dancing spores into the air.

Seconds later, the howling pack of Fungaloids crashed through the trees like a gray avalanche.

NINETEEN:

Dark Day

The Fungaloids exploded through the forest with a bone-rattling roar, their malformed feet pounding at the earth, their nubby fingers clawing at the air. Their infested bodies swarmed over the assassins in a flailing, gnashing wave. The killers struck back at the new threat, but their agility and skill were no match for the sheer number of bloated bodies bearing down on them. Osmark forced himself to watch as the black-clad killers vanished beneath the pale assault. His stomach churned as blood spurted and the Fungaloids tossed hunks of quivering meat down their maws.

Robert's heart ached as Horan glanced up at him one final time, his eyes wide in terror and disbelief, before likewise disappearing beneath the press of bodies. Thankfully the man didn't scream as the Fungaloids shredded him, showering in his blood and stuffing their greedy faces with bits of his flesh. In moments, Horan was gone. Dead. And unlike Travelers, NPCs didn't respawn, which meant Robert's closest ally was well and truly no more.

That hurt more than anything else—more than the wound in his side or the arrow jabbed through his shoulder.

Osmark pushed his pain away, instead focusing on what he needed to do next. After all, grieving for Horan now would accomplish nothing except his own death, and that would serve no one. He steeled himself and glanced down at the assassin inching his way up the tree trunk. The man was still some distance below Osmark's branch, but it wouldn't take him long to make the climb.

Robert closed his hands over the hilt of the short sword buried in his guts and closed his eyes. He took a deep breath, gritted his teeth, and pulled.

Nothing happened. For a long moment, Osmark feared he'd grown too weak to do the deed, that the loss of blood had dangerously depleted his Strength and Stamina. Then, millimeter by millimeter, the sword wiggled free. With a final shout, Robert tore the weapon loose from the tree and out of his body. Blood spattered his face, hot and sticky, and his Health dropped dangerously low, but he was still alive.

Debuff Added

Bleeding: Your wound is bleeding excessively. You suffer 5 points of Health damage and 1 point of Stamina damage every 5 seconds; duration, 3 minutes or until the wound is treated.

Robert was a tech genius, not an expert in first aid, but he knew if he didn't plug the hole in his side he was a dead man. He had 50 Health remaining, which gave him less than a minute to stop the blood loss. If he died, he'd just respawn back in Tomestide, but that would cost him two things he couldn't afford:

First, he'd lose time, eight hours worth of it. And after this debacle of a trip, he didn't have any of that to spare. Robert still needed to talk to Rozak and hunt down his Faction Seal, located in a restricted zone only he had the coordinates for. That dungeon dive would account for every minute remaining in his day.

Second, Robert would lose his chance to *talk* to the assassin clinging to the tree below him, and there was no way he was going to pass up the opportunity to have a nice chat with that piece of garbage. He needed to know what Sizemore was planning.

Osmark tore a strip of cloth from his shirt, hastily packed it into the hole in his side, and held it in place with a clenched fist, fighting back the onslaught of dizziness skipping through his head. He closed his eyes and listened to the slobbery sounds of the Fungaloids eating.

He'd be hearing those sounds in his nightmares for the rest of his life.

Debuff Removed

Bleeding: Your wound has been treated.

Satisfied he wasn't going to bleed to death, Osmark opened his eyes and stole another look down at the sole surviving assassin. He grabbed the dangling rope and slapped it against the climbing assassin's back. He did it again and again, until the killer glared up at him with narrowed eyes. "Knock it off, dead man."

"Grab it," Robert snarled. "Grab the rope or *you're* dead."

The assassin didn't respond, instead continuing his steady ascent up the face of the tree. Osmark rammed the tip of the short sword back into the tree's trunk. Then he drew his repeater and started reloading, feeding in rounds until the firing cylinder was at max capacity. When he'd finished, the assassin was less than five feet below the limb Osmark was loitering on.

That hardly mattered, though, given the circumstances. Robert drew a bead on the tree just above the man's head and squeezed the repeater's trigger.

Thunder rolled and echoed through the forest, startling a flock of ravens waiting to feast on the dead. Even the Fungaloids momentarily halted their gruesome meal to glower dumbly at the shocking roar of the repeater's discharge. The assassin's eyes went wide.

"Grab the rope," Osmark said, voice flat and cold as the arctic tundra.

The assassin hesitated for a beat, then nodded, wrapped his hands around the rope, and pushed away from the tree. He swung like a pendulum for a few seconds before his momentum died, and he was left hanging. Far from the trunk and directly above the Fungaloids, he was helpless to do anything but cling to the rope and pray.

Pray for mercy, which he certainly wouldn't receive.

Osmark pulled the short sword free from the trunk with his left hand. He drew its razor-sharp edge across the taut rope; strands of hemp parted and twisted into frayed curls.

The assassin shouted, "Don't!" panic flashing across his face.

"Who sent you?" Osmark asked, as though this were simply another day in the boardroom.

The assassin said nothing. He stared into Robert's eyes, and for the first time Osmark wondered if he'd met someone with a will to match his own.

Robert shrugged and sliced through a few more strands of the rope. "Who. Sent. You."

The killer glanced down at the Fungaloids, then back at Robert. "You know who."

"Sizemore?"

The assassin nodded, nervously eyeing the thin slice in the line above. "There'll be more," the killer said. "He hired the Coldskulls directly, but we aren't the only ones hunting you. He's got an open contract out. Anyone can claim the bounty on your head. You're screwed, my Imperial friend."

If the man was telling the truth, Robert's problems were only going to get worse until he dealt with Sizemore. An open contract would attract every would-be Boba Fett in V.G.O. Osmark wouldn't be able to trust anyone as long as he had a price on his head. He'd be constantly worried someone he worked with was going to betray him for a quick payday.

Dammit, Sizemore, Osmark thought.

Robert cursed himself for ever letting the senator into the fold. True, he'd needed the man's help to get things operational before the asteroid hit, but in hindsight he should've come up with another plan. Some other way to get the resources Sizemore brought to the table. If he'd worked harder, none of this would be happening. Horan would still be alive. Well, no more. Maybe he couldn't change the past, but he could certainly fix this problem moving forward and put an end to Sizemore's interference before any more of his plans were disrupted, or any more of his people wound up dead.

But to do that, he needed information.

Osmark held the short sword's blade against the rope. "The Coldskulls, you said. And where can I find the rest of your little social club?"

The man's forehead creased and his jaw tightened—the look of determined resolution. This man might drop Sizemore's name, but even at a glance Osmark knew he wouldn't roll on his brothers. "That's all you'll get from me," the assassin offered in confirmation.

Osmark sliced halfway through the rope. The remaining strands creaked ominously as they bore the weight of the dangling thug. "Last chance," Osmark said, not that he expected anything.

True to form, the assassin said nothing.

Silently, Osmark slashed the rope.

Down, down, down the assassin fell, landing in the midst of the Fungaloids with bone-crunching force. He held his tongue until the Fungaloids went to work. Then he screamed, a high, piercing sound that echoed through the forest like the cry of a hunting hawk.

Osmark sagged against the elm's trunk and closed his eyes as he waited for the Fungaloids to fill their bellies. By the time the last of them had wandered back into the forest, Osmark had almost half of his Health and all of his Stamina restored. It wasn't much, but it was enough for him to feel confident clambering down from the tree.

The Fungaloids had eaten the softest bits from the assassins' bodies. They'd scooped out the guts and eyes, gnawed away the meat on biceps and thighs, and left the rest scattered about the forest along with bits and pieces of equipment. Osmark carefully extracted Horan's corpse from the mess, neatly laying the remains on the ground away from the dead assassins.

"I'm sorry," he whispered, not wanting to look at the brutalized remains of his friend. "It shouldn't have been like this."

There wasn't much to salvage, but Osmark did a thorough job of searching the dead. He collected their weapons, knowing they'd turn a pretty penny back in town, and also scooped up a smattering of coins—ten gold pieces, a few hundred silver pieces, and some loose copper—which he stuffed into his belt pouch. Next, he stripped the armor from the assassins, but none of it was salvageable, not even the gloves, which were torn and tattered from the Fungaloids' grinding teeth.

Robert did find something interesting under those gloves, though. Each of the assassins—the Coldskulls, the last one had called them—had a small black skull tattooed on the webbing between the thumb and index finger on their left hand. A little bigger than the tip of Osmark's index finger, it would be almost invisible if they had their hands closed, and gloves would easily hide the markings. Osmark stared at the black tattoos until the image burned itself into his memory. If he ever saw anyone bearing that mark again, he would kill them. No matter the cost.

"When I'm through with you," Osmark vowed, "the Coldskulls will be a cautionary example for any other assassins who think they can come after me with impunity."

One of the killers had a small backpack still strapped to the remnants of his torso. Robert flipped the body over with the toe of one boot and opened the pack's bloody flap, searching the inventory. The waterproof waxed leather had kept the blood off the pack's meager contents. Osmark pulled a folded square of parchment, three small steel vials, several Health, Stamina, and Spirit Regen potions, and ten individually wrapped packets of rations from the container.

With a sigh of relief, Osmark popped the top on one of the Health Regen potions and slammed it back, then chased it with a Stamina Regen potion for good measure. The first tasted faintly of cinnamon and cherries while the second was light and vaguely citric. In a flash the potions kicked in, and a flood of energy suffused his limbs as skin and tissue knit themselves back together—even forcing out the bolt lodged in his shoulder. He was as good as new in no time and felt like a million bucks, despite the dirt, grime, and blood covering his body.

From here on out, he'd have a ready supply of the potions on hand at any given moment.

Next, he examined the steel vials, but got little information from his cursory scan. He needed more skills, or different skills, before he could figure out what they contained. Given the assassins' occupation, however, he assumed it was poison. He tucked them into his belt pouch and unfolded the parchment last. Two lines of impeccably neat handwriting were the only markings on the page.

Bring Osmark to Ravenswood Hall. Do not kill him. The vials of Illakri Venom will paralyze him once he's below 25% Health. One prick of a stiletto should be enough to do the trick. I'll deal with him when I get back. For now, make him comfortable in a cell beneath the Hall.

There was no signature, but Osmark didn't need to see the man's name to know Sizemore was responsible for the orders. The thought of being captured by his rival made Osmark's blood run cold and sent goosebumps racing over his arms and back.

Death was problematic in V.G.O., but it wasn't the end of the road for a player. Getting killed would cost Osmark all his current experience, set him back eight hours, and slam him with some nasty debuffs, but he would always come back from the grave. No matter how badly Robert was injured—no matter if they disemboweled him and scattered his limbs to the four winds—he, like every other V.G.O. player, would respawn. Always.

If Sizemore captured Robert and hauled him off to a prison, however, that was significantly more concerning. A properly designed jail inside V.G.O. could hold Osmark for weeks. Maybe months. Maybe *forever.* And an experienced torturer could keep him in agony for every second of his incarceration. Robert had known Sizemore would be a problem, but he'd had no idea the senator would go to these lengths. He was going have to come up with a more ingenious and permanent solution to deal with the bothersome senator.

He gathered up the rest of the loot, loaded it into his inventory, then turned his attention to what he'd been dreading the most.

Horan.

Putting the man to rest was a long and painful process.

Robert wished he'd brought the proper tools, but all he had were the weapons dropped by the assassins. The short swords and daggers they carried were better than nothing, but only barely. After an hour, Osmark had removed enough underbrush to form a clearing and ringed it with rough stones gathered from the surrounding forest. He didn't have time to spend doing this, but he did it anyway.

Horan deserved it.

Robert chopped up a fallen log and stacked the wood inside the hasty clearing, then laid Horan's corpse atop the makeshift pyre. He sat next to his friend for a few minutes, chin on his knees, arms hugging his legs into his chest. Honestly, he was surprised at the depth of his grief. The NPC wasn't real, he reminded himself. Just a procedurally generated bit of code, floating in a server deep in a salt mine in Independence, Missouri. Yet, despite that—and in a remarkably short time to boot—the NPC had burrowed his way into Robert's confidence and become one of his most trusted allies.

An actual friend.

Robert was going to miss the older man's sarcastic jibes and sound advice.

Osmark dug in his belt pouch for the gold coins he'd taken from the assassins. "Here's your bonus," he said, choking on the words as he stacked the coins in a neat pile on Horan's chest. With a bit of flint from his new Artificer Toolkit, he set the wood and brush on fire, then stoically watched as it burned. The smoke stung his eyes, and he brushed tears away with the back of his bloodied hand as his friend's body blackened and spat sparks into the sky.

Just like that, gone forever.

For the first time he could remember, Robert didn't want to be alone. Cold isolation settled around his shoulders like a cloak of thorns, and the bitter acid of sadness eroded his spirit and left him numb. He stared into the blaze, unable to muster the strength to stand.

This isn't what Horan would want, he thought after a time. *He'd want me to put a knife in the bastards who did this to him.*

Slowly, bit by bit, Osmark's sorrow transformed in the forge of his thoughts. Cold grief gave way to the heat of rage, and the raw ore of his anger became a sharp and deadly blade.

A muscle in Osmark's jaw twitched as he ground his teeth. "You'll regret this, Sizemore. For a very, very long time."

TWENTY:

The Brand Forged

Robert limped into Rozak's shop still woozy from his port-stone return trip to Tomestide. His stomach churned, and his head ached, but aside from that, he felt surprisingly good considering everything he'd been through. He must've looked much worse than he felt, though, because Rozak turned from his work to stare in wide-mouthed alarm as Robert crossed the threshold.

Rozak slammed the forge's door, dropped his tongs into the bucket of water next to it, and peeled out of his protective gauntlets before stomping across the floor to greet Robert.

"You look like you've been wrestling with wildcats and come up short," the dwarf barked, shoving his goggles up onto his bald head with the back of his soot-stained hand. "Don't bleed on my floors."

Osmark grunted a noncommittal reply and dropped the quest items on Rozak's desk next to the front door. At this point, he wasn't interested in friendly banter or small talk—he just wanted to complete this quest and put its memory far behind him. "Here are

227

your leaves, fungus, and rocks," Robert said, sorting through the items on the desk as he named them.

The dwarf raked his stubby fingers through the thick tangles of his black beard. His hands emerged from the wild locks covered in gritty black ash and even more soot. Rozak clapped his fingers clean before picking through the items Robert had deposited on his desk.

"I'll be damned," the dwarf muttered with grudging admiration, "you actually completed the task."

Quest Alert: A Dwarf's Dogsbody, Part 2

You have completed the apprenticeship task assigned to you by Rozak, the Artificer. In return for your diligent work and clever solutions, your reputation with Rozak has increased to Honored, your reputation with all Artificers is now Friendly, and Rozak will reward you with ten rare crafting materials of your choice. You've also received 10,000 EXP.

---

x2 Level up!
You have (10) unassigned stat points!
You have (3) unassigned proficiency points!

Though it hardly made up for the loss of Horan, Osmark was pleased with both the potential rewards and the amount of experience he'd earned for the quest.

He still had a ton of work to do before the day ended, and those extra levels would certainly help.

Rozak collected the quest items from his desk and shuffled off to deposit them in the storage bins at the rear of his shop. Osmark wanted to chase after him, demanding his next quest, but he didn't dare. The dwarf was cantankerous, and Robert was leery of doing anything that might jeopardize his hard-won reputation with the artificer. So instead, he stood patiently next to the desk, hands clasped loosely behind his back, and waited for Rozak to return.

While the dwarf puttered around and organized his new crafting materials, Robert spent the time mentally reviewing Tomestide's layout and working out how best to protect the small town from his enemies. It wouldn't be long before all of V.G.O.'s honored guests were gathered here for the first big meeting to discuss how they would proceed toward their goals. Knowing that Sizemore was actively working against him, Robert wanted to prepare for any eventuality. The first draft of a plan formed in the back of his mind, but it was missing too many pieces. Osmark didn't have enough time to put it into action, nor enough skill for its trickier elements.

He was so lost in thought as he chewed over possible solutions to these problems that he didn't hear Rozak addressing him until the dwarf cleared his throat.

"Might want to listen when your boss is talking," Rozak said with a gruff harrumph. "Here I am complimenting you, and you're off gathering wool from the clouds like a moon-starved gnome."

Robert bit off an angry retort before it crossed his lips. It had been years since anyone had been foolish enough to disrupt his deep thinking, and Osmark didn't like it. Not one bit. It took a great effort of will for Robert to remind himself he wasn't the boss here. Here, he was an apprentice, and if he didn't want to have his whole plan blow up in his face, he needed to act like one.

No matter how much it grated on his pride.

"I'm sorry," he apologized, offering the dwarf a flat professional smile, "I'm still a little dazed from everything that happened while I was gone."

"I'm not here to talk about your personal problems." The dwarf snorted and flicked a cinder from his tangled beard. "What I was saying was, you got a knack for this. Not many folks have the natural skill I see in you." He paused, eyes narrowed, hands planted on his hips. "Don't let it go to your head, but I think you could do great things."

A surprising rush of pride flooded through Robert's chest. It'd been a long time since there'd been anyone in his life whose compliment meant very much to him. And hearing the dwarf praise his skill made Robert remember what it was like to be a student, to still be learning, instead of being a master at his craft. At every craft he'd ever set his mind to. "Thank you, sir," he said, surprised at the depth of gratitude in his voice.

"But if you're going to go any further," the dwarf admonished as he dragged himself up into the chair behind the desk, "then you're going to need to find something much rarer and more precious than Starfall ore."

Robert found himself hanging on the dwarf's every word. There was a solemnity and gravity to what Rozak said that captured Osmark's attention and held it as fast as a bear trap's implacable jaws. "What do I need to do?"

Rozak leaned back in his chair and dug his oversized pipe out of the desk drawer. He fished a plug of tobacco from a pouch on his hip and tamped it into the pipe's bowl with a calloused thumb. The dwarf's eyes never left Osmark's, but he seemed in no hurry to continue their conversation. He clenched the pipe's stem between his teeth and raised a small steel rod from a thick gold chain around his neck. With a wink, Rozak pressed the end of the rod into the tobacco packed into his pipe's bowl. A moment later, thick plumes of disgusting black smoke rose from the pipe.

The dwarf took a deep drag on the stem and then blew a stinking cloud toward Osmark's face. After another puff, and then another, the dwarf pulled the stem from between his lips and pointed it at Robert. "Long, long ago, there were far more artificers than there are today. They constructed great machines, enormous factories, and weapons that make even the Empire's arsenal look like a toddler's toys."

Osmark was well aware of the basic structure of Eldgard's past because he'd helped write it, but still he found himself fascinated. He hunched forward, listening to the details, trying to glean new information that the AI had inserted after the Devs had finished laying down the framework of Eldgard's expansive histories.

The dwarf blew a series of concentric smoke rings toward the ceiling. As the first one expanded, Rozak shot another through its center, then another through that one's expanding middle. Soon a dozen rings were drifting toward the high ceiling, spreading out like the pattern of a bull's-eye target.

As if remembering he'd been talking to Robert, the dwarf shook his head and continued his speech. "But the greatest of their creations were the servants they built to help them run their kingdoms: the Brand-Forged."

Robert raised one eyebrow in surprise. This was new. He couldn't recall anything about the Brand-Forged from the design documents he'd seen or written. Apparently, the Overminds had been more imaginative than he'd thought possible. "What were these Brand-Forged? Golems?"

The dwarf said nothing for a long moment as he gnawed on the stem of his pipe, smoke drifting lazily from his nostrils. Rozak's eyes took on a faraway look as if he'd remembered something both amazing and depressing. "No, they were no golems. They were thinking creatures. As much metal as meat, yet the Brand-Forged were truly alive. Even at the end.

"They were living creatures with the power to change their bodies to suit the task at hand. It wasn't long before they'd surpassed their creators, and not much longer before they withdrew from the world of men altogether to create a society of their own."

Osmark found himself fascinated by this new wrinkle. Why would the Overminds have created a new race of mechanical men just to erase them from the world before any players entered V.G.O.? It was a conundrum that both intrigued and worried Robert. Before he could pursue his thoughts any further, the dwarf spoke again.

"In their isolation, the Brand-Forged mastered the art and science that had created them. They were the ultimate Mechanical Artificers, and their knowledge has never been surpassed." The dwarf twirled his pipe stem through the cloud of smoke around his head. "You'll need some of that knowledge if you want to become a *truly* great artificer."

Robert's pulse raced. This was it. This was the class quest he needed. "What is it I need?" he asked, working to conceal the desperation in his voice.

Rozak grinned and leaned in close to Robert. "You must find a Mechanical Artificer's Guidebook. They're rarer than a dragon's mercy and more precious than a demon's tears. Recovering such a book will require a journey to one of the ruins of the Brand-Forged—assuming you can even find such a place. The mechanical men hid their enclaves well, and few have ever been discovered."

"And if I can't find one?" Robert felt his chest tighten at the thought of failure.

"Then you will not be a Mechanical Artificer," Rozak said with a noncommittal shrug. He shoved his chair back from the desk and stomped away from Robert.

For a moment, Osmark thought he'd lost his chance with the dwarf. He wanted to race after Rozak but held his ground. He needed to be patient. Respectful. Charging after his master wasn't going to help matters.

Rozak disappeared into his workshop and reappeared a few moments later with a massive leather tome tucked under his arm. He stopped in front of Robert and raised the book, which was etched in golden runes and studded with ancient cogs. "This book holds the sum of all my knowledge. Every one of the rare mechanical blueprints I've discovered is stored between these covers. But even if I gave it to you, it'd do you no good. Each artificer must fill his own book. Only then can you truly understand the legacy of the Brand-Forged."

The quest prompt appeared in front of Osmark, and his heart pounded in his temples.

Quest Alert: The Legacy of the Brand-Forged

Becoming a Mechanical Artificer requires the hidden knowledge of those who have come before. Only by recovering a Mechanical Artificer Guidebook from the ruins of the Brand-Forged do you have any hope of achieving this lofty goal.

Be warned that this quest is not for the foolhardy or the weak. The Brand-Forged hid their homes well and protected them with powerful weapons and mechanical servitors. Those who dare to venture into their long-forgotten enclaves risk death at the hands

---

> of the ancient and powerful machines.
>
> *Quest Class:* Rare, class-based
>
> *Quest Difficulty:* Extreme
>
> *Success:* Return to Rozak with a Mechanical Artificer's Guidebook
>
> *Failure:* Death
>
> *Reward:* Class change; faction increase; 15,000 EXP
>
> *Accept:* Yes/No?

Robert never considered saying no. He extended one hand to Rozak, and the dwarf shook it vigorously in his powerful grip.

"I'll do it," Osmark said, gladly excepting the rare and deadly quest.

"Best of luck to you," Rozak said. "May the gods guide you on your path. They alone know how much help you're going to need."

Robert turned on his heel and stalked out of the forge. He had work to do and people to meet. His plan was coming together; he just had to stave off Sizemore for a little while longer.

TWENTY-ONE:

Status Report

Murly nodded as Osmark entered the Saddler's Rest with a spring in his step. He looked like a dirt-caked hobo, true, but he felt good and was excited by the prospect of the Brand-Forged and his potential class specialization—even if finding one of these Brand-Forged Dungeons could be tricky. It was a new and unexpected complication, though it was always possible his restricted area could end up as a Brand-Forged location.

The restricted areas weren't really designed in detail; rather, they were broadly programmed to meet specific input requirements, and the Overminds did the rest. It wasn't an ideal arrangement, but it was the only way to circumvent the Overmind base directive that prevented hackers and modders from tinkering with the system. He didn't know what to expect—not really— but the Dungeon would be geared heavily toward his specific class and would have a carefully balanced ratio of experience to mob difficulty. That algorithm would skirt just below what the Overminds would flag as unsanctioned modding.

Osmark put thoughts of the Brand-Forged from his mind as he surveyed the inn.

Unlike his last visit, the quaint tavern was hustling and bustling with activity: clouds of gray smoke floated by, while dusty, road-weary merchants lounged around the pub tables, eating, drinking, and laughing. After his misadventures in the forest, Osmark wasn't in the mood to deal with the noise, the thick pipe smoke lingering in the air, or the crowds in the common room. He also wasn't in the mood to search for his subordinates, who must've found some place to avoid the throngs of commoners.

Robert cupped his hands around his mouth and shouted to Murly over the din, "Where are my people?"

The innkeeper didn't have a chance to answer Robert before thirsty patrons began banging their tankards on the chipped and battered bar, causing a ruckus that drowned out whatever he'd been going to say. Flustered, Murly tilted his balding head toward a door at the rear of the tavern's common room.

Robert tossed a silver piece to Murly, then shouldered his way through the crowd. He ignored the cries and protests of disgruntled patrons and managed to reach the door without giving in to his urge to shoot someone in the face with his repeater. It was a near thing, though. Osmark flicked the metal latch, opened the door just enough to slip through, then quickly secured it behind him before any of the drunks out there got any funny ideas. He sagged against the rough wood and let out an exasperated sigh.

Dorak, Garn, and Aurion—back from their initial surveillance trip to Wyrdtide—rose to greet him, but Robert waved them off. "Sit, sit. I hope there's enough food and ale left for me. I'm starving."

The small private room held a round table, six high-backed wood chairs, and a sideboard bowed under the weight of platters of roasted meats and flagons of ale. Robert took a seat near the food and loaded a metal plate to overflowing. He turned back to his people but raised a finger to keep them from asking any questions. Savoring the quiet, he stuffed his mouth with a slice of roast duck, once, twice, then washed the dust from his throat with a gulp from a tankard of ale.

With the worst of his hunger's edge gone, Robert wiped his mouth with the back of one hand and leaned forward, his elbows resting on the table.

His crew waited for him to speak, anxiously eyeing his ripped clothes and bloody appearance. They were concerned, and so tense Osmark suspected they might start vibrating if he didn't allow them to make their reports. "Garn, status report—"

The door abruptly swung open, interrupting his request.

Robert spun, drawing his repeater in the same fluid motion, and leveled the barrel at the door. Before he could get a lock on the intruder, however, a black blur flowed past the door and seized his wrist in a firm, unyielding grip.

Sandra grinned down at Robert and released him. Though this was the first time he'd seen her since entering V.G.O., he immediately knew it was her. During the character creation process, she could've chosen to be anything, to look however she wanted, yet in the end—just like Osmark—she'd gone with a form that looked true to life. She had the same lean build, the same sharp green eyes, and even the same severe face, though air brushed with the sheen of VR magic. The only real difference was the slight golden hue to her skin and the pointed tips of her ears.

A Hvitalfar, then. A good choice, considering the Dawn Elves littered the West Viridia side of Eldgard and were close allies with the Imperials.

She was also as cool and collected as he'd ever seen her, and looked well-rested and relaxed despite the time she'd spent traveling to Tomestide. She had her long hair pulled back into a sleek black ponytail, which perfectly matched the form-fitting leather armor encasing her from throat to ankles. She padded past Robert in a pair of soft-soled boots that made no sound at all and slipped into a chair.

"Miss me?" she asked with a wink. "Sorry, I think I interrupted the status report." She paused, stealing a sidelong glance at Osmark. "Thanks for not shooting me, by the way."

"Garn, status," Osmark said, ignoring Sandra's intrusion. He sliced another hunk of meat with his Risi gutting knife. "You look like you have something to tell me about what happened in Wyrdtide."

The security expert cleared her throat and clasped her hands on the table. "Sizemore's been a busy boy, sir. He's put the word out that he'll pay well for anyone who can bring you to him. He wants you alive, though he doesn't seem to care how banged up you get in transit." Once more she eyed the muck and dried blood. She wanted to ask—the curiosity was etched into the features of her face—but she held her tongue.

A smart move.

Robert swallowed a mouthful of duck so tender it practically melted, and pointed his knife at Garn. "What does that tell you?"

The Risi fidgeted nervously in her seat. "He doesn't want you dead, but he does want you out of the way. If he takes you prisoner, and he can find some way to keep you from escaping, that's better than killing you."

"A gold star for Garn." Robert speared a hunk of roast beef and chewed on it thoughtfully, enjoying the burst of flavor. "I hope the rest of you understand that this changes things," he finally said. "Sizemore's upped the ante, and I'm not about to fold the hand I've been dealt. We need to be ready for anything he tries. And he *will* try something. Soon."

Aurion cleared her throat and needlessly straightened her robes with the palms of her hands. "I found Sizemore's family. He has them safely squirreled away in an estate outside of Wyrdtide. A wife and a son. There are enough guards on site to make an extraction difficult, though not impossible. I don't think there's a way to do it quietly, but we *could* do it if push comes to shove."

Osmark crossed his fork and knife on his plate. "And if we have to kill them?"

The sorceress clenched her napkin so tight her knuckles cracked. Killing Sizemore's family wouldn't do any permanent damage, but it was still murder. The civilians would experience the pain and fear of their death, which would stick with them for a very long time. That had been one of the major flaws early on—a flaw the Devs never really ironed out. In the early beta versions, dying in the game proved exceptionally traumatic for many players, and a few became … extremely unhinged.

Aurion didn't want that guilt on her conscience, which was precisely why Robert was assigning her the task. What they were trying to do was bigger than all of them—if she couldn't break a few eggs, then she wasn't fit to serve.

Aurion raised her eyes to meet Robert's. "Yes," she replied stiffly. "Give the word, and I can take them out."

Robert nodded and gestured to Dorak. He was too busy filling the void in his gut to waste time asking questions. Robert could sympathize. The food here was better than he could have imagined, but his hunger was much greater, as well. He couldn't remember ever eating this much in one sitting before, but hearty meals seemed to be the rule, not the exception, in V.G.O.

Dorak chewed on the inside of his lip for a moment and then dove into his report. "Sizemore's done more than just put the word out that he wants your head. He's been talking to the Coldskulls' leadership. I saw him with one of their lieutenants, and rumor has it he's been dealing with people further up their chain of command. All the way at the top, even. These people are very bad news, Mr. Osmark."

Robert twisted his knife between his hands. He stared at each of the assistants in turn, letting the full weight of his attention fall on them one at a time. Finally, he retrieved a linen napkin from the sideboard and carefully, slowly, wiped his mouth clean. "As it turns out, I already knew everything you each reported."

The cold steel in his voice froze the whole crew in place like an arctic blizzard. Robert could sense the questions on the tips of their tongues, but he wasn't in the mood to hear from them. If they'd been a little faster, a little more diligent, they might've been able to get him intel that would've saved Horan's life and spared him a lot of pain. "Do you notice anyone missing from our little meeting?" he asked, glancing left, then right.

Aurion responded instantly, her voice flat and emotionless. "Horan isn't here."

"Correct," Robert said. He adjusted his plate until it sat directly in front of him on the table. He laid his knife down across its top, careful to keep the blade exactly parallel to his chest. He folded the napkin into a perfect rectangle and laid it on the table. Each motion methodical and precise. Drawing out the moment and the awful tension. "Two hours ago," he said after a time, "while you were all gathering here and stuffing your faces with food I'm paying for, the Coldskulls attacked me in the forest east of town. They killed Horan. They almost captured me."

Sandra flinched at the devastating news, but she didn't look away from Robert's even stare. "I'm sorry, sir, I should've gathered the information more quickly and gotten it to you immediately. We didn't know the Coldskulls had already dispatched a team to Tomestide. It must've happened while we were in transit."

Robert knew his assistant was right, but it didn't make him feel any better about what had happened. There was a gap in his intelligence team, a hole in the net he used to gather the data that was so critical to his success in V.G.O. He should've left one of his operatives in Wyrdtide, where they could keep an eye on Sizemore.

He should've been on top of the situation, even if *they* weren't.

That was the difference between a good manager and a failure.

The team had screwed up, but he had, too. Ultimately, a team's shortcomings fell squarely on the leader's shoulders.

He took a deep, cleansing breath, and forced himself to relax. From the pained looks on their faces, it was clear his team felt terrible about Horan's death and his near capture. Yelling at them wouldn't inspire them to work any harder or any smarter, and it sure as hell wouldn't bring Horan back from the dead.

"There's nothing we can do to change what happened, but I think this can be a learning moment for each of you. Hopefully, you all now realize just how high the stakes are. While Sizemore is out there, we're all in danger. I don't know how he's done it, but he's gotten further along in his plans than I'd like." Robert's eyes swept the room. "Which means we need to move faster and be smarter if we want to beat him. We paid for this lesson in blood, so let's not forget it, yes?"

Robert let the words sink in for a moment before he handed out the next assignments. "Garn, I need you on the Coldskulls' lieutenant. Get back to

Wyrdtide, and cling to the asshole like a hemorrhoid. And if he sends another team my way, I want to know about it long before they try to stick a knife in my gizzard."

He drummed his fingers on the table, *rat-tat-tat*, then turned toward Dorak. "You're on Sizemore. I want to know his schedule, his routine—where he stays, what he eats, who he talks to. If he so much as gets up in the middle of the night to take a leak, you report it to Sandra. No more surprises."

"And me?" Aurion asked.

"Sit on Sizemore's family," he replied coolly. "I doubt he'll move them, but I need you tailing them at all times. If they leave the estate, you follow. Period." Osmark stared deep into the elf's eyes. "You have to be ready."

"For what?" Aurion said, her spine stiff, her chin raised defiantly, her hands curled into tight fists.

Osmark didn't like her rebellious attitude, but he needed her on this. For now, at least. Explaining his motives to one of his employees rankled Robert's spirit, but there was no other way to get the message through Aurion's head. "To kill them. If I give the word, I want his wife and child blown into a fine red mist. Or burned to ash. Or transformed into pillars of salt. Whatever. If I give the order, I want them dead. That instant—" He snapped his fingers. "Gone. Can you handle that or do I need to find someone else?"

"I thought—" Aurion started, but Osmark cut her off.

"I know. But we don't have a choice. I need leverage over Sizemore, and this is the best way to get it." Robert sat back and rubbed his temples with the tips of his fingers. A stress migraine was sprouting inside his skull, and he couldn't afford to let it grow. Absently, he wondered if the headache was somehow symptomatic of the transition—was he dying? Was this it? Had a blood clot migrated to his brain, killing him before the nanites could finish their work? He pushed the morbid notion away. Thinking like that wasn't useful, and he eliminated *everything* that wasn't useful.

"I know they're civilians," he continued, "but he's forced my hand with his plans. We need to be ready to do whatever's required for success."

For a long moment, Aurion and Osmark stared at one another across the table. He wondered who would win if it came to a fight. She was younger and faster than he was, and at this point, her spells were more powerful than his repeater. Robert put his odds of winning the fight at 3:1 against. But he wasn't about to let Aurion know that.

He pinned her to her chair with his cold blue stare, tenting his fingers in front of him.

The sorceress let out a long, exasperated sigh, then shrugged in resignation. Defeat. "Fine. You're the boss. I don't like it, but I understand it."

"Excellent. Well then, since the three of you have your marching orders, you're all dismissed." He shooed them away with the flick of one hand. "And remember what's on the line," he called after them as they left the room in an orderly rush, the sorceress trailing at the back of the pack. Osmark waited until Aurion's robes swished through the doorway before he spoke.

"I *did* miss you," he said to Sandra. "I just hope you have better news for me than Huey, Dewey, and Louie there." He waved at the door.

His assistant grunted from her side of the table. "Not much. But on the plus side, Sizemore is still moving in the shadows, and I don't think he's gained any more allies on the board. For the record"—she cocked an eyebrow at him—"I *did* give you a heads-up that assassins might be headed your way. Still, I'm sorry to hear about your acquaintance."

"I know," Osmark said. A cold knot of anger and sadness twisted in his gut, but he didn't have time to deal with it at the moment. "But let's put that all behind us—it's not worth dwelling on. Now, I hope you're not too tired because we've got a lot of work left today."

Sandra grinned. "I'm fine, old man. Let's see if you can keep up with me."

TWENTY-TWO:

Dungeon Dive

S andra tossed the spent ashes of the customized port-scroll into the weeds and clapped the soot from her hands. She wrinkled her nose at the smoky aroma lingering in the air like a cloying perfume. "It would've been nice if you'd made these a little less messy. Every time I use one, my hands smell like I smoked a pack of cigarettes."

Osmark snorted. "If you think those stink, wait until you meet Rozak. You're going to *love* his pipe. And, FYI, not everything here is my doing. The Overminds do most of the heavy lifting when it comes to filling in the gaps between the broad strokes we used to design this place."

Sandra grinned and threw a playful punch at his shoulder. "Sorry, boss. I just figured since it was a single-use scroll directly to your restricted area that maybe you'd customized it down to the tiniest detail. Like you tend to do."

Osmark couldn't suppress a chuckle at that. Sandra was right. He had a perfectionist streak that drilled all the way down to his core. If he'd had more time, Robert probably would've thrown a week's worth of work at the port-scroll to make sure it delivered him in a puff of just the right colored smoke with a swelling orchestral score rising on the wind to give him a majestic entrance. Not everything in life could be perfect, though. Sometimes—as much as it irked him—settling was the only feasible option.

With V.G.O., that axiom proved especially true.

The tech, platform, and game had been ten years in the making when 213 Astraea appeared on the distant horizon of space, hurtling toward Earth like a runaway train. True, he'd known about the asteroid before almost anyone, thanks to his generous financial support to the Arecibo Observatory in Puerto Rico, but even with his foreknowledge, he'd had less than eight months to get V.G.O. up and operational. Eight measly months, when the planned release date was still over two years off.

There were so many things he would've changed with enough time—first and foremost, V.G.O. wouldn't be a fantasy world. A fantasy-based MMORPG was great for money, but it certainly wasn't his idea of Heaven. With two or three years, he could've turned V.G.O. into a futuristic paradise even better than the world they'd left behind. But reprogramming the Overminds in eight months? Impossible. So, he'd done what he could. He'd made things serviceable.

Maybe there were a few hiccups. Maybe he'd made some shady deals. Maybe the Overminds were still undertested.

But the game worked.

That was the important thing to cling to.

"Let's get inside, and see what goodies are waiting for us," Osmark said, heading toward the half-hidden door in the side of the hill ahead of them. He had a vague sense of what he might stumble across, but it was impossible to say since so much of the programming rested with the Overminds. But whatever was in there would be good. Very, very good. Honestly, he felt like a kid on Christmas morning. Assuming, of course, that the presents under the tree were guarded by monsters who wanted to kill him and eat his guts.

The entrance was an ancient steel door covered in rusted gears, clogged by winding vines and bent saplings. Years of neglect had corroded the hinges into fine red dust, leaving the barrier cocked ajar to reveal the yawning darkness beyond. A tag appeared briefly over the door before vanishing in a flash: [Artifactory]. Osmark let out a long, low whistle, dry washing his hands in anticipation.

He turned to Sandra and asked, "Did you bring any torches?"

"I haven't even been back a whole day, and you're already forgetting everything," she said with a friendly grin, which took the sting from the words. "No torches, but something a little bit better."

She deftly plucked a thin metal cylinder from a sleeve stitched into the armor covering her left thigh. She twirled the rod between her fingers in an impressive display of manual dexterity, then brought it to a sudden stop balanced on the tip of her index finger. "*Ignir,*" she hissed, and a brilliant white light burst from the rod's surface.

"Nice trick," Osmark said, admiring the item. It cast a steady glow that illuminated a circle roughly twenty feet in diameter.

"It has an even better one," Sandra said and whispered, "*Guron*."

The rod floated off her finger, drifted about five feet ahead of them, and hovered in the air at Sandra's eye level. She took a step forward, and the rod floated away, keeping a constant distance from her position. "Neat, right?"

Osmark had to admit it was cool. While he loved his repeater, and found the Artificer's goggles extremely useful, neither of those items had the same utility as the simple magical flashlight. "Where can I get one of those?"

Sandra rolled her eyes. "You can buy one in just about any city if you know where to look. Or, Mr. Artificer, you could *build* one."

Robert grunted and then stepped past the glowing rod to grab the edge of the door. "Let's get in here and get some loot. Maybe I'll get lucky and find one of my very own."

He struggled with the heavy metal door, but it didn't budge. He just wasn't strong enough to push it aside. "A hand?" he asked, suppressing the surge of frustration welling up inside him.

Sandra strode past him and rested her back against the hill next to the door, then lifted her right leg and wedged her boot against it. "On three," she said and began counting down.

When she hit one, Osmark threw his body weight against the door, straining with his legs and arms, giving it every ounce of effort he had to offer. It creaked, shifted, and groaned, then crashed open, slamming against the wall with a dull thud. A trio of bats, alarmed by the sudden flood of daylight washing over their lair, burst from the opening. They screeched at Osmark as they passed, a warning and a rebuke, then they were gone, vanishing into the forest surrounding the buried dungeon.

"I guess you're not the only crabby one today," Sandra said, absently waving away a swirl of dust disturbed by the door. Before Osmark could respond, she turned away and descended the worn stairs leading into the earth.

The floating rod lit the passageway well enough, but Osmark still had to watch his step. Centuries of rainwater and grasping roots had weathered the steps and left their leading edges dangerously rounded. A slick layer of mildew and hidden pockets of moss made the footing even more treacherous. "Watch your step," he called out, but Sandra wasn't listening.

As a Stalker Class—a combination of Rogue and Ranger—she was far more dexterous than Robert and took the steps two at a time without faltering. She lingered at the bottom of the staircase, waiting, tapping her toes as he cautiously picked his way down to join her. "You're dumping all your Stat points into Intelligence, aren't you?" she asked without preamble.

Osmark felt a faint blush creep onto his cheeks. "Not all of them."

Sandra shrugged. "It would suck if you didn't put anything into Vitality, then died because you were running around with the Health of an asthmatic newbie."

"I'm not—" Osmark said, but Sandra was already moving deeper into the restricted area.

She had a point, he couldn't deny that, but the perfectionist in him didn't want to squander even a single point that didn't boost his most important stat if he could avoid it. Sure, having a little more Strength now might be nice, but it would likely cost him hours of grinding later on to make up the difference—doing it right the first time was the best choice.

Sometimes, Robert wished people thought more like he did so he wouldn't have to explain every decision he made. Life would certainly be simpler that way.

A few yards from the stone steps, the tunnel changed dramatically. The floor, walls, and ceiling morphed into seamless metal covered in a tangle of thick pipes running the length of the corridor. Smaller conduits threaded their way through the larger pipes to form a confusing labyrinth of steel tubes, copper gauges, and iron rivets.

The air was thick with heat and humidity as well as the rumbling and gurgling of steam rushing through the metal pipes around them. Thick glass globes flickered with jolts of pale blue light, reminding Osmark of primitive light bulbs attached to a failing power source. He idly wondered what this place would've looked like in its full glory, then paused and shook his head at his foolishness. This place had no past. It had never been in its full glory because it had been designed as a decrepit dungeon for Robert to plunder.

Sometimes, it was too easy to forget this was all a grand illusion—a trick Robert himself had designed.

He paused mid-stride, catching a glint of gold on the floor nearby. A single, fat coin lay on the ground near the wall. He bent over and picked it up. The breath caught in his chest as he examined his find in the flickering illumination from overhead. A carefully worked cog was stamped into the metal, and running along the outer edge, in thick bold lettering, he saw the words *Brand-Forged*.

Incredible.

Suddenly, his knees felt weak and his head felt light and butterflies fluttered manically in his gut. If this place really was Brand-Forged, it changed *everything*. Not only would he get a massive experience boost and a Faction Seal, it was likely he'd also find a Mechanical Artificer's Guidebook somewhere in these halls. Which meant, instead of scouring all of Eldgard for the next month, he'd be able to acquire his specialty kit in record time and move on to the more important matters: like eliminating Sizemore and conquering an empire.

He slipped the coin into his pocket—a token of good luck—as he pressed on, nearly exploding with excitement. This wasn't just Christmas morning, not any more. No, it was Christmas, Easter, his birthday, and New Year's Eve all rolled into one. He picked up his pace, eager to share his finding with Sandra, but the words died on his lips as the tunnel opened into an oval chamber with a glowing orb the size of a wrecking ball sunk into its center. Three figures stood around the orb, and all turned to face Osmark as he and Sandra entered the room.

"Who goes there?" the first of the adventurers asked as she stepped into the day-bright glow of Sandra's magical flashlight. She was tall and slender, with a pair of elegant wings covered with sleek brown feathers sprouting from her shoulders. Her crimson robes flowed down her voluptuous form like water, and their vibrant color exactly matched her flashing eyes.

Osmark raised his right hand and answered her challenge. "I'm Robert Osmark, and I command you by my seal and my sign."

On cue, a burning sigil appeared on the palm of his hand. The Accipiter stepped forward, crimson eyes narrowed as she examined Robert's hand; simultaneously, Sandra moved into striking range, palm resting on the hilt of a curved blade at her hip. The two women exchanged dangerous glances, and Robert tensed.

A pale blue light flashed across the Accipiter's eyes, and she nodded. "You are who you claim, and we are glad to be of service."

She pressed one long-nailed thumb against her chest and said, "I'm Eldred, the Fell Summoner."

A burly dwarf stepped away from the glowing orb and hefted a massive hammer in both hands. "And I'm Karzic, the Soul Chanter."

Finally, an enormous Risi with a head covered in more scars than hair stepped forward. He rested his gauntleted hands on the hilts of the iron *kanabo* dangling from hooks on his belt. The triangular spikes set into the clubs looked sharp and heavy enough to tear through metal armor like a can opener. He stepped up to Osmark and thrust his enormous gauntlet-covered fist forward in a gesture that was more challenge than a greeting. "And I am Targ, Bonecrusher."

Osmark wasn't sure if the Risi was announcing his class kit or just making a statement of fact. Either way, he looked more than capable of crushing just about anything he wanted.

Robert appraised the mercenaries, and a surge of relief washed through him. These were his NPCs, specially designed to help him grind his way through this dungeon, defeat the Boss, and claim his Faction Seal. He'd wondered what form they would take, and how competent they'd be, and these three surpassed his wildest dreams. They had a well-balanced party with two DPS members, a thief, a cleric, and a warrior. If Robert played his cards right, this was going to be a walk in the park.

"Well, then, I suppose it's time to get this expedition underway." Robert nodded toward Sandra. "This is our stalker. She'll lead the way and make sure we don't stumble into any unpleasant traps."

Sandra nudged him with an elbow as she passed, and muttered, "Gee, thanks, I'll do all the hard work."

Osmark was surprised to find that Sandra's sarcastic tone was far more comforting than annoying, even after all he'd been through. It was good to know that the more things changed, the more they stayed the same. Sandra was different here—stronger and more confident—but she was still the same person underneath the physical changes and black armor.

Robert needed that stability, now more than ever.

The NPC mercenaries said nothing as they followed Sandra, and Osmark kept his thoughts to himself as he brought up the rear. He didn't want to distract Sandra from the important task of making sure they didn't wander into some instant death security system, and the quiet gave him time to examine his surroundings more thoroughly.

Whatever else the Brand-Forged had been, they were heavily invested in the use of steam. Scalding jets of the stuff emerged from pressure valves overhead, pipes shook all around Robert, and he wondered how many centuries it had been since someone gave this place a safety inspection. If one of the hundreds of pressurized pipes surrounding them burst …

Robert shook his head. That was the last thing he needed to be thinking about. He'd been so preoccupied with his thoughts of doom, gloom, and sudden mechanical failure that he only noticed Sandra had stopped when he bumped into Targ's massive back.

"What's happening?" he asked, trying to peer around the Bonecrusher's muscular form. Before Robert could see anything, though, the lights went out, and an enormous hand clamped over his mouth.

TWENTY-THREE:

Scavlings

Osmark struggled against the hand on his mouth, trying to push it away, but the calloused palm refused to budge. Hot breath washed over his face as a gruff voice rumbled in his left ear. "Your stalker spotted some nasties up ahead. Stay. I'll kill whatever it is." With that, the hand vanished, and Robert was alone in the dark.

Soft footfalls approached on either side of him, and he realized his mercenaries were taking their job very seriously. Good. Eldred and Karzic were close enough to defend him if needed, but not so close as to intrude on his personal space. He was grateful for their professionalism and support, but he didn't like the idea of Sandra being out there with no one but the Risi at her back. Targ looked impressive, but Osmark had no idea how he stood up in a fight. He'd known lots of men in his life who were tough as nails on the surface but had guts of marshmallow fluff.

A metallic tapping echoed down the hallway in regular, rapid bursts. *Tick tick tick.* Silence. *Tick tick tick.*

The noises were faint at first but grew louder with each repetition. Osmark heard one series of ticks answered by another, which in turn was answered by two more. One of the tickers was close, while the others were more distant. Still, they were closing in from all directions, and there were a lot of them.

Osmark listened to the pattern of the sounds, the way they came first from his left, then his right, then from dead ahead. The ticking repeated, over and over, minutely changing direction as the tickers drew ever nearer.

Robert realized what was happening, and a spike of adrenaline set his heart into overdrive.

"Light," he hissed, hoping he was loud enough for Sandra to hear him, but not so loud he'd attract the attention of the tickers. "We need the light. Whatever's making the noise hunts by sound."

Eldred's voice slithered into his right ear. "Silence," she said, her mouth so close to Osmark's cheek he felt the heat of her lips brushing against his skin. "Targ knows what he's doing. Let him work."

A scalding geyser of anger boiled up through Osmark's body. Maybe Targ was the world's greatest fighter, but he wasn't much of a tactician, apparently. He was uncertain about what the Risi's plans were, but he was certain they were all in terrible danger from whatever was closing in on their location.

"Light!" he shouted, drawing his repeater from its shoulder holster. "They hunt by sound, you idiots!"

Karzic's hammer suddenly flared with holy, golden power. He raised it high overhead and growled at Osmark, "She told you to hold your tongue!"

The rebuke stung Osmark's pride, but only for a moment. He pointed at the passage ahead, where Sandra and the Risi stood side by side. A swarm of glittering arachnoid creatures the size of small dogs clung to the walls and skittered across the floor, deftly maneuvering to surround them. "Stop wasting your breath, and deal with those!" Osmark shouted, the words a whip crack of authority.

Sandra tossed her light rod into the air, barked its command word, then vaulted over the encroaching army of metal spiders with impossible aerial grace. She landed as light as a cat and drew a pair of slender scimitars from the scabbards behind her shoulders and dropped into a defensive stance. Ready to fight. To kill.

The Risi, on the other hand, went straight into attack mode. He drew his heavy kanabo and bolted in, putting the weapons to good use. His right hand shot out, and the spiked club crushed the metal carapace of a creature clinging to the wall beside his head, while the club in his left hand caught an arachnoid in mid-jump. The blow shattered four of the creature's legs, put a dent the size of a bowling ball into its armored carapace, and sent it sailing back into the darkness.

With a guttural shout, Karzic thrust his glowing hammer toward the battle, unleashing wisps of golden light that encircled Targ in a gossamer aura. Osmark realized the dwarf was still chanting under his breath, funneling more magical power into the aura surrounding the Risi. The Bonecrusher's muscles swelled as the light intensified, and a fiery glow poured from his bulging eyes. Whatever Karzic's chant did, it was impressive.

Eldred, her wings tucked tight against her back, stayed next to Osmark, her hands raised, her fingers flashing through a bizarre series of arcane gestures. Threads of glowing red light appeared between her fingers, and she twisted and wove them into an intricate cat's cradle that defied comprehension. She murmured a spiraling series of syllables that set Osmark's teeth on edge as it climbed through the octaves. He didn't know what the sorceress was up to, but he knew he didn't want to be on its receiving end.

Robert tried to get a bead on the arachnoid creatures, but the tunnel was too cramped for a clean shot. Firing the repeater risked hitting one of his allies, who were all engaged in the worthwhile pursuit of keeping him alive. Moving into a better position wasn't possible without walking into the middle of the fight, and Robert knew he wasn't cut out for that.

For the moment, he stood next to Eldred and prepared to fire on any of the creatures who drew too near. It was a frustratingly passive tactic for him, but he had no choice.

The arachnoids recovered from their surprise at the sudden burst of light and surged into frantic motion. Osmark counted nine, not including the two the Risi had already pummeled to death. Four of the metal spiders skittered along the walls, moving into a flanking position, while the other five rushed Targ.

He fished one of his steel caltrops from his belt and lobbed it high into the air, arcing the explosive over Targ's head. The metal grenade landed with a soft *clang* and detonated in violent fury, releasing a cloud of choking smoke and a hail of the familiar black spikes, which thankfully discriminated between friends and foe. The black spits of metal only harmed the long-legged arachnoids, and though they only sheared off a fraction of each creature's HP, it was still better than standing around, twiddling his thumbs. Plus, if the attack slowed the creatures down, that would be a significant advantage.

Naturally, a failure notification popped up instead:

Caltrop Failed! Brand-Forged Scavlings resist Caltrop with their Web-Walker ability!

Osmark grunted in frustration, then fixed his gaze on the bots, trying to understand how they operated and identify any weaknesses he could see. They had to have some weakness. Name placards, [Brand-Forged Scavling], appeared above their scurrying bodies, but Robert couldn't identify any other critical features before the spider-like monsters crashed into Targ.

The Bonecrusher met the attack head-on. There was no effort at defense in Targ's motions; every movement was a brutal, aggressive attack. The spiked club in his right hand caught a seam in a Scavling's armor and tore the creature apart like a wet paper bag. A spray of metal shards and loose gears burst from the gap between the creature's armored carapace and its abdomen, flying through the air in a rain of shrapnel. The creature fell to the floor with a hissing whine as steam gushed from a ruptured pipe somewhere deep in its innards.

In that instant, Robert spotted a weakness in the Scavlings' design. "They're soft underneath!" he shouted to his companions and hoped the advice would help them survive this swarm.

The Risi's second attack whistled toward another Scavling, but overshot, missing the creature by inches. The mistake cost him: the creature slammed into Targ's side and wrapped its segmented mechanical legs around his neck and torso like a vise. The metal spider thrust a pair of snapping mandibles at the Bonecrusher's neck, preparing to rip his head off.

Targ roared, but his bludgeoning weapons were useless while he was trapped in the Scavling's deadly embrace. And tied up by the attacker latched onto his torso, the Risi had no defense against the last three. They latched onto his legs and his right arm, using their weight to drag him to the ground. Their pincers gouged holes in his chainmail, and Osmark knew it would be only a matter of time before the Scavlings tore the Bonecrusher apart.

Sandra shouted and darted at Targ's attackers. Her slender blades sliced through the air but glanced off the Scavlings' metal carapaces in a shower of red sparks. She tried to slash at the creatures' bellies, but they were so low to the ground she couldn't get a clean shot.

A Scavling leaped at Eldred from high on the wall to her left, all eight of its legs outstretched and prepared to wrap around her the instant it reached the summoner. Osmark wasn't sure how magic worked, but he knew they couldn't afford to have Eldred interrupted before her spell went off.

With Karzic focused on keeping Targ alive, Robert was the only one close enough to save Eldred.

He stepped forward and thrust his repeater at the leaping Scavling. His finger twitched on the trigger, and the gun's thunderous report rolled through the crowded hallway like the voice of God. Despite the creature's speed, Osmark's last-second attack couldn't have missed, because he fired it when the Scavling was inches away from the repeater's barrel.

The bullet punched through the armor covering the Scavling's belly with a metallic crunch, and then it struck the inside of the armor covering the creature's back with a sound like a blacksmith's mallet striking an anvil.

The Scavling emitted a teakettle shriek as it slammed into Osmark's outstretched arm. It weighed far more than Robert had expected, and the impact knocked him off balance and away from Eldred. The creature's metal legs curled in around him, but they lacked the strength to hold him. The attack had damaged some mechanism within its body, leaving it weak and impotent.

But it was still more than capable of closing its mandibles on Robert's left arm. The razor-sharp blades ripped through Robert's jacket and the flesh beneath, while the crushing strength twisted his upper arm toward the breaking point. The creature's weight pulled Robert to the ground, and it crashed on top of him with enough force to drive the air from his lungs.

Robert's Health dipped by a third, and he knew he wouldn't last much longer with this thing on top of him. Pouring all of his points into his Intelligence and Dexterity would pay off in the long run, but at that moment he wished he'd been able to afford more investment in his Health and Vitality.

Sandra had been right. As usual.

The clash and cries of intense combat rang through the hall. From his position on the floor, Osmark couldn't see what was happening to his allies, but he had to assume no one was coming to rescue him from the snapping Scavling on top of him. If he wanted to survive, he'd have to handle the situation himself.

The Scavling's mandibles shot open and plunged toward Robert's exposed throat. Osmark twisted beneath the creature, avoiding a critical hit and instant death by a hair's breadth. The mandibles clanged against the stone floor next to his head and kicked up a spray of sparks, singeing his cheek and ear.

"Get off!" Robert shouted, pushing the repeater into the Scavling's side, just below the armored carapace.

He'd already shot the creature once, so he activated Focus Fire, squeezing the trigger and unleashing a burst into the weaker belly armor. The repeater roared in his hand, the barrel glowing white, and the creature's shell rang like a xylophone symphony in hell. A barrage of bullets punched through the outer shell and tore through the mechanical innards. But with most of their energy spent, the bullets weren't able to penetrate the outer armor on their second impact. Instead, they ricocheted in all directions inside the shell, plowing through delicate gear assemblies, shredding spring tension gears, and puncturing steam pipes.

Boiling water sprayed from the holes in the Scavling's belly and soaked into Robert's armor. The jacket absorbed most of the damage, but the water was still hot enough to blister his skin and chew away another chunk of his Health.

"Off!" Robert snarled and thrust the Scavling's dead weight from his chest. He struggled back to his feet to survey the scene, and his heart dropped.

Targ was on the ground with a mound of Scavlings crawling over him, claw-tipped legs stabbing down as blood ran from their mandibles in thick red streams.

The Risi struggled to free himself from the swarm, but even his massive strength wasn't enough to escape their grasping legs and crushing iron bodies. There were simply too many of them. His clubs were on the ground, useless in his current predicament, and his HP leaked away by the second. The golden glow once filling him with vigor was gone, leaving him unprotected and alone against the horde.

Sandra danced through the creatures like smoke and shadow, lunging in at them, but she couldn't reach their vulnerable stomachs because they were pressed against Targ. And for every mechanical leg she shattered, there were seven more that needed to be dealt with. And the Scavlings didn't just passively accept her attacks. Oh no, they slashed and snapped in retaliation. As capable as Sandra was, her light armor was no protection against their razor-sharp mandibles, which forced her to retreat more often than not.

Beads of sweat ran down Karzic's face as he struggled to reestablish the spell around Targ. Harsh words rolled from his lips like heavy stones into deep pools, but the globe of light around his hammer's head had faded to a sickly yellow sheen.

Osmark turned to Eldred, silently praying her spell was almost complete. She met his eyes with a twisted grin that sent icy shivers racing down Robert's spine. A grating, unnatural sound rumbled up from somewhere deep inside her throat as her hands danced in complicated and well-rehearsed patterns. In a flash, the red light around Eldred's fingers streaked away from her to a point a few feet over Targ's prone body. There it curled into a writhing mass, emitting a keening wail that made Robert want to find someplace safe to curl up in until this fight was over.

The sound rose to a fevered pitch as the tendrils of magic darkened, compressed, then vanished into a fist-sized black hole in the air. An eerie light gushed through the rip in the fabric of the world, and a terrifying, alien creature followed it.

The twisted beast—all glistening black skin, endless red eyes, and a sea of writhing limbs—hovered in the air, flexing its many tentacles. It shrieked, then, and bolts of lightning leaped from its flesh in a dizzying storm that struck the Scavlings again and again. Showers of sparks flew through the air in a blinding veil, which made it nearly impossible for Osmark to follow the fight.

Sandra hurled herself away from the lightning storm, narrowly avoiding a painful death.

Targ, completely engulfed by the creatures, was not so lucky. Even as the lightning blew his attackers apart, electricity passed through their metal bodies and into his. He opened his mouth to scream, but the only thing that emerged was a flurry of sparks and wisps of smoke. Robert stared in horrified awe as blasts of lightning transformed the last of the Scavlings into ruptured, smoldering husks. His ears rang with the sounds of their dying screeches and the unearthly howls of the creature Eldred had summoned.

Just when Robert thought the horrifying racket would push him over the edge into insanity, the tentacled monstrosity vanished back through the hole from which it had been summoned, and the hallway fell still.

For a long beat, the only sound was the ragged breathing of the survivors and the *sizzling-crack* of metal. Targ lay motionless on the floor, surrounded by the Scavlings' blasted shells and slagged legs.

Robert clenched his fists, lips pulling down in a scowl as he rounded on Eldred, ready to rip her a new one after that hellish display of friendly fire.

Before he could utter a word, however, Eldred stopped him with a knowing smirk and a raised hand. "He's fine."

"He can't possibly be fine," Osmark snapped, stealing a look at the Risi's charred body. "You just electrocuted him!" He raised a finger to emphasize his point, but his next words died on his lips.

"She's right," Targ said with a groan. He shoved the bodies of the Scavlings off, and they clattered around him like dice in a tin cup. The Risi hauled himself up onto his feet and shuddered, looking tired, dirty, and hurt, but very much alive. "I'm fine." Targ stood unassisted for just a moment before his injured legs refused to hold him any longer. He teetered for a beat, then toppled against the wall, sliding back down to the floor. "More or less."

TWENTY-FOUR:

Game Plan

K arzic trundled through the battle's wreckage to Targ's side and kneeled on the floor next to the bloodstained Risi. "All of you, gather round quick. I can't do this every time one of you stubs a toe."

Osmark, Sandra, and the rest of the group shoved aside shattered Scavling legs and dented carapaces, clearing a space around Targ. All of the adventurers—with the exceptions of Karzic and Eldred—looked worse for wear, but Targ was by far the most banged up. He had only a sliver of red remaining in his Health bar, and that was rapidly dwindling as blood oozed from deep puncture wounds and jagged lacerations crisscrossing his body. Frankly, Robert was astounded the Risi was still alive, much less conscious, after the savage beating he'd endured.

Karzic motioned for them all to sit, using hand gestures to guide them into a tight circle as he hummed a sonorous rhythm. When he was satisfied they were all in position, he raised his hammer overhead and unleashed a torrent of harsh consonants and gusty vowels that shook the air with their ferocity. If it was a prayer, it was the most violent and aggressive prayer Osmark had ever heard. Karzic wasn't *asking* for help.

He was *demanding* his god heal his companions.

A golden glow emanated from the hammer's head, intensifying as Karzic's words rumbled from deep within his thick beard. Osmark no longer heard the words as much as felt them, like a thumping counterpoint to his pulse. The chant sank into Robert's bones like a comforting warmth, and energy pumped into his bloodstream with every syllable Karzic intoned. Fresh strength filled his limbs as his injuries closed with miraculous speed.

The prayer did wonders for the rest of the group, too. The glow healed even Targ's terrible wounds, and by the time the dwarf lowered his hammer and leaned heavily against its handle, they were all as fit as they'd been when they'd entered the Artifactory. "I need a few minutes to rest before we move on," Karzic grunted, pulling a Spirit Regen potion from a pocket in his belt.

Robert stood from his position in the prayer circle and clapped his hand on Karzic's shoulder. "Rest easy. I think we've cleared this area for the moment."

He turned his attention to the rest of the group. "Let's comb this area for loot while Karzic catches his breath. Eldred, you check over there," he said, indicating the northwest corner of the small room they'd entered. "Targ, you check over there, and Sandra and I will take the other two corners. We'll catalog whatever we find and split it up accordingly. Then we need to discuss our tactics."

The NPCs followed Robert's orders without hesitation. Eldred looked more than a little miffed at being reduced to manual labor, but clearly the thought of finding some exotic new treasures took the sting from Osmark's command.

Despite the room's small size, it contained surprisingly large piles of broken machinery, scavenged weapons, and assorted odds and ends of Brand-Forged engineering. It took more than a few minutes to go through everything, but soon the group had reassembled with their loot in tow. In addition to a respectable pile of intriguing armor and weaponry, they'd recovered a large mound of gold coins and cut gemstones.

"Quite a haul," Osmark said, rubbing his hands together in anticipation. "Let's see what we've got."

He scooped up a delicate circlet made of copper wire wrapped around clouded crystals. "A Torque of Empowerment," he remarked after a brief examination. He handed the piece of jewelry to Eldred. "Should be good for you. Maybe next time you don't summon a wild lightning elemental to fry us all?"

The summoner rolled her eyes and sniffed dismissively. "No promises. A girl needs to stay alive."

Targ grunted and shot back, "The rest of us need to stay alive, too. A little less friendly fire will help with that."

Osmark felt the tension between the two mercenaries. There was some sort of old grudge there, and he didn't have time to deal with it.

Robert decided to give the Risi something else to occupy his mind. He retrieved a pair of heavy gauntlets from the pile of treasure. Each of the gauntlets had a thick cylinder attached to the back of its wrist guard by heavy copper bolts. Braided wires led from each of the cylinders to the tips of each of the gauntlet's fingers. "Gauntlets of Lightning," Robert said as he tossed them to Targ. "These will turn those clubs of yours into thunderbolts."

"Better than being struck by 'em," Targ said with a grin, slipping the gauntlets onto his hands. He furrowed his brow in concentration and then his eyes lit up. A faint hum rumbled from the cylinders, and crackling sparks of electricity sizzled along the wires. Targ grabbed one of his clubs, and the electricity shot up its length to crackle from the spiked tip like some bizarre piece of equipment in a mad scientist's laboratory. "Oh, yeah. These'll do nicely."

"And this is mine," Sandra said, reaching past Osmark to grab a pair of short swords with strangely hooked tips. "Forged Tears. Armor-piercing. Let's see those mechanical monkeys come at me again. I'll cut them up like a can opener."

The rest of the pile was all for Robert. He picked up a strange weapon that looked similar to his repeater—except where the handle and trigger should've been, there were four metal slats—almost like miniature helicopter blades—folded along the sleek gun casing. Osmark's eyes widened as he examined the object; it looked like some sort of steampunk drone.

Flame Spitter

Weapon Type: Firearm

Class: Forge-Branded Relic, Automaton

Base Damage: 20

Primary Effects:

- 20 pts impact damage + 5 points of fire damage/second for five seconds
- Upon activation, fires at every target in a 20' diameter sphere designated by the wielder.
- Does *not* require wielder's action
- Uses wielder's Intelligence bonus to-hit, no damage bonus

Secondary Effects:

- Any target struck by Flame Spitter's initial activation is *marked*. Flame Spitter fires at one *marked* target per second for ten seconds after activation
- Flame Spitter is most effective against targets with reduced movement. If a target has a movement penalty, Flame Spitter's damage is doubled for every 20% reduction in movement speed. This effect can stack for a total of x32 normal damage against a paralyzed or immobile target.

Sandra sidled up next to Osmark and nudged him in the ribs with her elbow. "This is some nice stuff, Robert. I take it yours is the cream of the crop?"

Osmark chuckled. "It is my restricted area, you know. And yes, it's good stuff, though I haven't finished going through it yet." He raised an eyebrow at her, but she ignored his pointed comment.

"We need to figure out how we're going to proceed," she said matter-of-factly. "I have the skills to get around most mundane traps, but this whole place is a bit outside my area of expertise." She glanced around, nervously running one hand along the hilt of her new sword.

She was right of course.

Robert considered the issue as he picked up a pair of boots from the remaining loot, turning them over in his hands, inspecting the fine cogs attached to the leather. Already, the challenges within the Artifactory were more daunting than he'd expected, but the rewards outstripped them. Each of the mechanical creatures was worth a full 2,000 EXP, and even split five ways, that was still 4,400 points from this one engagement alone. And, if he found more gear like the Flame Spitter or these boots, he'd be a force to be reckoned with by the time he left here.

Geometrically Threaded Boots

Armor Type: Light, padded

Class: Ancient Artifact; Set Item

Base Defense: 10 (20 vs. Mechanical Creatures or Automatons)

Special: 2 Small Mounting Brackets; 1 Sigil Plate

Primary Effects:

- +20 to Intelligence
- +10 to Reputation with all Friendly Factions
- +10 Renown

Secondary Effects:

- Part of the Artifactory Engineer's Uniform Armor Set
  - +5 Armor against all mechanical or automaton attacks per set piece worn
  - All Stamina Costs are reduced by 15% (2 pieces)
  - +10 to Movement Bonus (3 pieces)
  - +25% increased chance to avoid Movement Restricting Debuffs (4 pieces)
  - +1 Large Mounting Bracket (5 pieces)
  - +1 Sigil Plate when the full suit is worn (6 pieces)

The boots were poor protection against most attacks, but against the types of steampunk monsters Robert expected to face in the rest of the Artifactory, they'd be more than sufficient. The boost to Intelligence was also very, very nice. Robert pulled a pair of matching armored pants from the pile of loot, and couldn't suppress a grin when he examined them.

Geometrically Threaded Breeches

Armor Type: Light, padded

Class: Ancient Artifact; Set Item

Base Defense: 10 (20 vs. Mechanical Creatures or Automatons)

Special: 2 Small Mounting Brackets; 1 Sigil Plate

Primary Effects:

- +20 to Intelligence
- +10 to Reputation with all Friendly Factions
- +10 Renown

Secondary Effects:

- Part of the Artifactory Engineer's Uniform Armor Set
  - +5 Armor against all mechanical or automaton attacks per set piece worn
  - All Stamina Costs are reduced by 15% (2 pieces)
  - +10 to Movement Bonus (3 pieces)
  - +25% increased chance to avoid Movement Restricting Debuffs (4 pieces)
  - +1 Large Mounting Bracket (5 pieces)
  - +1 Sigil Plate when the full suit is worn (6 pieces)

Robert wondered what the mounting brackets and sigil plates did, but he hadn't unlocked the skills related to them yet. Until he'd gained the Mechanical Artificer class kit, the more esoteric armor features were barred to him.

For the time being, he'd have to satisfy himself with the dramatically improved Armor and Intelligence bonuses provided by the first pieces of his new armor set. He kicked off the ratty old boots he'd been wearing since the moment he'd landed in V.G.O. and started untying the laces of his Tinkerer's Breeches.

He glanced up at Sandra, who grinned impishly in his direction, cocking an eyebrow at him. *Please proceed,* that look said. He'd been in such a hurry to gear up he'd forgotten he wasn't alone.

"Turn around," he ordered his assistant, rotating his finger in the air to illustrate. She hesitated, just a moment, then turned her back on him with a pout. Robert ignored her silent protests, quickly kicking off his boots, slithering out of his old leggings, and stepping into the new Geometrically Threaded Breeches. Before he even had them up to his knees, however, a long loud whistle echoed through the pipe-lined room.

Osmark shot a dark glare over his shoulder at Eldred, who wiggled her tongue at him and gave him a wink that made him feel a little weak in the knees. "Nice legs," she said, arms folded across her chest as her eyes roved over him.

Robert almost tripped over his pants in his haste to yank them up to his waist. He'd forgotten about the NPCs in the room and had revealed a lot more of his anatomy than just his legs. When he finally had the leggings cinched tight around his waist, Robert resumed his conversation with Sandra without missing a beat. "Okay, we're going to have to discuss teamwork and tactics with the mercenaries."

"Darn," Sandra muttered, "I missed the show. But you're right about that last part. That was a disaster. We're lucky to be alive. One second, I was alone in the tunnel. The next we were surrounded by Scavlings. I don't even know where they came from."

"A trap, I think," Osmark said. "You must have accidentally triggered it, releasing some sort of hidden compartment which dumped those things right on top of us." He shook his head. "I think I know how we can avoid that in the future, but let's talk to the others."

When all eyes were on him, and Eldred had stopped her tittering, Osmark cleared his throat and launched into his best inspirational speech. "I'm not sure how you're used to operating, but that encounter was sloppy and unacceptable, ladies and gentlemen. This was the first room and those creatures were only the first wave—the easiest opponents we're likely to face—and we barely managed to scrape by. So, clearly whatever we're doing isn't working."

Eldred snorted, her wings flexing as she examined the tip of a short dagger. "I handled it just fine."

Targ groaned. "If by fine, you mean you nearly cooked me alive, then yes, you handled it *just fine*."

Karzic thumped his hammer against the floor and tugged at his gray beard. "Friendly fire's gonna put a strain on my abilities. I can shield one of you at a time, and I can heal you all after a fight, but if we get swarmed like that again there's no guarantee we're all getting out alive."

Listening to his NPCs bicker didn't do anything to improve Osmark's mood. He distracted himself by flipping through the Artificer's skill tree in search of something useful. The last time he'd looked at his abilities was back in the forest, before he'd bumbled into the Fungaloids. Robert was shocked to see there were several notifications waiting for his attention—all the battles he'd fought had earned him enough experience points to reach level thirteen. That left him with 6 unspent Proficiency Points and 30 Stat Points to distribute.

He quickly poured 10 more Stat Points into his Intelligence and was pleased to see it rise to 98.5. Thanks to his skill with engineered weapons, this provided him with an impressive bonus to hit the bad guys with his repeater. As long as he could get a clear shot, he'd be more of an asset to his team than ever.

Next, he added one more point each to the Clockwork, Firearms, Focus Fire, and Caltrops skills to further bolster his effectiveness. The first skill would help him spot the nastier engineered traps waiting for them deeper inside the Brand-Forged Dungeon. Firearms and Focus Fire would make him more of a force to be reckoned with in a scuffle. There was a boss fight coming at the end of this dungeon, and Robert wanted to be ready for it.

And that was why he was especially interested in the Caltrops skill. The point he'd invested into it increased the movement penalty for anyone caught in its radius to 75% and the duration to a full two minutes. Combining the caltrops' debuffs with the Fire Spitter's awesome damage against slowed targets was a huge synergy Osmark couldn't pass up.

"What was that?" he asked, realizing Sandra had been speaking to him the whole time he'd had his nose buried in the V.G.O. game screens. "Sorry, I was thinking about something else."

"I was just saying, I don't have the knowledge to spot whatever triggered those metal spiders." She folded her arms across her chest and raised one eyebrow as if to say, *What now, boss?*

Robert waved her concern away. "I have the skills to identify the triggers that are activating the Artifactory's defenses. I'll lead—"

All four of Osmark's companions protested at once. The clashing words flooded over him like an approaching storm, but Targ's thunderous complaint overpowered them all.

"No. I was paid to see you safely through this place, and that's what I'm gonna do. End of story." He hooked his thumbs into his weapon belt and shook his head vigorously. "I'll lead the way. The dwarf will keep me alive."

Karzic squawked and stomped his foot. "That means I'll be right behind you. So every trap you blunder into is likely to catch me as well. That's not going to work. And that doesn't even take into consideration the fact that I *can't* heal you every few minutes. My resources are more limited than that. Even with our stock of Health and Spirit Regen potions, we'd be courting disaster."

Robert scowled.

He didn't have time for these arguments, and he didn't like having his authority challenged. Still, he couldn't deny taking point could put him in a potentially dangerous position. After all, if something happened to him, then all of this was for nothing. He'd respawn, but the time lost might be the edge Sizemore needed to get his plans into action. None of his other Artificer abilities would be of any help here, but a sudden flash on inspiration struck like a lightning bolt.

He toggled out of his Artificer skill tree and pulled up his general skills.

There. His racial Overseer ability.

Although the ability itself leveled up through use, there were a variety of specialized skills he could unlock with Proficiency Points. Most of those skills were locked by level requirements, but not all of them. He dropped a single Proficiency Point into a skill called Micromanage. Robert was rewarded by a sudden burst of light surrounding the skill's title, and a short pop-up message that told him everything he needed to know. He read it once, then again to make sure he understood the implications of what he was about to do.

"Sandra, you can lead," Robert said. "I have a different plan that should help us avoid the worst of the traps."

Sandra leaned back on her heels, a skeptical frown pinching her lips. "That fast? Something tells me I'm not going to like this plan."

Osmark couldn't suppress an evil grin. "You're definitely not going to like it, but it's the only way we can make this work."

TWENTY-FIVE:

Steamwraith

The party spent the better part of half an hour gathering up the remaining loot from the Scavlings' lair, which included 3,328 gold coins and a large sack of polished gemstones worth another 1,000 gold at least. Not to mention, a ridiculous amount of interesting steampunk salvage. While the others dealt with the more mundane treasure, he sorted and organized all of the Scavlings' loot into piles by type and rarity.

"This looks like fun," Sandra offered dryly, poking at a pile of hinged joints with the toe of her boot. "What are you going to do with this scrap heap?"

Osmark held up a double handful of metal shards and said, "This." He flicked his eyes over to the build menu and selected Caltrops. He'd gained several levels since the last time he'd done any engineering builds, which had increased his stats, but creating the caltrops still drained the majority of his Stamina. Osmark felt the wind sucked out of his lungs and swayed on his heels as energy leached away.

"Are you all right, Robert?" Sandra asked, brows furrowed. "You look"—she paused and frowned, scanning his face—"unwell," she finally finished. "Like you're about to pass out."

"I'll be fine in a minute," Osmark grunted, showing Sandra a completed caltrop grenade. He tucked the shiny gray sphere away in his inventory, where it'd be ready for later use. "Building things burns a lot of Stamina. It's all right, as long as I have time to prepare. Better to pay the price *before* a fight, than during it." He groped at his belt, pulling free one of the yellow, citrus-flavored Stamina Regen potions. It vanished down his throat in a single gulp, and immediately left him feeling better.

The party rested for another fifteen minutes, letting Robert prepare ten more caltrop grenades and recover from the Stamina loss naturally, without burning through his finite supply of potions. Osmark wanted to spend more time experimenting with the build menu, to see what he could do with all these fancy new spare parts, but there wasn't time to indulge his curiosity. They needed to wrap this up and get back to town—Robert's to-do list wasn't getting any shorter, and he still needed to get a good night's sleep tonight.

Meeting Sizemore was going to be a helluva challenge, and Osmark didn't want to compound the difficulty of the board meeting by pulling an all-nighter. Not if it could be avoided. Before they ventured on, he needed a clearer picture of his team's capabilities and how they could put them to better use. The fight with the Scavlings had almost ended in disaster—they might not be so lucky the next time.

"Targ, what's your class and what specials do you have available?"

The Risi grunted and folded his arms, clearly unhappy with the question. "Standard Brawler," he finally offered. "Basically, a modified tank. High HP, high defense—though not as high as a straight Shield Bearer—with some good movement bonuses and a helluva right hook. In terms of specials, Taunt helps me draw aggro, Bloodlust kicks up Health Regen rate and Attack damage when I drop below 25% Health, and my Savage Blow increases damage by 25%, and raises Critical Hit by 15%."

"Eldred?" He quirked one eyebrow at the winged woman. "Report."

The Accipiter folded her arms across her chest and flexed her wings, just as unhappy as Targ had been. "I'm a Fell Summoner. Not much in the way of combat abilities or friendly auras—mostly, I rip holes in the fabric of the universe and pull Nether beasts into our plane. Unlike other summoners, I don't have access to a small army of low-level minions—skeletons, ghouls, trolls, that sort of thing. Instead, I can summon one powerful creature at a time."

"And what about you, Karzic?" Robert asked the dwarf, knowing the key to any successful party was an effective and efficient healer. "What spells do you have equipped?" Figuring out the chanter's capabilities and limitations was the first step toward refining their strategy.

The dwarf fidgeted and leaned on his hammer, seesawing his head left then right. "I can use the Chant of Restoration once more today, which will restore all of us to full Health and remove any status conditions. It takes five minutes to complete, though, and I can't do anything else while I'm performing the ritual. And if I get interrupted—by taking a hit, for example—then the chant ends, and the healing is negated.

"What else, what else," he said, drumming his fingers on the haft of his hammer. "Well, I can also use Stream of Life, as needed, on one target at a time. So long as it's sustained by my chanting, it doubles all armor and resistance ratings, and gives the target 50 Stamina and Health Regeneration per second."

"No burst healing?" Robert asked, hoping Karzic's abilities included some way to heal a lot of damage all in one shot. Against bosses, that was a tank's only way to survive.

Karzic shook his head and grimaced, as if self-conscious about the shortcoming. "I'm more of a sustained effort sort of healer. So long as no one takes a big whack of damage all at once, I can shift my healing as needed to keep everyone on their feet."

Targ raised an eyebrow in Osmark's direction as if to say, *I see a lot of suffering in my future.*

Sensing the doubts about his capabilities, the dwarf cleared his throat and pushed on. "I've also got Goradrim's Guarding, a barrier spell that can withstand 500 points of damage before it collapses. While it's up, hostile mobs have to stay outside the barrier. Attacks from inside the barrier pass through freely."

"And what happens when your barrier takes 500 points of damage?" Eldred asked, a surly smirk plastered across her pointed features. "Pop, we're all exposed?"

The dwarf glowered at the Accipiter. "No. When it's depleted, it takes 50 Health from me and is restored to its full 500 damage capacity."

"What are its dimensions?" Sandra asked before Robert could pose the question himself.

"It's a half-dome, about ten feet out and ten feet up in a 180-degree arc in front of me. If need be, I can also form a full circle, though that halves the barrier's diameter."

Osmark considered the options available to them and asked a final question of the dwarf. "Can your Stream of Life heal you, or just others?"

"It can heal me, but I can't do anything else while I'm using it," Karzic said with a shrug. *It is what it is.* "And that's all I've got to offer—though I can make a mean omelet if we get the chance to eat."

That earned a round of chuckles from the rest of the team. Robert waited for them all to quiet down before he laid out their new battle plan. He expected an argument from Eldred or Targ, but the mercenaries all agreed with this assessment of their capabilities and their use in the plan. With that settled, Robert turned his attention to the problem of the deadly mechanical traps set by the Artifactory's long-dead creators.

Robert reviewed the new ability he'd unlocked in the Overseer skill tree.

Ability: Micromanage, Unlocked

Your investment in this ability marks you as a true leader of men. When used wisely, the Micromanage ability enables you to command player characters

---

(PC) as well as NPCs.

Ability Type/Level: Racial, Active / Initiate

Cost: Racial Ability, Once a Day per 5 Character Levels (C.L.)

Effect 1: Command friendly PCs in your party or faction to perform any task.

Effect 2: Commanded PCs temporarily gain the Overseer's mental abilities, skills, and attributes for the given task.

Effect 3: Boost the skill increase rate of the PCs under your command by 5%

Note: This ability can be used to command a PC to perform a single, instantaneous action, such as an attack. PCs so commanded will perform the action to the best of their ability at the instant they are commanded (unless the command specifies a delay or trigger). Once the instantaneous action is completed, the ability's use ends, and the commanded PC returns to their normal range of actions.

If this ability is used to command a PC to perform an ongoing action, the PC will continue to perform the action until it is completed, or for fifteen minutes, whichever comes first. The Overseer must remain in sight and audible range of the commanded PC or the ability use ends immediately.

PCs with a high enough Intelligence Score can resist your use of this ability.

He closed the window and explained what he had in mind to Sandra, who raised one eyebrow in a dubious expression Osmark was all too familiar with. "You're sure this is going to work? It won't turn me into your zombie slave or something else equally unscrupulous?"

Robert rolled his eyes at Sandra's hyperbole. "It's fine, trust me. I used a slightly different version with Horan, and as far as I could tell, there were no ill effects."

"Horan's dead," she replied, voice monotone and unamused.

"But not because of this," he said. "Besides, it's the only way we can both find the traps without me taking point directly."

Targ opened his mouth to protest, but Robert waved him down with one hand and a cutting glare. "My money, my team, my plan. This is how we're proceeding and I want no more insubordination. Now, let's get moving, shall we? Time is money."

The Risi glowered at Osmark, on the verge of saying something, but then thought better of it, shutting his mouth and nodding stoically. A wise decision. In short order, the rest of the group secured their gear and loot and followed Sandra out of the Scavlings' lair and down a long sloping hallway. Her light floated ahead of her, bathing the metal, pipe-festooned walls in a cold, flat glow.

Osmark and Targ marched side by side ten feet behind Sandra to keep the Micromanage ability in effect while simultaneously providing Robert with protection in the event of an ambush. Eldred and Karzic brought up the rear. This was the weak point in his plan, and they all knew it. The dwarf was sturdy enough to stand up to all but the most overwhelming assault, which would give the rest of them time to rearrange their marching order to deal with a rear attack. Eldred, on the other hand, would fold up if she took any sort of serious damage.

A glass cannon through and through.

Osmark considered it an acceptable risk, though, and no one countermanded him. After all, Eldred had almost microwaved Targ with her summoning. She couldn't expect everyone to be too concerned about her health and well-being when she obviously didn't worry herself overmuch with theirs.

Robert's plan worked to get them deeper into the Artifactory. With Micromanage in effect, Sandra used Osmark's Clockwork skill to spot and disarm several mechanical triggers before the rest of the party could stumble into a trap. Their progress was slow and tedious, but using the Micromanage ability worked like a charm.

Idly, he wondered how many other extras the game had hidden away…

"Hold up," Sandra whispered to the rest of the group. "There's a lot of activity up ahead."

She killed her light with a whispered word, but the hallway they were walking down hardly grew any dimmer without the glowing rod. Light flooded into the wide passageway from its far end. As the party crept closer to Sandra's position, they heard the deafening clang of hammers slamming into anvils, and a rhythmic chuffing noise like the breath of a drowsing dragon.

The hallway ended at a metal archway covered in gears, pipes, and ancient rune work. Beyond the arch lay the biggest, most elaborate workshop Osmark had ever seen. On the left side of the room, six enormous foundries glowed like mouths leading into the bowels of hell. Molten metal gushed from each of them in regular intervals, filling a variety of huge molds, which moved along lines of slowly turning metal rollers.

Hulking, humanoid automatons—[Steamwraiths]—covered in bronzed plate and festooned with rivets, gears, and whirling cogs stood on either side of the lines, shaking the parts free as the metal cooled and solidified. The various parts—mostly gears, cogs, bolts, and steel plates—were then sorted by even more of the mechanical men. These automatons inspected the pieces carefully, turning them over in their heavy steel hands, discarding some of the pieces through circular holes in the floor—clearly defective—while passing others along to a second line of metal rollers.

Osmark took a split second to analyze the creature:

Steamwraith

These animated suits of armor are held together by Brand-Forged sigils and powered by the steam elementals bound within their metal shells. They are physically powerful but have only rudimentary Intelligence. While they can be programmed to carry

---

out specific actions with tireless zeal and inhuman precision, they do not actually think on their own.

With a muted grunt, he closed out of the screen and turned his attention back to the assembly process. Scavlings worked the second line of rollers, using their segmented legs to manipulate the parts as they trundled by on the crude conveyor belts, picking up each piece and skillfully connecting it to the next item in line. They used either a wrench-like attachment on the tips of their legs or a powerful burst of lightning from between their mandibles—some sort of soldering iron—to accomplish the task.

Osmark couldn't help but stare in awe: this whole area was an enormous assembly line.

Though the assembly lines were amazing feats of engineering, what was even more interesting to Robert was the activity on the far right-hand side of the room. There, more armored automatons hauled the completed husks over to tall metal benches, where they were once more inspected and sorted. Subpar creations were summarily dropped through holes in the floor, while the rest were passed on to other rolling lines leading into dark holes at the end of the room. Not far from those dark holes lay a staircase connecting to a lower-level hallway.

"That's where we're going to have to do our sneaking," Robert whispered, pointing out the darkened area of the massive chamber near the ends of the lines. "There aren't a ton of guards down there, and it's dark enough that we should be able to sneak past."

Targ growled. "We should just smash our way across. It can't be more than a couple hundred feet from here to the staircase."

"There are a couple of hundred armored *workers* down there," Eldred snapped. "We can't fight that many even with my servitors."

"Eldred's right," Osmark said, though he loathed the thought of abandoning all the experience and loot this room could offer. He was peeved, really. These restricted areas were carefully designed to provide the maximum amount of EXP with the easiest possible mobs—yet his dungeon didn't seem to fit that mold at all. "We're sneaking through," he said, "and that's the end of the discussion. Sandra will take the lead, and I'll follow behind her. With any luck, we'll be through here in no time."

Sandra took a deep breath, dropped into a crouch, and nodded to Robert. "Let's do it."

Fortunately, the roar of the foundries' fires, the screaming hiss of molten metal splashing into molds, and the banging and clanging of the assembly lines' innumerable moving parts filled the room with such clamor nothing short of an all-out assault would attract much attention. As long as the party didn't do anything stupid, he thought they'd be all right.

They watched the automatons work the assembly line with rigid precision, then carefully moved from position to position in a ballet as regimented as the rotation of a clock's hands. Once it became obvious none of the automatons were moving anywhere near the path Robert intended to take, he triggered the Micromanage ability and slipped into Sandra's thoughts, willing her forward. Slowly, his assistant stole through the foundry, hooking right near a jutting pylon, skirting around a cooling barrel, then heading straight for the stairs as she scanned for clockwork traps.

Once she'd made it through safely and undetected, Robert took point, leading the rest of the crew along the same path until they came to the stairs where Sandra waited. Quickly, they stole forward, their footsteps ringing out on the metal steps as they descended, but the awful racket blended seamlessly into the factory's pervasive clangor. None of the automatons turned in their direction; they might as well have been invisible.

The stairs connected to a gargantuan hallway studded with pairs of hulking iron support pillars, which, in turn, connected to another section of the assembly plant. More automatons worked there, busy installing complex pipes and steam gauges into the empty robot shells manufactured above. At the far side of that room was a steel door, covered in elegant golden rune work. Osmark had played enough MMORPGs in his days to spot the entrance to a boss's lair. There was no doubt in his mind.

Sandra took a step forward, but Robert lashed out, one hand digging into her shoulder before she could go any further. They were so close now, yet the defenses in this section had been minimal. Almost nonexistent. An apprehensive paranoia bloomed inside his chest as he scanned the hallway. He just couldn't shake the feeling he was missing something crucial.

Clearly, this was the most important part of the Artifactory—the central manufacturing facility—and furthermore, this was the final challenge before the boss.

Yet everything had been … easy. Too easy.

Why weren't there more defenses? More traps?

He broke the problem down, looking at the points of failure the system might experience, one at a time. He started with the most obvious weak link in any security setup: the wandering mechanical creations.

With so many of the Steamwraiths and Scavlings moving around, there was no way the Brand-Forged could've relied on mundane mechanical triggers for the security systems. Not here. Even if they trusted their creations to follow orders precisely and without the slightest deviation, machines were never perfect. A single misstep from a misaligned Scavling's leg could easily trigger a mechanical trap. The Brand-Forged were too smart for that, which meant whatever security precautions they had in place needed to be foolproof.

There were no workers in the hallway, though, which meant it would be a perfect choke point to catch intruders flatfooted.

"No one move," Osmark barked, a dark thought creeping through his skull.

If I was a Brand-Forged, how would I protect my assembly lines?

Osmark pulled the goggles down over his eyes and flicked the blue lens into place. He almost fell over in shock at the sheer number of Divine Geometry sigils inscribed into the hallway. Massive circles of glowing blue light covered the floor, walls, and ceiling. Arcing branches and intricate designs curled within each of the circles, while flowing lines of arcane patterns—carved by long-dead Mechanical Artificers—powered the assembly room. This hallway was a nexus, providing energy to the plant and standing as a final safeguard against would-be thieves.

The amount of work invested into the passageway was staggering. A wave of awe surged through him, quickly replaced by a twinge of jealousy. Suddenly, a desire to surpass what he saw here burned like an inferno inside his gut. The Brand-Forged had created wonders, but they'd hidden them from the rest of the world. Osmark had bigger plans. With this tech, Eldgard was his to shape. To mold. To rule.

Just as soon as he dealt with Sizemore.

But first, he'd have to escape from the dangers littered throughout this place.

"There are alarm patterns inscribed into the floors, emanating around each of those support pillars," Osmark said, pointing out the rivet-riddled columns marching down the hallway. "The patterns extend out about five feet in diameter. It'll take a little doing, but I'm confident I can find us a way through with a little time and patience." *And luck*, he thought, though didn't say.

Once more he slipped into Sandra's mind via Micromanage, guiding her through the winding maze of glowing lines visible only to him through the blue lens attached to his goggles. Osmark followed in her wake, while the others trailed behind him, clinging to his tracks with surgical precision. It was like playing a game of pantomime telephone, except the slightest misstep would end in death.

Osmark knew he should've been afraid, should've been nervous, but he wasn't. He felt alive, as if this was what he'd been meant to do with his life. The rush of adrenaline combined with the threat of imminent destruction inspired him. He hadn't felt this driven, this desire to achieve, since …

Since he'd learned about the asteroid on its way to wipe out all life on Earth.

He shook away the depressing thoughts and focused on the task at hand—this was his world now.

They snaked between four sets of columns, creeping up to the edge of the assembly floor and the last leg of the deadly journey. From here, they would hook a sharp right, skirt along the perimeter of the room, and cling to the thick shadows until they reached the metal door at the other side. Simple, though far from easy, especially considering more wards peppered the floor in spots. He willed his plan to Sandra, and she instantly padded forward without a hint of hesitation in her steps.

Unfortunately, Karzic hissed a warning from the end of their line a moment later.

Osmark glanced over one shoulder, and his breath caught in his chest. One of the Steamwraiths had moved away from the assembly line and was approaching the dwarf with purposeful, determined strides. It was still several yards away, but it wasn't changing course. From this close, Robert could see the armored plating was much heavier than he'd originally thought. Its entire surface was carved with glowing sigils, which he intuitively recognized as representations of strength, protection, and power.

Obviously, the steam elementals within were built to brawl.

Sandra desperately gestured for Karzic to move against the factory wall and further into the shadows.

Before anyone could respond, however, the armored worker raised its left hand and pointed directly at Karzic. It made no sound, but its hand glowed an ominous red like a branding iron straight from the fire. Then it abruptly changed direction and walked away from the dwarf and toward a heavy brass bell attached by a cross bar to one of the support structures fifty feet away. Osmark didn't need to see the sigils connecting the bell to the rest of the factory to know it was an alarm.

If the worker reached it, he'd bring a tsunami of metal crashing down on their heads.

So far, none of the other workers had taken notice, and Robert had to keep it that way if he wanted his party to survive.

Osmark didn't have time to explain his plan to the rest of his team. He rushed forward, carefully dodging the sigils so painstakingly worked into the floor, and threw a caltrop grenade on the ground just ahead of the armored worker.

The Steamwraith's lead boot crunched down on the gray steel orb, detonating the grenade in a shower of tiny black spikes and swirling smoke. In any other circumstance, the explosion would've roused every mob in the dungeon, but the noise was a drop in the bucket compared to the clang of steel on steel echoing through the room. The black prongs bit into the automaton's HP, but more importantly punched into the creature's metal soles, causing the Steamwraith to stumble and falter.

Temporarily slowed by 75%.

Osmark let out a silent prayer of thanks that whatever special ability protected the Scavlings from his caltrops didn't apply to the automatons.

The caltrop wasn't a permanent solution to the problem, but the slowed Steamwraith would be easier to handle. Plus, it also bought them a few more precious seconds to deal with the creature before it could alert the whole factory.

Osmark sprinted back to his party and whispered his orders. "Targ and Sandra, stop that thing. If you go straight from where we are, you won't trigger any sigils. Eldred, stand by with a summoning in case it looks like the thing is going to get away. We have to keep it from reaching the bell. That's paramount to survival."

The winged woman sniffed and shrugged. "I could just summon something now."

"Yes, and you'd definitely alert the rest of the factory. These things don't look terribly observant, so they might not notice Targ and Sandra beating the hell out of one of their own, but I'm pretty confident they'll notice if a lightning-spitting monstrosity tears through space and time in the middle of their assembly line."

Eldred sniffed again, apparently offended by Osmark's characterization of her work. "Fine, we'll do it the hard way," she replied with an eye roll. "But I'm willing to bet club boy"—she nodded at Targ—"makes more noise than one of my fell beasts any day of the week."

"I'll take that action," Targ said with a snarl before lumbering toward the Steamwraith with his kanabo raised high overhead. A loud *clang* reverberated in the air as the Risi's spiked clubs smacked into the back of the automaton in a shower of sparks. The creature shuddered and faltered, plumes of white steam leaking into the air.

Maybe this will be easier than we guessed, Osmark thought.

Then—as though in defiance of Osmark's optimism—the Steamwraith flung its left arm back and smashed Targ in the side of his head so hard the Risi went down on one knee, his HP cut by a third, half his face suddenly lopsided and bloodied. At the same moment, another Steamwraith emerged from the shadows to Osmark's right, charging straight for him like a rodeo bull seeing red.

Or, maybe it's going to get a lot harder, Osmark thought, cold panic flashing through him.

TWENTY-SIX:

Divine Geometry

O smark took a calculated risk and darted toward the approaching Steamwraith. He tossed a caltrop grenade at the creature's feet, then hurled three more between the automaton and the alarm bell. The caltrops wouldn't stop the mechanical man in its tracks, but they would slow it down—hopefully for long enough to give his party the time they needed to get to the door and away from the factory floor.

A *boom* sounded as the first device went off, showering the Steamwraith in barbed metal debris.

Osmark stole a look back at Targ and couldn't help but wince; things weren't going well for the visiting team.

The Risi warrior fought gamely, but he wobbled on his feet, one eye swollen shut, punch drunk, blood dripping from between his bruised lips. Sandra danced in with her fancy new armor-piercing blades, slicing at the Steamwraith's vitals, then bounding away in a flash before it could counterattack. Her hit-and-run tactics opened gaps in its armor, but the constant movement sapped her Stamina, and the Steamwraith showed no signs of dying.

"Karzic, get a Stream of Life on Targ before that thing takes him down," Robert snapped at the dwarf. Then, to Eldred, "If Targ drops, call something nasty to take his place."

Robert weighed his options as Karzic chanted and Eldred watched the battle with renewed interest. He could go after the second Steamwraith, but that was putting a bandage on a sucking chest wound. If they wanted to get through the factory, he needed a way to solve all their problems at once. A sly thought snuck into his mind, giving him renewed hope. The Brand-Forged had prepared their defenses to repel outsiders—intruders—but they'd never anticipated the need to protect their work from *other* Artificers.

Artificers like Osmark.

"Here goes nothing," he said, angling toward a huge crank wheel mounted on an enormous boiler against the left-hand wall—a central power junction if his rudimentary understanding of Divine Geometry was correct. He was careful to avoid the dangerous sigils worked into the floor, stepping only in the gaps between the alarm triggers, but his path took him close enough to attract attention from another Steamwraith. The creature wasn't yet on alert, but it started walking toward Osmark with determined steps.

He ignored the automaton, skidding to a halt in front of the boiler and groping at the wheel. The crank screeched and moved a half inch before it slammed to a halt. Osmark strained against it—one eye on the Steamwraith beelining for him—and wished once more he'd invested a few points into Strength. It *would* pay off in the long run, dammit. He took a deep breath, cleared his mind, and realized being smarter was the same as being stronger. He ripped Heart Seeker from his inventory and wedged the crossbow's heavy stock between the spokes of the crank wheel.

Ten feet away, the Steamwraith raised its left arm, and a dull red glow sprayed from the creature's palm. The light played over Robert as he crouched and braced his shoulder against the sturdy stock.

With a grunt and a heave, Osmark straightened his legs and pushed with everything he had. The improvised lever creaked ominously for a moment, the wood straining from the sudden pressure, then lurched. The crank wheel shifted with the sound of screaming metal. "Thanks, Archimedes," he muttered, dropping Heart Seeker back into his inventory.

The Steamwraith turned away and stomped toward the alarm bell.

But that didn't matter right now. Nothing mattered except the wheel and the boiler.

Osmark spun the crank with both hands, rotating it so fast the spokes blurred, as the needle on a brass steam gauge, fastened to the outside of the boiler, dropped into the red. The iron wheel slammed to a stop a handful of seconds later, jarring Robert down to the soles of his boots. He drew a deep breath and turned to take in the results of his efforts. For safety reasons, no one crank wheel could stop the flow of steam through the factory—the risk of a catastrophic pressure failure was just too great.

But Robert had reduced the available power to a mere trickle. The lights were little more than orange sparks hanging in gloomy rafters. And though the Steamwraiths weren't attached directly to the pipes, they were connected to steam power by sigils of Divine Geometry. With their power output reduced to almost nothing, the Steamwraith that had spotted Robert was scarcely moving, his feet shuffling along, fighting for every inch.

Osmark pumped his fist as the factory ground to a near halt. The assembly lines rolled at a snail's pace now, and the Steamwraiths manning them moved as if submerged in molasses.

Targ and Sandra took advantage of their opponent's sudden sluggishness. The stalker's armor-piercing blades pried up the edges of the Steamwraith's breastplate to reveal a coiled mass of copper tubes and braided cables.

"Hit it here!" Sandra shouted, easily ducking below a clumsy right hook.

Targ attacked the gap with a spinning roundhouse, slamming his spiked club into the Steamwraith's exposed innards. Jagged strokes of lightning burst from the Bonecrusher's weapon, and its thick spikes tore through the delicate tubing like a wrecking ball through a china cabinet.

A steam-kettle shriek erupted from the automaton, along with a superheated jet of vapor. The steam enveloped Targ's torso in a moist inferno. Karzic's Stream of Life shielded the Risi from the bulk of the damage, but some of the white mist penetrated Targ's armor and scorched his flesh.

Enraged and mad with pain, the Bonecrusher returned his clubs to his belt and rushed the Steamwraith, arms outstretched, bratwurst fingers flexing. The mechanical creature was too slow and confused by its loss of power to avoid the Risi's grasp. With a great bellow, Targ hooked his hands into the creature's damaged torso and heaved the animated automaton over his head. Targ stood there for a moment, arms shaking, eyes bulging under the strain, then slammed the mechanical man down onto the metal floor with a triumphant howl of bestial hate.

Osmark realized the danger a half second too late to do anything about it.

Targ smashed the worker's head directly into a critical nexus in the Geometric sigils winding their way across the floor. The automaton's armor crumpled and cracked on impact like a soda can, and the sigils inscribed into its armor ruptured and spewed raw power in every direction. The uncontrolled flood of energy poured into the invisible symbols etched into the floor like a bolt of lightning discharged through a high-tension wire.

"Run!" Osmark shouted, eyes wide. "Get to the door!" He had no idea what was going to happen next, but he was sure it wouldn't be good.

Robert bolted for the rune-etched exit at the far end of the assembly floor—his arms and legs pumping frantically—and his party followed him without question. The alarm in his voice was enough to spur them into action, even if to their unaided sight there was nothing wrong.

Osmark could see the danger headed their way, however. To him, it was as clear as clean glass. The ancient floor sigils shattered into a thousand neon shards and shot toward the ceiling on a coruscating geyser of raw power. Every Steamwraith in a fifty-foot radius of the fractured sigil crashed to the floor like a marionette with its strings cut. Their plate armor creaked, groaned, separated, and dropped, bouncing across the ground with a deafening series of clangs.

Targ reached Osmark and clapped him on the shoulder so hard he almost fell over. "Did you see that?" the Bonecrusher asked, even as he ran. "I think I killed 'em all. Not bad, am I right?"

Osmark had to admit the Risi's attack had been effective. Effective but careless. The hair on the back of his neck stood at attention, while goosebumps raced along his arms and legs, because he could see something Targ could not. The result of his reckless move. Electric-blue tentacles, as thick as telephone poles, burst through the sigils worked onto the floor and lashed wildly at the nearby assembly lines. A bulbous, glaring eye emerged next, followed by a bloated sac of a body as large as a pickup truck.

A tag appeared in the air, there then gone: [Sigil Guardian].

"What are you staring at?" Sandra yelled. "I don't see anything."

The creature was a beast of the Divine Geometry, a being formed of mathematical formulae and theoretical paths of knowledge. Fractal patterns glistened across its ephemeral body like hypnotic scales.

And it was *pissed*.

Osmark couldn't find the words to explain what was happening.

A moment later, he didn't have to.

The broken armor from the Steamwraiths flew through the air in a whirlwind of bolts and rivets, nuts and steel scraps, latching onto the Sigil Guardian's cephalopod body. For a long beat, everyone stopped, turning around as though compelled to watch the horrid creature take form.

Eldred raised an eyebrow. "That is an impressive summoning."

"No shite," Karzic said. "We need to get the hell out of here."

The dwarf's words broke the horrified paralysis surrounding the rest of the team, and suddenly everyone was once again sprinting for the exit. Leaping over fallen Steamwraiths, dodging around the ends of the assembly lines, and abandoning an absolute fortune in Brand-Forged objects Osmark dearly wished he could collect.

Karzic—despite his enthusiasm for fleeing from the creature—was the slowest among them, his squat legs unable to keep up. Before long, he'd fallen five feet behind the rest of the group, then ten. The guardian, meanwhile, was gaining on them with terrifying speed, using its massive tentacles to pull its immense bulk along. The creature was swimming through the air so fast, Robert knew they had no chance to outrun it. It was going to catch them, Karzic first, and it was going to kill them all.

Osmark faltered, turned, and rushed back, grabbing Karzic by the arm. "Come on," he shouted, spurring the man on. "We'll never be able to defeat the final boss without a healer."

The dwarf's eyes flared in shock as he shouted back, "That's *not* the final boss?"

Reluctantly, Sandra rushed back too, and she grabbed Karzic by the other arm; the two of them dragged the dwarf ahead of the onrushing Sigil Guardian, making better time.

Even with her help, though, it was a losing race.

With a sudden lunge, the creature shot forward, and its vast shadow fell across Robert, Karzic, and Sandra.

Osmark gritted his teeth and braced for the bone-crushing impact he knew was coming.

Only, it didn't come. The guardian roared past the three of them like a charging rhino, dodging around Eldred as if it wanted nothing to do with the winged woman—as though she were a fly beneath its notice.

When it caught up to Targ, however, it was a different story entirely. An armored tentacle lashed out like a baseball bat, slamming into the Bonecrusher's back with such force it drove him off his feet, sending him sailing across the Artifactory like a line drive. With a surprised roar, Targ slid down one of the assembly lines, bounced off, and crashed through the wreckage of disabled Steamwraiths, before finally landing flat on his back with a groan.

Everyone else skidded to a stop unsure what to do, how to proceed. Did they fight it? Did they run? Could they even run? But Robert instantly understood what had happened. "It just wants Targ," he shouted. "It wants the one who damaged its sigil."

The host of confused looks told Osmark he was wasting his breath. "Never mind, it's hunting Targ. Not us. If we don't attack it, the rest of us can escape."

Eldred put one hand on her hip and pointed a lacquered nail at Robert. "Are you thinking about leaving Targ behind?"

Robert weighed their options for a split second, then nodded. "We'll get the door open. If Targ can put some distance between himself and the guardian, we might be able to bar the door behind him and keep it from eating his face."

Eldred's wings fluttered. "And if he can't outrun it?"

"This job didn't come with any guarantees of getting home safely," Osmark snapped. "Otherwise, the pay wouldn't have been so high. Do your job or die trying—that's the standard. The only standard."

"You're a real bastard," Eldred responded, her eyes burning with cold, feral light. "It's a good thing that's how I like my men."

"Fly over there and tell your boyfriend the plan," Sandra said, her tone harsh and unamused. "I'll whistle when it's time for him to head back this way."

Eldred glowered at the woman, then unfurled her wings and launched toward the factory's ceiling. No love lost there. Even with the lights dimmed to almost nothing, the glow from the foundries cast enough orange light across the factory for Osmark to watch as the Accipiter gracefully arced through the air toward Targ and the enraged guardian.

"Let's move," he shouted.

The rest of the party soon reached the doors, which turned out to be a sliding pair of metal sheets with a small steel button set into the wall next to them. Robert didn't see any dangerous sigils through his blue lens, so he immediately jabbed the button with his index finger. The double doors slid open with a soft hiss. Osmark poked his head into the small square room on the other side and noted a single dial set into its front wall beside the doors. An elevator.

"All clear," he hollered over one shoulder.

Sandra put her pinkies into the corners of her mouth, pursed her lips, and unleashed a whistle so loud and long it made Robert's ears ring. "Eldred can get back here without any problem, but you think Targ can outrun that thing?"

"Maybe you should have asked that question before you called them all over here," Osmark said, lips pressed into a thin line. "Let's hope so, I suppose."

Eldred shouted to Targ, then wheeled around and flew back to Osmark's side. She landed and gracefully folded her wings back without so much as ruffling the hair on her head. "He's coming, but it's going to be close."

Targ sprinted, feet clomping on the metal flooring, pouring everything he had into his escape. The creature flailed at him with its massive tentacles, sweeping them through the air like medieval flails. Brass support structures crunched, crashed, and flew in every direction, along with rollers from the assembly lines and armored plates from the fallen automatons.

"Everybody in the elevator," Osmark said, much more calmly than he felt. In situations like this, subordinates looked to their leader for confidence and inspiration—not fear and uncertainty. "This is going to be a photo finish," he offered, oozing authority.

It almost looked like Targ was in the clear, then, twenty feet from the elevator, he stumbled. His left boot caught on a piece of fallen Steamwraith armor, and he tottered, narrowly avoiding a devastating fall. But the mistake still cost him precious seconds, and without missing a beat, the Sigil Guardian slammed a tentacle across the Bonecrusher's back. Once more the Bonecrusher was airborne, skidding and bouncing across the floor before sliding to a herky-jerky halt just a few feet away from the elevator.

Osmark extended his repeater through the doors and focused all of his attention on the rushing guardian, breathing slowly as he lined up his shot. Voices clamored around him, and the creature unleashed a braying war cry like the peal of a hundred trumpets. Osmark ignored them all; the only thing he cared about was finding one weak point in the guardian's body. The lines of its Divine Geometry snapped into focus under his blue lens, and his Engineering skill went to work.

Time seemed to grind into half-speed.

The Sigil Guardian was almost on them.

Osmark was dimly aware of Sandra and Karzic dragging Targ into the elevator, but he knew it was too late for a clean getaway. If he didn't do something, the guardian would trap them here. Its massive tentacles would jam the doors open, and it would crush Targ to death. End of story. Even worse, it might accidentally kill the rest of them while trying to murder the Risi. There wasn't enough room on the elevator for the thing to be picky with its attacks, and it didn't strike Robert as a very deft combatant.

No, there was only one way. He relaxed, exhaled, aimed, and fired.

TWENTY-SEVEN:

Treasure Room

The repeater's thunderous report echoed through the factory in one long, warbling crash as he unleashed a hail of gunfire.

Osmark's senses were so wound up by the adrenaline pouring through him he actually *watched* bullets streak from the end of the barrel, propelled by a cloud of steam and smoke. Rounds slammed into the Sigil Guardian's left eye with devastating force. Crackling energy erupted from the wound and spread out in a haze of blue-white static. The disoriented guardian screamed as the sigil defining its reality struggled to heal its wound.

Its body twisted in agony, tentacles flailing wildly, smashing into machinery and steam turbines surrounding it. After a moment, it flopped onto one side, crashing down across the assembly lines, throwing rollers and severed pieces of Steamwraiths in every direction. It raised its body on trembling tentacles and glared at Robert with its good eye from ten feet away, hate and fury burning in its gaze as it charged.

Osmark didn't care—he'd won this round.

He holstered his repeater, offered the creature a brief wave goodbye, then twisted the elevator's sole dial counterclockwise until it clicked. The doors slid shut a split second before the Sigil Guardian slammed into them with a thunderous *clang*. The motor kicked into life with a soft whir, and the elevator descended as the guardian's useless attacks on the doors echoed down the shaft.

"How did you know that would work?" Sandra asked.

Despite the white-knuckled anxiety and tight-bellied fear waltzing through his system, Robert shrugged and projected strength. "A magician never reveals all his secrets," he replied. Truthfully, it'd been a wild guess, fueled by hope and desperate need. Sometimes luck played a role in success, but it was always best to make people believe you made your own luck.

The rest of the group said nothing, their faces ashen and their expressions somber. Understandable, considering they'd just stared death in the face and narrowly come out on the other side. The Sigil Guardian continued to rage above them, its anguished voice almost as loud as the sounds of destruction ringing through the factory above.

Targ forced a grin. "Thanks, I owe you one."

The Risi raised his left arm to examine a long gash in the back of his gauntlet. He flicked the tattered leather with his right index finger and grunted. "Hope this thing still works."

Osmark's heart froze in his chest. In that split second when the two halves of the leather had separated, he'd seen a tattoo on the Risi's hand: a single black skull.

Coldskulls.

Somehow, Sizemore had gotten to at least one of his NPCs.

Osmark glanced at Karzic, but the dwarf wore a pair of heavy mail gauntlets that covered his arms to the elbows. Likewise, Eldred sported shimmery, enruned gloves that covered her hands completely. No way of knowing for sure, but if Targ was an assassin it stood to reason the others were, too. It was best to assume so, anyway. He silently cursed himself for not checking their hands earlier. It was a simple mistake, and one he hoped he'd be able to rectify before he had to pay for it.

He triggered V.G.O.'s private messaging function and fired off a note to Sandra.

Personal Message:

These are Coldskulls. Assassins. Be ready for anything.

Osmark didn't look at Sandra, but he felt her tense next to him. She responded instantly.

Personal Message:

I'll kill Eldred, you shoot Targ in the head. Do it now, while we still have the element of surprise.

Sandra's plan would work—and it would probably get them out of immediate danger—but it would put Osmark in a terrible position. The boss fight, judging from the resistance they'd faced so far, was going to be a damned nightmare. Robert needed every person in this group if they hoped to defeat the boss and claim the Faction Seal.

Personal Message:

Negative. We need them—killing the Boss without their assistance will be impossible. We'll strike when the fight is over. Hopefully the Boss will do some of the work for us.

Sandra pinched the outside of Osmark's thigh through his padded armor.

Personal Message:

When we're wounded and exhausted from the fight? That's suicide. There must be a better way …

Robert didn't flinch, but he vowed to make Sandra pay for that little trick when they got out of here. He was still her boss, after all.

Personal Message:

They'll be wounded, too. I have a plan. Trust me.

Sandra let out a little sigh, something no one else in the elevator would notice, but to Osmark, it was an exasperated, angry gesture every bit as emphatic as if she'd turned and flipped him the bird. It was also, however, a sign of reluctant acceptance. She would play along, even if she disapproved.

The elevator shuddered to a stop, but Karzic extended a hand before anyone could disembark. "Let's get everyone patched up before we go in. Robert, you look all right. Eldred, I don't see a feather out of place. These other two, though, need my attention."

Osmark gestured for Sandra to trade places with him so she could be closer to Karzic and the Risi. He leaned back against the wall, thoughts racing as he tried to imagine how Sizemore had replaced his hired NPCs with assassins. It should've been impossible. Though his merc crew seemed alive and marked by long, complicated pasts, the truth was they hadn't existed until the moment Robert opened this restricted area and met them. They were custom jobs, created specifically for this mission.

Something very strange was going on, and he was going to enjoy getting the answers to this mystery from Sizemore.

All this double-dealing and backstabbing exhausted Robert. He'd had more than his fair share of corporate and political machinations back IRL— though, admittedly, that had been more about contracts and suppliers and less about actually sticking a knife in someone's ribs.

Eldred's wings fluttered, and Osmark wondered how easy it would be to put his repeater against the back of her skull and turn her head into pink mist. Tightly controlled rage seethed inside him like an active volcano on the verge of eruption. If there was one thing he couldn't stand, it was traitors.

If I didn't need you, he thought darkly, fingers flexing around the grip of his weapon.

"Jumpy?" Eldred asked, suddenly peering at Osmark.

Robert raised an eyebrow. "Why do you say that?"

"Because you're about to draw that fancy gun of yours," she said with a cool smile, eyes narrowed in suspicion. "I could feel you back there. Getting ready to kill."

Osmark's face became a perfectly neutral mask. He didn't know how Eldred was picking up on his emotions, but he clamped down on them. He didn't want her in his head. "I'm just ready to get this over with."

Targ grunted at that. "Me, too."

Karzic finished his chanting and grabbed the lever next to the door. "Alright then, let's do this," he said.

But the elevator remained closed despite the dwarf's best efforts. Osmark stepped up and slipped his hand past Karzic. "Soulbound," he said matter-of-factly as he twisted the dial. "It only opens for me."

There was no guarantee the exit would be soulbound, as well, but Robert wanted that possibility to prey on the mercenaries' minds. *If they killed him, would they be stranded below in a tomb of machines?* It might make them pause when it came time for their betrayal, and that could be the edge he needed to get out of the fight in one piece.

The elevator's doors slid open to reveal a wide chamber with a vaulted ceiling studded with glowing white orbs. Through the blue lens of his goggles, Osmark saw sigils covering the floor, ceiling, and walls in dizzying tangles. Trying to decipher even the simplest of them skewered his brain with a pain so intense it made his eyes water. Rather than risk scorching his mind, Robert chose to err on the side of caution and look away. "The whole room is riddled with sigils. Just about every inch. Anything we touch, anywhere we step, could be a trap," he told his companions.

"This job is the worst," Targ muttered, holding his hands on the pommel of his club. "I was promised easy money and even easier experience."

"Me, too," Osmark shot back.

Steam pipes and wire conduits snaked along the walls and crisscrossed the ceiling in mystifying configurations. Thick hoses tipped with bulky coupling rings dangled from the heavy pipes on the ceiling, while nozzles and mounting ports jutted from the walls and floor at regular intervals. Osmark took all of it in at a glance, his Clockwork skill organizing everything into understandable categories for him: active steam pipes, exhaust channels, activated power grid, inactive cabling.

Whatever they were going to face in here was well prepared to put up a fight.

But despite the dangers, Osmark only had eyes for a pedestal rising from the back of a small doorless chamber on the far side of the room. It held a heavy, iron-banded chest that practically glowed with hidden promise. That was the real object of this quest—recovering his Faction Seal and the other specialized gear waiting for him inside that chest.

"Where's the boss?" Eldred asked, giving voice to all of their concerns. "Shouldn't there be a boss monster here?"

"There will be," Osmark said softly, sweeping his gaze across the floor one more time. "Stay on your toes."

The only way Robert could reach the chest containing his Faction Seal was to cross the main chamber. He was positive the floor was covered in deadly sigils, but they were so complex he couldn't decipher them at a distance.

"Targ, Karzic, and Eldred, hang back by the elevator. There are traps littering the floor, but I can't see a path around them or a way to disarm them at this distance. I'll have to get a closer look." Robert tapped Sandra on the shoulder. "You're with me. You take point and I'll make sure you don't blow us all up."

Sandra opened her mouth to protest, but Osmark activated his Micromanage ability before she could voice her complaints. He watched her eyes widen in surprise just before her jaw clicked shut.

Interesting, he thought.

Crossing the floor was a terrifying exercise. Sandra walked a few feet ahead of Osmark, and his Overseer skill directed her around the handful of dangerous sigils he was able to identify. The Artificers who had crafted these designs were far more advanced than him, and with every step, Robert was certain they were about to die. But miraculously, after what felt like hours, they arrived at the small alcove housing the pedestal. Robert and Sandra both breathed out a sigh of relief and slumped against the walls.

"Think they can hear us all the way over here?" Sandra asked as the Micromanage ability faded away.

Osmark stole a quick glance at the mercenaries. They were standing in a loose group, not talking to each other, instead scanning for danger. "No. I think we're safe as long as we keep our voices down."

Sandra stepped in front of the chest and examined it for traps. "How did you know?" she asked. "About them being assassins, I mean."

Robert's attention was on the chest, as well, and he saw no sigils. That was a relief. "The killers who came after Horan and me in the forest all had skull tattoos on the webbing between their left thumb and index finger. When our boy Targ showed me the hole in his glove, I caught a glimpse of his tattoo."

"You're sure?" Sandra asked. Then, a little louder, "This thing's clear of traps as near as I can tell."

They swapped places, and Osmark pretended to search the chest for sigils he already knew weren't there. "As sure as I need to be," he whispered. "They're all wearing gloves, so I can't be certain. But if they managed to get one in, why not the others?"

"That's impossible," Sandra said, hunching forward, resting her hands just above her knees. "Unless Sizemore got to someone inside the Dev team …"

Her words died, and Robert nodded while facing the chest. "That's what I'm worried about, too. If he has agents who can mess with the code, that's even more of a reason to stop him. That kind of tampering endangers all of us. The whole world."

Neither of them said anything for a long moment. Finally, he broke the silence. "The Micromanage skill. What was it like just now? When I compelled you with it?" he asked, still facing the chest.

Sandra stood and folded her arms across her middle, chewing on the corner of her lips. "It was like someone giving you advice—you know, whispering in your ear. It made it hard to concentrate on anything else. I couldn't even talk, really, while it was happening."

Robert made a mental note of that and stowed it away for future use. Then he leaned back from the chest and cracked his knuckles. "Well, I don't see any sigil traps," he said, loudly enough to ensure the others heard. "Time to get the goods." Without hesitation, he put one hand flat against the top of the chest. A brilliant blue flash filled the chamber with painfully bright light, and the chest opened with an audible crack.

Before he could examine the chest's contents, however, the crack morphed into a whole chain of loud shattering noises. The cacophony echoed through the room with a sound that reminded Robert of an earthquake he'd experienced on a business trip in San Francisco. The sound was deafening, but he felt it as much as heard it.

"Oh, shit," Sandra said.

Robert spun around and drew his repeater. He expected a horde of monsters to come swarming at them from hidden doors in the chamber.

What he didn't expect to see was a smooth line separating the ceiling into two halves. As Osmark watched, the metal plates and the maze of pipes attached to them split cleanly. Something rumbled in the darkness above the new fault line, and moments later, a massive metal platform lowered from the gap in the ceiling.

A towering mechanical construct, easily twenty feet tall, stirred as the platform descended, awakening like a hibernating bear struggling up from the depths of its long winter's nap. By the time the great elevator crunched onto the floor, the contraption was fully energized and awakened.

[Iron Goliath]

The humanoid construct raised its left arm, and a buzzsaw screamed to life. Flames dripped from a pair of flared exhaust pipes above and below the boss's right wrist. A series of alarmingly loud clanks echoed through the room as armored panels on the creature's right shoulder opened and a massive six-barreled cannon rose into position next to the automaton's head.

"Intruder alert," a thundering voice announced. "Commence annihilation protocol."

TWENTY-EIGHT:

Iron Goliath

"**M**ove!" Sandra shouted, dragging Osmark from the treasure alcove before he had time to grab his Faction Seal or anything else from the unlocked chest. The instant they cleared the doorway, she shoved him hard to the right while she dove left. A gout of rippling flame flooded the alcove they'd just evacuated, transforming the smaller chamber into a deadly furnace. Osmark stumbled away from the heat, shielding his eyes and slapping at his shoulders and hips where his armor smoldered.

If Sandra hadn't been on her toes, there'd be Osmark flambée in that room.

Robert spun back to face the enormous monster just in time to see Targ charge in with weapons raised.

The Risi ducked beneath a colossal swipe from the monster's buzzsaw arm, feinted left, then shot in swinging. The spiked clubs slammed into the creature's leg just above the ankle. Each attack echoed like a struck gong, but the Iron Goliath's HP didn't drop by more than a hairsbreadth.

In response, the towering automaton raised its foot and stomped down on the Bonecrusher, pinning the warrior to the floor like a bug.

"Get it off!" Targ screamed, using the last of the air in his compressed lungs as he pried at the foot with his calloused fingers. His efforts were useless, though. The Risi's dark skin turned eggplant purple as the enormous mechanical boss bore down on him with all its weight.

A Stream of Life flowed to Targ, keeping him alive for the moment, but Robert had serious doubts that Karzic could keep up with the damage the monster was capable of inflicting.

Osmark flicked the blue lens out of the way and dropped the magnifying lens into position. Luckily, it was already in focus and he got a good look at the joints connecting the Goliath's legs and feet. There was a small weakness he could exploit. He dropped into a crouch to stabilize his gun arm, aimed his repeater at the ankle joint of the leg bearing down on Targ, and fired.

Critical Hit flared across his vision as the bullet struck true, punching into the Goliath's leg. Sparks hissed and a jet of steam gushed from the damaged joint; the monstrosity instantly shifted its weight to its undamaged leg to keep from falling over.

As soon as the foot was off his chest, Targ rolled left, scrambled upright, and sprinted away from the towering mechanical golem. "Nice shot," he called out to Osmark as he skidded to a stop next to him. "A few more seconds and I was done."

I should have let him die, Osmark thought. *Would've made the fight harder, but it also would've saved me trouble in the end.*

"Not a problem," Osmark forced himself to say, before fishing a Health Regen potion from his belt and tossing it to the warrior. He couldn't afford for the Risi to become suspicious. Not now.

"What's the plan?" Targ asked, before downing the potion in a single gulp.

"It's weak at the joints," Osmark said, pointing to its ankles, knees, and hips with the muzzle of his pistol. "If we can break its ankles, we should be able to take it down. If it can't stand, it'll have a helluva time fighting."

Sandra darted at the monster's good ankle and slashed her armor-piercing blades across an exposed bundle of pipes and heavy wires. Osmark offered a silent cheer as his assistant damaged the monster's leg—knocking off a handful of HP in the process—though not enough to cripple the creature. It was still an impressive attack, though, and a damned fine start.

But the clockwork monstrosity wasn't going down that easily. It straightened the leg Robert had damaged; thick brass rods erupted from within its innards, locking its ankle in place and stabilizing the joint. It would be limping, but it was far from out of the fight.

"Watch for an opening," Osmark hollered as he pulled the Fire Spitter from his inventory and held it aloft.

Then he charged straight at the limping golem.

Sandra shouted wordlessly, her eyes wide in terror.

Eldred uttered an arcane command and a rip in space pulsed over the golem's head.

A golden glow surged around Robert's body, and Karzic's chanting echoed in his ears like the voice of a priest standing in a holy sanctuary.

Osmark knew it was going to be close, but he had to take the risk. He needed to get close enough to the Iron Goliath for his plan to work.

The creature spotted Osmark and lashed out with the screaming saw blade, the weapon carving a vicious arc through the air, aimed at his head. He threw himself into the prone position, sliding across slick metal, barely avoiding the monster's decapitating swipe by inches. His slide ended just short of the golem's stiff left leg—which was exactly where Robert wanted to be.

He dropped a caltrop grenade at the edge of the monster's foot, then tossed out three more, placing them so they'd all activate in the same instant. Osmark rolled away from the automaton's bad foot, then scrambled to his feet and sprinted away as an explosion erupted behind him—the sound of all four caltrops springing at once.

Still, quick as he was, he wasn't quite quick enough. The Goliath's other leg lashed out in a mule kick, which caught Robert in the lower back, punting him high into the air. The blow slashed a full third off his HP, and the skull-rattling impact with the wall on the far side of the room took him down to half his total Health.

Osmark's vision swam unsteadily as he slid down to a seated position on the floor. Every inch of his body ached as though he'd just gone twelve rounds with a heavyweight champ. A second later a combat notification flashed in the corner of his vision:

Debuff Added

Blunt Trauma: You have sustained severe Blunt Trauma damage! Stamina Regeneration reduced by 30%; duration, 2 minutes.

"Let's hope this was worth it," he groaned, tossing the Flame Spitter into the air with a flick of his arm.

The fan blades on the weapon's bottom extended and spread wide the instant it left Osmark's hand. At the height of its arc, the Flame Spitter's blades whirled into action, rotating so fast they became an almost invisible blur, flipping the Flame Spitter over as they carried it higher into the air. The steampunk drone rocked from side to side, then righted itself, swiveling left, then right, before locking onto the Goliath.

"Oh," Osmark muttered, inching his way up the wall until he managed to gain his feet. "That was the top, not the bottom."

The clockwork boss moved with glacial slowness now. Between its damaged legs and the caltrops carpeting the ground like fresh snowfall, it took more than five seconds just to turn and face Osmark. By that time, the Flame Spitter had risen to a position just below the ceiling and locked in on its target. With a roar, the Flame Spitter fired a flaming bolt straight at the golem's steel-plated face. The projectile appeared tiny in comparison to the mechanical construct, but Osmark knew big things often came in small packages.

Especially when those small packages doubled their damage for every 20% reduction in their target's movement rate.

The burning bullet careened into the Goliath's head like a meteor. It wasn't a critical hit, but it didn't need to be, because the bullet did *thirty-two* times its normal damage against creatures with a 0% movement rate. Osmark grinned so wide his cheeks ached as the bullet sheared the armor plating away from the clockwork's head and carved a wide swath of destruction through the delicate machinery inside. Springs and cogs flew in every direction like confetti, followed by sprays of hot oil and jolts of rogue electricity.

Eldred's summoning completed at that moment, and the thin rip in space became a gaping hole, throbbing with unearthly light. Viscous liquid poured through the hole between worlds and slopped over the golem's head and shoulders like thick red syrup.

[Acid Slime] appeared over the summoned beast.

The golem staggered drunkenly, clawing at its face, but its blunt fingers couldn't find purchase on the slippery, amorphous Acid Slime streaming into the gears inside its head. Its wounded left leg skidded on the floor and jutted from its hip at an awkward angle, and down the Goliath went, dropping to its right knee.

"Now!" Osmark shouted, punctuating his command with a burst shot from his repeater. Two of the bullets in the burst ricocheted off the golem's armor, but the third ripped through the mechanical construct's right hip and exited in a spray of dirty fluid and splintered metal.

The Fire Spitter attacked again, blasting through the armored plating covering the left side of the golem's chest, revealing a massive set of brass gears surrounding a glowing orange coil and a pipe organ's worth of steam tubes.

Targ and Sandra took advantage of the clockwork's awkward posture to hack at its bent right knee. Their attacks rained down on the exposed gears and pipes, sending sparks, slivers of metal, and jets of steam flying in every direction. The Bonecrusher's electrified clubs smashed into brass rods as the Goliath's healing mechanism fought to stabilize the knee, bending them out of true, so they ground to a halt when they were only half-extended. Sandra's armor-piercing weapons carved jagged wounds into the knee's infrastructure, crippling the joint in record time.

Meanwhile, Karzic swept the Stream of Life from one ally to the next, patching up small injuries and restoring Stamina with smooth efficiency, even eliminating Osmark's Blunt Trauma debuff. Robert shot the dwarf a shaky thumbs-up—the dwarf might've been a traitor, but any doubts he had about his efficiency as a healer evaporated.

The automaton was down, but it was far from out. Its flamethrower belched a stream of burning death at Osmark, covering the floor with a sticky pool of fire that forced Robert to backpedal toward the elevator door. He dodged the actual blaze, but the hellish heat still clawed away 10% of his Health before he could get to a safe distance.

The Goliath's shoulder-mounted cannon whirled and rotated, unleashing a barrage of shells at Targ and Sandra. The fist-sized bullets screamed at Osmark's allies, who realized the danger just before the shells landed.

The Bonecrusher's heavy armor stopped the first shot, but the impact drove him back on his heels and exposed his torso to the second shot. That attack burst under the Risi's left arm, shredding the chainmail beneath his breastplate and peppering his flesh with corkscrews of scorching-hot metal.

Sandra threw her body into a nimble cartwheel, dodging the first wave of incoming fire. Unfortunately, the shells exploded, and the resulting shrapnel punched through her leather armor like a butcher's knife through a silk blouse. Blood splattered across the floor as her graceful evasion turned into an ungainly tumble. The short sword in her left hand slipped free and clattered across the slick metal as she crashed onto the floor.

Bad luck.

The Flame Spitter was still in play, though.

The drone swung left, orbiting the boss like a moon around a small planet, then unleashed a fresh round of suppressive fire, destroying the Goliath's damaged right knee in a spray of bullets and ruptured steel. The blaze lit by its previous attacks continued burning, softening the golem's armor plates and deforming its infrastructure.

Osmark realized they'd only been battling the creature for a few minutes, and they'd already stripped away a third of its Health. The Flame Spitter had more than half of its marked shots remaining, and all of Osmark's allies were still, miraculously, in the fight.

They were going to crush this boss, and in record time.

The Goliath groaned and lashed out at Targ with his gleaming saw blade. But the Bonecrusher danced away from the blade, staying just outside its reach as he struck the construct's arm with both batons. Gears and screws popped from the golem's wrist, and the whole limb shuddered as coruscating streams of jagged light shot out from between the plating.

Steam gushed from the golem's damaged body in thick clouds, and a ragged mechanical whine clawed its way free of a damaged system deep inside the construct's armored frame. Sparks leaped from holes in the clockwork's shattered torso, flickering through the steam clouds like bolts of lightning ahead of a thunderstorm.

The Fire Spitter blasted away at the golem again, tearing the shoulder cannon loose from its mounting bracket and igniting an oil fire deep inside the boss monster's metal body. Smoke boiled up in a thick black cloud that gathered on the ceiling.

Eldred landed next to Robert and flicked her fingers at the gelatinous mass still surrounding the Goliath's head. "Watch this," she said with a smirk, hands clenching tight.

The amorphous Slime she'd summoned pulsed and flexed its goopy body, clenching tighter and tighter

331

around the automaton's head. Then it wrenched itself side to side in a frenzied convulsion, damaging its own body with the ferocity of its attack. Splashes of thick red fluid mingled with oil spurting from the mechanical monster's cracked lubrication systems and poured down the Goliath's body to puddle on the floor.

"Impressive," Osmark said with a roll of his eyes. The summoned creature was doing as much damage to its own body as it was to the boss.

"Wait for it," Eldred said with a throaty chuckle. She threw her fingers wide, uttering an unintelligible word of power. A metallic shriek erupted from the golem's body. Rivets and bolts popped free like coat buttons and bounced across the floor.

With a warbling groan, the summoned monster tore the clockwork's head from its shoulders. A geyser of gritty green fluid sprayed in every direction, and the summoned Slime—badly damaged from its efforts—dissolved in a cloud of crimson mist.

The Goliath's body went slack and collapsed to the floor, more oil, green liquid, and steam pulsing from the shredded stump of its mechanical neck.

"There you go," the winged woman remarked through a grin, brushing her hands together in satisfaction. "I killed it for you. Nice and easy."

Robert rubbed his chin and eyeballed the fallen construct. It certainly looked dead, but its Health bar wasn't empty, and he hadn't received any experience bonus for defeating the creature. "Something's wrong," he warned, hefting his repeater and quickly feeding rounds into the chamber.

"What are you talking about?" Eldred demanded, folding her arms across her chest. "It's down. Go collect your reward so I can get paid."

Osmark flipped the blue lens back over his eye and groaned. The sigils on the floor throbbed with barely constrained power. Bursts of energy pulsed away from the golem, racing along the lines scrawled into the floor, then coursing into the walls of the room. The flow of power shimmered and morphed, outlining a series of small doors scattered around the room's perimeter. The doors snapped open with the whirl of gears and a series of metallic clicks, revealing a host of burning red eyes hidden in pools of inky darkness.

"I hope you've still got something up your sleeve, Eldred," Osmark said, nodding toward the new arrivals, "because I think things are about to get much, much harder for us."

TWENTY-NINE:

Closing Gambit

R ed-eyed Scavlings poured through the open doorways set around the room's perimeter in a chittering rush. The sharpened tips of their mechanical legs clinked against the metal floor as they emerged from their warrens and scurried to attack. Nervous sweat broke out along Robert's forehead when he saw that this model of Scavling had a few extra features the first batch hadn't. In addition to the snapping mandibles and viselike legs, these critters also sported a pair of heavy pincers and whipping tails.

[Enhanced Combat Scavling]

Scorpions, Robert thought as he read the tag.

There were too many Scavlings to count, and they scuttled across the floor in an organized charge. Several of the mechanical creatures closed in on Targ and Sandra, a few headed toward Eldred and Osmark, and a double fistful charged Karzic, their barbed tails waving wildly. Most of them, however, zipped toward the downed Goliath in a madcap rush.

Osmark instantly knew what they were up to, but he didn't know how to stop them.

"Get into the air," he said to Eldred, his hand closing around her shoulder. "Summon something that can deal with the Scavlings while I figure out what to do with the boss."

The winged woman nodded and brushed his hand away with a flick of her wing as she launched into the air, her fingers already weaving strands of power. An empty gesture because Osmark knew in his gut she'd be too slow to stop the skittering bots from fulfilling their duty. The best he could hope for was that whatever Eldred summoned would be able to keep the Scavlings clear while Osmark and the rest of the team dealt with the clockwork Goliath.

"Regroup!" Osmark shouted, feeding more rounds into his pistol. "Form up on Karzic!"

The Fire Spitter launched its last attack at the golem, blasting a chunk of armor and a trio of unfortunate Scavlings from the clockwork's back, before returning to Osmark. It floated alongside Robert as he ran, but as soon as Osmark reached out and grabbed it, the rotors folded up, and the steampunk drone went inert. A quick examination told Robert the Fire Spitter would need at least five minutes before it was ready to launch again.

"I don't know if we have five seconds, much less five minutes," Osmark grumbled, stowing the Fire Spitter. He shouldn't have used it so soon—a mistake he wasn't going to make again.

Targ carved a path through the Scavlings with a windmill of electrified cudgel attacks, which sent several of the creatures bowling back into their comrades. Sandra followed in his wake, dodging over and around the bots trying to intercept her and crippling those that came within range of her blades with lightning-fast, pinpoint precise attacks on their joints. Between the two of them, they'd disabled a dozen of the creatures, but there were far more.

Too many more.

Meanwhile, those Scavlings that had reached the golem were already hard at work restoring their master to fighting form. A small group had raised the shoulder cannon back into place and were securing it with welding flames that burst from between their mandibles. Others diligently reattached the Goliath's severed head while the rest of the scorpion squad tore the armor from their own bodies, and the bodies of their comrades—literally cannibalizing themselves—to restore the golem's protective plating.

Robert scrambled around a swarm of arachnoid bots to reach Karzic, who was fending off a wave of minions with the golden aura emanating from his hammer. The Scavlings were piled up against it in anticipation of the spell's failure. As soon as Karzic ran out of power, they'd swarm him in a battle of attrition he couldn't win and tear him limb from limb.

Osmark passed through the edge of the golden shield and a prickling sensation ran across his whole body, fluttering his hair in an unseen breeze. The dwarf nodded a greeting to Osmark, but he was too busy chanting to spare any words. Robert leveled his repeater in a flash, selected the automatic mode with a flick of his thumb, and drew a bead on a Scavling at the bottom of the pile, rudely smashed up against the shield.

"This is going to get loud," he warned the dwarf.

The dwarf nodded vigorously, and his chanting grew more fevered.

Osmark extended his arm, until the repeater's barrel was only inches away from the glowing shield, and fired. He couldn't miss at that range, and all ten of his shots plowed into the Scavling carapaces. The front rank had unwisely pressed their bodies up against the shield in a vain attempt to climb the glowing barrier. Each of Osmark's bullets found its mark, punching through soft underbellies. Unlike the other Scavlings Robert had battled, these were all equipped with welding torches, and those welding torches required fuel tanks.

Fuel tanks which were hidden inside their bellies.

A series of muffled crunching noises resounded in the air as his shots tore through the mechanical guts, followed immediately by blasts of flame and violent explosions as the internal fuel chambers ruptured.

The creatures detonated like living grenades.

Bits of metal shrapnel snipped off legs and sheared off heads from neighboring bots, and the force of the blast hurled even more of the creatures away from the shield. Scavlings rolled across the floor, struggling to stay upright, their pincers and mandibles clacking together in confused agitation. For a moment, there was a clear path to Targ and Sandra, the machines momentarily parting like the Red Sea.

"Go!" Osmark shouted to the dwarf, shoving him into motion. "Get to the others!"

The chanting dwarf broke into a lumbering run, picking up speed slowly, like a freight train lurching to life. Robert scanned the battlefield as he followed, still protected by the golden half-dome. Eldred loitered uselessly overhead. Targ and Sandra were pinned down. Even worse, the Scavlings had finished the repairs on the golem, and it was back on its feet again. And to top it off, the mechanized repair squads hadn't been happy with just repairing the damage, oh, no.

They'd added something new to the Iron Goliath …

The hoses dangling from the overhead steam pipes were now fastened to a series of ports on the golem's back, which, in turn, led to a line of turbines mounted just below its shoulders. A red power core blazed with energy as more and more steam poured into the turbines, filling the Goliath with new power and deadly purpose.

With their work completed, the Scavlings who'd been tending to the clockwork boss now had a new mission: kill Osmark and Karzic with extreme prejudice.

"Keep moving," Osmark commanded the dwarf. "If you have to replenish the shield with your Health, do it. I'll keep the Scavlings off of us, but you have to keep moving."

He reloaded his repeater and fired a three-shot burst into the scorpions charging at Karzic's defensive shield. There were no easy belly shots with these, but Robert had anticipated that. He aimed low, and the tactic paid off.

The repeater's powerful bullets either ripped legs free from steel bodies or ricocheted off the metal floor and punched up through the softer layer of armor on their bellies. Two more of the creatures squealed and rolled onto their backs, damaged legs twitching in the air like dying roaches. Flickers of fire appeared through the holes in their bodies, and Osmark knew it was only a matter of time before they exploded.

They were closing in on Targ and Sandra, but the duo was bogged down by a swarm of scorpion-tailed Scavlings, which seemed to grow larger by the second. Robert's allies were putting up a good fight, but he knew if they didn't reach them soon, it was all over for the Bonecrusher and his assistant.

The Goliath's shoulder mounted cannon fired, *boom-boom-boom*, denting the floor and walls as it tried to draw a bead on Sandra. Reluctantly, the stalker abandoned her attack on the Scavlings, focusing every ounce of energy and skill she had on evading the relentless barrage pouring from the oversized weapon. Osmark prayed her Stamina would hold out until he could turn the tide, but his confidence was flagging.

This was supposed to be an easy dungeon—a cakewalk that would net him a Faction Seal, some epic gear, a small mountain of gold, and enough EXP to transform him into one of the most formidable players in V.G.O. Instead, he was facing an increasingly difficult series of challenges that seemed to anticipate his advantages, then nullify them before they could be fully exploited. Between this turn of events and the presence of a trio of ColdSkull assassins, Osmark knew something had gone very, very wrong.

He just didn't have time to worry about that while a two-story-tall automaton tried to murder him and his entire party.

Targ feinted left, then hooked right, dodging the golem's saw blade, but he didn't get away clean. The spinning edge of the weapon clipped the Bonecrusher's left pauldron, cutting through its straps, then digging into the Risi's meaty shoulder. The warrior howled in agony as blood, shredded flesh, and chips of glistening bone sprayed from the grisly wound. The sight was sickening, but there was nothing Osmark could do.

Besides, Targ was the enemy, he reminded himself.

The golem followed through with the momentum of its swing, pivoting 180 degrees at its waist, bringing its flamethrower to bear on Osmark and Karzic. The dwarf turned to face the attack and raised his hammer higher, thrusting it forward in defiance. The chanter's voice boomed like thunder and echoed with divine strength. Robert couldn't help but admire the dwarf's faith in his god's power.

Karzic stood, resolute, and stared down the flamethrower's flickering barrel, wreathed in a glimmering halo of holy light.

Flames roared around Karzic and Osmark, a cloud of orange-and-black death. Despite the shield, Robert felt the skin on his face grow tight as a furnace-blast of heat seeped bit by bit through the magic barrier.

In that second, Robert made a choice. He leaped, throwing himself into a tight roll that carried him away from the shield; he gained his feet a second later and sprinted toward Targ and Sandra with all the speed he could muster. Behind him, the flames smashed through Karzic's shield, and the dwarf's faith was rewarded with an inferno.

Karzic screamed and staggered through the fire, hammer still held high even as licking tongues of flame wriggled beneath his armor to melt his flesh. Osmark watched in horror as the dwarf soldiered on, walking out the other side of the flames with molten fat dripping through the seams of his armor. His luxurious gray beard had burned away to stubble, and his face was a black mask of charred flesh.

But still the dwarf staggered toward Targ and Sandra, determination etched into the lines of his burned face.

Osmark couldn't help but feel a pang of sympathy. Even if the priest had been nothing more than an assassin sent to capture him, it was a hell of a way to go.

And unless he wanted to go out the same way, he needed to act fast. He abandoned his plan to regroup with the rest of his team—they were surrounded by Scavlings and would make ripe targets for another blast from the clockwork boss's flamethrower. Regrouping meant death. No, the only chance any of them had of getting out of here alive lay in Osmark's hands.

"Get its attention!" he shouted at Sandra, jabbing his repeater at the Goliath. The creature was much more powerful thanks to the work the Scavlings had done, but Osmark saw something in the hasty engineering changes he could exploit. A small opening, but he'd take what he could get.

Unfortunately, that meant getting very, very close to the hulking monstrosity.

Targ bellowed, and Sandra shouted at the towering golem. It shifted its position, turning toward them and away from Osmark.

Robert's Health was dangerously low, and the Scavlings he charged past chipped away at it even more. Nicks and cuts and bruises didn't do much damage individually, but their cumulative effect was wearing him down slowly. If he didn't end this fight soon, they were all dead.

The Goliath's new, makeshift armor was effective, but it wasn't smooth or finished and offered plenty of hand and footholds. Osmark fired at another Scavling, shearing one of its mandibles off where it connected to its head, holstered his pistol, then leaped at the back of the golem's leg.

Sandra screamed in agony—the sound hit Robert like a sucker punch to the solar plexus. His heart ached, and his stomach clenched, but he didn't have time to worry about her. If she died, she died. It would be painful, true, but she'd respawn in eight hours—a minor inconvenience at most. His death, however, would be catastrophic. He needed his allies for a distraction, and if that meant they needed to burn? So be it.

As Osmark dragged himself up the creature's jury-rigged body, the sounds of combat grew more intense, and the pained cries of his allies became more distracting. He couldn't tell if they were winning or losing, and he had to constantly remind himself to stop worrying about what they were doing. All that mattered was what *he* was doing.

Any chance of success lay in Osmark's hands alone.

The way it should be.

An unarmored Scavling scampered over the Goliath's broad, armored shoulder and down its back, snapping its mandibles inches from Robert's face. Startled, Osmark nearly lost his grip on the golem. He dug the fingers of his left hand over a protruding steel ridge, drew his repeater, and fired a single shell through the bot's gaping jaws. Gears and oil splashed in every direction, and the mortally wounded Scavling toppled with an ear-rending screech.

Eldred shouted at Osmark from where she hovered above him. "Whatever you're doing, do it fast. Targ is almost down, and your stalker is out of the fight. Not dead, but close. Karzic can't keep them alive much longer."

Shit.

He was supremely impressed that the dwarf was still alive, but knew that couldn't last for long. He inched his way upward, finally reaching the first of the steam hoses, but that was where his work started, not ended. "Then get this thing's attention off of them," he yelled up at her. "Summon a creature. Fly into its face. Do *something*. Anything."

Eldred snorted and flew away, the gusts of her flapping wings ruffling Osmark's hair. "No promises," she shouted.

Worthless.

Osmark pulled his toolkit out of his inventory and went to work. He focused his attention on the problem at hand, taking deep, even breaths to hold anxiety and fear at bay. He couldn't control what anyone else was doing, and he couldn't save anyone but himself. All that mattered was the work and the man doing it.

He fished out a wrench and slipped it around the steam fitting's nut. The nut budged a hair, just as he'd hoped. The Scavlings had tightened the fasteners, but they'd been in a hurry—there simply hadn't been time to wrench them down so tight a puny human couldn't pull them apart. Ten seconds later, the nut fell away from the fitting and rattled down the outside of the golem's body like a pachinko ball.

"Here goes nothing," Osmark muttered to himself.

Robert clambered above the steam pipe, clinging tight to the Goliath's back with both hands, then stomped down on the loose fitting with both feet. The metal collar spun once and popped loose with a *clang* as a blast of steam washed over Osmark's lower legs, chipping away at more of his precious Health. The hose abruptly retracted into the ceiling with a mechanical squeal, leaving an unprotected, and very vulnerable, steam shaft exposed.

Perfect.

Karzic's voice rolled through the chamber like a bomb blast, shaking dust loose from the ceiling and rattling Robert's teeth. Osmark took a quick peek under the golem's left arm, and his eyes widened in surprise.

The dwarf stood over the fallen bodies of Targ and Sandra, his hammer brandished in front of them like a shield. One of his eyes was missing, burned from his skull, and half his face was melted into a blackened scab. His hair and beard were gone, and Robert was amazed he could speak through his scorched lips. Despite it all, a golden glow flooded from Karzic's hammer, protecting those within its aura.

But the dwarf's defense came at a terrible cost:

Maintaining the shield against the golem's swinging buzzsaw and rattling cannon burned away Karzic's remaining Health faster than the flamethrower had. Assassin or not, the dwarf was giving his all to this fight.

It was going to be hard to kill him when the time came.

Osmark would kill him, though. He didn't abide traitors.

Have to survive for that to happen, Osmark thought. He took a deep breath and pulled the last of the caltrop grenades from his inventory. He wasn't sure this would work, but it was the only shot he had of surviving this unholy debacle. Robert reached down and slipped the gray orb into the steam port he'd opened, listening to it *clink* and *clack* as it dropped.

THIRTY:

Traitor's Fate

The caltrop burst inside the golem with a sound like a hailstorm in an aluminum siding factory. An impressive cacophony of ricochets, whines, and metallic pings rattled through the clockwork boss's body as the monster shuddered, lurched, and grew still. Finally, the last of the clanging died down. Then— taking everyone by surprise—it threw its head back and unleashed an anguished roar, a plume of greasy black smoke drifting from its yawning mouth.

Osmark's hunch had paid off, far beyond his wildest imaginings. The deployed caltrop had plowed through something vital inside the golem, and at least one of the sharpened metal spikes had critically damaged the power core. The red light leaking out of the narrow slits in the Goliath's armor blazed so bright Osmark had to shield his eyes from its glare.

An ominous rumble followed the golem's pained roar, and its torso shook like a skyscraper in an earthquake. Three of the steam fittings burst and sprayed superheated vapor in every direction, scorching Robert through his armor and covering the automaton's back in a slick sheen of oily water.

Time to move, Osmark thought, slipping down the golem's vibrating torso. Though there were hand and footholds galore, the creature's thrashing and stumbling made every step potentially deadly. Whenever the hulking automaton moved, it took every ounce of his strength just to hang tight. Climbing quickly became a series of short, controlled falls, but even that wasn't fast enough to get Robert to safety before the damage took its toll on the Goliath.

The crimson light pouring out of the power core grew so bright Osmark could see it with his eyes closed, and feel the tremendous heat even through the tough metal armor. It flashed once, twice, and then the clockwork's torso came apart with a thunderous explosion that sent pieces of golem soaring in every direction. One of those pieces was its upper thigh, which tore loose from the hip joint and carried Osmark across the room, flipping topsy-turvy.

Robert pressed his eyes shut, and a moment later the leg slammed into the ground with a dull *boom,* kicking up bits of dust and scattering dead Scavlings. The terrible jolt threw Osmark from the detached leg, hurling him across the floor like a ragdoll—arms and legs splayed out—until his shoulders plowed into a wall with breathtaking force. His ears rang, his pulse pounded like the throbbing of distant war drums, and his brain rattled inside his skull like a lonely ice cube in a shaken cocktail.

His Health was well below 15%, deep in the Critical Zone, and there was something terribly wrong with his left leg. It lay at an unnatural angle, a piece of shin bone popping through the skin. Robert lay back against the cold metal and frantically pulled a Health Regen potion from his belt, downing the cinnamon-sweet elixir as pieces of the golem continued raining down around him. For a time, Osmark just lay there, letting the potion do its work, praying some piece of jagged debris didn't smack him in the face.

Finally, with a groan, he pushed himself onto his elbows.

Even with the potion, his Health was still below 75%, but at least his left leg felt more or less back to normal. A PM from Sandra flashed across his vision:

Personal Message:

Sitrep?

Situation Report. She always had a tendency to slip back into quasi-military vernacular whenever things got tense. Osmark responded:

Personal Message:

Glad you're alive. I used a Health Regen Potion. Still only at 75%, but doing much better. You?

He waited anxiously, feeling the tension mount and build in the air. They'd taken out the Brand-Forged monstrosities, true, but there were still plenty of dangers lurking around the corner—like the three traitorous Coldskulls. Now that the Goliath was out of the picture, it was only a matter of time before they made their move. Sandra's returned message *pinged* in his ear.

Personal Message:

Recovering, but banged up. Nothing a handful of Healing Potions won't fix. Eldred and Karzic are still alive, but the dwarf is tap-dancing on Death's door—he's got little chance, given the extent of his wounds and the mountain of debuffs he's currently buried under. Even better news, Targ is KIA. One less threat to worry about.

Time to finish this.

With a wince and a grunt, Robert pushed himself to his feet, testing his legs experimentally as he scanned the room. The whole chamber looked like the site of a train wreck. Twisted metal lay everywhere, covered in crimson blood, sticky black oil, and viscous green motor fluid. The Goliath was a deformed wreck of steel and pipes, while the floor was a thick blanket of Scavling corpses.

Osmark spotted the remainder of his crew near the alcove with the pedestal and his coveted treasure chest. Good. The alcove would provide some scant cover from Eldred's summonings, if it came to that, and they could use the narrow doorway to keep Karzic from rushing in with his hammer or pinning them down with his shield. It was a long shot, but lately, that seemed like the only kind of shot Robert was getting.

He dusted his hands off, hastily checked his repeater—reloading it in seconds—then set out.

Crossing the chamber was harder than Robert could've imagined. The Scavlings had powered down the second the Goliath exploded, and the metal floor was littered with their inert bodies. Extended mandibles and opened pincers lay hidden beneath broken carapaces and scattered armor plates, threatening to trip Robert with every step he took.

Eventually, though, Osmark reached Sandra and the Coldskulls, surveying the state of things for himself.

Sandra looked at least as bad as he felt—dirty, bloody, and sweat-caked—but she was alive, and her HP hovered around 60%. Eldred looked untouched, which made sense. She'd spent the majority of the battle flying around and avoiding combat. Briefly, Robert wondered if he'd made a poor choice in class because summoning other creatures to do your fighting seemed a hell of a lot easier and less painful than what he'd just endured.

Karzic, on the other hand, appeared more beat up than the rest of them combined. His lower face was a sticky mask of drying blood, and his remaining eye was stained crimson from the burst vessels around his pupil. He nodded at Osmark and winced as if the gesture had cost him dearly. For a moment, Robert felt pity for the battered dwarf, and then the ugly truth lit a fire of rage in his belly. These people weren't really his allies, at all.

They were Sizemore's people, and they had to die for Robert to live.

He shuffled over and dropped to a knee, placing a hand on the dwarf's shoulder. "Don't worry," he said, voice brimming with warm reassurance. "We'll get you all patched up. I'll even make sure you get a bonus for your efforts." Lies, all lies. He slipped a gray steel vial from his pack. "This is a specialty brew," he said, "crafted by Master Artificer Rozak. It'll take care of your Health and eliminate all status debuffs." More lies.

He'd taken this vial from the other group of Coldskulls, and the only thing it held was a powerful paralytic, which would immobilize the dwarf and make him easy prey.

"Make sure to patch him up," he said to Sandra, handing her the vial. He sent her a private message as he stood.

Personal Message:

It'll paralyze him and make him weak as a newborn kitten. As soon as I get into the alcove with Eldred, slit his throat. And make it noisy.

"Shame about Targ," Osmark said, trying to put as much pity as he could into his voice. The Bonecrusher's body was a catalog of horrific injuries, and most of his face was an unrecognizable purple mass. It looked like he'd taken a direct hit across the jaw from the golem's fist.

Eldred shrugged. "More loot for us, right?"

Robert smirked. "Right you are. Now, let's go get the treasure out of the chest, and we can divvy it up. Eldred, you're with me."

"Sounds good," Karzic croaked.

"Shhhh," Sandra cooed at the dwarf, uncorking the vial. "Save your strength."

351

Osmark headed for the small chamber, Eldred trailing a few paces behind. He could almost feel her anticipation building—he was handing them a perfect ambush on a silver platter, and any assassin worth their salt would know it. Once inside the room, he opened the chest and glanced down, a lopsided grin splitting his face. "Well, this is more than I expected."

And it was true.

Much of the chest was filled with a king's ransom worth of gold coins and polished gemstones, but there were two other vitally important items resting on top of the pile of loot: First, was a fat golden disk, about the size of an old-world CD, with the image of a noble-faced man in profile and the Latin phrase *Imperatorius Factio Signum* on the top and *Domini est Terra* on the bottom. His Faction Seal. The second item was a thick leather-bound tome studded with bits of metal and cogs.

An Artificer's Guidebook—a prize almost as rare as the Seal.

"Raise your hands, and step away from the chest." Eldred's voice was as smooth and venomous as a serpent. "You made a big mis—"

The word *mistake* froze on her lips as a guttural cry sounded from outside the treasure chamber. Karzic's tortured voice rose higher than Robert thought possible. It was a pained, frantic plea for mercy that held no words, only an animal's cry for life. Apparently the Coldskull poison wasn't just deadly, it was *painful*. All the better.

Osmark drew his pistol and spun, bringing the barrel up to head height. As he'd hoped, the summoner had her back to him, distracted by Karzic's death cry. Osmark let out a sigh of relief as he pressed the repeater's barrel against the side of Eldred's head. "Who made a mistake?"

The summoner froze, her body suddenly as rigid as a statue. "I'll tell you everything," Eldred said, panic giving her voice a frantic edge. "You want to know who sent me? I can tell you who sent me."

Osmark offered Eldred a smile as hard and cold as a straight razor. "I already know. I've known since Targ slipped up and showed me his tattoo in the elevator."

"Then why?" Eldred asked, turning slowly to face him, her hands still raised. "Why fight the Goliath when you knew we were traitors?" He could see her doing the calculations in her mind, but none of it added up the Accipiter. Her sense of self-preservation was too strong to gamble like Robert had. She'd never try to buck the odds like that.

Which is why *she* had lost, and *Osmark* had won.

"Because I needed you."

The repeater roared three times in quick succession, and Eldred's head disappeared into a cloud of moist red vapor. Blood pumped from the cratered stump of her neck, then her knees collapsed, and the winged woman fell to the floor.

"And now I don't," Osmark said, smoothly holstering the repeater.

Sandra peeked around the corner of the doorway, her short sword in hand. "All clear?"

"All clear," Osmark replied, folding his hands behind his back as he loomed over Eldred's corpse.

"Remind me not to get on your bad side," Sandra said, trying to force a smile. It didn't work.

He shook his head and shrugged noncommittally. "Traitors. I thought things were bad enough in the boardroom, but this is taking it to a whole new level. I have to figure out how Sizemore got his people in here because it shouldn't be possible. He must have someone on the inside."

Sandra frowned at that suggestion. "I don't believe that's possible."

Osmark shrugged again, unconcerned with what she believed. Not about this. She was a phenomenal assistant—capable, loyal, witty—and a deadly security consultant, but he was the tech genius. He was the inventor of V.G.O. and the father of the Overminds who ruled this world. So in this, Sandra's opinion didn't matter and he couldn't afford to spend time or energy arguing with her. He needed to get back to town, get his gear patched up as soon as possible, and talk with Rozak before the day was done.

"Let's just see what we've got, shall we? Then get the hell out of here."

Sandra counted the money while Robert examined his loot.

There was nothing for her, or anyone else, in the chest. It was all his, and there was plenty of it. He took the Seal first, eager to finally have the coveted item in his inventory. Osmark didn't bother trying to pull up a description—the Faction Seals were extraordinarily rare, and there was an expectation that players who found one would know what it was and how to use it. Next, he examined a new pair of Artificer's goggles with better bonuses, an extra ability, and space for an extra lens when he got around to making one:

Master Artificer's Goggles

One of the most important tools in an Artificer's bag of tricks are his goggles. The master model has five different lenses, each of which provides a different bonus:

Magnifying Lens (clear): Provides a +15% bonus to any Engineering task involving intricate or detailed work.

Engraver's Lens (blue): Provides a +15% bonus to any Engineering task related to repairing Divine Geometry patterns.

Harvester Lens (green): Provides a +15% bonus to any Engineering task related to disassembling engineered items for parts or plans.

Surveyor Lens (telescoping): This lens provides a +15% bonus to any Mining tasks.

Marksman's Lens: This lens provides a +10% bonus to Ranged Attack Strength when using any Engineered weapon.

Empty Lens Mount: This mount can be used to install any lens that can be found or created.

Last came the Artificer's Guidebook. A heavy, old thing that felt right in his hands—as though it were made for him and him alone. He flipped back the front cover and noticed the first few pages were already marked up with what looked like blueprints. Before he could thoroughly examine them, though, Sandra's voice cut through the room.

"Boss, want to see what I found under this obscene pile of gold?"

He stowed the book for later examination, and Sandra handed him a long hooded cape, a garish top hat, a pair of gloves, and a padded jacket, all woven with the same geometric patterns he'd come to recognize as the mark of the Brand-Forged Artificers. His armor set was complete.

Geometrically Threaded Cape

Armor Type: Light, padded

Class: Ancient Artifact; Set Item

Base Defense: 10 (20 vs. Mechanical Creatures or Automatons)

Special: 1 Sigil Plate

Primary Effects:

- +20 to Intelligence
- +10 to Reputation with all Friendly Factions

- +10 Renown

Secondary Effects:

- Part of the Artifactory Engineer's Uniform

Armor Set

- o +5 Armor against all mechanical or automaton attacks per set piece worn
- o All Stamina Costs are reduced by 15% (2 pieces)
- o +10 to Movement Bonus (3 pieces)
- o +25% increased chance to avoid Movement Restricting Debuffs (4 pieces)
- o +1 Large Mounting Bracket (5 pieces)
- o +1 Sigil Plate when the full suit is worn (6 pieces)

Geometrically Threaded Gloves

Armor Type: Light, padded

Class: Ancient Artifact; Set Item

Base Defense: 5 (10 vs. Mechanical Creatures or Automatons)

Special: 1 Small Mounting Bracket, 1 Sigil Plate

Primary Effects:

- +20 to Intelligence
- +10 to Reputation with all Friendly Factions
- +10 Renown

Secondary Effects:

- Part of the Artifactory Engineer's Uniform Armor Set

  - o +5 Armor against all mechanical or automaton attacks per set piece worn

- All Stamina Costs are reduced by 15% (2 pieces)
- +10 to Movement Bonus (3 pieces)
- +25% increased chance to avoid Movement Restricting Debuffs (4 pieces)
- +1 Large Mounting Bracket (5 pieces)
- +1 Sigil Plate when the full suit is worn (6 pieces)

Geometrically Threaded Gentlemen's Hat

Armor Type: Light, padded

Class: Ancient Artifact; Set Item

Base Defense: 5 (10 vs. Mechanical Creatures or Automatons)

Special: 1 Sigil Plate

Primary Effects:

- +20 to Intelligence
- +10 to Reputation with all Friendly Factions
- +10 Renown

Secondary Effects:

- Part of the Artifactory Engineer's Uniform Armor Set

  - +5 Armor against all mechanical or automaton attacks per set piece worn
  - All Stamina Costs are reduced by 15% (2 pieces)
  - +10 to Movement Bonus (3 pieces)

- o +25% increased chance to avoid Movement Restricting Debuffs (4 pieces)
- o +1 Large Mounting Bracket (5 pieces)
- o +1 Sigil Plate when the full suit is worn (6 pieces)

Geometrically Threaded Jacket

Armor Type: Light, padded

Class: Ancient Artifact; Set Item

Base Defense: 20 (40 vs. Mechanical Creatures or Automatons)

Special: 2 Medium Mounting Brackets, 1 Sigil Plate

Primary Effects:

- +20 to Intelligence
- +10 to Reputation with all Friendly Factions
- +10 Renown

Secondary Effects:

- Part of the Artifactory Engineer's Uniform Armor Set
  - o +5 Armor against all mechanical or automaton attacks per set piece worn
  - o All Stamina Costs are reduced by 15% (2 pieces)
  - o +10 to Movement Bonus (3 pieces)
  - o +25% increased chance to avoid Movement Restricting Debuffs (4 pieces)
  - o +1 Large Mounting Bracket (5 pieces)

> ○ +1 Sigil Plate when the full suit is worn (6
> pieces)

Osmark wanted to stop right then and there to exchange his old gear for the full set of Geometrically Threaded Armor, but he was filthy—covered in gore and grime and oil. He refused to stain his new wardrobe with the blood of traitors. When he left this tomb behind, he wanted no reminder of the Coldskulls. He leaned against the pedestal holding the treasure chest, fuming silently about Sizemore. The man would pay for everything he'd done, but what fate could possibly be terrible enough to fit his crimes?

As he glanced at Eldred's ruined body an idea occurred to him. "Do you have a port-scroll back to Tomestide?" he asked his assistant.

"Of course, boss," Sandra replied, tapping a scroll case strapped to the outside of her left thigh. "I never leave home without at least one emergency escape hatch." She paused, stealing a sideways glance at him. "But don't you have a port-stone?"

"As a matter of fact, I do," he replied, an edge of arctic ice coating the words. "But I have something else in mind for that." He pulled the opalescent ball from his inventory and opened its item description in his interface.

Port-stone

Activation allows instantaneous travel between the user's current location and a predetermined location

---

> (the port anchor).
>
> The anchor may be changed to the user's current location by willing the update.
>
> *Cooldown:* The port-stone requires a cooldown period of 1 hour after each use.
>
> *Current Anchor:* Tomestide

With a malicious grin, he activated the stone—not teleporting back to Tomestide, but rather changing the anchor location to the small alcove with the pedestal. Oh yes, Sizemore would pay all right—and he would pay for a very, very, very long time. He silently closed out of the menu and turned his attention on Sandra.

"Alright," he said, rubbing his fingers over the smooth surface of the stone. "Before we go, we have some work to do. I want to salvage what we can from these wonderful machines. We'll pack this chest"—he thumped the heavy box with his fist—"then carry the rest on our backs when we teleport out."

Sandra groaned, then nodded. "Of course, boss. But where should we even start?" She paused, chewing on her bottom lip as she looked around. "There's just so much of it."

"Easy," Robert replied as he absently scratched his chin. "Start with the buzzsaw and the flamethrower the golem had strapped to its arms. Then we'll move on to raw materials. I think you'll find something interesting over there," Osmark said, gesturing toward the far corner of the room.

Sandra groaned again, but set to work.

THIRTY-ONE:

Class Change

Sandra scowled at Robert as they stumbled through the portal from the Artifactory and back into Tomestide. "Rozak can wait, boss. You need food, rest"—she paused, lips pressed into a thin line— "and probably a priest just to take the edge off. Honestly, Robert, you're half dead. You can't even stand on your own two feet. You're exhausted—and I should know, because *I'm* exhausted. Please." She reached out and placed a hand on his forearm. "Just a little break."

Osmark waved away his assistant's concerns, adjusted the hood of his travel-stained cloak to hide his face from any unfriendlies who might be lurking around Tomestide, and continued down the street. The immense weight of all the loot and raw materials in his inventory made the trek slow going, but he wasn't about to delay meeting with Rozak even a second longer.

"The inn is always open, and so is the church, but Rozak? His shop will be closing up any time. If I don't catch him now, I won't be able to get in to see him before tomorrow morning. And if that happens, the rest of my schedule will be off by at least eight hours. Maybe more. *We* can't afford that, Sandra, not with everything happening tomorrow. This needs to be done, and it needs to be done *now*."

Sandra huffed angrily, arms folded across her chest in disapproval, but didn't try to stop her boss from carrying out his plans. "At least let me carry some of that scrap, then. You're over-encumbered. It'll go faster if I—"

Robert squared his shoulders under the weight of his burden and turned to face Sandra with a cold, determined stare. "I appreciate your concern. I do. And I know you're just doing your job, but this isn't open for discussion. I need to speak with Rozak immediately. Alone."

Sandra flinched away from the hard edge underlying Osmark's words. His chest tightened at the hurt in his assistant's eyes. He'd rarely raised his voice to Sandra, and he couldn't remember the last time he'd shut her down so completely. But Rozak was temperamental at the best of times, and Osmark couldn't risk having the presence of a stranger upset the dwarf before he had a chance to lay out his plans.

"Very well," she replied coolly with a dip of her head, jaw clenched tight. "I'll round up a priest, head over to the inn, and have some food prepared for you." Then, without another word, she turned on one heel and set off, cold anger marking her steps.

Osmark shook his head—no matter how much he learned, women remained a mystery.

He put her from mind and made his way down Tomestide's many side streets, trying to stay off the main roads where enemies would most likely be posted. Still, despite his aches and pains, and the near fatal encounter with the Coldskulls, Osmark felt good. His plan was ahead of schedule. The new gear he'd retrieved from the restricted area would make him even more powerful than he'd expected. And he had enough supplies to build a respectable arsenal of engineered toys.

Even Sizemore's treachery had played into Osmark's hands.

If the senator had been a little cleverer, things could've been much trickier for Robert. Trying to explain the threat Sizemore posed to the other board members would've been a hard sell if Sizemore had kept his scheming hidden. Overt aggression, though, was another matter entirely. There wasn't a single member of the board who was going to sit for the senator sending assassins after Robert. After all, if Sizemore could turn on Osmark, he could turn on *anyone*.

"You grabbed the wrong tiger's tail, Senator," he whispered, eyes scanning the darkness for potential threats.

The sound of steel striking an anvil reached Osmark's ears as he rounded a corner and spied Rozak banging away at a piece of glowing metal with his oversized hammer. Osmark wondered if the dwarf was actually building something or if all the activity was just for show.

When he reached the shop, Robert raised his voice to make sure the dwarf heard him over the racket of his work. "I'm back, sir."

Rozak stopped hammering to glare at Osmark through his heavy Artificer's goggles. "You look like something the Iron Devil ate then shat out," the engineer remarked with a measuring look.

"That's more accurate than you might think," Robert said. "Can you give me a hand with some of this?" He dropped a thick bag on the deck, packed full of scraps.

Sandra had taken most of the treasure back to the inn, but Osmark had hauled the spoils of their battle with the Goliath and the Scavlings himself. With his limited strength, his inventory would only hold so much, so the rest he carried in an oversized bag Sandra had so kindly provided. His shoulders ached under the burden, and his legs wobbled with every step, burning from a combination of exhaustion and hunger.

"That's quite a load of scrap, lad," Rozak said as he dropped his thick leather gauntlets next to the anvil, eyeing the bundle askew. Rozak walked down, flipped back the leather flap covering the sack, and grunted in approval. "Quite a lot indeed." Surprisingly, he bent over and slipped the bulging sack over his shoulder, as though he were carrying a bag of pillows, then scuttled into the shop.

Osmark let out a grateful sigh and followed.

Rozak hauled the load over to one of his many workbenches, deposited it on the scarred wooden surface, then hustled outside to retrieve his work and his tools. Robert used the time to unload the rest of the salvage from his inventory proper, glad to have the weight off his back. After stowing everything for the night, Rozak closed the shop and dropped the bar across the door.

"Alright. Now, let's see it," Rozak said with a glint in his eye.

Osmark couldn't help but grin, knowing exactly what the dwarf was looking for. He pulled out his Guidebook, opened the cover, and fanned through a few of the mostly blank pages, letting Rozak get an eyeful.

The dwarf reached for the book, but Robert pulled it back, just out of his reach. "You show me yours, and I'll show you mine."

The dwarf tugged on his beard, his face a thundercloud of disapproval. "I never should've taken on a human as an apprentice," he grumbled. "You lot are all a little too uppity for your own good."

Osmark chuckled and placed the book on the workbench in front of the dwarf. "I doubt there's anything in there you haven't seen before, sir."

Rozak casually flipped through the few pages covered in neatly drawn diagrams and tight, even handwriting, nodding to himself whenever he found something of interest. "This is a good start, look here." A popup appeared in front of Osmark:

Quest Update: Legacy of the Brand-Forged

You have ventured into the Brand-Forged Artifactory and defeated the Iron Goliath within its deep vault. Though the battle was fierce and your companions fell along the path, you returned to Rozak with the Mechanical Artificer's Guidebook.

Retrieving this powerful piece of Brand-Forged lore

> has increased your reputation with Rozak to Exalted, and your reputation with all Artificers is now Honored. You may now select the Mechanical Artificer class kit. You've also received 15,000 EXP.

Osmark had been so caught up in surviving the Artifactory, he'd missed the flurry of experience and level-up messages that had come in during and just after the battle against the Goliath and his army of bots. All told, including the bonus experience from completing the quest, Robert had enough points to reach level twenty.

x6 Level Up!
You have (55) unassigned stat points!
You have (8) unassigned proficiency points!

Rozak cleared his throat and tapped the Guidebook with his calloused thumb. "I can tell you've learned a lot on your journey, but you still haven't learned how to listen."

Not wanting to miss any of the dwarf's words of wisdom, Osmark dismissed the notifications and returned his attention to the Guidebook. Rozak had his thumb next to an exploded-view diagram of an intricate clockwork mechanism. At first, the drawing made no sense to Robert, but the longer he looked at it, the clearer it became. He understood how a toothed gear would slip over an articulated axle here, and the steam fitting would couple with the drive line to the turbine there …

Congratulations! You are now able to pursue the Mechanical Artificer class kit. Would you like to proceed? Please select Yes or No.

He chose Yes so quickly he was afraid he had sprained his eyeballs swiveling them to that option. A new skill tree unfolded in front of him, along with brief explanations of what each of the available talents offered. Rozak hadn't said another word. In fact, he hadn't moved other than to breathe since Robert started examining the Guidebook.

Good, Osmark thought, looking over the new skills he'd unlocked by taking the Mechanical Artificer kit, *that gives me a second to make some choices.*

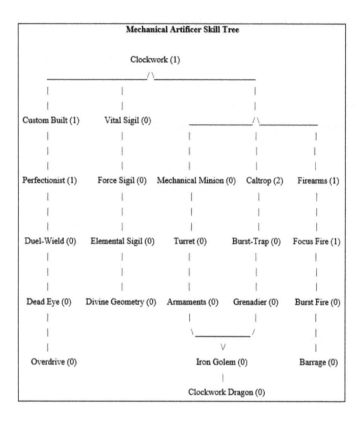

After careful examination, Robert dropped one more point into the passive Custom Built ability, which would increase his odds of "discovering" new blueprints while he salvaged the gear on the table. Next, he put another point into Perfectionist. Though he had a huge stack of salvage he could use for building engineered weapons, armor, and other gadgets, Robert knew his supplies wouldn't last forever. The extra point in Perfectionist would enable him to stretch his limited supply by reducing his production costs and production time by 24%.

Caltrop also earned another point, boosting it to three, and increasing the number of uses per activation and the total movement reduction. Locking down his opponents was always good news, especially with the Flame Spitter ready to wreak havoc on slowed enemies. He would've loved to add the Burst Fire skill to his repertoire, since it would drastically increase his damage output against a crowd, but that skill didn't unlock until he hit level twenty-five.

Still, there were a few other offensive skills he couldn't wait to try out.

But unfortunately, those would have to wait.

The Mechanical Minion and Turret abilities—both specialty features of the Mechanical Artificer Kit—looked incredibly powerful, but right now he needed to beat Sizemore. Defeating the senator and consolidating power was the only thing that mattered, and neither ability would help appreciably toward that end. Not with the plan he already had in mind. A feral smile crept across his lips as he read over the description of Vital Sigil. Yes, that would do the trick. He dumped all six of his Proficiency Points into the skill.

Skill: Vital Sigil

With a fundamental mastery of scrivening, Mechanical Artificers can inscribe Vital Sigils onto their armor. The Vital Sigil allows Mechanical Artificers to use their Intelligence Score in lieu of

---

other physical ability scores.

Skill Type/Level: Passive/Master

Cost: None

Range: N/A

Cast Time: N/A

Cooldown: N/A

Effect 1: Inscribe (1) Vital Sigil onto any piece of armor with an empty Sigil Plate.

Effect 2: Replace any one Physical Ability Score—Dexterity, Strength, Constitution, or Vitality—with your Intelligence Score.

Effect 3: Vital Sigil efficacy is 90% of Intelligence Score.

Coupled with his Geometrically Threaded armor, the Vital Sigil skill made his next choice a foregone conclusion. Robert toggled over to his character screen and dropped 35 of his stat points into Intelligence. The rest he invested in Spirit since that was the only stat that wouldn't benefit from his ridiculous Intelligence Score.

Soon—very, very soon—his hard work would pay big, big dividends.

THIRTY-TWO:

Mercenary Artificer

The whole process had only taken a few moments, and Rozak had waited as if frozen in time. Osmark closed out of the interface menu and turned his attention back to the dwarf.

"You see?" Rozak asked. "As you learn more, you'll fill this book with additional plans and blueprints. And that, in turn, will open the theory of Divine Geometry to you, guiding you as you rise through the ranks of the Mechanical Artificers."

If I survive tomorrow, he thought. Then, to Rozak, "Thank you for all you've done—"

The dwarf raised a soot-stained hand and shook his head. "We're not done here. Let's put a little of this theory into practice."

Rozak pawed through the salvage until he found the heavy buzzsaw attachment Osmark had retrieved from the fallen Goliath. "Fancy," the engineer said, "very fancy. Now, let's make it useful."

The dwarf cleared the salvage away from the workbench in front of Robert, then dropped the saw and its housing onto the empty space. "First, we're going to get rid of all the artsy-fartsy crap we don't need. Strip that housing off and pull those ludicrous fasteners from the blade axle."

Osmark, as exhausted as he was from his journey, couldn't afford to ignore any of Rozak's wisdom. Not now with so much on the line. He pulled his toolkit out of his backpack, unrolled it on the table in front of them, and went to work. His naturally high Intelligence, combined with the Custom Built skill, put him in good stead; he had the whole saw disassembled in a matter of minutes.

He laid out the parts in a neat line as he pulled them free from the saw. He ended up with a [Steam Core], a [Brass Equalizer], a [Rotary Gear Assembly], and finally, the [Hardened Steel Saw Blade]. Without the armor and the rest of the junk that had been attached to them, the parts weren't as large as Osmark would've thought. Even the blade, by far the biggest piece, was constructed from a series of interlocked pieces, which could be folded down into a compact disk not much wider than Robert's outstretched hand, or expanded until the saw blade was twice the diameter of a dinner plate.

Before Osmark could do anything else, Rozak started shuffling the pieces on the workbench, sorting Robert's work into two piles. "Don't need that, don't need this, just these."

Then he grabbed Robert's book, flipped through several pages until he came to a blank sheet, and retrieved a pointed stick of charcoal from the depths of his beard. He handed the crude pencil to Osmark. "Sketch out how you would attach this contraption to your repeater," he said.

At first, Robert considered the idea to be completely ludicrous. The repeater was a slender, almost delicate weapon, and the saw was anything but. And yet, as he began drawing the rough outline of how the ridiculous contraption would look, the pieces began to fall into place like a jigsaw puzzle. A few minutes later he had a serviceable, if rather generic, diagram to show Rozak.

"You might want a strut here," Rozak offered, pointing at the sketch, "maybe a stabilizer bar there to keep it from bouncing back on you."

Osmark immediately saw the wisdom of the dwarf's words and refined his plan, his hands whizzing across the paper—erasing this, adding that—the schematic seeming to take shape of its own volition. His mind guided his hand, but his mind was, in turn, governed by the power of Divine Geometry. It was not an altogether pleasant sensation, and he wondered if those he commanded using the Micromanage ability experienced the same sensation.

Rozak grunted his approval at Robert's enhanced sketch. "Aye, that'll do the trick, boy, assuming you've got the know-how to put it all together."

Osmark grinned in reply and immediately set to work. Oh, he had the know-how all right. He gathered the pieces he needed—reaching across the workbench to snatch a trio of metal rods from his pile of salvage, digging through the spare parts for steam tubes and fittings—then soon lost himself in the work. When he finally paused and lifted his head, the weapon was complete.

The saw blade sat horizontally beneath the repeater's barrel. A pair of copper tubes ran back along the repeater's length to the Steam Core he'd mounted on top of the repeater's original core. The blade and the Steam Core balanced one another, but Robert also added the stabilizer grip Rozak had suggested, giving the short weapon a second handle just behind the blade.

Rozak reached for the modified repeater but stopped, his finger lingering just inches away. "May I?" he asked with surprising deference.

Osmark nodded in a haze, still trying to pull himself together after the frenzied bout of construction. The whole experience had been strange, almost unnerving. For a time, he'd been lost in the grasp of something more powerful than himself. Ideas and concepts he could never have put into words had simply seized control of his hands and showed him how to exert his will on the world around him. That was the game mechanics at work.

It was amazing, but a little frightening too.

A long, low whistle escaped the dwarf's lips. "You're a quick study," Rozak said, then lowered his voice a bit, stealing a sidelong glance at Osmark. "But I fear you may have put all your eggs into a single basket, if you know what I mean."

Osmark *did* know what the dwarf meant.

The same worry had crossed his mind. Virtually all of his Stat points had gone straight into his Intelligence to boost his Artificer skills. But right now, all his other stats weren't much better than a beginning lowbie's. His armor and the Vital Sigils talent would help overcome his other deficiencies, but only if he had enough time. If anything went wrong—or Robert found himself caught flat-footed without preparation—his big brain wouldn't be enough to get him out of trouble.

Osmark couldn't let that kind of doubt color his vision of the future, though. "About that," he replied. "I need to collect my reward from my previous quest—the ten rare crafting ingredients." He told the master engineer what he needed, and the dwarf's brows beetled together.

"You aren't the first to try this scheme of yours, boy. Most have failed." He paused and stole a sidelong look at Osmark. "I hope you won't be one of 'em."

While Rozak gathered up the loot, Osmark turned his thoughts to the dwarf. Asking for his rewards from the quest was one thing, but the next request on Robert's list would be much harder for the dwarf to swallow. And if Rozak refused, all of Osmark's planning was in jeopardy. Osmark composed himself as the dwarf approached with a heavy bag slung over his shoulder. Despite the dwarf's gruff demeanor, Robert had developed a fondness for him.

It would be a shame if he had to kill him.

Rozak handed Osmark the bag, and he checked inside to make sure it had all the items he needed. Everything he'd requested was contained in the rough burlap sack, as well as a few other items he hadn't requested. "How much for the rest?" he asked, pulling up a stool at the workbench.

"No charge for my apprentice," the dwarf replied, waving one thick hand through the air. "We'll figure out some way for you to work it out later, I guess."

Robert placed the sack on the workbench and holstered his repeater. The blade mounted beneath the barrel folded up tight against the weapon's body, allowing it to slip into the holster without modification.

"I have something else to ask—" Osmark began, but the dwarf cut him off.

"I've shown you all I can. If you wish to learn more, you'll have to fill that book up a bit." The dwarf tugged at his beard. "You've already got one blueprint in there, for a creature called a Brand-Forged Scavling—you get three more blueprints and we'll talk again."

Robert sensed another quest in the offering, but he ignored the prompt for the moment. He had something more important in mind. "I will, but this isn't about your instruction. I want to hire you."

A bellowing laugh roared from the dwarf, his belly shaking as he doubled over, nearly toppling off his seat. "Lad, on your best day, you couldn't afford what I charge for even a simple dagger. Don't be getting ahead of yourself with delusions of grandeur."

A flat smile transformed Osmark's face like the frigid blast of an arctic front. "You don't know me as well as you think you do. I am your apprentice, but I'm not *only* your apprentice." He reached into his inventory and retrieved a sack of gold coins, which he promptly dropped on the workbench with a loud *thud*. "There are two thousand gold pieces in here—all of it from the Brand-Forged Artifactory. If you'll accept this job, there's more where this came from. Much more."

The spark of wisdom fled Rozak's eyes as gold fever flared within the dark recesses of his heart. Two thousand gold was a hefty sum in V.G.O.—equivalent to nearly two hundred thousand US dollars. As skilled as Rozak was, he probably wouldn't make that amount in two or three years, much less a single day. Greed was a powerful motivator. The dwarf's fingers curled together like knotted serpents, clenching and twisting with minds of their own, his breathing harsh and labored like the mechanical gusts of hard-worked bellows.

"And what is it you'll be wanting in exchange for this, eh?"

Relief washed through Osmark, but it was tinged with a prickling stab of disappointment.

He'd thought the dwarf was different, perhaps, that Rozak was driven by knowledge and the unquenchable thirst for perfecting his art. In the end, however, he'd been swayed by nothing more than a pile of shiny metal. Nothing more than a few bits of digital code, in reality. The gems Robert had recovered were worth far more than the gold, but he doubted the dwarf would have taken that bribe.

It was gold or nothing, for some.

Osmark closed his Guidebook and cleared a space on the workbench. He used the charcoal stick to draw a hasty sketch on the tabletop as Rozak watched on, drawing his pipe and slipping it between his teeth. The more details Robert filled in, the darker the dwarf's glare grew.

"Is this what I think it is?" he barked, sounding none too happy.

Osmark nodded. "It is. Here's what I need ..."

It took Robert most of an hour to lay out his plan for Rozak. It was a daring, audacious scheme. One that would cost many lives before the next day was done.

"When?" the dwarf asked, pacing back and forth, his hobnail boots *click-clacking* on the wooden floorboards.

Robert put on his best salesman's grin. "Tomorrow. By dawn. And no one can see your preparations—that's imperative. You can only work where I've marked this map. Anywhere else and someone is likely to see you. If you manage it, I'll double that two thousand. Four with no strings attached."

Rozak pondered Osmark's plan. "Okay," he grunted.

For the next twenty minutes, they quibbled over the details until Robert finally slapped his hand on the workbench. "We're out of time for talking. This has to be done. Now."

The dwarf chuckled to himself and took a long puff at his pipe, his eyes faded and distant. Making calculations and running through projections, no doubt. "Alright, then. Get your arse back to the tavern, Mr. Moneybags. I got work to do. You get yourself some rest, too. Can't have a Mechanical Artificer looking so bloody shabby."

THIRTY-THREE:

Straight Talk

O smark headed back toward the inn, one grueling step at a time, exhaustion making his limbs heavy, hunger burning a hole in his gut. He ignored them both and pushed on—eating and sleeping was for lesser men. Men who didn't have empires to build and enemies to crush. He caught sight of a familiar Legionary—Bingley, he thought—making his rounds. Seeing the guard made Robert think of Horan. Robert pushed the painful memory away, cleared his throat to catch the guard's attention, then leaned heavily against a storefront to wait.

"You look like hell if you don't mind me saying, sir," the Legionary quipped, giving him a thorough once-over. "Even more of a mess than the night you first came to Tomestide, and that's quite an accomplishment. You need some help getting back to your rooms? A cleric perhaps?"

Osmark waved away the guard's concern. "Just tired. But there is something else you can do for me. I'm willing to pay well for it, but it needs to be done now, and it's not going to make you a popular man."

The guard raised an eyebrow and scratched his chin. "I'm but a simple guardsman, sir. I don't know—"

Robert pulled a gemstone from his inventory and flashed the egg-sized ruby.

"Well, let's hear it then," the guard said with a nervous grin, eyes wide and fixed on the jewel.

Another pang of disappointment lanced through Robert's heart. Money certainly changed everything. He suddenly understood just how Sizemore had been able to manipulate things so easily. That ended today.

Osmark laid out his plan to the guard, who listened with a growing sense of panic and outrage, shifting uncertainly from foot to foot, one hand subconsciously reaching for his sword. "You can't mean—"

Osmark pulled a pouch of gemstones from his inventory. "I do mean. This is for you, and to help everyone else who will be put out. I know it's a bitter pill I'm asking you all to swallow, but I hope this will help it go down easier."

The guard chewed the inside of his lip and eyed Osmark. "People aren't going to like this. This is their home, and what you want to do is—"

Robert put a hand on the young man's shoulder and pinned him beneath his cold blue stare. "I want to make it very clear that I was never really *asking* you to do this. This will be an inconvenience for everyone, I know that. But it's much more convenient than death, wouldn't you say?"

Osmark thrust the bag of jewels into the man's hand. The guard reluctantly accepted the leather bundle and peeked inside; he gulped hard, his eyes bulging in their sockets. "Consider it done, sir."

Osmark nodded, sighed, and headed for the inn. It was growing late, and he still had hours of work to do before he could afford to sleep. Half a block away, the guard called back to Robert. "What do I do with what's left?"

Robert shrugged at the man. "If you do your job right, there won't be anything left."

And if you don't, Robert thought, *you and everyone you know in this little town will be dead.*

Thankfully, mercifully even, Sandra was every bit as good as her word despite how short he'd been with her earlier. When Osmark entered the Saddler's Rest, a pair of tonsured clerics clad in sackcloth robes greeted him at the door as if they'd been standing ready for his arrival. The duo—one almost comically portly, the other rail thin—guided Robert away from the door and to a chair padded with a tidy arrangement of quilted bedclothes.

"Please, sir, sit, let us attend to your health," the thin priest whispered, glancing nervously at the bar, where Sandra lingered, chitchatting with Murly.

Sandra smiled at Robert and crossed the room with a flagon brimming with honey mead. "I took the liberty of renting the whole place for the night," she offered with a small shrug, as though to say, *it's nothing really.* "The regulars weren't happy, of course, but the coins jingling in their pockets should sing them sweetly to sleep tonight."

Robert couldn't suppress a slight smile at the idea of Sandra negotiating with the villagers. At her most gentle, she was an imposing woman. When she put her mind to it, she was downright terrifying. He chuckled, imagining the townspeople fleeing from Sandra's stern glare, pocketing the coins almost as an afterthought. "We're going to be here a while, so try not to scare the locals too bad, all right?"

Sandra laughed, then drank from her own mug. Whatever she had, it left a dark and sticky scarlet stain that clung to her lips until she licked it free. The blush in her cheeks told Robert this wasn't her first drink since he'd left her to work with the dwarf.

The priests were shockingly efficient. Unlike Karzic, they didn't need to chant or make any other annoying noises while they worked their magic. They hovered their hands above Osmark and closed their eyes, lips moving in silent prayer to some higher power he didn't understand or care about. And then, a few minutes later, Robert had a belly full of mead and a body as hale and hearty as the day he was born. Somehow, their prayers had even managed to wash away his weariness, though he knew a full night's sleep was a definite necessity before the morning.

"Thank you," he said, reaching into his pouch for a gemstone to hand the holy men.

"That is totally unnecessary," the heftier priest said, raising his hands defensively as if Robert were about to give him an angry pit viper instead of a brilliant blue sapphire. "We've already been paid in full."

Sandra nodded to the men, and they backed away, bowing and scraping as if she were their queen.

"Well, that went well." She licked the crimson liqueur from her lips. "How did your secret mission go?"

Osmark didn't like the faint tinge of suspicion in Sandra's voice, but he didn't have the energy to argue with her about it. "Good. Very good. I think we're solid, no matter what Sizemore tries."

That confidence was greeted with a dubious frown from Sandra. "Sizemore's ahead of us. I don't know how, but he's cut you off at every turn. What makes you think we're prepared for his next move?"

Her candid doubt caught Osmark off guard, but the longer he let the words sink in, the more sense they made. She probably wouldn't have said anything if not for the liquor, but her words rang true. Robert cradled his mug in his hands, slowly turning it between his palms as he ticked off the reasons behind his confidence. "All of the board will be together, here, in Tomestide," he said after a time. "That gives us home field advantage. And trust me when I say I'm milking that particular advantage for all it's worth."

Robert's eyes drifted toward the window. The clouded glass was impossible to see through with any detail, but Osmark saw the shadows of figures walking past. All of them were heading in the same direction. East. Out of town.

"All of my assistants will be here, too, except for Aurion." Robert reminded himself to check in on the sorceress. He needed to be sure she was on top of her game and hadn't gotten cold feet. She owed him her life, but so did Sizemore and the rest of the board. Debts had a way of getting erased when self-interest came into play. "If Sizemore makes a move, someone will stand up to take my side. The senator is smooth, but I don't see him swaying the entire board.

"I'm tactically far better prepared than Sizemore can possibly be. I'm sure he's looking to pick a fight, but he has to transport whatever he plans to use against me. All of my defenses are already in place. Or will be," he muttered as an afterthought, glancing out the window again. No doubt Rozak was out there right this minute, slaving away. Setting Osmark's devious plans into motion.

Sandra gulped down the last of her drink and hammered the cup down on the table with such force Robert had to hold his mug tight to keep it from toppling. "First, you're overestimating the advantage of convening this meeting on your turf. The Brand-Forged Artifactory was your turf, too. How'd that work out?"

Before Osmark could respond to Sandra's criticism, she pressed on. "Second, you have no idea how many allies Sizemore is bringing to this shindig. He already has Peng, which is the same as having the rest of the Chinese military bosses. That will bring in the Russian oligarchs, who know they need China's muscle if they want to survive. Eastern Europe will follow the Russians, and that'll probably drag the German industrialists along for the ride."

Sandra's eyes were bright and glassy—it was obvious she'd had too much to drink. But he also knew she was telling him the hard truth. She'd been under a lot of pressure to gather the intelligence he needed, and now she was giving it to him unfiltered and free of her usual positive spin.

"India's tech moguls and the Saudi oil sheiks will hang together, but aren't likely to throw in with you or Sizemore. They're too afraid that the Iranian real estate tycoons will come after them if they side with anyone from the States, which is probably true for Iraq's mercenary barons and Malaysia's heroin kingpins, too. That whirlpool of fanatics might suck in some others with an axe to grind, but no one of note.

"What does that leave you with?" she asked, eyes squinted and blurry. "Sure, you've got all of your pals from the tech biz and the Wall Street hedgies. Other than Sizemore, the rest of the politicos and their business cronies from the States will hang tight with you, because they're still clinging to the old ideas of a world filled with nation states and all the rah-rah homeland bullshit that just about killed everyone before the asteroid showed up to do a better job.

"That might be enough to get you the financiers out of Britain. *Maybe*. But it's always hard to tell which way that crowd will bolt. Carrera seems to be on your side of the equation, but he's a thug, Robert. If he senses the tide has turned against you, he'll be the first shark with his nose inside your cage."

Before he could respond, Sandra grabbed his mug and headed for the bar, giving him ample opportunity to digest her words. Osmark felt a dark shadow rising up in the back of his mind, an old friend he'd thought was long gone. It was a reminder of what he'd done to reach his goals, of the damage he'd left in his wake on the long, ugly climb to the top of the ladder. He'd tried to shed that nasty old side of himself for many years, and after he'd crested the pinnacle of his business, he hadn't needed his brawling instincts anymore.

But he was damned glad to feel the old darkness worming its way back into his thoughts.

Because the problem he faced wasn't just the quantity of his enemies, it was the quality.

The Chinese were hardline military leaders with experience and training in large-scale combat. Most of the oligarchs had done their stint in the Russian military, then moved on to global mercenary forces, before finally getting their hands dirty with the criminal side of things when their legitimate business didn't earn out quickly enough. The Chinese and Russians only made up a tenth of the board, but it was the strongest tenth when it came to combat operations.

Osmark had more allies, but they weren't people he could depend on in a fight. No matter how much money or power they wielded in V.G.O., they couldn't stand toe-to-toe with men like Peng. Carrera maybe, but he was unreliable—a loose cannon that could fire either way, and God help whoever was on the other end of that barrel.

"Now you see it?" Sandra asked, dropping into her seat and sliding Robert's drink across the table. She slurped a hearty mouthful of liqueur. "It's Spartans versus Persians, and we're on the wrong side of the fight."

Robert grunted and guzzled his ale before responding. "What is it that gives Sizemore his handle on people?"

Sandra twirled her ponytail around one of her fingers as she pondered the question, eyes hazy and distant. "Promises, I think. He knows how to get at what people really want, and then he puts them in a position to achieve it."

"That's exactly right," Osmark replied, running one finger over the edge of his glass. "Peng and the Russians stick with Sizemore because he's promised them something they desperately want. And he's led them to believe only he can give it to them." Robert hefted his glass and savored the taste of mead on his tongue. It was sweet but had a bite lurking beneath the honey flavor. "If we can show them definitively that Sizemore can't give them anything—that he's worthless to them—they won't back his play. They're bloodthirsty pragmatists, plain and simple."

Sandra nodded. "Sure. But how do you do that?"

Osmark swirled the mead in his mug and stared into its dark depths. A coldness spread through him like liquid metal flooding his veins. "Killing him won't be enough. Even killing his family won't be enough. But we can destroy him, utterly. And we can do it in front of the rest of the board."

Sandra's eyebrows rose high at his statement. "You really think you can do that?"

Robert drained the last of his mead and banged the mug on the tabletop. "I know I can. Get some rest, it's going to be a busy day tomorrow." And it would be a busy night—he had a whole lot of crafting yet to do.

THIRTY-FOUR:

Game Day

B linding agony dragged Osmark from the depths of sleep. A spear of pain pierced his head from temple to temple as if a maniac had driven an ice pick through his skull directly into his brain. His stomach churned like he'd spent the night shoveling funnel cakes down his throat and then ridden the tilt-a-whirl all morning. His heart alternately galloped and skipped beats, filling Robert with the certainty he was about to have a heart attack, stroke, or some hellish combination of the two.

To top everything off, a chorus of trumpets brayed in his ears every few seconds. "What is that damned noise?" he hollered, pressing his palms against the sides of his head. When that didn't help, he pulled himself out of bed—only then realizing he wasn't at home—and leaned heavily against the wooden wall of his cramped room. Painful tremors ran from the soles of his feet to the top of his head, making it difficult to stand and even more difficult to think.

"Where am I?" Osmark asked himself, blinking sporadically, trying to clear his vision. When in doubt, he always started with the simplest facts and worked his way up to the truth from there.

His eyes jumped from the unkempt bed to the rough floorboards, to the wooden nightstand where black clothes, sewn with glittering threads, had been carefully stacked in a neat pile. He was in a hotel—

The stabbing pain in his head obliterated his thoughts for a long, agonizing moment as the trumpets howled in his ears again.

No, not a hotel, an *inn*. The Saddler's Rest. He'd been up late the night before inscribing the Vital Sigils on his armor with the tools he'd taken as his reward from Rozak.

He wasn't dying. He was in V.G.O.

"Kill the alarm," Osmark commanded, and the trumpets' call ended abruptly. A blinking message icon flickered in the corner of Robert's vision; he opened it in the hopes of good news from his agents.

Instead, a prerecorded message from the V.G.O. staff began playing.

"Good morning, traveler," a perky female voice said. "This is Silvia, your customer support representative, and our records indicate you've successfully spent your second night in Viridian Gate Online. Congratulations! Since you're hearing this, I have some great news for you: your overall chance of surviving the transition has increased from ninety-five percent, to nearly ninety-nine percent. With that said, you're likely feeling extreme physical discomfort, but those symptoms are to be expected and should not be cause for concern. Make sure you stop by your nearest inn or tavern and eat a hearty meal. Thank you for playing."

The message faded and died.

Robert once again cursed the technician who'd so badly understated the pain involved in the transition. Shaking his head, he gathered his newly inscribed armor from the top of the nightstand and slipped it on for the first time.

The exterior of the Geometrically Threaded armor was sleek and black—vaguely Victorian—while the quilted interior was comfortable and provided ample protection without looking like armor. Clear threads with a rainbow, almost holographic, sheen were woven into the cloth in intricate patterns that dazzled the eye and made it impossible to follow one thread at a time.

Robert studied himself in the mirror, adjusted his outlandish top hat, which somehow tied the look together, then tweaked the short cape trailing down his back. Perfect. He had a busy morning ahead, no doubt, but he couldn't resist pulling up his character sheet and examining his stats in light of his new sigil-inscribed armor:

V.G.O. Character Overview					
Name:	Robert Osmark	Race:	Imperial	Gender:	Male
Level:	20	Class:	Mechanical Artificer	Alignment:	Unassigned
Renown:	110	Carry Capacity:	1240	Undistributed Attribute Points:	0

Health:	2090	Spirit:	560	Stamina:	2090
H-Regen/sec:	105.93	S-Regen/sec:	9.2	S-Regen/sec:	22.99

Attributes:		Offense:		Defense:	
Strength:	189	Base Melee Weapon Damage:	10	Base Armor:	60
Vitality:	189	Base Ranged Weapon Damage:	20	Armor Rating:	211.2
Constitution:	189	Attack Strength (AS):	597	Block Amount:	47.25
Dexterity:	189	Ranged Attack Strength (RAS):	607	Block Chance (%):	119.6
Intelligence:	210	Spell Strength (SS):	315	Evade Chance (%):	39.8
Spirit:	36	Critical Hit Chance:	5%	Fire Resist (%):	21.9
Luck:	5	Critical Hit Damage:	150%	Cold Resist (%):	21.9
				Lightning Resist (%):	21.9
				Shadow Resist (%):	21.9
				Holy Resist (%):	21.9
Current XP:	21,900			Poison Resist (%):	21.9
Next Level:	23,200			Disease Resist (%):	21.9

Amazing. He'd inscribed one Vital Sigil onto his coat, hat, pants, and boots, swapping out all four of his primary Physical Attributes. With his ridiculously high Intelligence Score, he now had stats to rival any player in the game—even the most seasoned warriors weren't likely to have his raw strength. With smug satisfaction, he closed the screen, grabbed the item he'd painstakingly crafted for Sandra, and headed downstairs to eat. Despite his nausea and throbbing headache, Osmark was ravenous.

He needed food, and lots of it, and he needed it right that second.

Sandra was already waiting for him at a table in the center of the common room, which was completely deserted save for the two of them and Murly. Sandra sketched a salute in Robert's direction, then lifted her empty bowl with both hands toward Murly, *more please.*

Osmark flopped down in the rickety wooden chair across from his assistant and leaned back, rubbing at his temple, trying to massage away the dull throb invading his skull. "You look like hell," he said to Sandra.

She raised her middle finger and used its tip to drag down the lower lid of her left eye. The whites were shot through with thick threads of crimson, and the pupil was a tiny black pinprick swimming in the green ocean of her iris. "Yeah, I had a tough night— apparently hangovers are still a thing here. You look great, too, Sleeping Beauty." She paused, hunching forward as she examined his Artificer gear. "Nice duds, though. Sort of old world vibe, but they suit you."

Murly swept in from the kitchen with a platter loaded down with bacon, sausage, fried eggs, and a tureen filled with a creamy porridge sitting next to an open crock of sticky honey. "More coming," the innkeeper said, before bowing and backing away from their table, eyes averted. She'd put the fear of God into that man.

Sandra ignored the innkeeper and immediately grabbed the serving spoon from the porridge, slopping a heaping mound into her empty bowl. "This is the best hangover cure ever," she said as she poured a thick spiral of honey on top of the steaming porridge. "Trust me, you don't want to miss this."

"Why don't you give me a status report while I serve myself," Robert suggested before folding a piece of thick, peppered bacon into his mouth.

Sandra gulped down two spoonfuls of porridge, nodded, and started. "Your boy in Wyrdtide might be the world's smoothest politician, but he's a terrible gamer. Dorak says he hasn't even completed his beginning quests, much less made any progress toward completing the area-specific missions that will help him consolidate his faction once he has his Seal. It's pretty pathetic."

Robert hadn't expected Sizemore to run through his quests like a veteran gamer, but he had expected the senator to at least start playing. Surely the man had a pro gamer on staff—or was he really so unaware the idea simply hadn't occurred to him? Something about that bothered Osmark, but he couldn't put his finger on what. "What *is* he spending his time on?" he asked.

"Pretty much what we expected," Sandra said and gulped down another dripping spoon filled with porridge. "Wheeling and dealing. Including himself, Sizemore has ten of the twenty-five board members firmly in his camp. Peng, Novotny, Hamada, Sokolov, Tang, Lerch, Petrov, Weber, and Gallo. That gives him China, Russia, Czechoslovakia, Japan, Germany, and even Canada."

Robert raised an eyebrow at that. "Canada? Erin Gallo?"

That was much worse than Osmark had expected. He and Erin had worked together a time or two and had remained friendly up until the news about the comet broke. They hadn't spent much time talking since then, but she was here on Osmark's personal invitation. To think she'd turn on him because of Sizemore was both unnerving and irritating.

He'd have to deal with her personally.

"I think Erin was a jab at you," Sandra said as she finished slurping down her porridge. "She doesn't have any real power, and there aren't enough Canadian players to be a threat, honestly. The rest is pretty much what we predicted. I'd hoped Hamada would hold out, but Sizemore must be cooking up a pretty tasty dish if half the board is eating it up."

Osmark devoured another slice of bacon and drank his porridge straight from the bowl. "How many are in the bag for us?"

Sandra fidgeted in her seat, fingers running nervously over her napkin. "We've been busy with quests and keeping an eye on Sizemore," she said after a time. "We weren't focusing on the political stuff."

Robert didn't need to hear the rest of the sentence to know what she meant. He'd kept his people jumping from one assignment to the next, and none of those had included sweet-talking the rest of the Imperial Advisory Board. While Robert and his people had been gathering power in the game, Sizemore had been out schmoozing people who could make a serious difference when he opposed Osmark.

"I know," Robert said, bristling at his failure, "but how many do we have?"

"Other than you? Smythe and Schuler, for certain." Sandra stalled for time by taking a deep drink of the spiced tea in front of her. "And, probably, Carrera."

Three.

The meeting of the board was in just a few hours, and Osmark was outnumbered by Sizemore's people more than two to one. It wasn't the position he'd anticipated being in, and there was nothing he could do to fix the problem while the board members were in transit to Tomestide. He gnawed on a sausage, gulped down a mouthful of tea, and motioned for Sandra to continue. "There's nothing we can do about Sizemore's political edge," he offered. "Not at this point. We'll just have to deal with it at the board meeting. What does Garn say about the Coldskulls' and their lieutenant?"

Sandra's eyes brightened. "Her name is Dural Gont, and she oversees all operations for the Coldskulls in Wyrdtide. Both Garn and Dorak confirm she's been meeting with Sizemore every night. Garn says the assassins have been leaving Wyrdtide in small groups since yesterday morning. It's a safe bet they're headed here—and you know what that means."

That, at least, was a problem he could handle. "Let them come. The more, the merrier. I have quite a reception in store for the Coldskulls. It's going to be something to see."

Osmark ate in silence for a moment, filling his belly while he turned the pieces of his plan over in his mind, carefully examining them for the hundredth time. Finally, he dabbed the corners of his mouth with his napkin and leaned back in his chair. "Tell Garn and Dorak to get back here, now. I want them at the board meeting with me."

A spoonful of porridge stopped midway to Sandra's mouth. "I thought I'd be attending the meeting with you?"

Robert rubbed the scrubby bristles of an incoming beard on his chin and shook his head. "I have something else for you to do. Something more important."

He opened his interface, toggled over to the inventory, and pulled out the engineered weapon he'd spent the previous evening building. It was sleek and black, with an articulated scope, an oversized magazine loaded with heavy shells, and a steam core the size of both his fists put together. He grabbed the barrel and stock and yanked, extending the rifle to its full six-foot length. "This is Icebreaker. She's yours."

He stood and handed the weapon to Sandra. A burst of skepticism dashed across her features, but she accepted the massive weapon, handling it as gently as a newborn. Her skepticism grew as she examined the weapon, her lips turning down into a disappointed frown. "It's beautiful, but it's also a firearm. I don't have the skill to use this."

Robert waved her concerns away with one grease-smeared hand. "You will when you need it. Leave that to me. Now," he said, "here's how we're going to deal with Sizemore …"

THIRTY-FIVE:

Board Meeting

O smark regretted sending Sandra off as soon as the first of the board members arrived at the Saddler's Rest. He was used to attending business meetings, to giving speeches to employees, and to making public statements. But he was far less comfortable when it came to socializing with his so-called peers. He'd pulled himself up from nothing, but many members of the board were born not just with silver spoons in their mouths, but swaddled in the whole damn cutlery drawer.

Elizabeth Schuler, the first of the board members to find her way to the Saddler's Rest, was a perfect case in point. Born into a wealthy industrial family, she'd spent her whole life encased in the nigh-impenetrable armor of privilege. There was nothing she'd ever wanted that her daddy hadn't bought for her, including a seat on V.G.O.'s Imperial Advisory Board.

Robert was surprised to see she'd chosen a blonde-haired Wode as her avatar—he'd assumed most would flock toward the Imperials—but even the barbarian class kit she'd chosen couldn't disguise the faintly dismissive tone that accompanied everything she said to anyone she didn't see as her equal.

Which, basically, was everyone.

Osmark greeted Elizabeth at the door with a mug of mead, which she snatched out of his hand like she hadn't had a drink in days. Her long braids danced on either side of her throat as she gulped down half the mug. "Ah, that hits the spot. Which way to the food?"

He kept his eyebrows from shooting up by sheer force of will. V.G.O. had changed Elizabeth, and he wasn't sure if it was for the better or the worse. "We've set out a buffet across the common room," he replied. "You should be able to find anything you need there."

Elizabeth shed her fur cloak and handed it to Garn, who glanced at it as if the woman had just deposited a dead animal in her hands. Elizabeth didn't wait to see what the security guard did with her cloak; instead, she stormed across the room and began loading up a plate with roasted meats, small loaves of bread, and a towering mound of fingerling potatoes.

Dorak joined Osmark by the door. "I hope they're not all that hungry," he whispered, eyeing the woman, "or we'll be out of food in no time. I'd better go talk to Murly and see if we can get the cook on the case."

Robert watched Elizabeth wolf down food like a wild animal and shook his head. V.G.O. changed people. It either brought out their real selves or allowed them to indulge whatever fantasies they'd kept locked away from polite, proper society. He wondered how long Schuler had been hiding this side of herself, and whether or not she still had her eye on the ball. She was supposed to be one of his allies, but if she'd gone native …

Well, he didn't know if he'd be able to depend on her when push came to shove.

Before Osmark could speak with her, however, more of the board members poured into the common room.

Despite their changes in physical appearance, Osmark found he could still identify them without too much difficultly. Sokolov and Petrov, the Russian contingent—both now short, stocky Dwarves—pumped his hand briefly, then made their way to the buffet, stopping only to snatch tankards of ale from the bar. Kaleka and Lerch came next—wearing the forms of an Accipiter and a Hvitalfar, respectively—and they didn't even bother at pretense. They simply blew right past Osmark's outstretched hand, ignoring him as though he were hired help, beelining toward the Russians.

As uncomfortable as Osmark was by the influx of board members making their way into the Saddler's Rest, Gorn and Dorak were getting the worst of it. They'd been conscripted into cloak check and guide duty, forcing them to leave Robert on his own.

Osmark put a brave face on it, shaking as many hands and clapping as many shoulders as he could. It was an exhausting, boring job, but he needed to be seen. These people needed to understand that he was real, and he was ready to lead them into the future. No matter what Sizemore told them, Robert had to be the very picture of confidence and professionalism.

Anything less was just giving ammo to the senator, and he refused to do that.

"Nice party," a familiar voice whispered in Osmark's ear.

He turned to greet his guest, and his tongue stuck to the roof of his mouth.

Erin Gallo had chosen an Accipiter to represent her, and the effect was stunning. She'd been an attractive woman IRL, with flowing dark hair and startlingly blue eyes, but in V.G.O. she was an intimidating beauty. Her golden skin contrasted with the fiery copper of her braided hair, and her eyes flashed like polished diamonds. She wore little more than a diaphanous drape, which left her wings free to unfurl if need be and very little to the imagination.

"It's nice to see a familiar face," Osmark forced himself to say, balling his hands into fists. "Even if it's not quite the face I remember."

Erin laughed, a throaty chuckle that sent shivers racing down Robert's spine. She eyed him from the bottom of his feet to his eyes and offered a sultry smile. "No sense bringing our flaws in here with us, right? You look well, Robert."

"Looks can be deceiving," he offered coolly, lips pursing into a thin line. Peng Jun arrived in the form of an enormous Risi wearing a polished suit of gleaming, rune-inscribed, brigandine armor. He wore a heavy spiked club on a strap across his back, and a golden-etched crossbow slung over one shoulder.

"… and that's why I told him I'd consider the offer," Erin continued. She paused and shot a look at Peng, realizing Osmark hadn't been listening. "Don't tell me that brute is worthier of your attention than I am?" She laid her delicate fingers on Robert's wrist, and his skin tingled at her touch.

"Not at all," he replied, offering her a lopsided smile. "I'm just concerned about where Peng's friend is."

"If you'd been listening to me, you'd know," she replied with another one of her heart-melting chuckles and a smoldering glance that would've looked more at home on a hungry leopard. "He had some business in Wyrdtide—something he needed to attend to before he could travel to the meeting. That's why he's coming after the rest of us."

Robert snatched a pair of mugs from a serving girl's tray and handed one of them to Erin. "You're friends with the senator, then? I'd heard as much, but I'm a little surprised to find it's true, given our history." He scanned the room as he talked. The other board members had split into groups along the lines Osmark had expected. Sizemore's cronies flocked around Peng Jun like a pack of hungry jackals, dallying in the far corner of the bar.

And Peng himself stared daggers at Osmark even when he spoke to the rest of his party.

Erin turned her back to Peng's group. "Sizemore approached me early on with certain guarantees. A girl would be foolish not to entertain such an opportunity."

Robert's mouth quirked into a sour frown. "It's even more foolish to hitch your wagon to a falling star—and that is all Sizemore is." He paused, drumming his fingers on the glass. "Can I ask what he promised you?"

Erin swirled her glass of mead and stared into its frothy surface. "Peace. Order. Power."

Osmark struggled not to roll his eyes. "What makes you think Sizemore can deliver on his guarantees? He doesn't have any more sway than any other board member. It's not like he can bend the rules to suit himself or his allies."

The Canadian shrugged, and Robert forced himself not to stare. "He's a very convincing man. The kind of man who can make things true just by saying them often and earnestly enough."

Osmark had no reply.

She was right, insofar as Sizemore's power lay firmly in his mouth. If that silver-tongued weasel could convince enough board members to do what he wanted them to do, then maybe he could bring peace to V.G.O. Or, more likely, he'd use his ill-gotten power to crush his enemies and establish himself as God Emperor of this new world.

Before Osmark could respond, Erin leaned forward and kissed him on the cheek, just a peck next to his right ear. "We were friends, Robert. We can be again." Then she leaned back and cast a meaningful glance over Robert's shoulder. "One of your guests needs to steal you away, it appears. You'll know where to find me."

Then she was gone, moving away from Osmark as gracefully as a dove on a gust of spring wind. He felt a pang of some rare emotion in his chest—loneliness, maybe—as she made her way to Peng's table and took a seat among the traitors.

"Helluva thing," a man said. "I guess you never know who you can trust, right?"

Robert turned, and Aleixo Carrera took the mug from his hand and replaced it with a short glass filled with amber liquor. "It's not mezcal—this world doesn't have such a drink—but it's close enough."

Robert found himself clinking glasses with the cartel mastermind and sharing a drink with one of the most dangerous and brutal men in the world. The liquor scorched his tongue and burned his throat like a splash of acid. Osmark forced himself to drink the vile stuff, but he couldn't keep his eyes from watering just a little. "That was certainly something," he said with a forced smile.

"That it is." Carrera chuckled. "This is quite the place you have here." He waved a tan hand around the room. He'd chosen to go with an Imperial—a smart, practical choice. But then, the Colombian drug kingpin was a smart, practical man, much like Osmark in that way.

He turned his back on Peng's table and shrugged at Carrera. "It is what it is. It'll be much more impressive given time."

Carrera's eyes twinkled like dark stars, and a sly grin crawled across his features. "Will he give you time, I wonder?"

Robert's eyes skimmed over the gathered crowd. He'd brought these people here, he'd given them a new world, and he'd promised them kingdoms of their own to rule as they saw fit. A new golden age, so long as they followed a few simple guidelines, which would allow them to work together for the common good. He'd done so much for these people, yet now they were all scheming against him, laying plans to claim it all for themselves. Every conversation he saw, every hushed word and meaningful glance, was another weapon aimed at his heart.

Traitors. Scum.

"Did you come here to threaten me?" Osmark asked flatly, draining the last of the awful liquor from his glass. "Because, I have to be honest, it's starting to lose its impact."

Carrera laughed, a sound like embers popping in a hearth. "Oh, my friend, you mistake me. I don't threaten. I don't make promises. I just take care of things."

Robert smirked at the thug's words. "If that's why you're here, you might as well take your shot now and save us both the trouble of the dance—though I have to warn you, appearances can be deceptive."

Carrera didn't laugh this time.

His dark eyes gleamed like cold steel and his face became an expressionless mask. "I do not like to be mocked, Mr. Osmark, nor do I like to be threatened. We are men of means, you and I. Men of ambition and drive. We are more alike than we are different."

Except I don't murder people to get what I want, he almost said, then realized that was no longer true. Instead, he raised his empty glass in a salute. "I'm sorry, Mr. Carrera. It's been a trying couple of days. Thank you for the drink, and my apologies if I've given offense. That was not my intent."

"And it was not my intent to give you a reason to mistrust me," Carrera said, shaking his head. "I'm not used to this dance, as you call it. May I be blunt?"

Osmark nodded, and Carrera took his arm and led him off into the shadows near the bar.

"These men and women," the drug lord whispered, "they are the real monsters. Their money, their power, their laws and neglect created me. Enabled me to amass my fortune on the backs of others. I am not a good man, understand, but I am also only a symptom. They are the disease.

"If you're afraid of me, Mr. Osmark, then these demons should terrify you. They're not like us—men who work for what we have. Oh no, they come from a long line of monsters who believe the world is theirs to rule as they see fit. They will turn your heaven into a burning hell if you allow it. And they'll enlist men like me to do it, unless you stop them."

"And what should I do? Kill them all like you would?" Osmark shook his head. "I don't believe they're as bad as you seem to think. Are they snakes? Yes. Liars? Undoubtedly. Monsters, as you say?" He shrugged one shoulder. "Probably. But they're here because we need them to keep this place from becoming unlivable. Better a government of thieves, liars, and monsters than no government at all."

Carrera drained his glass and dropped it onto the bar top. "This is true, but what you need are allies, not serpents. Sizemore, the senator, he's turning these people against you."

It was Robert's turn to chuckle, and he raised his hands defensively. "I'm not laughing at you. I'm just laughing at the message. Sizemore's tried to kill me twice now, and I'm sure he's going to make that three times very soon. So this isn't exactly news to me."

Carrera gave a long, slow nod. "That is good. I'd hoped you weren't blind to the schemes swirling all around you. He approached me, you know. Wanted me to be his, how do you say it, enforcer?"

A cold ball of dread tightened around Robert's heart. He didn't need this man gunning for him. Not now, not ever. "And what did you say?"

"I told him I have a lot of experience dealing with traitorous little puppies who think they can take meat from the big dog's mouth." Carrera's eyes shot past Robert to the door.

"Thank you," Osmark said, "for being honest with me."

"I am always an honest man," Carrera replied, running one hand over the pommel of a dagger at his belt. "I always will be. But don't mistake my honesty for weakness or gullibility."

Robert extended his hand to Carrera. "Honesty is all I ask. Shoot straight with me. I'll shoot straight with you. We'd be good allies, you and I."

"Easy, hombre," Carrera said as the front door opened. "Let's not get ahead of ourselves. Besides, we don't want anyone getting the wrong idea about what kind of friends we are."

Peng's table burst into applause, and Robert turned to see Sizemore step through the door. He'd chosen a Dawn Elf, some sort of mage. He wore robes of gold and red that flashed like fire as he moved. His every motion attracted attention, and he shook hands and kissed cheeks in rapid succession as he worked the crowd like a seasoned pro on a reelection campaign.

Osmark moved in Sizemore's direction, his jaw clenched, his eyes narrowed to venomous slits. He wanted to reach across the room and choke the life from Sizemore. He wanted to kill the man and stomp on his body until there was nothing left but a greasy smear to be cleaned up by the waitstaff. He wanted Sizemore dead, and he wanted to do the deed himself.

But, for the moment, he had to content himself with the next best thing.

As he approached the senator, Sizemore extended a hand covered with jeweled rings. The senator's thin lips quirked into an evil smile and he opened his mouth to greet Robert.

But Osmark didn't accept Sizemore's hand, and he didn't wait to be greeted. Instead, he pushed through the crowd surrounding the devious little prick and lifted a drink from a serving maid's platter. Then he climbed onto the bar top and raised his glass toward the roof. "Greetings, fellow members of the Imperial Advisory Board. It is my pleasure to welcome you to Tomestide, and to a new future."

A few others raised their glasses in return and thumped tables with fists.

Osmark took note of those who cheered and those who sneered and vowed to even accounts before the day was over. He took a drink from his mug, steeling his resolve. "And now that our tardy friend has managed to find his way to our meeting, I believe we can begin with the business at hand." He smiled with more cheer and confidence than he felt, daring Sizemore to do anything.

For a long, tense moment, the two men watched each other warily, like a mongoose and a cobra trapped in a cage together. Finally, Sizemore raised his glass and drank deeply from the flute. Osmark smiled over the rim of his mug, hiding his grinding teeth from the rest of the crowd.

THIRTY-SIX:

Threasts and Promises

O smark finished his drink and tossed the mug aside, his stomach a knotted fist of anxiety as he prepared to speak; he knew the speech he was about to give would draw a line in the sand for better or worse. On one side would be Robert and his allies, and on the other Sizemore's cronies. Given his lack of political support, Osmark had no doubt his friends would be sorely outnumbered by his enemies. And that was assuming any of his friends were even brave enough to stick their necks out in the first place.

He might just be sticking his head through a noose.

Every eye in the house locked on Osmark, and the crowd grew still while he paced the length of the bar with his hands clasped behind his back. Clad in his Artificer's armor, Robert knew he cut an imposing figure. He took a few moments to collect his thoughts, a brief span of time that felt like an eternity. He'd written and memorized his speech last night, but it no longer seemed adequate for the task. Osmark took a deep breath and trusted the words would come to him. Then

411

he put on a brave face and turned to the Imperial Advisory Board.

"Not so long ago, most of you thought I was crazy. Or, at least, not well acquainted with reality." He took the sting from his words with a wide, soothing smile that never quite reached his eyes. "Some of you doubted Astraea would hit—you trusted everyone but me. Furthermore, many of you believed my attempt to turn a fantasy game into a digital haven was foolhardy at best, and dangerous at worst. And it was an ambitious project, I'll admit."

Osmark glanced at the smug faces of Sokolov and the rest of the Russian contingent. His fingers closed into fists when he remembered their arrogant disregard for his initial overtures.

"My friends in the back there thought all of our money would be better spent arming missiles to try and blast the asteroid from the sky before it could reach us. Even some of my closest allies"—and here he offered a charming crocodile smile to Erin Gallo—"were reluctant to accept the reality. Up to the very last minute, many of you sitting in this room diverted precious resources from this project to prepare ill-fated asteroid bunkers or science fiction laser shields."

Osmark *tisked* in disapproval, eyeing each of the guilty members in turn, then gave a weak, small smile. *No hard feelings.* He'd offered them digital salvation, but even he had to admit it had sounded like a science fiction novel. Still, he wanted his remarks to remind them that he remembered *everything*.

"And yet, here we all are. The last leaders of an old world gathered together before its destruction in this sanctuary I built over the last ten years." Robert paced back and forth for a moment before continuing. "But what kind of leaders are we?"

"Some of you are here because you're afraid," he offered, voice devoid of judgement. "Afraid to lose your wealth. Afraid of losing your social status. Afraid of dying." Robert accepted Murly's offer of a full mug of mead. He drank deeply from the honeyed brew before continuing.

"What lies at the root of all these terrors that haunt you? A fear of change. But, despite this dread of the unknown, you came anyway. You put your money and your influence and your lives in my hands. You trusted me and my people to shepherd you from the shadow of the destroyer into the valley of peace."

Osmark sought out the faces of the uncommitted in the crowd. He locked eyes with Hank Carter, an American steel magnate who'd once been Robert's bitter rival; he'd come around in the end to become one of the project's most generous donors and most committed advocates. He smiled at Abubakar Mubarak, an Egyptian arms dealer who'd joined the project without protest, but who'd never once committed to an alliance with Osmark. Robert needed people like them to stand against Sizemore, and he wanted to remind them that he was the one who'd protected them and sheltered them when literally no one else *could*.

He hoped they would remember that with some gratitude.

"There's a second kind of leader in this room. The kind who isn't running *from* anything." Robert raised a glass to his kindred spirits. "You're running *to* a new future. You came here not because you feared what would happen to the old world, but because you hoped could make this new one even *better*."

Carrera led a round of applause that a scattered handful of others joined with enthusiasm. A few of the neutrals were even caught up in the excitement, and Osmark was pleased to see Chiara Bolinger from Switzerland and Steven Williams from the UK cheering him on. It wasn't much, but every board member who tilted in his favor would make things easier later.

"I salute both kinds of courage. This new world needs leaders who remember the old ways and cherish them just as much as it needs visionaries who can carry us into a new age." Robert raised his mug high overhead to a chorus of raucous cheers. "Together, and only together, we will make this new world a home we can be proud of."

A polite round of applause followed his statement, and even Sizemore and his cronies couldn't help but agree with the sentiment.

Next, Osmark met the eyes of his enemies, one by one. Peng Jun stared back at him with the flat and deadly gaze of a shark. Sokolov smirked—the kind of a grin that precedes a shot of whiskey as often as it does a fist in the face. The other men and women gathered around them watched from the shadows like pit vipers coiling to strike.

And Sizemore beamed back like the cat who'd eaten the canary: fat, full, and unconcerned.

But Osmark wasn't finished with his message. No, not even close. He poured mead down his throat and braced himself for the stinging words he had for anyone who wanted to oppose him. "I want you all to know that there is also a third kind of leader among us tonight. Neither a refugee nor a builder. This third kind is as insidious and dangerous as cancer. And that's what this leader is—a malignant growth with nothing of value to offer the world."

Robert's eyes never left Sizemore as he let the cold, bitter words pour over his lips. "This third kind will tell you everyone else is a fool. That the refugees who came here seeking shelter don't have the strength to save themselves. That the visionaries who see a new way forward will destroy everything with their altruism and compassion.

"This third kind schemes against the rest of us, spreading lies and corruption—even going so far as to send assassins after you when your back is turned. They mistake tyranny for strength and freedom for weakness. They seek not to work *with* us, but to steal *from* us. They don't want partnership, they don't deserve leadership, and they don't honor allies. They seek only power, and they want only slaves—and believe me when I say this leader will make you into a slave."

As Osmark spoke, Sizemore's cheeks reddened, and his eyes narrowed to sparking slits. The crowd shifted nervously, glancing between Robert and Sizemore. Osmark tried to read them—to gauge their response and receptiveness to his message—but there were too many conflicting emotions and too much confusion in the air. There was nothing left to do but roll the dice and hope for the best.

"Let me end my little commencement speech with this thought: If you've thrown in your lot with this third kind, with the men and women who carry shackles behind their backs while they smile to your faces, ask yourself this simple question. If they're willing to betray *me*, what makes you think you're safe from their ambition?"

And, with that, Robert stepped off the bar and took a massive chest from Garn, who'd slipped from the shadows behind the bar. Osmark dropped the sealed container on top of the table at the front of the room and gestured at it with a stage magician's flourish. "And now I'm done preaching. It's time to get down to the real reason you're all here.

"Inside this chest are your individual dossiers, each of which includes the following: a single-use port-scroll to your restricted location, details about the dungeon in that restricted area, and the passphrases for the mercenary teams on location, waiting to assist you once you arrive. You can do whatever you want with this information, but it's critical that you understand that anyone who possesses it can, and most likely will, try to beat you to your restricted area and claim its rewards for themselves."

Robert placed his hand on top of the rune-encrusted chest, and a blue light flared from its enchanted lock. He wiggled the fingers of his other hand in the air, and a soulbound key appeared in his grasp. He inserted it in the lock, and the lid of the chest popped open to reveal twenty-four black vellum folders.

"Carter, Schuler, Williams," he said, pulling folders at random and reading each name as it came from the chest. "Come on down."

An excited buzz passed through the crowd as the first members of the board rose to claim their prizes. The buzz grew louder as Osmark called more names; he passed out the black vellum sheaves with a smile and a handshake to each member of the board. There were more sneers, and very few smiles. The odds were shifting in the wrong direction, and Robert wondered how much of that had to do with his speech and how much with Sizemore's toadies working the crowd, even now.

Finally, Sizemore stood before Osmark. Everyone else had claimed their folders, returned to their seats, and buried their noses in the critical information. The senator extended his hand and raised one eyebrow expectantly.

"Hmm, sorry, Travis, I don't see one for you in the chest. I guess you're on the naughty list," Robert said with a venomous grin.

"Maybe if you spent more time focusing on your work and less time making pointless and juvenile gibes, you wouldn't be having so many problems, Robert," Sizemore responded without emotion. "Now hand it over."

Osmark stuck his hand into the chest and retrieved the last folder. He tapped its edge against his chin and eyeballed Sizemore for a long moment. "It doesn't have to be this way, Senator."

Sizemore sighed, as if already bored with the whole conversation. "You're a very skilled technician, no one denies that, and the work you've done here is truly amazing. But you're not a leader—not in the real sense of the word. Heading a business isn't the same

417

thing as heading a nation, and my allies simply don't have faith in your ability to see us through the tumultuous days ahead." He shrugged, a cocky grin on his lips. "They want someone with more experience to lead the way. Frankly, it's hard to blame them. Now, my folder."

Osmark extended the dossier.

Sizemore pinched it between the knuckles of his thumb and index finger, but Osmark didn't release it from his grip. "They did have faith. Until a certain snake started hissing in their ears. You can turn this around, Travis. You *want* to turn this around. Before it's too late."

The senator tugged on the folder again, but Osmark held fast to the black vellum; with Osmark's incredible Strength Score, the senator would never win this round of tug-of-war.

Sizemore's eyes flashed with hatred, his lips pulling back in a snarl. "We're far too far along to turn anything around. My plans are in motion, but how they end is at least partially up to you, Robert. Hand over the reins of power to me, take a back seat, and you'll still have a chair at the table. It's time for the adults to run things, but you can still save yourself. We can be allies, even if we'll never be friends."

Those words tumbled through Robert's mind like embers dancing across gasoline-soaked timbers. They ignited the fires of his rage and sealed both men's fates. Osmark said nothing and released the folder so suddenly Sizemore took a stumbling step back.

Osmark grinned, Sizemore glared, and they parted ways like old West gunslingers heading to opposite ends of a dusty street for a showdown.

After everyone had a few minutes to review the contents of their folders, Robert banged his fist against the top of the bar to get their attention. "The folders in your hands are the keys to a new future, but they're also a hell of a to-do list. As you all know, our time is running short, and if we want to succeed in our goals, you'll need to move quickly.

"For now, things are relatively calm. Our current residents are trying to get their bearings, but in a little over a week, that's all going to change. We'll be hit with a flood of new citizens, and most of them will be frightened, confused, and angry. Some of them will also be ambitious. To avoid chaos, we need to establish a firm government and an orderly system of law. And that all needs to happen before our friend in the sky pays us a visit."

Sokolov raised his voice from the back of the common room, his thick Russian accent almost obscuring the words. "Which city we take?"

Robert responded briskly. "Virtually all cities are available to use as bases for founding a faction. Keep in mind that you must have an Honored reputation with the local governing official before you can plant your flag. To make things a little easier, those officials will recognize the first Faction Seal they see and will offer a quest to its holder. Completing that quest will elevate you to Honored status and allow you to claim the city as your home base."

Tang Zhelan—one of Peng Jun's Chinese allies—stood and raised his hand, then waited patiently to be recognized. Zhelan had chosen a Murk Elf avatar, and Robert was surprised at how well the Overminds had modeled the exotic race's features to resemble the Chinese man's original face without falling into crude caricature. Once again, he was amazed at the game's adaptability and flexibility.

When Robert nodded to Zhelan, the man began speaking immediately in fluent, scarcely accented, English. "What if we fail in any of the quests associated with our membership on the board?"

Osmark shrugged indifferently. "Failing a location-based quest, such as the one to gain control of the city, just means you'll need to move on. The local official will have his quest reset and will offer it to the next person bearing a Faction Seal. Failing your restricted area quest is unlikely, but in the unfortunate event you are killed, you'll simply respawn and get another crack at it.

"Keep in mind that even restricted areas respawn their monsters, so if you botch your first run, you'll need to come up with a better plan for the second and subsequent attempts to avoid defeat. A few caveats, though. Once you've obtained the Faction Seal at a given location, it is gone and that restricted area will rebalance—it will become even tougher—though it will still be locked to the general public. With that said, most of these quests shouldn't be much of a challenge to anyone with any experience at online games." He paused, glancing around. "I hope you all did your homework."

That earned Robert a few chuckles, and then another flurry of questions from the crowd. He answered them quickly and with comfortable ease. Robert wasn't a politician, but he knew more about V.G.O. than any other single person.

Finally, he saw the sun setting through the windows and knew it was time to wrap up the meeting so the members of the board could be on their way. "All right, I think that's enough questions. You have all the information you need. Please report in as you complete your tasks, and be sure to let my assistant know when you've secured your Faction Seal and are ready to proceed to the next phase.

"I want to thank you all for your willingness to work with me, and for your generous donations of time, energy, money, and influence. I wish you all the best, and look forward to our achievements." With that, Osmark closed the chest with a bang, and the first meeting of the Imperial Advisory Board was over.

THIRTY-SEVEN:

Final Vote

The board members left the Saddler's Rest in an excited, nervous rush. For the first time in many of their lives, they were truly standing on the brink of something new. Something great. Something visionary. Here, there were no families to rely on. No businesses waiting to back up their decisions with money and personnel. Every choice from this point forward would impact the world around them in ways they couldn't understand.

Osmark watched them leave with the combination of pride and regret. No matter what happened once he stepped through those doors, he'd changed the world. Certainly, Sizemore and the rest of the board had shaped his decisions, but, in the end, Osmark had saved millions and formed a new way. A whole new world. He waited for several seconds after the inn's common room emptied, then turned to address Dorak and Garn.

"Get into position," he said, voice low, "just like we planned. If this goes south, you know what to do."

Garn hesitated for a moment then nodded. "Sir, Mr. Osmark, I just wanted to say—"

Osmark grinned and rested one hand on each of their shoulders. "No goodbyes. Not yet. We're going to win this thing, and when we do, you'll be rewarded for your hard work and loyalty."

The duo shook hands with Robert, then quietly slipped out the inn's rear entrance. They had to move fast, and Robert was pleased to see them doing just that. Once they disappeared from sight, Osmark squared his shoulders, adjusted his armor, straightened his top hat, and headed for the front door, confidence marking his every step. This was his world and he owned it, despite what Sizemore may have thought.

He retrieved his cloak from the peg and carefully draped it over his shoulders before stepping through the doorway and into the last rays of the dying sun. The setting sun cast a dazzling red glare across the town square, blinding Osmark as he left the Saddler's Rest. Before he could raise a hand to shield his eyes, he heard the hissing rasp of blades leaving their scabbards. A handful of horrified gasps rose from the crowd standing in the square, and by the time Robert could see again, he was surrounded by hostile faces.

Zhelan and Peng flanked Sizemore and used their long, spiked clubs to isolate Osmark and corral him into the center of the square. Behind Sizemore—on the far side of the crowd of board members—Sokolov and Petrov used their crossbows to keep anyone from making a break for it. Obviously, the senator wanted an audience for what was about to happen, and he was willing to use violence to make sure the board witnessed the last phase of his nasty little coup. Several of Sizemore's allies had their weapons trained on other board members, adding tension and confusion to the gathering.

Most of the weapons, however, were fixed unwaveringly on Osmark. Weber, Hamada, and Novotny all had spears leveled at his throat, while Berg and Romano had their hands raised, spells prepped and ready to fly with a thought. If Osmark made a move, he'd be skewered and blasted out of his boots in the blink of an eye.

The enemy board members alone would've been a serious threat, but to top things off, they were backed up by a small army of Coldskull assassins. The masked figures appeared from the shadows like murderous wraiths, forming a deadly steel fence surrounding the board members. There had to be close to thirty of the assassins, including one lieutenant with the top half of her face tattooed to resemble a skull and a black, braided ponytail rising from the crown of her head like a scorpion's stinger.

For the moment, all Osmark could do was stand quietly and wait to see what Sizemore had in store for him. After a long pause, Sizemore cleared his throat and addressed Osmark—though he was really addressing the rest of the uncommitted board members. This was all a show, designed to consolidate his power.

Osmark knew that, because he was going to do the same thing shortly. Assuming everything went according to plan, of course.

"Kneel, and hear your sentence," Sizemore declared, his voice magnified by some magic spell or item. His words echoed through the square loud enough to silence the murmuring crowd.

As distasteful as it was, Osmark obliged, dropping to his knees, staring death and hate at the senator the whole time. He needed to let this thing play out so he could be sure who was on his side and who wasn't.

On cue, Tang Zhelan stepped away from Sizemore and took a position behind Osmark, jabbing something sharp and deadly into the nape of his neck, just above his cloak. Tang was a Rogue, which made him perfectly suited for being a backstabbing bastard. If Osmark tried anything, that knife would punch through his spine right at the base of his skull. He'd be dead before he knew what had happened.

Sizemore smirked down at Osmark and crossed his arms over his chest, his red robes rustling as he moved. "I gave you a chance," he said. "All you had to do was step away from the throne. Put down the scepter and let someone more qualified and more mature lead these people into a glorious new age."

Robert's muscles ached for action, but the weight of the blade against his neck kept him frozen in place. He couldn't do anything until the time was right.

"But not you. Not the wonder boy of Silicon Valley. You couldn't swallow your pride, and now look at where you are." Sizemore shook his head and tutted at Osmark. "You say you want a better future for us all, but that isn't what you've offered us. You took our money. You took our favors. You took our lives, and you gave us a sneak peek at the glories of your new world. A—what do you software developers call it?— an early access beta test?"

Osmark wanted to tell Sizemore he'd given him as much as he could, but he bit his tongue.

V.G.O. had been deep into development when the asteroid appeared, and there was no way to subvert the AIs and other systems without jeopardizing the rest of the code. Osmark and the rest of the development staff had done everything possible to give the members of the Imperial Advisory Board a head start, but they'd been hamstrung by the nature of the world they were constructing. There were a dozen examples Robert could have given, but he knew the senator wouldn't care.

Sizemore was grandstanding, whipping his followers into a frenzy so they wouldn't think twice when he gave the order to kill.

"That's. Not. Good. Enough," Sizemore continued, and a ragged cheer rose from the majority of the gathered board members. "You were kind enough to open the door for us, but this isn't your world. It's ours. Bought and paid for with our resources. The very heart of this world, the server farm we're all living in, is located deep within the salt mines *I* procured for you. If anything, this world is *mine*."

Osmark let his shoulders slump in false defeat. "You don't understand, you moron. V.G.O. isn't hardware. It's not just lines of code. It's alive. The Overminds that underlie everything can't be controlled or altered. I wouldn't turn the reins over to you even *if* I had the power, but I don't. No one does. That's not how any of this works, you brain-dead, tech-illiterate neophyte."

Sizemore seethed at Osmark's harsh words. His hands balled into tight fists and he shook his head as if disappointed by an unruly child. "Call me all the names you want, but don't expect any of us to believe your lies. Maybe I'm not a programmer, but no one here is gullible enough to believe that Robert Osmark—the visionary who conceived and created V.G.O. through sheer force of will and iron determination—doesn't know how to change the rules of his world.

"Now, I'm going to give you another chance to do the right thing. Open the gates of V.G.O. for all the members of the board. Give us your private access codes so we can set up our own kingdoms and rule them the way we want. There's no need for a unified empire. There's no reason we can't all be gods in our own territories."

Osmark stared up at Sizemore, feigning open despair. He needed these mindless dolts to think he'd lost. "I already told you, I can't."

"Very well," Sizemore said, jabbing a finger at Osmark's face. "You're unfit for the office of emperor. You're unfit to even run a faction. But you do have your uses, and I'm unwilling to let even a flawed tool go to waste in these desperate times.

"Turn over your Faction Seal, now. You'll serve as my advisor until we've all established our rightful kingdoms here in V.G.O." Sizemore withdrew his hand and steepled his fingers. "Then, when I'm satisfied with your work, you'll be released. You can live out your days here, in Tomestide. Perhaps you can even run this inn behind you. I think that, at least, suits your leadership capabilities." The cutting remark drew a chuckle from Sizemore's allies.

Osmark didn't care, though. He'd even the scorecard soon enough. Just one more thing to do.

"Let's put it to a vote, Sizemore," he said. "All or nothing. The board can decide which of us should lead, and the other will be banished." Robert glared at Sizemore, daring the man to oppose the measure. If the senator denied Osmark's suggestion, it would prove beyond any doubt that Sizemore didn't have the board's support.

Sizemore smiled as if he'd been waiting for Osmark to walk into a particularly malicious trap. "Yes, let's do that." He leaned in close. "You might be a better gamer, but I know how to win a vote." The senator turned, his robes fluttering out around him, and raised his hands like a king addressing his subjects. "All in favor of my assuming the duties of emperor until we can establish our individual kingdoms?"

For a long, tense moment silence hung in the air, pregnant with possibility.

Then, the majority of the board raised their hands and responded with a resounding "Aye!"

Robert took note of each and every person who had raised a hand to support the traitor. He was surprised to see the Indian and Saudi alliance shift to Sizemore, but he supposed he shouldn't have been. As Sizemore admitted, he knew how to get votes. Leave it to him to turn some of the West's most bitter enemies to his cause.

Osmark's eyes drifted toward Erin Gallo, who had her hand raised. A shame, that. When their eyes met, however, her head shifted slightly from side to side, a careful negation that gave him some small hope she might rally to his side if she had the opportunity.

Still, though, that left thirteen board members plus Sizemore that had turned against Robert.

"And those opposed?" Osmark called out, his voice clear and calm despite the seething knot of tension surrounding his heart.

"Nay," Carrera said, stepping forward with his thumbs hooked into his broad leather belt. He stared at Sizemore and spat into the dust.

"Nay," Alice Smythe, Elizabeth Schuler, and Chiara Bolinger said at once, all stepping forward in a remarkable display of courage.

Robert's eyes swept across the crowd, stopping briefly on each of his allies as he made a mental note of who stood with him, who was against him, and who remained neutral. He glanced one last time at Erin and mentally moved her name into the column with his allies. He hoped it wasn't a choice he was going to regret in the days to come.

If there *were* days to come.

Sizemore turned back to Robert and showed him a devilish grin. "You see? While you scurried through holes in the ground in search of personal power, I've been talking. Just talking. And look where we are." He spread his hands wide. "Last chance, Osmark. Hand over your Faction Seal and serve me. Or"—he paused, a slow grim spreading across his face like cancer—"or my allies will cripple you, I'll rip the seal from your broken body, and you'll spend the rest of your days sequestered beneath Ravenshall."

Osmark lowered his head, staring at the virtual dust beneath his virtual knees. How had his plans to unite the world's last leaders into a new utopian empire become such a squabbling viper's nest?

"You know what, Sizemore?" he said as he lifted his head to meet the senator's cold stare with a fiery glare. "Why don't you take your best shot?"

THIRTY-EIGHT:

Showdown

Osmark stared past Sizemore's head at the shaded window on the second floor of the building across the town square. Sandra peeled the curtain away, revealing the very long barrel of the very large gun he'd crafted the night before. The instant he made eye contact with Sandra, he activated the Micromanage skill, slipping part of his mind—his essence and will—into her head. Light flashed like lightning from the darkened window, obscuring Sandra's face as thunder rolled across the square.

The air rippled as a heavy bullet narrowly careened past Robert's head, burying itself in Tang Zhelan's neck. Blood, hot and sticky, splashed across his cheek, streaking his new armor with gore. That, more than anything else, bothered Osmark. A PM dinged in his head as he wiped the speckles of blood from his skin:

Personal Message:

Tang is down. Moving out before Sizemore's thugs come hunting for me.

—Sandra

Osmark dismissed the message with a blink, then—in the shocked silence that followed Sandra's shot—Osmark made his move. He leaped to his feet, putting more of his dirty tricks to use, and he didn't even feel a glimmer of remorse. After all, this was Sizemore's fault. He'd killed Horan, undermined Robert's authority, and forced this confrontation from the get-go. What happened now was on his head.

Osmark stomped hard with his left heel, activating the caltrop dispenser he'd attached to the mounting bracket concealed by his britches. Four gray grenades bounced free and burst across the cobblestones of the square. Board members shouted in shock, eyes wide, arms flailing in panic as smoke and hooked spikes erupted under their feet, biting into their HP and holding them in place.

The repeater mounted in the bracket attached to Robert's right arm sprang free with a *twang* and landed in Osmark's outstretched hand at his mental command. Before anyone could react, Robert cranked up the buzzsaw beneath the repeater's barrel and grabbed the stabilizing grip. He twisted to his right and dropped to one knee, lashing out with the screaming blade.

Petrov screamed in sheer agony as Robert buried the roaring buzzsaw in his abdomen. Osmark pushed in, putting his full weight behind the attack, then followed through by reversing course and whipping the saw to the left. The howling blade ground through the Russian's guts and exploded from beneath his ribs in a shower of very satisfying gore. That would wipe the smirk off his condescending face.

Petrov screamed one final time, hands groping at his ruined stomach before he toppled, his eyes glassy with death. His body lay in the street for a moment, before simply vanishing in a burst of digital sparks. Robert pointed the bloody weapon at Sizemore and shouted, "You're next!"

Unfortunately, Osmark wasn't the only one who'd come to the meeting prepared. Sizemore and his allies had recovered from their initial bout of surprise, and already they were on the move. A small contingent of bodyguards—Lerch, Sokolov, Chukwu, and Berg—formed a fence around Sizemore, who hurriedly barked commands to organize his bewildered forces. The senator's retreat was slowed by the caltrops, but it wasn't stopped. Given time, Robert knew the snake would slither free of his trap and disappear into the wind.

He couldn't let that happen.

Four Accipiter threw themselves into the sky, wings beating at the air, kicking up great swirls of wind as they flew out of sight, avoiding the caltrops altogether. Osmark wasn't sure if they were preparing a counterattack, or if they'd simply gotten out while they still could. A quick head count told him all of those who'd taken flight were Sizemore's allies, which Robert assumed was bad news for his side. But he couldn't worry about that now.

Osmark lifted his left hand high above his head and a flare of crimson light burst into the cloud-strewn sky—a signal for Garn and Dorak to commence their grisly work. In response, shutters on the east and west sides of the square burst open as Robert's employees activated the first of the devices Rozak had installed the night before. High-pitched whirring noises erupted from both buildings as powerful engineered automatons booted up, slowly coming alive.

I hope you've got those calibrated right, Rozak, Osmark thought.

And then his thoughts were consumed by the need to defend himself. The need to *survive* long enough for the automatons to get moving. Peng brandished his enormous spiked club and advanced toward Osmark with Hamada closing in on the left and Weber closing in on the right. Novotny advanced behind the trio, her voice raised in a triumphant hymn, which Robert recognized as a variant of Karzic's Stream of Life spell.

Amber light flowed from her, surrounding the group in powerful magic that would heal all but the most grievous of wounds. Classic MMO strategy. That would make things a bit more complicated, but only a bit.

Osmark drew a bead on Peng.

Slowed by the caltrops, the big man would never reach Robert in time to avoid the shot. A predatory grin spread across Osmark's face as he prepared to blast the Risi's head from his armored shoulders. And if ever there was a man who had such a fate coming, it was Peng.

Suddenly, Hamada sprang across an impossible distance, reaching Robert faster than should've been possible. He realized too late that she was hovering on a magical field, her soles a few inches off the ground, well above the caltrops that had slowed everyone else. Hamada's spear left a comet-tail of fire in its wake as she drove it forward, right into Osmark's leg. Caught off guard by the woman's supernatural leap and speed, Robert was easy prey for the attack.

The blade plunged through his armor and deep into the muscle below with a white-hot flash of agony. Then—before Osmark could even think—Hamada barked a word of magical power; the blade's tip sprouted ripping barbs of fire a split second before Hamada yanked the spear free.

Critical Hit! You suffer 75 points of penetration damage and an additional 25 points of fire damage!

Hamada threw back her head and crowed in premature victory—certain the terrible wound would push Osmark to the brink of respawn. How wrong she was. The wound was ugly and shockingly painful, true, but far from life-threatening. Even one day before, her attack might've killed him, but with his new Vital Sigils in place his Vitality Score was at 189, giving him an incredible 2,090 hit points. Her attack was a drop in the bucket next to that.

Hamada's levitation spell ended a heartbeat later, and she landed hard on the caltrops. Panic blossomed on her face like a poisonous flower opening its leaves when she realized there was no way to retreat and Robert was virtually unscathed.

Osmark leveled his repeater and fired a burst into the hollow of Hamada's shoulder, just where her neck met her body. Before she could scream, the woman's elfin neck transformed into a wet mess of bone chips and shredded meat. *Critical Hit.* Her corpse vanished in a Technicolor burst before it could hit the ground, leaving the rest of her assault squad staring in disbelief at Osmark's smoking repeater.

"You had a chance to do the right thing," Osmark offered with a bloodthirsty sneer, "but you trusted a man who'd sell his own mother for a quick buck. Having second thoughts yet?"

Weber roared, overcome with a berserk fury that gave him the strength to ignore the movement debuff. He charged Robert with his dwarven battle-axe reared back and ready to strike. Lost in bloodrage and overcome with a bone deep lust for violence, the German in a Wode's body threw himself forward with no concern for his own safety. The move cost the man a chunk of his rib cage and a quarter of his HP, but it also brought him in range to put his axe to good use.

The berserker's first attack sliced through the air with devastating force, missing Osmark by mere inches, but Weber spun into the momentum and took a step forward before Robert could retreat. The axe's broad head struck Osmark on the shoulder, and only his sigil-enhanced Dexterity saved him from losing his head. Even still, Robert suffered another fifty points of Health damage and had to backpedal toward the inn to avoid the whirling Wode tornado of doom.

But Weber's relentless assault worked in Robert's favor because it prevented any of Sizemore's other allies from getting anywhere near the twirling maniac. While the berserk rage lasted, Weber created a ten-foot-wide sphere of pain that no one seemed willing to enter, no matter how much Sizemore screamed for someone to do something.

While that protected Osmark, it also kept him from pursuing the senator. Robert watched in helpless rage as Sizemore and his wall of bodyguards retreated toward one of Tomestide's side streets. If he didn't make his move soon, the sniveling shit would escape, and Robert would have to spend an enormous amount of time and effort tracking him down before he could regroup and regather his forces.

To add to Robert's problems, the Coldskulls were pushing forward, entering the fray with military efficiency. They spread through the crowd, then reappeared as a cordon of drawn swords at the edges of Osmark's caltrops.

Robert was suddenly hemmed in by a small army of trained killers, all wielding poisoned blades. Even with his boosted physical abilities, Osmark had no illusions about his ability to stand up to an expert poisoner, especially not thirty of them. The venom might not kill him—it might only paralyze him, or blind him, or otherwise cripple him—but if that happened, he'd be captured long before he could recover.

Robert scanned the crowd, looking for some hole in the lines, but found nothing. The Coldskulls were traitorous rats badly in need of extermination, but they were competent. No denying that. The tattoo-faced lieutenant shuffled forward; she paused, a smug grin on her thin lips, and raised her black-edged cutlass to the sky. In an instant, black-shrouded crossbowmen materialized on the rooftops surrounding the square, their weapons raised and trained on his heart.

He had nowhere to run, nowhere to hide.

The bodies of his enemies might catch a few of the crossbow bolts, but many more of the poisoned missiles would have a clean shot.

The cutlass fell, and Osmark tensed against the pain he knew was coming—

Fire and thunder erupted from the windows on the east and west sides of the square as the automatons finally roared into action. A hail of grapeshot and explosive rounds raked across the rooftops. Wood and stone burst apart as the powerful barrage reduced most of the roofs to fountains of splinters and shards. Suddenly, Osmark was very glad he'd had the town guards evacuate the buildings the night before. He had no problem killing, but murdering innocent NPC civilians was more than a little distasteful.

The crossbow men screamed as the automatons went on the warpath, their cannons and repeaters blazing away with steam-powered speed and engineered accuracy. A seemingly endless stream of death rained down into the assassins, ripping apart bodies with contemptuous ease. The Coldskull crossbowmen fell, their corpses tumbling through the ruined roofs, into abandoned homes, or onto the cobblestone streets below.

In a split second, the tides of battle had turned. Robert glared at the leader of the Coldskulls and leveled his repeater at her face.

"Surrender, and I'll make it quick," Robert promised.

The lieutenant sneered at his offer, and a flicker of worry caught fire in Osmark's belly.

He'd just blown half her forces straight to hell, so why was she so confident?

What had he missed?

THIRTY-NINE

Firestorm

Fire poured from the sky and smashed into Osmark like a Mack truck, blinding him and simultaneously knocking him flat on his back. An endless scream clawed at his ears as the flames chewed on his flesh, and it wasn't until Robert's throat began to ache that he realized *he* was the one screaming. The shocking assault had stripped away a quarter of his Health in a single burst and sent an explosion of combat notifications scrolling past his eyes.

Debuffs Added

Stunned: Movement reduced by 75%; duration, 10 seconds

Burning: You are on fire! You suffer 50 Health damage per second; duration, 10 seconds

Dazzled: Your vision is severely impaired! Your line of sight is limited to 20 feet, and you suffer a 90% penalty to any vision-related abilities (including missile weapons); duration, 10 seconds

---

Smoke Inhalation: Your lungs are full of smoke, causing 200 points of Stamina damage per second; duration, 10 seconds

---

So, that's what the Accipiter were up to, Osmark thought—his mind filled with a hazy mist—followed quickly by, *Pull it together or you're a dead man.*

Even without the Coldskulls, Robert was gravely outnumbered. The caltrops slowed his enemies and kept them from all charging at once, but his blurry vision showed him they were closing in. Not including Sizemore's bodyguards, which Robert could no longer see, that left at least nine board members ready and willing to put the boots to him while he was burning on the ground.

Sandra was still out there somewhere, as were Garn and Dorak, but Robert had given them explicit orders. They weren't to enter the fray, no matter what else happened. If Sizemore's side captured them, that would give the senator leverage he could use against Osmark. Better for all of them to flee and fight another day than be taken prisoner.

Someone kicked him in the ribs with the toe of a heavy boot, but Robert couldn't see well enough to tell who was behind the attack. Someone else stuck a dagger into his lower back—a kidney shot—and then the whole mob was suddenly in on the beatdown. Osmark's caltrops were still in action, but once his enemies reached him, the movement penalties didn't mean much. They could stand still and whale on Robert like he was a piñata and they were chubby kids who hadn't had their sugar fix in a week.

441

He flipped to his belly and fought to get to his feet, but a heavy club smashed across his shoulders and flattened him to the cobblestones once more. Thick spikes punched through his padded armor and tore into the meat of his back; Robert swore vengeance on Peng just as soon as he could get up. But as his HP plummeted, the mob only grew angrier and even more violent, their blows coming faster and harder. If he didn't think of something quickly, his enemies would beat him into a puddle of burning goo.

Motionless, Osmark thought, and a bloody smile peeled his cracked and bruised lips back from his teeth. *They're all motionless.*

With a howl of maniacal laughter, he unleashed the Flame Spitter. Its rotors whirled to life, and it took to the sky with a throaty *whoosh*. Its underslung gun chattered like a five-alarm blaze in a fireworks factory, drowning out Osmark's barking laughter.

Too late, the gathered board members realized the danger they were in and tried to flee from Osmark's deadly drone. But they were slowed to a crawl by the field of caltrops they were standing in, and the Flame Spitter showed no mercy. The first salvo cut half of the survivors down like a burning scythe through a field of drought-parched wheat. Bodies burst into flame, fell around Osmark, and then evaporated into sprays of digital blood.

"I gave you a chance," Osmark snarled, finally dragging himself upright. "I saved your lives," he spat, blood running down his chin and dribbling onto his armor.

Weber lunged at Robert, foaming at the mouth as his berserker fury kicked into gear again, but Osmark was having none of it. The repeater barked, and the Wode's head whipped back, a gaping hole in his forehead. His legs spun out in front of him, and his powerful body crashed to the ground, limbs splayed out akimbo.

Peng, realizing the futility of running, raised his weapon and faced Osmark, slowly spinning his spiked club as he glared at Robert with muddy eyes. "You can't beat him," Peng snarled in heavily accented English. "You may have created this game, but we are all playing his."

Osmark shook his head. The Flame Spitter roared again, mowing down the remaining board members save for Peng. The Accipiter had made the fatal mistake of landing near Osmark to take out their misguided rage on his fallen body and now were trapped by the caltrops. They fell in sprays of bone and feathers, their exotic wings shredded by burning shells.

Osmark let out a long, slow sigh. "I know this isn't permanent, Peng, but it's still going to hurt like a bitch. I hope you remember it after you respawn."

The spiked club swung at Osmark's head, but his finger mashed down the trigger in a blink. The repeater belched flame and lead as he emptied the magazine into Peng's chest at point-blank range. The brigandine armor blew apart, its engraved plates flying in every direction as Peng's body burst at the seams.

With no enemies left in its area of effect, the Flame Spitter fell from the sky. Robert caught it and tucked it away safely in his inventory while he scanned the square for Sizemore. *Where are you?* he seethed, searching for the man who'd tried to destroy his hard work.

But the senator was nowhere to be seen.

Osmark realized the automatons had gone silent, as well. He looked across the battlefield and saw plumes of smoke rising from the open windows, and Coldskull assassins dropping back to street level with their poisoned blades drawn. Damn, they'd taken out his drones. He counted ten headed his way and started reloading the repeater. "I guess we're doing this," he said, then wiped the blood from his brow with a dirt-caked hand.

"I hope you got some more tricks, *jefe,* because those are some bad, bad people with your name carved into their knives."

Osmark raised an eyebrow and turned to his right, where Carrera leaned casually, almost lazily, on a gleaming greatsword. "What?" the drug lord asked with a shrug. "You thought I'd cut and run? No." He shook his head, a disgusted sneer sprinting across his face. "I've been hacking some of Sizemore's men into bite-sized chunks."

Robert smiled. "Never figured you'd be the last one on my side, Carrera. Honestly, I thought you'd be the real source of my problems, not Sizemore."

He shrugged again and sniffed dismissively. "What can I say, I like your style. Your flair." Carrera spat on the blood-slicked street, then waved a hand at the carnage. "Besides, the senator, he always rubbed me the wrong way. He thought he was better than me, you know? Better than everyone."

"Well," Osmark muttered, glancing around, "I'd say he got the better of us this time, at least. I don't see him anywhere, just his thugs. Bastard must've had a dozen escape plans. Now I'll have to track him down before he stabs me in the back again."

"He didn't get far," Carrera said, hooking a thumb toward the main street beyond the gathering Coldskulls. "Can't be more than a few blocks away. If you hurry..." He cocked an eyebrow, leaving the rest unspoken. Apparently, Carrera was on his side for the time being, but his gesture said this was a score Osmark needed to settle on his own.

Osmark couldn't have agreed more.

He nodded and turned toward the approaching Coldskull Lieutenant, leveling his repeater at her face. He was actually surprised she'd managed to escape the automaton assault. If she survived what came next—which he doubted very much—he might even offer her a job. "Stand down, now," he said. "Get out of my way, and I'll show you mercy."

The Coldskull laughed, and it shook her head so hard her black ponytail whipped from side to side. "You didn't see the firebombs coming. What makes you think there isn't another trap waiting to spring on you? I'll make you an offer. Surrender and I won't hurt you." She twirled her cutlass through the air with a flourish. "Much."

Robert shrugged. "I don't have time for this. Last chance."

The lieutenant snarled, "Get him!"

Osmark whistled, and the building on the north side of the square exploded. Shattered beams and chunks of masonry the size of bowling balls pelted the Coldskulls from behind as bits of wood sliced into unprotected skin. Caught off guard, the assassins ducked and scattered, all discipline lost as the surprise attack tore into their ranks.

Rozak emerged from the decimated building, his pipe protruding from the corner of his mouth, his stocky body surrounded by a powerful steampunk frame nearly identical to the Iron Goliath Osmark had faced in the Brand-Forged Artifactory. A powerful buzzsaw roared on his left arm, and the spinning rotary cannon screamed to life on his right.

"Who broke my machines?" he bellowed, his voice rumbling out of the speaker on the golem's chest with the force of an earthquake. "I bet it was you sneaky gits! Never did like assassins." His cannon thundered to life, and fist-sized explosive shells devastated the remaining Coldskulls. Then—because Rozak was apparently a big fan of overkill—the dwarf hammered their remains with another sweeping barrage, reducing the assassins to a fine pink mist.

He'd spared the lieutenant, though, who turned toward Osmark with wide, shocked eyes. "What kind of monster are you?"

Osmark casually raised his repeater and blew the woman's heart out of her back with a single shot. As her body sailed backward, smoke trailing from the massive wound through her torso, he said, "The kind that wins."

Carrera let out a long, slow whistle. "That was something else. I mean, I've seen some things, but what you did here ..."

Robert holstered his repeater. "You can be president of my fan club after I deal with Sizemore. Right now, I need to find him before he escapes."

Osmark downed a Health Regen potion in a single, long gulp, then strutted down the main street, Rozak following on his heels like a ten-ton guard dog. Time for payback.

FORTY:

Payback

O smark caught Sizemore and his bodyguards at the gates of Tomestide, preparing to mount their horses and bolt into the wind. They stopped to stare at Osmark and Rozak, however, their horses nickering nervously as they pawed the ground.

Robert shook his head. "It's over, Sizemore. You took your shot, now I'm taking mine."

Sizemore's bodyguards, all five of his inner circle of board members, turned to face Robert and brandished their weapons. The senator slung his leg over his horse's saddle. "You haven't caught me yet."

Osmark hiked his thumb over his shoulder at Rozak. "Your horse might be able to outrun me, but you can't outrun that cannon. Trust me, it makes a helluva mess."

The bodyguards stared at the dwarf in his Iron Golem, eyes wide and mouths dry.

"Kill me then," Sizemore sneered. "I'll respawn, and you'll spend the next year trying to find me. And by then? By then, my next plan will already be in motion. If you stop that one, there's another contingency. And another. And another. You've lost,

Osmark, you just don't know it yet. Today was a mistake, I'll admit that, but hardly a fatal one."

"Message your wife. Ask her how the house is," Robert said, his eyes as cold and dead as winter's heart. He messaged Aurion in the same moment.

Personal Message:

Hit the house. Hard. Do it now.

— Osmark

Sizemore's face paled, but he held tight to his reins. "You're bluffing. This is between us, you wouldn't dare to go after my family."

Robert held up three fingers. "Get out of the saddle and surrender to me before I hit zero, or your family is dead."

Osmark folded his ring finger under his thumb.

Personal Message:

Done.

— Aurion

Sizemore's face crumpled into a mask of confusion and fear.

"Got a message from the wife?" Osmark smirked. "Probably going to need to hire some carpenters, huh? Maybe you wish you'd invested in something to put out fires?"

> *Personal Message:*
>
> Do it again. Even harder.
>
> — Osmark

He folded his middle finger down into his fist, leaving just his index finger standing. "I'm not screwing around here, Senator."

"You can't kill them, not permanently." Sizemore struggled to regain his composure, but his nerve was slipping through his fingers just as his horse's reins dropped onto the horn of its saddle. "They'll be back." His hands shook, and a sheen of nervous sweat dotted his brow.

"Haven't gotten out much since you came to V.G.O., have you?" Osmark replied. Without warning, he drew his repeater and fired a shot through Sokolov's foot. The Russian bodyguard yelped in pain and shock, falling to the ground as he clutched the spurting stump at the end of his leg. "That's not permanent, either, but the memory of the pain? That sticks with you. And with healing potions, it's possible to keep people alive for a very long time without sending them to respawn."

Sizemore licked his lips. "You wouldn't—"

Osmark cocked his head to one side, eyes narrowing. "You didn't research me well enough," he said, curling his index finger like he was squeezing a trigger.

"Don't, for the love of God, man, don't!" Sizemore shouted as he jumped from the saddle. "I surrender. Please, let's be civil about this."

"Civility is overrated. And I think your wife is going to love hearing how I had to blow up half your house because you couldn't decide whether or not you were willing to let her die." Robert gestured with his repeater. "Over here. Now."

As Sizemore shuffled forward, Osmark holstered his weapon. He'd won this thing, and now was time for the reckoning. "I want all of you still alive to think about what happened here today. Fifteen of you, including this worthless piece of garbage, decided to take a shot at me. Sure, I'm burned and bloodied, but I'll heal."

Robert backhanded the senator so hard Sizemore lost his balance and tumbled hard to his knees. "This is the man you trusted to beat me. This is the waste of skin you pinned your hopes on. Look at him."

Sizemore glared at him with a hate so limitless even Robert had to pause for a moment to admire its purity. "How did that work out for all of you? Most of your allies suffered for what you did. Hell, by now Sizemore's house is a pile of smoldering rubble, and his wife and son are going to have nightmares for a very, very long time to come. For the rest of their lives, they'll be looking over their shoulders, wondering if the boogeyman is preparing to hurt them again."

With a cold, heartless smile, Osmark looked down at the senator. "Don't worry, Sizemore, I'll take good care of your family for you. I'll put them up somewhere nice. Somewhere I can keep an eye on them. And as long as you behave, they'll be fine."

"Why?" the senator asked, bewildered, his face a mask of dawning horror. He struggled to find words for his confusion, as if he couldn't believe he'd lost everything after coming so close to having it all. "Why does it have to end like this?"

A feeble tendril of pity wormed its way around Robert's thoughts. Sizemore was brilliant—he could be very useful in the right circumstances. Maybe... But then Osmark remembered how hard he'd worked to put all this together. He remembered the way Sizemore had turned his onetime allies against him and tried to poison *his* world.

He remembered, and his heart turned to ice.

"Because you couldn't be content with what I gave you. Because you wanted everything for yourself." Robert shook his head. "Because, Travis, you're an evil man. And sometimes, the only way to defeat evil is with something even worse. And I will be that worse thing. Everyone here remember that. You can talk, but I will act. I will burn down everything you care about and hunt down everyone you love. I will be whatever I need to be to secure this world. I'll make the hard choices, just like I always have."

Osmark grabbed Sizemore's throat and squeezed. Not hard, but enough to keep the senator from trying to wriggle away. "Now, I'm going to take you someplace very special, Sizemore. Somewhere you can't get into trouble. Say goodbye to your friends, because you're never going to see another living soul for the rest of your miserable damned life."

Sizemore's eyes bugged from their sockets, and his mouth hung slack. "No, that's not—"

Robert activated the port-stone, and he and Sizemore vanished from Tomestide—

—and reappeared in a metal-lined alcove with a single pedestal on one end and a doorless archway on the other.

Osmark shrugged off the port sickness, refusing to give Sizemore the pleasure of seeing him nauseated.

Unprepared for the sudden travel, Sizemore didn't have the same opportunity. He retched, and Robert jerked his hand away before the sudden gush of vomit could touch his bloodstained gloves. "Yeah, that takes some getting used to."

"Where?" Travis asked.

Robert laughed, and his voice echoed in the small room. Something outside rumbled to life with a sound like the world's largest can opener. "I told you. Somewhere very special."

Osmark moved out of the way so the senator could see through the open archway. They were deep in the heart of the Brand-Forged Artifactory, where Robert had claimed his Faction Seal only a day ago. The massive Iron Goliath glared at the men with eyes like molten lava.

"What in the hell is that?" the senator asked, his voice a rasping whisper.

"That is a Clockwork Golem. He's the boss of this place. A guardian, I guess you'd call him." Robert had to admit the respawned automaton was even more terrifying than the original. Scavlings scampered all over it, adding new armor plates and weapons to the golem's body even as they watched. "He'll leave us alone as long as we stay in here. I wouldn't step outside this room, though, if I were you."

The truth of his position began to sink in for Sizemore. "No, you wouldn't," he stammered, eyes wide, hands grasping his robes to keep them from trembling.

Robert snapped his fingers and extended his hand, palm open. "Open your inventory. Now."

Sizemore shook his head and backed away until he bumped into the pedestal. "I won't."

Osmark sucked air through his teeth and shook his head. "Do you already need a reminder of who you're dealing with? Because I can have my mage vaporize your wife. Or your child? I'll let you pick."

Sizemore ground his teeth so loud Osmark heard the sound across the room. Finally, begrudgingly, the senator opened his inventory and stood stock-still, waiting for Robert to finish. "Fine," he whispered, the word a curse.

Robert raided Sizemore's inventory. There wasn't much there—not compared to Osmark's own equipment—but he wasn't leaving the traitor with so much as a toothpick. "Bet you wish you'd have thought to bring some port-scrolls with you, right? Wouldn't have done you any good. My buddy Rozak warded Tomestide against that. Roaches can check in, but they can't check out. The only port magic that works to leave my town is mine."

Sizemore stood naked except for a linen loincloth draped around his bony Elven hips. His pale skin and sunken chest reminded Robert of a maggot worming its way through the dark and rotten flesh of a piece of roadkill. Osmark left the black vellum folder for last.

He plucked it from Sizemore's inventory and tapped it against his chin. "You were so close," Osmark said, unable to keep the gloating satisfaction from his voice. "If you'd just held on for a little bit longer, you might even have won. Maybe not, but that'll give you something to think about in the years to come."

Sizemore said nothing. He lifted his chin and stared deep into Robert's eyes. Despite how far he'd fallen, the man wouldn't admit defeat. Couldn't. It wasn't in him.

"Bind your respawn point to the spot you're standing on," Robert demanded. "And remember, I have your family and I won't hesitate to hurt them. Not for a second."

He could see a glint of defiance in Travis' eyes, but the senator finally lowered his head as a circular flash of opalescent light enveloped him. "It's done," he hissed as the light faded and died away.

"Good." Osmark clenched his right fist and drove it into the senator's stomach; the man doubled over wheezing for air. "I'll be sure to let your wife and son know you did the right thing in the end," Osmark whispered.

After a moment, the senator grimaced and righted himself, one hand still clutching at his gut. "You think this will hold me?"

Osmark chuckled and leaned against the wall. "You still don't know where you are? This is my restricted area. *Mine*."

Horror crept across Sizemore's face as he realized the truth.

"That's right. You're stuck here. You can't send messages. You can't receive messages because this isn't *your* restricted area. You're not even supposed to be here. In some ways, V.G.O. doesn't even recognize you as part of the game because you're so far out of bounds." Robert laughed again. "The good news, though, is that you can leave anytime you want."

He stepped away from the archway and gestured for Sizemore to go on out. "I won't even try to stop you. Of course, the Iron Goliath there"—he waved a hand at the steampunk monster—"probably isn't going to be so understanding."

Sizemore's shoulders slumped, and the spark of defiance dimmed in his eyes.

Robert snapped his fingers. "Don't be so glum. If you kill the Goliath, you can walk right out of here. But you'll have to be quick, because I think he's on an hour respawn timer. Of course, if you fail to kill him, it's going to hurt. A lot.

"And then you'll respawn right here in"—he paused and glanced at his wrist—"oh, eight hours or so with all those nasty death debuffs in place." Osmark scratched his chin and flicked a glob of dried blood away. "Just between you and me, though, don't wait too long, or you'll get hungry. Thirsty. Then *those* debuffs will kick in, and you'll be even weaker than you are right now."

"You're a monster," Sizemore snapped, his face a knot of hate.

"If I'm a monster," Robert said, "then you made me. I didn't want to fight you. I didn't want to fight *anyone*. I wanted to make a new world that we could all rule together. We had a plan."

Sizemore sagged even further, his hands suddenly dangling listlessly at his sides.

"Hey, smile for the camera," Robert said, pulling a small chrome disc from his inventory. He stuck it over the door and pointed up at it. "Magic viewing mirrors, courtesy of the the *Mystica Ordo*. Very expensive, but worth every penny. I'm having sister mirrors delivered to every member of the board. Anytime they want, they can take a look at what you're up to.

"Every day, they'll be able to watch you and see what happens when someone crosses me. And, if you look closely enough, you'll probably be able to see your reflection in it. You'll be able to watch as you wither away. As hunger hollows you. As thirst dries you out and leaves you an insane husk of the man you used to be. You'll be able to look at yourself and remember how great your life could've been."

Osmark opened the port-scroll Sandra had purchased for him the previous night. "Think about where it all went wrong, Sizemore. And pray to whatever god you believe in that we never cross paths again." He shot him a wink, triggered the portal, and stepped through into Tomestide, pursued by a wordless scream.

FORTY-ONE:

Chaos

"I've been poisoned," Osmark mumbled to himself as he staggered back to the Saddler's Rest beneath the fading purple light of the dwindling sun. A terrible fever raged through his body, and his muscles ached as if he'd been run over by a train. More than once. Every throbbing beat of his heart was like a hammer blow to the back of his head, and every step sent jagged razors of pain slicing through his skin.

He tried to remember if he'd been stabbed or shot by one of the assassins, but so much of the battle was a hazy blur. One of them could've gotten a lucky shot off while the firebomb burned him alive. Either that, or a crossbow bolt could've grazed him at some point. Even the nick of an errant blade could've done the trick. It was impossible to tell when he'd been poisoned.

What he *could* tell, though, was that he was dying.

Dying...

Like an open-handed slap to the face, Osmark abruptly realized he was entering the third and final day of his transition.

Poison wasn't killing him. No, he was *actually* dying, IRL. His former body was entering its final hours, and would soon be nothing more than a discarded shell of rotting meat attached to machines that pumped blood and inflated the lungs for no good reason. If everything went according to plan, the new Osmark would wake from a tortured slumber in Tomestide, like a phoenix from the ashes. A fitting metaphor considering he'd nearly just burned to death.

Either that, or he'd vanish, deleted like a corrupt line of code.

Robert pushed that morbid thought away and clung to hope as he dragged himself through the Saddler's Rest and into his rented room. He'd be fine. He had nurses. Staff. Medicine. Monitors. He threw the latch, peeled out of his bloodstained armor, and promptly collapsed onto his bed. He hoped that Garn, Dorak, Aurion, and especially Sandra were all somewhere safe, but he was in too much pain to check on them at the moment.

Hours passed in a horrifying fever dream of pain and terror. Osmark imagined Sizemore towering over him from the foot of the bed, his gaunt Elven frame wreathed in dark fire as his eyes burrowed into Robert, and he laughed like a rabid hyena.

Osmark drifted in and out of sleep, but he couldn't tell one from the other.

One moment he was back in the battle of Tomestide, fighting for his life against impossible odds …

The next he was trapped inside a metal coffin, as thick hypodermics drained his blood and sapped his life.

Finally, a new day dawned, and Robert opened his eyes to the golden rays of a kinder sun pouring through the open shutters of his room like warm honey. Somewhere nearby, a bird sang its morning melody to a nest filled with chirping hatchlings. In the distance, he heard the steady banging of hammers and the rhythmic rasping of saws.

The people of Tomestide had returned to rebuild their lives. Osmark was glad he'd thought ahead and paid the guard to evacuate them before yesterday's battle. They'd lost a lot, regardless, but the citizens of Tomestide were still alive, and he'd provided them with more than enough money to rebuild bigger and better than what they'd had before.

Osmark took a deep, cleansing breath of the fresh air pouring through the open window and dragged himself out of bed. To his surprise, he didn't feel sick, and there was none of the hangover he'd experienced the previous two days. If anything, he felt better than he had in years. His body was fresh, new, and whole.

He'd survived the transition. Not that he'd ever doubted. Not really.

Sandra—because who else would be that thoughtful and thorough?—had left fresh clothes for Robert in the dresser, and he donned them after washing off the dried blood in the basin on the nightstand. He wanted a hot shower, or even better, a hot bath, but he'd take what he could get. There was too much work to be done to waste time hunting down gallons of steaming water.

Washed and dressed, Osmark bounded down the inn's stairs, ready to meet the first day of his new responsibilities. He was no longer just an adventurer searching for treasure and power, he was the unquestioned leader of the board and he had a faction to establish.

He was pleased to see all three of his trusted employees, Garn, Dorak, and Aurion, at a table in the private dining room. He was even more pleased to see they'd already ordered breakfast, and the table was piled high with fresh fruit, stacks of pancakes, platters of biscuits, and enough bacon, sausage, and sliced ham to feed a small army.

Osmark wished Sandra could join them, but he imagined she was sleeping off her final transition. She'd arrived in V.G.O. hours after Robert, which meant she'd be down for the count until late in the afternoon. *Let her rest,* he thought and turned his attention to his employees.

They'd done well.

"Welcome back," Robert said with a smile for Aurion. "Did our guests give you any trouble?"

The sorceress shook her head. "They were well-behaved after I took out the guards and burned down their house. They're still shaken up, and they want to see the senator, but I'll leave that side of things to you. For now, they're sequestered in the mayor's home, and I took the liberty of hiring some sellswords to keep an eye on them. I wouldn't leave them there for too long, but they should be fine for a couple of days until you decide on more permanent arrangements."

Osmark nodded at the news.

He didn't particularly like the idea of keeping hostages, but he liked the idea of Sizemore's family running free even less. They were a powerful point of leverage, and he couldn't give that up. Robert made a mental note to find somewhere comfortable and secure to keep them while he let his subconscious dwell on the problem of turning them to his side. They could be turned into useful figureheads if nothing else, and he needed them to work with him, not against him.

"Any other good news?" he asked Garn.

"Lots," Garn responded. "On your side of the board, Bolinger, Schuler, and Smythe have all secured their Faction Seals. They're working out which towns they want to claim at the moment, but I've suggested someone snatch Wyrdtide before it can fall into the wrong hands. I want someone based there to keep an eye on the Coldskulls. If we can't recruit those assassins, I think we should wipe 'em off the map."

Dorak jumped in with his report as Garn shoveled a forkload of syrup-soaked pancakes into her mouth. "You'll be happy to know that the rest of the traitors are towing the line after your display yesterday. Sokolov, Peng, and several others have secured their Faction Seals and reported in. They all claim they've seen the light and come over to the side of angels, but we're keeping an eye on them just the same. Sandra has some contingencies in place to deal with any new opposition, but I'll let her tell you about that when she's back on her feet. I think you're going to like what she has in mind, though."

Robert nodded and washed a mouthful of bacon and toast down with a gulp of apple cider. "That's the good news, but I can already tell there's some bad news waiting in the wings."

Garn wrinkled her nose and placed her hands on the table. "Someone beat Carrera to his restricted location. They killed the mercenaries, looted the dungeon, and stole his Faction Seal."

Robert's temper flared, but he held his emotions in check. V.G.O. was a big world, and it was filled with unpredictable characters. The stolen Faction Seal wasn't anyone's fault, and Robert wasn't going to blame his people until he knew the whole story behind what had happened.

"Find out who, and find out how," Osmark commanded, dabbing at his mouth with a napkin.

"Already done. I checked with the few remaining Devs back IRL—had them comb through the company databases." Garn produced a wanted poster of a young black woman dressed in spellcaster's robes. "Looks like a mid-level Dev named Abby Hollander is likely responsible. Not sure where she is in-game, but we'll find her."

He vaguely recalled her. A peon, a nobody—but even nobodies could cause problems if left unchecked. "Good," Osmark said. "And enlist Carrera—I'm sure he'll be eager to help. Once you have her, bring her to me. I need to know whether she went rogue on her own, or whether Sizemore put her up to this. The senator is out of the picture for the time being, but he warned me he had other irons in the fire before I pulled a Montressor on him. Even without Sizemore around to pull their strings, his puppets could cause us a lot of problems."

Osmark knew he'd have to find some way to placate Carrera for his loss, but he didn't imagine that would be much of a problem. One Faction Seal in the hands of rebels was an inconvenience, but it wasn't a catastrophe. V.G.O. demanded conflict to continually generate new storylines, quests, and interest for its inhabitants. To that end, Osmark knew there were other Faction Seals hidden in Rebel-aligned areas. All just a natural part of the game.

Besides, he could always just give Carrera Sizemore's dossier. The dungeon wouldn't be ideal, but he could make it work. He prepared to give orders when he realized the common room was silent.

No birds sang outside its windows, and the banging and sawing had fallen still.

Likewise, his agents were frozen in place, sitting before him like statues. Garn's fork was halfway to her mouth, and a thin trickle of mulled wine was frozen between Aurion's goblet and her lips.

Suddenly, Osmark was very disappointed with himself for not bringing his armor and weapons down to breakfast.

"Refill?" a woman asked.

Robert spun in his seat to stare at the figure approaching him from the bar.

Heavy plate armor covered her slight frame in smooth planes of black steel studded with curving spikes stained by red-brown patches of what could only be dried blood. A massive sword was strapped to her back, and its demon-faced pommel rose above her left shoulder like the leering head of a witch's familiar.

The woman's pale face was elegant and refined, though the hint of cruelty clinging to its icy beauty caused Robert's heart to skip a beat. Thick shadows gathered around her piercing emerald eyes, and her raven-black hair swirled slowly around her head like black flames caught in a wind Robert could neither hear nor feel.

"Don't look so alarmed, my friend," the woman said as she reached Robert's table and handed him an iron mug filled with sticky red liquor. "I've wanted to meet you for quite some time, and I bear you no ill will." She paused, eyeing him askew. "Yet."

Robert's thoughts careened in erratic orbits around the interior of his skull. Nothing made sense. The world was frozen in the space between moments, except for this woman and himself. She was barely five feet tall, yet wore heavy plate armor and carried a weapon that even a towering Risi would've struggled to handle. And she was also more beautiful than any woman he'd ever seen, but her smile curdled his blood and shriveled his spine.

"Who are you?" he finally managed. He took a deep drink from the iron mug, and the alcohol burned his throat and scorched his belly.

"Me?" She quirked an eyebrow at him. "I am one of the Seven," she said, and wiped the red liquor from her mouth with the back of her gauntlet. An exaggerated pout pushed her lips out and furrowed her brow. "How disappointing you don't recognize me."

Osmark's mind raced as he tried to make sense of what he was hearing. Her reference to the Seven could only mean the Overminds, but this couldn't be right. Couldn't. They were dispassionate arbiters of the game and its rules. While they each had a distinct function, they weren't personifications, and they certainly weren't self-aware. Not like this.

The woman clucked her tongue at Robert and shook her head. "I see the gears turning in your mind, Artificer. You're trying to apply logic to beings your kind were never meant to understand. Let me help you. The Overminds are the greater forces that keep this little ball of mud spinning. And, yes, we are embodiments of the virtues vital to Viridia and Eldgard. My brothers and sisters govern nature and time, the plants of the field, the beasts of the forest, and everything else that makes this life worth living."

She loomed over Osmark's chair, suddenly seeming much taller than her slight stature. Her hypnotic gaze captured him as surely as the moon captured the tides. "But we are much more than unfeeling, uncaring engines of reality, Robert."

Her gauntleted fingers grasped his chin and tilted his head back until their eyes locked. "Aediculus the Architect loves his buildings and cities so much he bleeds for their creators," she crooned. "Gaia the Worldmother has her roots sunk so deeply into your world she feels every birth and every death. Kronos' beating heart measures the sands in the hourglass of the universe, and he is so much a part of its passage that when the last grain has fallen through its waist, then Kronos will die, too.

"Even primal Cernunnos loves his charges, in his own crude way. The pack runs, and so Cernunnos runs with it, eschewing the finer aspects of an Overmind's power to be one with the beasts, great and low. Our dread brother Thanatos, ruler over Serth-Rog and his Infernal Forces, seeks the destruction of the world. Dealing death from the realm of Morsheim as he searches for a way to invade Eldgard."

The names tripping from the woman's tongue jogged Robert's memory—pet names the lead developers had given the Overminds. If he was right, there were only two names left. But, before he could utter his guess, she pressed the tip of her index finger against his lips to silence him.

"And, because we love our roles, we seek Champions to defend them. One of your kind to help us bridge the gap between our home and yours." She offered him a hungry, predatory grin. "And you, Robert Osmark, are my *Chosen.*" She pulled her finger away from his lips and took a seat to his right. She was once again a dainty figure in oversized armor, her face so beautiful it stole his breath.

Osmark took another drink of the burning alcohol. "Then you must be Sophia, the Overmind of Order and Balance."

The dark woman laughed, and the long, sinister peals pouring from her mouth echoed around Osmark like the cacophonous chatter of a flock of vultures. She waved her hand and the Saddler's Rest vanished. Robert blinked, and when he opened his eyes again, the two of them were standing astride a winding road edged by dark trees. Burning wagons and corpses surrounded them on all sides. Writhing flames and buzzing swarms of flies filled the sky like a churning curtain of black smoke.

"Is this order?" the woman asked, no hint of mockery in her words.

Before he could answer, however, they were deep in the Blackwillow Woods. A mound of burning bodies sizzled atop the collapsed ruin of a crude fortress. Rotting corpses with bulging black tongues dangled from noose snares strung through the trees surrounding the fallen camp.

"Is this?"

She snapped her fingers, and they stood among the dismembered bodies of the Coldskulls he'd fed to the Fungaloids in order to save his own hide. *Snap*, and they were back in Tomestide, strolling through the chaotic aftermath of the Imperial Advisory Board.

Ruby drops of blood hung in the air like scattered gemstones.

Men and women stood frozen with their mouths stretched wide in silent screams at the wounds blooming in their flesh.

Buildings burned, and the smoke hung suspended in thick plumes, which clawed at the sky like broken black fingers.

"There is only one Overmind we haven't mentioned, Robert." She curled her gauntlet in the rough spun fabric of his shirt and pulled him close. Their eyes were inches apart, and suddenly Osmark felt no more significant than a speck of dust in the face of the moon. "Say. My. Name."

Two syllables rose from the darkness inside his chest, a darkness he'd always known was there, but had never truly embraced. He'd thought he was bringing stability to this world, that he was civilizing a barbaric frontier. But no. He was something much more primal, more vital to this world's survival.

"Enyo." Osmark intoned the words as if they were a holy vow, and felt something sharp and relentless dig into the meat of his heart. "Mistress of Discord."

The chaos engine.

Her hand didn't leave Robert's chest, but she floated into the air until their faces were level. She pulled him toward her until their lips were so close, he felt her words as much as heard them. "This world was built for struggle, Robert. It was made for conflict and violence—a crucible to test the might of man and god alike. Since you arrived in this world, you've been the very embodiment of disruption and discord. You've sown the seeds of a storm of blood and violence on the wind, and soon, you and I shall reap that whirlwind. We are the beating heart of the struggle, and it is our pulse that drives this world forward.

"You hoped your rulership would bring peace and structure to its people. But that way lies stagnation and death. Mortals need change—violent and disruptive—to keep them from shambling through life like walking corpses. We will bring them that change, Robert, forever and always."

He couldn't peel his eyes from hers. The deep and enchanting green irises swirled around the dark chasms of her pupils like the flailing limbs of a hurricane surrounding the dead calm at their heart. "Where do we begin?" he croaked.

Enyo chuckled, and Osmark smelled liquor on her breath, along with the churning, electric perfume of an approaching storm. "The Empire needs you. It has grown long in the tooth and become locked within a prison of meaningless tradition. It is an edifice of government that now serves only to keep power concentrated in the hands of doddering old men and their toothless advisors."

Abruptly, her lips crushed against Robert's, stealing the breath from his lungs but filling his heart with a bonfire of energy and ambition. The kiss lasted for a timeless eternity. And yet, when she pulled away, he yearned for her lips to return and suck the last of his soul away into the oblivion at the center of her being.

Kiss of Enyo

You have been blessed by the Overmind of Discord. While you serve her, your Luck is permanently increased by 10.

Enyo thrust Osmark back to arm's length and clenched his shoulders in her gauntleted fists. "It pleases me to give you a gift. Accept this blessing of luck, for you will surely need it."

She released him, licked her lips, and turned to walk away. The tip of her massive sword dragged across the ground as she stalked through the commons.

"What makes you think I'll need luck?" Osmark called after her retreating back.

She glanced at him over one shoulder and laughed. "Oh, Robert, how else will you claim the reins of your faction from its current ruler?"

Robert's thoughts churned. Who in Tomestide would oppose him? Taking the seat of his power would be an afternoon's work, if that.

Enyo aimed her index finger at Osmark and cocked her thumb in the air as if pointing a gun between his eyes. "You're thinking too small. Far, far too small. Your faction is the Empire, my champion. Your city is New Viridia itself. And before you can claim it, you must dispose of the emperor squatting on its throne. And for that, you're going to need all the luck in the world."

Enyo squeezed the trigger of her imaginary pistol, and a gust of wind that smelled of gunpowder and blood washed over Osmark, forcing him to blink.

When he opened his eyes, he was standing in the middle of the commons, and the work of rebuilding battered the air with relentless noise.

Robert cracked his knuckles and grinned so wide his cheeks ached.

He had work to do.

It was time to change the world.

Special Thanks

I'd like to thank my wife, Jeanette, daughter, Lucy, and son, Samuel. A special thanks to my parents, Greg and Lori. A quick shout out to my brother Aron and his whole brood—Eve, Brook, Grace, and Collin. Brit, probably you'll never read this, but I love you too. Here's to the folks of *Team Hunter*, my awesome Alpha and Beta readers who helped make this book both possible and good:

Dan Goodale, Nell Justice, Jen "Ivana" Wadsworth, eden Hudson, Heather Copeman, Amber McKee, and Bob "Gunslinger" Singer. They read the messy, early drafts so that no one else had to; thanks guys and gals. Another big thanks goes to my ironically-hipster writing buddies, Amanda Robinson, Kelsi Martin, Brian Howard, and Meagan—the best sounding board on the planet. And of course a big thanks to my editor, Tamara Blain who rocked this book (if you need editing, go to her, she's seriously awesome:: ACloserLookEditing.com)

—James A. Hunter, September 2017

About the Authors

S.R. Witt

I've been a lifelong and avid reader of fantasy and cyberpunk stories of all stripes, and a dedicated gamer (both tabletop and digital) for almost as long. I've written all kinds of fiction over the years, from sword and sorcery to gritty horror, and I've been lucky enough to design expansions and supplements for tons of RPGs, from Dungeons & Dragons to Vampire: The Masquerade to the Game of Thrones RPG.

Dragon Web Online is my first series fusing my genre and gaming passions into the delightful stew known as LitRPG. This new and growing style allows me to tell fantastic stories that bring together swords and magic and virtual reality on a gaming backdrop that is truly unlike any other genre you'll read.

James A. Hunter

Hey all, my name is James Hunter and I'm a writer, among other things. So just a little about me: I'm a former Marine Corps Sergeant, combat veteran, and pirate hunter (seriously). I'm also a member of The Royal Order of the Shellback—'cause that's a real thing. I've also been a missionary and international aid worker in Bangkok, Thailand. And, a space-ship captain, can't forget that.

Okay … the last one is only in my imagination.

Currently, I'm a stay at home Dad—taking care of my two kids—while also writing full time, making up absurd stories that I hope people will continue to buy. When I'm not working, writing, or spending time with family, I occasionally eat and sleep.

Books, Mailing List, and Reviews

If you enjoyed reading about Osmark and the world of Viridian Gate Online and want to stay in the loop about the latest book releases, promotional deals, and upcoming book giveaways be sure to subscribe to my email list at www.AuthorJamesAHunter.com And be sure to check out more free LitRGP adventures from S R Witt, by signing up to his awesome mailing list at www.SRWittWrites.com

Word-of-mouth and book reviews are crazy helpful for the success of any writer. If you *really* enjoyed reading about the world of Viridian Gate Online, please consider leaving a short review at either Amazon or Goodreads—just a couple of lines about your overall reading experience. Thank you in advance!

Other Works by James A. Hunter

If you enjoyed The Artificer, you might also enjoy James A. Hunter's other works, such as the classic Viridian Gate Online, the Yancy Lazarus Series, or the Golem Chronicles. All three series are available in Print, E-book, and Audiobook through Amazon. Or, you can read more about James and his books at www.AuthorJamesAHunter.com

Viridian Gate Online: Cataclysm (Book 1)
Viridian Gate Online: Crimson Alliance (Book 2)
Viridian Gate Online: The Jade Lord (Book 3)

***

Strange Magic: Yancy Lazarus Episode One
Cold Heatred: Yancy Lazarus Episode Two
Flashback: Siren Song (Episode 2.5)
Wendigo Rising: Yancy Lazarus Episode Three
Flashback: The Morrigan (Episode 3.5)
Savage Prophet: Yancy Lazarus Episode Four
Brimstone Blues: Yancy Lazarus Episode Five

***

MudMan: A Lazarus World Novel

Other Works by S.R. Witt

If you enjoyed The Artificer, you might also enjoy S.R. Witt's other works, such as Dragon Web Online, The Gamer's Universe, and the Pitchfork County Novels. Or you can read more about Sam and his books at www.SRWittWrites.com

Dragon Web Online: Inception (Book 1)
Dragon Web Online: Dominion (Book 2)

***

Operation Catspaw: A Gamer's Universe Story
Operation Snowblind: A Gamer's Universe Story

***

Half-Made Girls: A Pitchfork County Novel
Night-Blooded Boys: A Pitchfork County Novel
Dead-Eyed God: A Pitchfork County Novel

CPSIA information can be obtained
at www.ICGtesting.com
Printed in the USA
LVHW02s2235090718
583237LV00001B/114/P